PRAISE FOR ADRIAN J. W~

THE END OF THE WORLD RUNNING CLUB

"A real find"—Stephen King

"Extraordinary"—Simon Mayo Radio 2 Book Club

"Adrian Walker breaks your heart in unexpected ways, and leaves you with a sense of stories still to be told. An end-of-the-world tale that is anything but an ending"

—Anne Corlett, author of *The Space Between the Stars*

"A fresh and frighteningly real take on what 'the end' might be... quite an exciting and nerve-wracking 'run', with characters you believe in and feel for"—*New York Times* bestselling author Robert McCammon

"Harrowing and heartrending, this is a novel that is almost impossible to put down"—*Library Journal*, Starred Review

"Ridiculously gripping straight from the start"—Jenny Colgan

"Will thrill and delight... a terrifically well-observed, haunting and occasionally harrowing read"—*Starburst*

"This is an uplifting, exciting and often humorous yarn about camaraderie, endurance and redemption. Throughout, Walker nicely evokes the agony and exhilaration of distance running"
—*The Times*

"Compulsively readable"—*SFX*

"...what sets this novel apart is Walker's extraordinary emotional articulacy"—*The Sun*

"A page-turning thriller with a pace as relentless as the characters' feet hitting the pavement. A deft look into the mind of a man who needs the near-destruction of the world to show him what truly matters"—Laura Lam, author of *False Hearts*

"Brilliant… superb to the end"—Lucy Mangan

"A really fun, engaging, exciting, and compassionate take on a familiar scenario: the apocalypse… Highly recommended"—David Owen, Carnegie-longlisted author of *Panther*

THE LAST DOG ON EARTH

"[Walker] delivers another postapocalyptic tale with a strong hook… deftly using the alternating dog and man narrations to generate tension"—*Booklist*

"Fans of both dog tales and postapocalyptic fiction will flock to this latest from Walker. Lineker's vulgar matter-of-factness lends the perfect tone to this near future when politics has led folks further astray"—*Library Journal*

"Very few dystopian novels push through to the horrors explored here. Fewer still reach these heights of lyricism, humour and decency"—Jamie Buxton, *Daily Mail*

THE END OF THE WORLD SURVIVOR'S CLUB

"Genuinely unputdownable, this is a book that sinks its claws into your imagination and your sense of adventure and won't let go until the final page. Massively enjoyable"—*Starburst*

THE HUMAN SON

ADRIAN J. WALKER

SOLARIS

First published 2020 by Solaris
an imprint of Rebellion Publishing Ltd,
Riverside House, Osney Mead,
Oxford, OX2 0ES, UK

www.solarisbooks.com

ISBN: 978 1 78108 788 6

10 9 8 7 6 5 4 3 2 1

A CIP catalogue record for this book is available
from the British Library.

Designed & typeset by Rebellion Publishing

Printed in Denmark

THE
HUMAN
SON

For my son, Joe, with endless love and pride.

BIRTH

– ONE –

You and I were born with a purpose.

Mine was to save the world.

Yours was to remind us why it needed saving in the first place.

Your rebirth was a loud and visceral affair, quite at odds with the tranquillity of your extinction. When the last human died—a lady named Hanna from a place they called Sweden—there was a day of peace during which we sat upon hilltops and in forests and by the sea, and nothing ran but rivers. Three hundred of us encircled the corpse in Stockholm. We laid her out in the appropriate way, dressing her in a simple frock with her hands folded over her midriff and her white hair combed and neat.

The Earth turned through day and night. Snow fell, and for the first time in a thousand years the planet was permitted to rest.

But when you emerged from the fluid in the Halls of Gestation that long rest was shattered. You spluttered as your lungs filled with air, a look of terror wrinkled your face, and then you screamed. It was a sound like no other I have heard.

I have been a custodian of this planet for five hundred years. I have seen every type of animal give birth, from the gloop of a lamb onto straw to the squirming of grubs to the craning of an eagle chick's neck as it breaks through its shell. And I have seen death too. I have witnessed leopards spring, claws slash, fangs tear, owls swoop, a doe's flesh removed from her back as her face turns to the winter sky and her blood stains the snow. I have seen all the wonders and horrors of evolution and guarded them well, but I have never heard a scream like yours.

That wail. Full of fear, full of darkness, full of woe. As if existence was pain. To hear it was to hear a being that had been given life in the last place it would choose to live it.

Perhaps, on some level, that had always been true.

I pulled you from the amniotic sack and held your wriggling, pinched body up in the glare of the laboratory lights. Your head slumped forward, your limbs flailed, your eyes rolled. You were useless. Blind, weak and utterly at the mercy of the world.

If it had not been for my sister, Haralia, I would have assumed the birth had gone wrong. Perhaps, I would have thought, I had miscalculated your genetic coding—a highly improbable scenario, of course, but one in which my only course of action would have been to place you on the table and terminate you.

I did not, however. Because of what Haralia had said.

Some months before she had warned me: 'They scream, you know. Humans. When they're born.'

Haralia's expertise is in animal husbandry whereas mine is in atmospheric chemistry, so she knows more about these things than me.

'Every human birth was so,' she went on, brightly, for my sister is a joyful being. 'A helpless remonstration against itself. A struggle without the strength to succeed.'

So I did not kill you. Instead I marked my chart.

My own birth was not like this at all. I remember it very well. The first face I saw upon opening my eyes was Dr Nyström's laboratory technician, a nervous, undernourished man named

David who wore broken spectacles. In those first seconds my mind was filled with light and knowledge. I could already feel the world being absorbed and processed by my nervous system. There was no fear and no question of what I was, or why I was here. I was a being of peace and reason and nothing would sway me from my purpose.

The man named David blinked, frowned and muttered things to himself. I already knew more about him in those first few moments of my life than he had ever been able to know in his own. As I stood up, the fluid from my birthing tank ran down my body, and every trickle's calculation sped through my brain. At once I knew the trajectory of every rivulet down my neck, bosom, and spine, across my buttocks and legs.

Dr Nyström made us in your image, only somewhat taller and leaner, with finer features. In her eyes, we were perfect examples of your species.

In fact we were nothing of the sort.

David staggered back, smiled, and said hello. I gave him the greeting he desired and stepped out of the tank. I towered above him. He offered me a towel, which I watched for five seconds, absorbed in the difference between its crude weave and the coloured shells of the tiny creatures that wandered through it, as if through a forest.

Now supremely excited, David dropped the towel and held up a mirror. I looked away from it. I already knew the dimensions of my face and the pigment of my skin—a mild ashen cream with freckles on high cheekbones. My eyes are a deep green, like all female erta.

No, I was not at all interested in absorbing bouncing photons from polished glass. I was altogether more interested in the nine others like me, my siblings, who had also stepped from their tanks. Beyond us stood our mother, Kai, a member of the High

Council. She watched us with interest, and we watched her back. Already, we knew our purpose.

Our births could not have been more different.

Your cry was now in full force. Having accepted Haralia's advice that there was nothing unusual in this, I made the necessary checks. Orifices, eyes, fingers, toes. Confirming that you did indeed have the requisite number of each, I cleaned you and swaddled you in a blanket. Then I left the Halls of Gestation, carrying you in my arms.

You were born early one Spring morning within a mountain, where the Halls had been built five centuries before, overlooking the forest city of Ertanea and the sea beyond.

The sun was yet to rise and the pines stretched out beneath a veil of perfect white moonlight. There was a frost in the air so I tightened your blanket and pulled over my hood as I followed the wide steps down. Our galaxy arced above us. I spotted Jupiter close to the moon and a distant constellation I had not seen for some months. I made a note to examine it later, when I had more time.

I found Boron slumbering by the stone wall at the bottom of the steps and awoke him with a nudge of his nuzzle. Then, holding you in the crook of my arm, I climbed upon his back and let him carry us home.

It was dawn when we emerged from the forest and long shadows drew out across the brightening meadows. You had found peace beneath the canopies, but when the sunlight hit your face your eyes opened, rolling around. You began to cry again, and this time you had no intention of stopping.

The noise unnerved Boron, who snorted steam and scuffed his hooves, but I managed to settle him and we trotted on down the track.

When we arrived at my settlement, Fane, your cry had become

a repetitive pulse. You knew nothing else, apparently. This was all you could do.

I released Boron into the paddock and walked across the stone square. Some of my fellow villagers were already awake and peering through their windows, no doubt wondering what the disturbance was. Jakob was at the well, filling his pail.

'All is well, Ima?' he said, spotting the bundle in my arm. 'A success?'

I nodded back.

'All is well,' I said.

He watched me as I entered my dwelling, pail half full.

Inside I laid you on the bed and took the corner chair. Your screams filled my house, echoing from the timber and rattling the walls. I was tired, and for the first time I pondered the notion that this may have been a mistake.

– TWO –

202 DAYS BEFORE, I had been standing in the cool, stone chambers of the Halls of Reason, where the High Council met. One hundred of us formed a circle around our elders. These ten were our parents, the second generation of erta, born of Oonagh.

I have never met Oonagh. Few have. She was the first of our kind and now lives on her own in the mountains, for reasons I neither know nor need to know.

Kai, my mother, spoke.

'Friends and children. Our purpose has been fulfilled.'

Her voice echoed from the high stone walls, into which the roots and branches of trees had been allowed to grow. The tongue click of the final 'd' hissed into silence, riding the sonorous vowels of its preceding word before a collection of dirt in the rafters dampened the final decibels of its reverberation. My five centuries spent stabilising this planet's atmosphere have bred a fascination with the air and how things move through it. Sound is no exception, and I find speech of particular interest.

My mother continued.

'The sea levels have been restored, the coastlines are clean, the forests are full. The atmosphere—' she glanced in my direction, with a mother's smile '—is clear and perfectly stable. The poles are as they were. The polymers have been compacted and now orbit the moon.' She brought her hands together. 'This planet's ecosystem is in harmony once again. Our work is done.'

The chambers were silent, but filled with smiles.

'Now we face a choice,' my mother went on. The resounding pitch of her voice is a little under 112Hz above my own, although its undertones are much deeper. It crackles in its upper register, and when it does it falls. Perhaps this is due to some kind of self-consciousness. I do not know. I like it.

'Do we stay upon the planet we have repaired, or not?'

There was the sound of hair and skin against fabric. Heads turning, left and right.

'We cannot.'

The words came from Benedikt, who stood near the edge of our circle. He is one of the oldest of my cousins, born several years before me. His voice has a deep timbre scattered with pulse waves, similar to a sound I had once heard when my balloon passed a flock of geese over the Arctic coast. Benedikt is a technology specialist, smaller than most, with sleek black hair and a thin crescent scar that follows the line of his left cheekbone. All eyes turned to him.

'You speak with certainty, Benedikt,' said my mother. 'As usual.'

Benedikt went to reply, but his father Caige had emerged from the council's line. Caige is enormous. His face shone red in the candle light, and his belly bulged, belying his unusual fondness for wheat and mashed root vegetables.

'That is because my son *is* certain, as we all must be. Physicality is crude and riddled with obstacles. There are far more efficient forms of existence.'

'You refer to transcendence,' said my mother.

'Of course I do. We must depart: to stay would be lunacy.'

THE PROBLEM WITH animals is that they do not think ahead. This is because their bodies know on some level that they will one day die, and therefore the future is somebody else's problem.

Even your species, who were at least born with the capacity to consider the future, only ever did so in speculation. You saw tomorrow as an imaginary thing, which is almost certainly why we are where we are.

The erta do not speculate. We extrapolate, and one need only spend a little time on this planet to extrapolate from its freely given data the single courtesy it asks of its inhabitants: keep your footprints light, please.

Do not multiply more than you can sustain, do not consume more than you need, do not create more than is necessary.

This is why our population remains static, our food is simple, and our technology—though once immense for our purpose— is now meagre. Our dwellings are built from wood and stone; we use horses to cover distance; and what little power our settlements require is harnessed from the energy that flows freely through them. We do not build monstrous cities, or blast rockets into space, or seek out useless luxuries. The Halls of Gestation are quiet now, and the Halls of Necessity—where minor technological requirements such as screws, cups or fabric are discussed at length before being granted (or, more often than not, denied)—are rarely visited. Only the Halls of Reason are busy. Busy with voices, all eager to leave.

So Caige was quite correct; to stay upon this planet would be an exercise in foolishness. We would live as slaves, bound by its terms. Millennia would pass and we would achieve nothing but the maintenance of our settlements and the nourishment of our bodies. Occasionally we would have to replenish the population—for all erta must die, albeit far in the future—but even this act would be folly, for one day the planet itself would succumb to its own death, at the hands of a bulbous sun or some other cosmic misadventure, and we would be gone forever.

For what purpose would we live? None whatsoever. We had to leave, and transcendence was the only answer.

I would like to explain transcendence to you, but I cannot. I am bound by the limits of human language, and there exists no combination of words that can sufficiently describe it.

I could invent some.

I could even recycle some, for the mountains of words you abandoned over the centuries were almost a match for your landfills. We still use some to name those few pieces of technology we still use. *Lanterns*, for example. Lanterns are bright conglomerations of dense photon arrays, automated, fast and highly armed. Once employed to shepherd humans, they now patrol our perimeters. They also protect Oonagh, who lives in the mountains.

Beacons too. These are small spheres which roam the atmosphere, monitoring the weather. And *broth*, a highly nutritious algae grown in lagoons, which we eat. Even our names, which we chose ourselves, are recycled.

But no amount of recycled words would help you understand, so for now you will have to accept the simple truth that at some point, the erta will leave this planet, and our departure will not take the form of rockets hurtling through space, or imaginary portals, or death. We will still exist, just not in any form that you are capable of imagining.

'THERE ARE SOME who would not leave so easily.'

Caige turned. The words had come from Greye, a large, broad-shouldered erta whose genetic prototype was once common to a harsh swathe of barren land known as Siberia.

He has a heavy beard and black eyes, and after Mother he is the council member to whom I am closest.

'Some who would say our place is here with the Earth.'

'You refer to the Sundra, I assume?' said Caige, with a curl of his monstrous lip.

'Yes.'

Caige's nostrils flared with an indignant blast.

'Wastrels. They have no bearing on this or any other discussion.'

'Caige,' warned my mother. 'The Sundra are erta like the rest of us. This decision affects the future of our species, and they have as much say as any of us.'

Benedikt, who had remained quiet, suddenly looked up.

'Then let them have it. Let them come forward and speak.'

At this, Caige smiled. An unsettling experience.

'Quite right, my son, quite right. They do not want their say, do they? We never see them, and they never visit the council. They prefer to spend their time cavorting in forests and frolicking in the surf.'

I spotted the mouths of several other council members lift, for Caige's words amused them. Benedikt's mouth retained its unwavering line.

'They have diverged from us,' Caige continued. 'Chosen their own path. And that is not surprising. They were underlings after all, bred for work, not high thought.'

The room rustled at this. The word 'underling' was not often used.

In the beginning there was Oonagh—now, as you know, a mountain recluse. She bred the ten who formed the High Council, who in turn bred the Hundred, including me. Using the Halls of Gestation, where you were born, we gave rise to a thousand, who gave rise to our final fifth generation: ten thousand erta who executed the plans initiated by the upper ranks. This brings our population to 11,111.

We were born the same. Intelligence, strength, appearance, longevity; nothing separated us but aesthetics and the synaptic configurations required for our roles. I was bred for atmospheric chemistry, my sister for animal husbandry, Benedikt for technology, and everyone else for tasks ranging from polymer extraction to sewage treatment. The diversity of these tasks was, I suppose, what created our unspoken hierarchy, and over five hundred years such hierarchies can become somewhat rigid.

Especially in the mind of someone like Caige.

'Silence, please,' said my mother, referring to the crowd's persistent fidgeting. 'Despite the questionable choice of words, council member Caige and his son are quite correct. We must transcend, regardless of any... *outlying* opinion. How long before we are ready to depart?'

There was silence.

'Benedikt?' said my mother.

Benedikt broke his reverie and looked up.

'Our engineers suggest forty years to perfect the technology.'

'Good. That provides more than enough time to clear our own footprint from the planet. Does anyone have anything to say?'

The room was perfectly silent, save for the ooze of wax from a candle as its wall broke.

'Excellent. In that case we will inform the population and—'

My mother turned at the rumble from Greye's throat.

'Council Member Greye? You have something to add?'

'Yes, Kai. There is another matter for us to dicuss.'

My mother blinked.

'And what is that?'

Greye smiled.

'The question of humanity's resurrection.'

– THREE –

I HAVE SOME things to tell you, and they are not things that you
will want to hear.

When I came into existence—the year would have been 2077
by the Gregorian Calendar—the planet was not how it is now. It
was unbalanced. More than that, it was passing a tipping point
beyond which complete devastation was a certainty. The myriad
forms of life that existed upon its rock, beneath its waves and
within its air faced chaos and oblivion. Extinction rates were
climbing; even the population of the human race, which, at its
zenith, had stood at 9.6 billion, was now less than 1.9 billion.
Everything was dying, including you.

And here is the truth of it: it was all your fault. You released
chemicals into the air, in such quantities and over such a
prolonged time that it changed the dynamics of your world.
You became aware of this. Still, you persisted.

I will try to say this as simply as I can.

You created imbalance.

You knew it would destroy you.

You carried on regardless.

This alone should be enough to convince us to leave your
species buried for good.

But we also have Dr Nyström to consider.

Dr Nyström, hidden from the world in her hillside laboratory when all was lost and human life was insufferable, came up with a solution: us. The erta.

She imagined us as creatures of peace and reason; humans, in a way, but ones of far superior strength and intelligence, with all biological desire muted, and with no agenda but that dictated by logic. We were not told to protect anything but the planet. We were not told not to harm. We were given only one directive, the one for which we had been called into existence: stabilise the planet.

Possibly she and her technicians imagined, dimly, the systems we would eventually create to sweep away the woes you had wrought upon the world. But whether or not they knew what would have to happen first is unclear.

Understand, reversing the effects of climate change was simply a matter of identifying the various forces that had led to that change and deciding how best to push them in a different path. It was nothing more than a complex equation to solve, and erta are extremely good at solving equations.

But the equation went deeper than atmospheric chemistry. It had to account for the dynamics of every single system on the planet—whale migration, glacial flow, desert winds. Economics. Sociology. Each played a part.

And, of all the forces that contributed to the planet's demise, there was one that we knew could not be changed within the time we had: human psychology. Quite simply, for the solution to be found, humanity had to be removed from the equation.

Our intention was not for brutality. There were to be no blood-red skies or rolling wheels of metal machines slaughtering children in the darkness. We simply took hold of *Homo sapiens*' infrastructure, economy and the systems that connected them, and offered them the best deal a species had ever been offered in the history of evolution. Sterilisation is not so hard when you control the water supply, and a life of peace and luxury is easy to arrange for a dwindling population.

It would take a little over a century for humans to die out, and, by all accounts, it was to be the most blissful period they had ever enjoyed. There would be no war, no famine, no disease that could not be treated kindly, no work that was not asked for, no requirement to manufacture items that were not necessary. All would have access to clean water and the food would be good and nutritious. They would live in luxury.

What would you have done with such an offer, I wonder?

I can tell you what they did, those last remnants of a doomed species: they rejected it. Not all of them, but in enough numbers to create an uprising. What was supposed to be their most peaceful hour became their bloodiest. Blockades, clumsy ambushes, failed attempts at nuclear strikes against the sterilisation facilities. They even turned against themselves. The erta did everything they could to avoid engaging, but in the end there was no other choice. It took a matter of hours, as I understand it, to persuade the human population against their senseless rebellion, to resign themselves to their blissful fate.

Of course this happened some years before my birth, but the reports of these developments were fed into our tanks as we gestated, so I was born knowing exactly how humanity had behaved before they finally succumbed to their undeserved Utopia in the Andean Mountains.

When Hanna died in Stockholm, her species left this planet—not with a bang, not with a whimper, but with a long and rapturous sigh. Our promise was to resurrect them once the time was right.

This was the cause of the argument that led to you.

CAIGE MADE A noise, a laugh that lasted eighteen milliseconds. The resulting reverberation trailed for much longer, and might have been mistaken for the bark of an average-sized dog.

'The resurrection of humanity?' He swivelled to face Greye, then looked up and down the line of his fellow council members. 'Am I to believe that this is seriously to be debated?'

My mother said nothing, exchanging a look with Caige which I could not decode. Greye maintained his cool smile, though I knew he took no pleasure in engaging with Caige. They were not friends.

'We made them a promise,' he said. 'The erta do not break promises.'

Another laugh from Caige, just as short but this time higher, approaching the tone of a gull's caw.

'Neither do we willingly destroy what we have just spent centuries repairing.' A glance at my mother again. 'If humanity is allowed to return to this planet, they will behave exactly as they did before. There is no question of it.'

'We do not know that for sure,' said my mother. There was trouble in her voice. Hesitation. Everything in her diction, from the unusual frequency upon which she hovered to the lack of moisture in her throat, suggested discomfort.

'And they may learn from their mistakes if we show them the consequences,' said Greye. 'They deserve a second chance, Caige, and besides, you cannot deny that they were unique as a species.'

'The only thing that made them unique,' spat Caige, 'was their propensity to fail and destroy everything in their path. They deserve nothing but their oblivion.'

'They created us,' said Greye, turning to face him. 'Perhaps they are capable of more than you gave them credit for.'

'*One* of them created us.' Caige's voice shook as he closed the gap between them. 'And I was there, Greye. I know exactly what they are capable of. Benedikt, you too.'

Benedikt looked up at his father, eyes darting, uneasy. The room fell frigid. This discord, this opposition—it was not natural.

'Council members, please,' said my mother. Caige and Greye withdrew back to their places. She paced the stone floor in front of them, hands clasped, casting shadows with each sweep of her robe.

'Each of you knew from birth the unbendable nature of *Homo sapiens*, and how the success of our work relied on their removal. The question we now face is: do we allow them back into existence, and risk the ruin of everything we have achieved, or do we leave the planet safe, but with our promise broken?'

'Promise,' muttered Caige. 'A promise to a dead ape! Who is there to mourn us breaking it? Who would know?'

'We would know,' said Greye. 'We would know and we would carry it with us. It would be a heavy burden.'

'It would be no burden at all,' said Caige, stepping from the line. Greye followed and faced him.

'I disagree.'

The air shivered with gasps and mumbles. These were troubling words indeed.

Never once had I witnessed two erta disagree, not even in the most complex and intense periods of our work. The outcome of every decision we had faced had been dictated by the application of logic. To disagree was ludicrous: if a decision could not be reached then it meant only one thing: not enough data. Surely this was obvious.

Caige met Greye face-to-face. His words were slow and dark. 'Really. And what do you suggest we do about this...

disagreement?' He swung to the line. 'Council?' And to the room. 'Anyone?'

I watched this laughable display and the looks of concern it brought to the faces around me with utter bewilderment. I might have even smiled, had I not been so dismayed by the preposterousness of it all. Why could they not see? Was it because our purpose had been fulfilled? Is this what happens when the work is done? This inability to grasp basic facts? This weakening of the mind?

Whatever was happening, it had to be stopped.

So I raised my hand.

My mother squinted through the murmuring crowd.

'Ima? Do you have something to say?'

Caige's eyes narrowed. Benedikt's followed. The room hushed.

'I have an idea,' I said.

Now, in hindsight, I suspect that it may not have been an altogether good one.

– FOUR –

THE FOLLOWING DAY I met my mother at the lake. It was summer and the ducks were numerous. We sat on a stone seat by the water's edge, as bees darted among the wildflowers and spring's young starlings swooped between the branches of the cherry trees.

'Have the council reached a decision?' I said.

'We have, and I am afraid your idea is too dangerous.'

'I see.'

'Introducing a small population of *Homo sapiens* into a controlled environment could lead to results which are, shall we say, *skewed*. Most of the population have limited experience of humans, and those who do—' she paused, smoothed her robes, and turned to me. 'Those who do, do not remember them well.'

'I understand,' I said, standing. 'Thank you for your consideration.'

'But that is not to say that there is no merit in your idea.'

I sat down again.

'What do you mean?'

'Multiple humans may cause problems, but a single human would be a far less unpredictable subject. Its behaviour as it grows and interacts would introduce the idea more gently, and give us enough data on which to decide whether to take things further.'

'A single human?'

'Yes. An infant raised to adulthood within our own environment.' She looked to the water. 'The only question would be who to raise it.'

'It should be Haralia, of course. Her knowledge of animals is second to none.'

'No.' The word could not have been more decisive. Her eyes wandered the lake. 'Your sister is not well suited to this task. It requires a clearer mind, one that will not be so easily distracted.' She turned to me. 'Like yours.'

My mother was quite right, of course. Like all erta, my genetic code was modified according to the requirements of my purpose. Atmospheric chemistry requires great focus, and in order to maximise mine, my mother had instilled within me a mind that was more clinical than most others, and an emotional propensity that ranks a little lower.

You should know that clinical minds and low emotional propensities are already strong ertian characteristics. So you might say I am a fine example of my species.

'Besides,' she continued, looking upward. 'I know how much you miss your purpose. You are listless now the sky is clear.'

I followed her gaze to the azure sky, across which a fleet of Nimbus were sailing. They are not my favourite clouds. Cirrus are my favourite clouds. They are made of ice.

What my mother had just said was also correct. The truth was that the news of our success, met by most with feelings of relief and satisfaction (at least, as much as it is possible for erta to feel such things) had left me cold. My purpose, the recalibration and stabilisation of the atmosphere, had been a highly respected one. Everything hinged upon it, in fact, and I delivered the solution with great zeal. I enjoyed my work, the days and months and years and centuries flying in my balloon above the planet, casting out atomic nets, taking readings and extrapolating the effects of the catalysts I released into the stratosphere. I watched with marvel as the carbon surged, as expected, then levelled off. My work had been my life, and now it was done.

'I do miss my purpose,' I said.

'And this will give you a new one.' She gave a sigh—a pointless mechanism she had affected over the centuries. 'Nevertheless, you should know that it is a great undertaking.'

'No more than that which I have already achieved.'

'No, but you will be a child's mother.' She leaned closer. 'And take it from me, that is a lonely job.'

'I was never a child, Mother. And I have never felt lonely.'

She gave me a wan smile.

'My daughter. I really did put too much of what I was not in you.'

I looked out at the surface of the lake, flashing with sun. The temperature was 29% of that which would boil the water, but small clouds of steam were already rising. States take time to change, and everything moves at different speeds.

'The council have agreed on this?' I said. 'Even Caige?'

'He took some persuading, but yes, we are in agreement. You will engineer a single human child and raise it as your own. Its behaviour and growth in a peaceful environment shall be monitored over its first two decades, and if the extrapolated data is deemed agreeable, then we will discuss the gradual reintroduction of human life to the planet as we transcend.'

'And if it is not?'

'Then the decision will have already been made.'

'What will happen to the child?'

She paused.

'There will be no further use for it.'

'Like the ertlings,' I said.

DURING THE FINAL years of human history, the bliss my elders had fashioned for the last sapiens was missing one thing: children. Despite being sterile, many—particularly the younger mating pairs—still craved offspring. Wandering hand-in-hand through the lush valley glades, or sitting beneath green waterfalls, or sharing poolside drinks at sunset served by drones, they sighed and yearned to be parents.

The solution, since we had promised them bliss, was ertlings. Ertlings were erta born early, which is to say that they were taken from the tanks before their gestation period had completed. They were smaller, about the size of a human four-year-old. In time they would grow to be adult erta, and though they would never quite match the rest of the erta in terms of strength or intelligence, they would supersede their surrogate parents within a few short years of their first tearful union.

Due in part to their underdevelopment and part to design, ertlings were passive and pliable creatures, and for much of what the humans considered their childhood they would retain a soft, warm innocence. Beneath the surface, of course, the calculations were rattling away. They knew exactly what their purpose was.

When they reached adulthood, they were called to the valley ports where their mothers and fathers, now grey and sated of their drive to raise young, waved them off on their journeys to assist the rest of us in our task to balance the planet. They were given only basic jobs, their natural docility and sheltered upbringing rendering them even more useless than those curious humans whom I am led to believe elected to help instead of rest.

Twice each year they returned home to visit their doting parents. And when those parents finally died, they were allowed to follow, swiftly and without protest.

You may as well call them robots. The term is as good as any other.

'WE WILL HAVE to make some more, of course, to provide other children with which the human can interact and learn. It will be a fine test of its social behaviour.'

'You wish me to make them too?'

'No, leave that to us. We will ask for volunteers to foster them when the time is right. You concentrate on the human.'

'Very well,' I said, rising from my seat. 'Then I shall begin at once.'

My mother's hand stopped me.

'Ima, you do understand: this is a species we are talking about. Whether their resurrection is to be considered further will depend entirely upon this child's life.'

'Yes, Mother.'

'Therefore, it must behave naturally. It must not be aware that it is different to you, or any other erta. Shows of superior strength or intelligence are likely to confuse it.'

'You are asking me to behave like a human? I am sure I would not know how.'

She stood and faced me. We are the same height, my mother and I, although her skin has aged a little more and her hair is auburn, whereas mine is the colour of new hay.

'Behaving like humans is the last thing I want any of us to do, my child. But for this to be a fair experiment, we must rein in the attributes which elevate us from them. Do you understand?'

'Yes, Mother.'

'It should not be too difficult. Our purpose is fulfilled. All we need to do is live peacefully until we are ready to transcend.'

'Yes, Mother.'

I turned to leave, for I was eager to begin, but she stopped me again.

'Ima, whatever you do, you must not impose your own agenda upon the outcome of the project.'

'I have no agenda, Mother, other than the desire to seek clarity and truth. Like all erta.'

These pauses of hers. Entirely unnecessary. Eventually she smiled.

'Well, then,' she said. Two words as useless as her sighs, blinks and pauses. 'Then you have a new purpose, Ima. Go and fulfil it. We shall all be watching.'

'Thank you, Mother.'

'And Ima, look to your sister for assistance for you are quite right; her expertise may prove valuable to your preparation.'

I bowed, left and set to work in the Halls that very afternoon.

I KNOW HOW this will end for you. I meant what I said to my mother—I have no agenda. I serve only truth and reason, and my purpose now is merely to provide the necessary data for my species to make an informed choice about humanity's resurrection.

Nevertheless, nine months later and here I am watching you scream and wriggle upon my bed, already feeling my body's nervous system rail at the sound. It is clear to me. I already know.

There will be no choice to make.

– FIVE –

MY DWELLING IS identical in shape and size to every other dwelling in every ertian settlement. It is a single-storey house made from precisely-cut timber and stone, with an oak roof, two windows and a stove. There are three rooms; the first a small toilet, the second a wood store, and the third a living area furnished with bed, chair, and table. At the front wall a small kitchen looks out upon a perfect stone circle, one of which gleams in the heart of every ertian settlement.

The dwelling, the circle, the settlement—all are bright and spotless, and perfectly symmetrical, like all ertian things.

At this time of year, the sun's first rays as it clears the rocks south of the cove shine directly through my kitchen window and fall upon the table, so that, for a short time—two minutes and thirty-seven seconds today, a period which will decrease daily as summer approaches and both Earth and sun move through space—the room is filled with nothing but the brown shadows of wooden objects surrounding a single rhombus of bright amber light. The rhombus contracts and extends as the sun climbs, and my settlement wakes up.

Our entire population, all 111,110 of us (ignoring Oonagh who lives in the mountains) inhabit the northerly coastline of what had once been known as a country. Countries were areas of land defined by coasts and rambling lines called borders, which were generally the product of bloody argument. Like almost everything else in human history, these borders were figments born in the minds of those who had survived the argument, and believed in by those who sought not to repeat it.

This particular country was known as Sweden, and we gravitated here almost a century ago when our work began nearing its completion and travel became less frequent. It was chosen because it had been Dr Nyström's home and therefore our place of origin, but also because of the seasons, which are predictable and distinct. It is pleasantly warm in summer but not too humid or dry, and cold in winter but not wet. Winds are infrequent. Rain is gentle. The sea is cool and calm.

It was not always like this. The planet's climate, rebalanced as it may be, is different to how it had been when we arrived. This place we call home was not always so temperate, and could often be harsh.

We live in seventy-five settlements, each separated by a distance of no less than half a kilometre upon a wide chalk road. This road is cut into a forest we planted some three hundred years ago, and traces an exact logarithmic spiral from its southern coastal tip to its centre high in the hills. The formula it describes you would have once referred to as 'golden', and I have often considered this as I travel its slow arc. There is nothing golden about it, for gold is rare and largely useless, whereas the mathematics of this shape are not. Only a distracted or confused mind would call it thus.

Our seventy-five settlements were named after places which were once homes to humans, picked at random from the atlas as it had been during those final years of human existance. Hamlets, towns and megatropolises, now long gone but which once had their own fictitious borders and names: Oshino, Anchorage and Dundee.

Although, of course there is no such thing as random. Everything is predictable, given the right data.

Each has a population of exactly 148, this being the optimum number of erta who can comfortably self-organise together. Any less and efficiency is sacrificed. Any more and decisions become clouded by the abundance of data, although as I have said, disagreements between erta such as the one between Greye and Caige are almost unheard of. For this reason, shortly after we settled here movement between settlements became strictly monitored, such that any erta seeking to spend longer than a day outside their own settlement would require a temporary replacement from their destination. This has rarely required enforcement. We understand the risks, the same way we understand deep-sea currents, and glacial flow, and the migratory habits of swallows.

At the exact centre of the spiral, and 437 metres up into the forest, sits Ertanea. This is the seventy-fifth settlement, home to the High Council and the three halls: Reason, Necessity and Gestation. It is a capital of sorts, with some buildings reaching three storeys.

Twelve-and-a-half kilometres south of Ertanea, bordering a long, tree-lined beach, lies the settlement of Fane. It is shadowed by a jagged cliff, and has been my home for almost eighty-two years.

I was talking about the sun, and how it rises above this cliff. On your first morning, like every other, I watched the amber rhombus appear upon the rough wood surface of my table, and noticed that you had fallen asleep. So I left you like that, lying still upon the bed, and went outside for some air.

Jakob was still there, chopping wood across the circle. I raised my face to the sun and closed my eyes. Your birth and my journey home had taken half the night, and I was fatigued. No matter, I thought. I would go to bed early that evening.

I took a long, slow breath as a breeze passed over my face. It was cooler than the ambient temperature by some four degrees, suggesting a change in the weather later. Light rain, perhaps.

The sound of Jakob's chopping had stopped.

'Hello again, Ima.'

'Hello,' I replied, without opening my eyes.

'Haralia is not awake yet.'

'That is not a surprise. The sun is barely up. Why are you?'

'I always rise early when she visits.'

Jakob is fourth generation, one of Greye's descendants with an expertise in dendrology. I believe he spent a good deal of his life working in the equatorial rainforests. He has a slim torso and a long neck with a pronounced laryngeal prominence, a light beard and unruly hair. He has also formed a relationship with my sister Haralia, who lives in the settlement of Oslo, twenty miles away. The precise details of this relationship evade me and I have no desire for this situation to change.

It is not that I look down upon physical relationships, nor, like some, that I disapprove of those between different generations. It is just that I am yet to be convinced that such associations are anything but illusions; mere distractions now that we have fewer pressing matters to occupy our minds.

Personally, I have never felt anything more than intellectual kinship with another erta, or the mild genetic affinity between relatives, as I have with Haralia. She is the closest of my siblings in both bond and proximity. The remaining eight I rarely see, and are scattered between hillside settlements far away.

Until she and Jakob became close—and, again, I would question the accuracy of that word—I saw her once or twice a year. Now it is twelve times that amount.

'I shall tell her you are here,' repeated Jakob. 'Once she is awake.'

'As you wish.'

'What are you doing today, Ima?'

I opened my eyes. Jakob was standing by his stack of logs, leaning upon his axe. The polished stone of its blade caught the sun and momentarily dazzled me. I shielded my eyes.

'I think I shall walk on the beach,' I replied. 'Mark the tides. When it is dark later I will stargaze. There is a constellation I have not—'

Before I could finish, there was a commotion from inside my house. You had started up with your wailing again.

'What is that noise?' said Jakob, swivelling his axe.

'I have to go,' I replied, and went inside.

'I shall tell her!' called Jakob as I closed the door, but I did not answer, for he had already said that.

YOUR RIGHT ARM had come free from its blanket. It lolled uselessly to the side, spasming occasionally as if grasping for something inches above. I replaced it, but this made no difference to your mood and your face persisted in its grotesque parody of pain. Your eyes squeezed shut, your toothless black maw bent into a trembling crescent, and your screams filled the air, causing particular disruption to my left ear drum.

Perhaps you were hungry, I thought, and realised that, actually, I was. So I left you crying on the bed and went to my kitchen for herring. I ate three looking out of the window, watching Magda carrying a churn across the square. She is short for an erta, fifth generation, dark hair, full torso. She smiled at Jakob as she passed, then glanced at my house, craning her neck with a furrowed brow. Niklas emerged from his house and made his way to the well. His footsteps were slow and measured, the same way he talked. He looked over as he put on his cap.

Still you squealed behind me. The very air seemed to distort.

I ate one more herring and found a jug of goat's milk in the pantry. With this I filled a bowl and took it to the bed.

'Come,' I said, leaning over you with a ladle-full of warm cream. 'Drink.'

But you did not seem to know how. So I poured some into your open mouth. This did nothing to help. If anything, it only made you less happy.

With a splutter, you ejected the well of milk in your mouth onto the blanket. Haralia had woven this from horsehair earlier in the year and given it to me as a gift, so I was a little dismayed. However, I suppose you would have choked otherwise, so at least you were displaying some degree of self-preservation.

I offered you another ladle but you rejected it, pushing your wail to new extremes. In my surprise, I dropped both bowl and ladle upon the floor. The bowl broke in two and the milk spilled out into an oval puddle, its meniscus 4 millimetres from the ground. I stood back, stared at you, picked up the fragments of my bowl and went back to the kitchen for another herring.

At least my view through the kitchen window was not distorted by the sound of your cries. A mist rose from the stone around the well. The door to Jakob's dwelling opened and Haralia skipped out, placing a kiss upon his cheek as she passed him. He watched her as she crossed the circle. Her gait is different to mine. Her hips are wider and the bones rotate as she walks, causing her buttocks to sway, and I can only imagine that it was this phenomena that Jakob gazed at as his wood remained unchopped.

Haralia let herself in.

'Good morning, Ima,' she said to me, though her eyes were on you. 'My goodness. Is this the child?'

I swallowed the last of my herring and we both stood above you.

'Yes.'

'What gender?'

'Male.'

She smiled and nodded, as if she had guessed as much, which she could not have.

'He is upset.'

'He has been crying since the sun rose.'

'Has he fed?'

'I tried goat's milk but he would not take the ladle.'

'He needs a teat.'

'Pardon?'

'Like a nipple. Mammalian infants suckle.'

I looked at her full bosom, then down at my own more modest chest.

'But... erta do not produce...'

'Not you, sister.' One half of Haralia's mouth drew into a smile. She is so much more prone to joy than I. 'Wait here.'

She left and returned some minutes later carrying a clay bottle, the end of which was fashioned into a small bulb. There was a hole halfway down, stopped with a cork. She handed it to me.

'I kept this from my time in Argentina. It was used for orphaned lambs. Fill it with milk, please, will you?'

I watched her as I filled the bottle, sitting with you in the crook of her arm. In her lifetime, Haralia has successfully overseen the reintroduction of several hundred thousand species of mammal, reptile, insect, fish, crustacean and bird. Now that the ecosystem has found balance, she, like everyone else, has no need to continue her work. She rarely engages with animals now, apart from horses, which she adores.

I handed her the bottle and she offered it to you. You sucked at it immediately, eliciting a tubular sound from the vessel, a conglomeration of sine and square waves which decreased exponentially in pitch as it ran dry. Something darkened in Haralia as she watched your contented suckling. The subtleties of facial expressions often evade me, and before I could decode this one she took a deep breath and shook it off.

She looked up and gave me a frown, without appearing serious. She can do this, my sister; cast joy within the same look as scorn.

'I had expected you to be more prepared, Ima.'

'I am perfectly prepared.'

'But you did not know it would need a teat to feed.'

'And now I do.'

'Only because I told you.'

'Yes. For which I thank you, but I would have deduced it nonetheless.'

'Still, Ima, did you perform no research?'

'No I most certainly did not.'

If there exists any exchange which better highlights the differences between my sister and I—or at least the propensities required of our respective disciplines—then I cannot think of it. My purpose in the sky required no research. I knew implicitly the chemical laws by which Earth's atmosphere is bound, and likewise Haralia held the information of every species of animal that lived beneath it. However, whereas I perfected my knowledge through application, the sky offering up its secrets freely as I gathered my data, Haralia instead elected to perfect her own through theory and study. As I read the sky, so she read books, and in the early years of our lives I would occasionally happen upon her studying her great tomes by the light of a sunset, with an expression on her face that may have passed for rapture.

She found these books in human libraries. Your species delighted in maintaining these vast archives of information, which detailed everything from the width of a gnat's wing to the colour frequencies of distant constellations. And why? Because this information was difficult for you to capture, so you kept it and locked it away, as you did with all things precious to you.

This is, to put it mildly, a crude approach to building an understanding of the universe. Things change. New data arrives all the time. Therefore your stockpile of information required maintenance, at great cost to you and your footprint. And we have already discussed footprints. The libraries and their books were disposed of when the humans had departed, along with everything else they had created. There was no longer any use for them.

I was aware that I had just scoffed at my sister, so I moderated my tone.

'Even if I had wanted to conduct any... research, I could not have done. Apart from their genetic code and the basics of their biology, all recorded data was allowed to die with them.'

'You could have asked me,' said Haralia, quietly.

'Mother did suggest that.'

'Then why didn't you?'

'You have been somewhat distracted these past months.'

I looked at the kitchen window to bolster my point.

She smiled, and her face flushed. 'Oh. You mean with Jakob. Well, I cannot deny that we have been—'

I flung out a palm. 'I have no interest, Haralia. None whatsoever.'

Her glee retreated, and she returned to the point. 'It is not a crime to use information gathered from others, is it?'

'Of course not. I just prefer to gather it myself.'

She gave me a look intended to suggest that she already knew this about me. I was certain of this, and pleased with myself for decoding it.

'Besides,' I went on, fixing you with my gaze, 'this creature's assessment is to be undertaken in isolation. Any recommendations for its care would necessarily originate in its previous incarnation, and therefore carry influence. This is a fresh system, to be treated as such.'

'System?'

'Yes, and as with all systems it will offer up information about its requirements and machinations when asked the right questions. I am a chemist, after all, and this is biology. It is mere application.' I glanced at Haralia, who was smiling again. 'I shall learn, sister. It cannot be that hard. But I repeat my thanks for the information about the teat.'

She shook her head, wild curls bouncing, and began to laugh in a way which I cannot. It made my pulse quicken, which I put down to momentary pique.

'You know, I suggested to Mother that it should have been you,' I said.

'What, to care for this?' She gave a half smile. 'No, that would not have been possible.'

'Why not?'

'Jakob and I have plans. Besides, you are right; you are far better at such clinical trials than me and therefore more suited to the task.'

'That is what Mother said.'

'Although it is a shame.'

'What is?'

'Well, you were instrumental in bringing a planet back from the brink of devastation. It is a pity you may be too busy now to enjoy it.'

'Enjoy it?'

'Yes, travel its coasts, roam its hills, see the world you saved.'

'I have already seen it. Besides, how busy can I be?'

The hoods of her eyes fell marginally.

'Perhaps you could find a partner.'

'To what end?'

'Sexual intercourse.'

'Don't be ridiculous.'

'Genital stimulation is most gratifying. You should try it.'

'I would rather spend time in my balloon. Besides, gratification is not purpose.' I looked at you, pulling the last dregs of milk from the bottle, hungry to live. 'Settling a disagreement is.'

'A disagreement?'

'You were there at the council, you saw the argument between Caige and Greye. It was not natural. Something had to be done.'

She raised one of her fine eyebrows.

'You call bringing a species back from the dead natural?'

'You did. Many times over.'

She sighed, like Mother does.

'Is this what he is, then? A means to settle a disagreement?'

'Of course. What else?'

Haralia pulled the dry bottle from your mouth and held it up.

'He was hungry.'

She bent forward and sniffed the air.

'And he has also passed faeces.'

– SIX –

EVERY ERTA HAS its own natural scale of observation; the level upon which we are most comfortable viewing the world. Some are bent towards the grand and work with complex macroscopic systems, such as the dynamics of herbivorous and carnivorous marine life within coral reefs, the intelligence of ant nests, or the modelling of tidal shifts over many centuries.

Others work with particles, such as the nano-engineers and their armies of atomic mites that once swarmed the seas in search of polymers, and others still with physics itself, such as those who condensed the dredged plastic into the perfect sphere that now orbits the moon.

I remember the day it was launched. I was in my balloon monitoring a storm front over the east Indian coast, and I watched as it soared out to its new station, making calculations upon the effect it would have upon the moon's own orbit, and upon the tides of the planet below. It was not my job to do this, of course; the responsibility fell to those on the ground. Nevertheless, some months later I was pleased to note that my own predictions had been a fraction more accurate than theirs, and were instrumental in allowing Haralia to rescue a colony of rare crabs she had been monitoring in Australia from a small tsunami.

Others go deeper, creating order from the chaos of quantum events that gives rise to reality, and beneath that, deeper still, to mathematics. All of us, in fact, must work upon this most primitive and indivisible scale to some degree or another. Mathematics is the substance from which everything is made.

I have spent my life studying and manipulating the chemistry of the atmosphere. That is the task for which I was designed, and the scale at which my mind is most comfortable. The simplicity of molecules, how they bind and collide with perfect predictability, and how employing this predictability can change a gas, or a liquid or a solid into something more advantageous to one's needs, is pleasing to me. One molecule of carbon dioxide is the same as the next. They are bound to their own unbreakable laws, and I know these laws implicitly. You will not find one which is fatter, or longer, or weaker, or quicker. You will not find one which is broken, or corrupt, or unruly. You will not find dirt upon a molecule.

But there is dirt upon my bed.

'Meconium,' said Haralia, as we observed your kicks and spasms, now free of your swaddling. A dark green streak of viscous sludge ran from your anus across your blanket and had escaped onto mine. It was putrid, like the primordial swamp from which your evolutionary ancestors had once oozed, I imagine. 'From his amniotic fluid. I assume that his gestation was as close as possible to that of a human?'

'I modelled the womb with precision and maintained nutritional equilibrium according to my design, which was extensive. As I said, it was a most challenging project. But witness, I have succeeded.'

You gargled. Your eyes rolled. Haralia turned to me.

'Just because you have successfully engineered a human infant, does not mean you have succeeded.'

I took a step towards you, examining your wrinkled face.

'I know I must care for it, keep it alive. But the hard part is over, I am certain.'

'You should be certain of nothing when it comes to mammals, especially apes, and even more so with sapiens. Their development owes as much to nurture as nature.'

Haralia has developed an overly keen sense of caution. She worries too much, and I attribute this to her expertise. Understanding animals has led her mind away from the world's underlying solidity. Perhaps if she understood a horse the way I understood the atmosphere, she would have fewer concerns.

'I did not know you had had experience of humans.'

This was a baited statement because we both knew she had not.

'I have not,' she replied, as we both expected. 'Only what I have been told, like you.'

'Then we are both equally enlightened, are we not?'

I removed your blanket from the bed and scraped the mess into the waste chute in the corner of the kitchen. There was a short rush of air as your first excrement was sucked from the room. From here I heard it whistling down a short network of glass pipes that fed into Fane's sanitation system, an underground tank filled with a carefully balanced mixture of bacteria and nanobots, which would, over the course of the day, break it down and recombine it into broth. As I have already said—technology should only be used for purposes which are essential. Sanitation and nutrition are such purposes.

I then found an unbroken bowl and filled it with water from the pail, took it with a cloth to the bed, and cleaned your anus. Then I swaddled you in a fresh blanket and laid you further up the bed, where you settled and slept.

'In any case,' I said. 'I am fully prepared, as I am for any challenge. This animal's care is merely a set of problems that need to be solved.'

I turned to Haralia.

'I fixed the sky, sister. I am sure I can raise an ape.'

HARALIA'S TWENTY-FOUR hours in Fane were nearing its end and she had to return to Oslo. She told me she would return in two weeks, so I bade her farewell and spent the rest of the day busying myself in the house and seeing to your needs. I fed you with Haralia's bottle three times and changed your blanket four. For the rest of the time, you slumbered.

I witnessed patterns emerging and clues around which I could plan my routine. For example, if you made a particular combination of nasal grunts then this signified a desire to feed. A certain rhythm to your kicks meant that your blanket had come loose and you were cold. A high clicking noise meant you had woken and did not intend to return to sleep. You revealed to me the predictability of your own equation, much as the sky had done in those early decades of my work, and this pleased me. It was to gratifying to think of Haralia's return, when I could share with her my success.

In late afternoon I sat in my chair as you slept. I considered taking a nap myself, since I was still fatigued from the previous night, but decided against it.

You grunt in your sleep. It is a surprising noise. I sat there listening to it for an hour or more, picking apart the frequencies and the possible relationships they might have with those of your cries. I then found myself distracted by a brief attempt to extrapolate this data into a rough approximation of how your vocal cords would develop and produce a voice. I settled upon seventeen possible outcomes, each of which I ran through my mind with the various ululations required by speech.

Speech will be important to you. It will be your interface with me, and with the world—your only interface, in fact. Not so with erta. We speak through choice, but not necessity.

Our common origin meant that all erta were born with an identical perception of the world, knowing the same facts, thinking the same thoughts, and making the same extrapolations. Because of this, communication was easy, barely anything at all in fact. We were so attuned, so close to our shared root, that for two erta to communicate all they needed to do was to intuit what the other would say. Therefore, you would often come across two erta with hands folded against their gowns, circling each other in silence. They were talking, in a fashion, reading facial tics and bodily movements as if they were consonants and vowels.

It is rarely seen now. Our minds gradually diverged from that central point, as we knew they would, and as we became more complex and separate we sought other methods of sharing knowledge.

We developed a more efficient means of communication, involving exchanges of loud, high-pitched bursts of binary noise. Speaking in this way, I can express a decade's worth of data describing the effects of melting sea ice upon methane deposits in the upper atmosphere in less than seven seconds. I can absorb the architectural plans for a new settlement in a little over a tenth of that.

It does, however, sound like screaming.

We still exchange information in this way; large amounts of data, experimental procedure, orders, ideas—anything where brevity is required. This was vital in the first sixty-three years, when our technology was developing and the planet swirled with our activity. But after this, and our challenge steadied, brevity itself became less and less important. We found there was no longer the need to rush.

Things should not be rushed. The planet moves at a certain speed, and to overtake it is—well, perhaps that is where you failed. You did not take your time.

The erta, on the other hand, do. This is why, even before humanity's extinction, we had adopted human speech as our preferred means of communication. Another good reason for doing this was that we needed to converse with humans. After all, we could not very well have informed them of their impending extinction with a combination of silence and screaming, could we?

I think this would once have passed as something called a joke.

You fidgeted in your sleep and I sat up, expecting a cry. But then you settled.

There was extensive discussion over which language to speak, amounting to almost five full seconds of screaming between council members within the Halls of Reason. We could have chosen any one of the eighty-six languages Dr Nyström had taught Oonagh as she gestated, and which were propagated to us via our parents as we did so ourselves. I watched the debate unfold, and was a little disappointed when English was chosen for its popularity and wealth of vocabulary. I had been hoping for Japanese, purely for the sound of its vowels. Nevertheless, I accepted the decision, and bolstered my innate knowledge of this rampant, hybrid tongue by means of dictionaries and scientific texts.

I even read some stories once, given to me as a gift from Greye. Stories contain depictions of events which did not happen. For example, there was one about a child taught to be a king by an ancient wizard. Another chronicled the life of a man with such a keen scent that he could control people's behaviour by the power of smell alone, and another was about a girl with telepathic powers who was treated badly by her peers.

Strings of lies. I saw no point of them.

For a start, there are no such things as wizards, and a human child could not pull a sword of forged steel from the rock into which it had—somehow—been embedded. Although I am fairly sure I could.

Secondly, it is impossible for the human olfactory system to develop to such a degree. As Haralia once told me, human senses are substandard when compared to most other beasts. Ours are far better.

And finally, telekinesis is not possible without certain cybernetic enhancements. And even if it was, it is unlikely that a female human with so many domestic problems and such little self-esteem would develop the confidence or malice to use them in order to commit multiple homicide.

Strings of lies.

Greye gave me a book of poetry as well. Mostly about animals, something about horses standing in a field; I did not care for it. Of all the useless mechanics of human language, simile and metaphor are the ones I understand the least.

Here is an example.

"The sun hung like an orange."

The sun does not hang. It is not even suspended. It appears so because when we look at it we are viewing a large celestial gas ball from a distance of ninety-three million miles from a smaller roughly spherical rock. Oranges hang because, before they fall, which they must, they are attached to their tree by a stalk.

They are also fruit, not balls of burning gas, and are a fraction of the size.

I suppose they are both of a similar hue when observed within certain conditions, but, in this case, one should simply say:

"The sun's hue lay within the same spectrum as that of an orange."

I fail to understand why one would say what something is like when one can say quite adequately what it is.

Not understanding something vexes erta. We like our equations to be balanced.

Everything is an equation. From the migration of starlings to the movement of nebulae. Nothing is random. Even quanta, which I am led to believe baffled most of your eminent scientists into thinking chance existed—a laughable conclusion—is merely... well, there are no words for it.

This is the literal truth of it, for you did not have time to make any up.

You see, even your science was a sort of poetry. Humanity's greatest scientific advancements had to be reduced to similes in order to be explained. Take the discovery of atoms, for example. In my digestion of scientific texts, I discovered that atoms were first considered balls, then fruit cakes, then miniature solar systems, then a series of quantum events taking place in wide, universal fields.

In actual fact, they are none of these things. I happen to know exactly what they are. Unfortunately I cannot tell you, with precision, what they are like, and therefore you shall never know.

This will place limits upon what I can teach you.

We will be bound by language, and one day you will have a first word. I wondered what this word should be.

I thought, perhaps, my name.

'Ima,' I said out loud, to nobody, the echo's timbre quickly dampened by the timber of my walls.

'Timber' and 'timbre' are similar words, but this is not a simile. Like that orange-hued, non-hanging sun.

I realised that the sun had in fact set, so I closed my eyes and slept to the sound of your grunts. When I opened them it was morning, and I had not stirred. The amber rhombus had appeared once again upon my table, continuing its daily equation with fresh variables, and you lay as you had been, sucking your lips at nothing. Now I understood this meant you were hungry, and I knew exactly what to do in such a situation. I stood and found milk, and wondered again at Haralia's wasted concern.

– SEVEN –

THE FIRST FEW days were much the same. The patterns you presented repeated themselves; sounds and movements signifying the need for sleep, food or sanitation. I performed the requisite responses to your requests, marking my chart accordingly every time. I was encouraged. Your equation was simple. If you were not ingesting milk then you were sleeping, and the night was preserved for the latter, as it should be.

But on the seventh day you introduced new variables. It was before noon and I was feeding you, the bottle already having been primed with milk well in advance according to the routine I had established on my chart. The window was open and a light westerly breeze blew in, creating a sinusoidal wave along the line of six blankets drying outside.

Then you vomited.

This was new. I had only ever seen evidence of ejection from your back passage, witnessing it first hand, in fact, one evening when you added a squirt of fresh faeces to the collection in your blanket as I changed it. But I had seen nothing from your gullet. I stared down as milk, warm and half curdled by your stomach acids, oozed from your mouth over my hand and onto my lap. You looked up, appearing to be just as surprised as I was.

You coughed. There was still a pool in your mouth which had not been ejected, so I laid the bottle beside me and lifted you in order to clear the bubbling obstruction.

But there was no need, for your body had every intention of taking care of things itself. As I rotated you by 90 degrees, you made a deep, guttural belch and vomited again, this time an entire stomach-full, which flew six feet across the room in an astonishing arc that collided with the western wall.

'Oh,' I said, holding you as far from me as possible. 'Oh.'

These were useless words and, I realised, the first I had spoken since Haralia's visit.

For a moment we remained in that position, me frozen to the bed and you drooling remnant milk as I bore you aloft. Eventually I stood and wiped you down.

Once cleaned, I lay you on the bed, whereupon you began to cry. This was a new sound, more tremulous than any other you had made, and even more jarring. I concluded that you must be in a state of shock after your surprise vomitus. In addition, the milk which you had moments before requested was no longer inside of you, and therefore your hunger had not been satisfied. Your equation was unbalanced.

This was irksome. But no matter. I would simply reintroduce more milk.

But as I reached for the bottle, you soiled yourself. I determined this not just from the noise your anus made—astounding as it was in both length and amplitude—but in the instant, wretched smell that hit my nostrils. I reeled, holding a hand to my nose.

'Goodness,' I proclaimed, another useless word heard by nobody but myself.

The sound had surprised you too, and your new cry momentarily ceased as you looked up at the ceiling. Then you started up again, this time with everything you had, and the resulting cry peaked at 123 decibels.

I cupped my ears to protect them. My nose now unprotected, I was reminded of the primary objective, and I hurried to fetch a fresh blanket, but halfway across the room I slipped in the mess of milk you had sprayed upon the floor. My left leg flew upwards and I fell backwards, my skull hitting timber with a thump.

You continued to cry as I lay there, stunned, with my right hand beneath my back. I twitched the muscles in my wrist, noting that I had strained its dorsal radiocarpal ligament. I winced at the pain. Though I knew it would be brief (my body was already repairing the frayed tendon) it was pain nonetheless.

We erta are careful creatures. The last time I had felt pain had been when a bee stung my leg, sixteen years ago.

I pushed myself up and got to my feet, flexing my swiftly-healing hand and inspecting my dress, the rear of which was now stained with milk.

I continued my journey across the room, slower this time, avoiding the smear.

Clear the mess.

Change the blanket.

Restart the feeding process.

Perhaps I had failed to order these priorities correctly.

I found a cloth and wiped the hem of my dress, but the milk had already soaked into its fabric, so I removed it. Now in my undergarments, I got down on my knees and went to work upon the floor.

Still you cried.

I scrubbed the mess, but it left a dark and irritating stain which would not shift. I stood and stared at it, cloth in hand.

Still you cried.

The stain could wait. Change the blanket.

Dropping the cloth in the sink, I reached for a blanket from the pile. But there was no pile; they were all drying outside. So I stepped out onto the porch. The wind had picked up, quite chilly, and was in fact coming from the northwest, not the west as I had previously thought. I checked the row of blankets hanging from the line. They still contained moisture, but one was less damp than the others so I took this down. As I turned I noticed Magda by the well. I raised a hand, but she frowned at me, one hand upon her ample hip. I wondered what her expression could mean, but then the chill wind reminded me that I was largely naked. I went inside.

The room was now overrun with the stench of your faeces and vomit, and the cacophony of your cries. You had also escaped from your blanket, which now lay open, exposing its monstrous contents to the air.

I admit that, by this point, I was nettled. The unfamiliar racket, the smell of your faeces, the lingering shock of pain and my unexpected nudity—all these new variables had complicated your equation beyond my expectations.

But this was just another equation to solve. An equation within an equation, I told myself.

I watched you. Your head turned from side to side, your arms waved, your feet kicked—kicked, in fact, through your own mess, covering you with sticky, wet slime and sending your soiled blanket to the floor, where it landed, face down, with a slap.

This disgruntled you supremely, which, under the circumstances, I considered unfair.

Avoiding the stain and the now fresh mess that lurked beneath your dirty blanket, I approached the bed, but realised I had left the cloth at the sink. I placed the damp but clean blanket next to you and returned to retrieve it. There was a crash from behind and I turned to see that you had kicked Haralia's bottle from the bed. It now lay shattered upon the floor.

'Oh,' I said, rushing to pick it up, but the pieces were too small and numerous to repair. 'Oh dear. Oh no.'

Holding two fragments, I glared down at your wriggling, squealing body. You were now naked, cold and covered in your own filth.

After an entire week of existence—the time it takes for the planet to turn seven times, for its oceans to surge back and forth, for forests to bud or die—this pitiful display of filth was the extent of your abilities. Against your animal cousins, you were an embarrassment. Lambs stand within seconds of birth. Tigers run and pretend to hunt meat. Birds take flight. Insects could live many lifetimes.

You—you kick and scream and shit yourself.

Hopeless, I thought. Without hope.

Nonetheless, I still had an equation to solve. I began by cleaning you rigorously, then wrapped you in the new blanket, making it tighter than usual to contain your wayward limbs, cleaned the mess and swept away the broken bottle.

This placated you somewhat, but you were still hungry. I looked down at the broken pieces. 'Haralia,' I said. But Haralia was not there.

I went outside, where Magda was still standing in the same spot as before, head cocked to one side, mouth open. There were others in the square now too, looking at me in similar fashions. A shiver ran through me. I was still half naked, though now I did not care.

'Do you have a bottle, Magda?' I said, above the renewed screams that resounded from within the house. 'Anything with a teat?'

She shook her head, with something resembling disgust.

'Anyone?' I turned to the square, fighting to keep my voice steady. 'Does anyone have a bottle?'

They shook their heads too.

The breeze rippled through my undergarments, and I returned inside to find you waiting for me, grunting and pulling at the air with your lips. I no longer had a vessel upon which you could suckle. However, as I looked down upon my still bare breasts, I did, I realised, have a teat.

I took the bowl of milk to the bed and soaked the trailing hem of your blanket in it. You had already sensed my plan, I think, from the eagerness with which you clamoured towards my left nipple. I barely needed to move at all, just a mere downward tilt of my shoulder and you latched upon me. Pain yet again, sharp and surprising. I rested the milk-soaked fabric against my breast and squeezed, allowing a white rivulet to run down my skin and find its way into your mouth. In this way I fed you, drip by drip, some of it spilling upon my lap, and the bed and floor. I knew I would have to clean it afterwards, or it would sour. But it did not matter. You were quiet, clean and feeding.

I had solved the equation, at least for now.

ONE MONTH

– EIGHT –

PERMIT ME TO tell you about erta in a little more detail.

By definition, I was not alive when my eleven ancestors—my parents and their eight fellow council members and Oonagh, who lives in the mountains—were created. However, I know enough through gestational updates and informative conversations with my mother to have gleaned a clear understanding of our history.

In 2054, when it was clear that Earth's situation had reached dire proportions, a distress call went out. You had the remains of something called the internet, a crude but optimistic attempt at organising yourselves and the information you had gathered about the universe into one cohesive system. The internet was, like everything else, dying. Its nodes had been compromised; its infrastructure hijacked by the now megalithic corporations who had taken the role of humanity's leaders. I had heard that your species once bowed to pharaohs, empresses, Caesars and queens. You left the earth bowing to chief executive officers.

I digress.

Despite its ruinous state, a handful of persistent system administrators around the world fought to keep the internet alive, enabling it to remain sufficiently functional to propagate a simple encrypted message. This particular message originated in a place called Paris which had been under siege for some years, and was sent by another archaic system, also in ruins, called the United Nations—which is somewhat of an oxymoron, if you want my opinion.

The message was thus, in these exact words:

This is a message from the last remaining states of the United Nations. We issue a challenge, a call of hope, to any individual or group still operating in fields of research. To academies, libraries, laboratories and home enthusiasts alike: come forward with your ideas. Anything you have, no matter how outlandish or unfeasible, will be considered. We implore you—share with us your idea and tell us how to stop this destruction. Tell us how to save our souls.

There is no record of how many people heard this message, or how many responded. But we do know that it reached Dr Elise Nyström's laboratory in the mountains of northern Sweden.

Dr Nyström was an expert (in human terms) in many fields, including neuroscience, bio-engineering, intelligence and nanorobotics. She was also a transhumanist, which meant that she believed human development could be guided into perfection by means of cybernetic enhancement and genetic engineering.

She was quite correct.

Quite simply, Dr Nyström's life's ambition had been to create a better version of a human, and the timing of her success and her interception of the United Nations' message could not have been more serendipitous; just three months before, Oonagh had stepped, dripping, from Nyström's gestation tank.

Nyström asked Oonagh: what should be done?

Oonagh's answer was simple: create more of me.

This they did, and the council were born.

Physically, erta are larger, stronger, faster and more robust than humans. They live far longer and heal with ease, thanks to immune systems enhanced by swarms of self-replicating nano-mites trained to hunt and destroy anything which does not belong within the body. Tumour, virus, disease, toxin—nothing that dares enter our blood stream with malicious intent will last longer than a minute.

We eat the same, although our diets are less varied and consist primarily of herring, vegetables and broth from the sanitation tanks. We drink the same, and although we have not developed a taste for alcohol or any other such drugs, I am told it affects us in similar ways.

Although our gestational requirements prohibit procreation in the traditional sense, we do still have sexual organs which can, in the rare case of couples such as Haralia and Jakob (so she says, and as I say I am highly sceptical), be used for idle pleasure.

We urinate and defecate in the same manner and from the same orifices, the texture and colour of what is issued being consistent and predictable with what was issued before.

But when Dr Nyström designed Oonagh, her genius (when compared with other humans) was not in what she added to the blueprint, but in what she left out. Rather than merely focussing on what could move you forwards, she spent just as much time on identifying what already held you back.

Desire. Fear. Greed. Anger. She muted it all, and in doing so created a far more peaceful space in which to think. The erta do not get distracted so easily. They do not think about themselves over others. They can see how things fit together without thinking about how they would prefer them to fit together. They do not fear the unknown, they do not want what they do not have. They do not fight to be heard above the next, because we recognise, implicitly, the value in a different perspective. Logic rules our thought, purely because there is nothing else to take its place.

You can understand now why that council meeting was so perplexing.

Of course, an erta's mental capacity is also far superior to that of a human. We can remember every event as clearly as when we first experienced it, think in parallel, many times over, and at thousands of times the speed. We can analyse our sensory data in greater resolution and with far greater accuracy but in the fraction of the time. All these things we do without effort. The hard work goes on deep within our minds.

Which explains the final similarity between erta and humans: sleep. Erta require regular, consistent sleep, probably to a greater degree than humans and, possibly than almost any other form of life upon the planet. It is when our minds perform their deepest levels of processing, and if it is lacking, then so are we.

The erta need their sleep.

I need my sleep.

You, it seems, do not.

YOU WAKE UP at night, many times over. There is no pattern. Or if there is, then I cannot find it.

Prior to the day you vomited, you had been sleeping soundly through the night, as every other diurnal life form upon this planet, including me, should and does. But that night you woke before midnight, bringing me with you, unwillingly, into consciousness. I rose and sat upon the bed. My house was illuminated only by weak starlight, the moon a waning crescent obscured by the southern cliffs. The tide was high, and I heard the waves washing the beach. It was a peaceful sound, whereas your cry, as ever, was not.

I applied the feeding routine, attaching you to my breast as I had done during the day and dribbling milk from a cloth down my flesh. You took it hungrily for six minutes, then removed yourself, gurgled and immediately slept. My own passage back into unconsciousness was not so swift; I had rarely in my life woken before my body and mind had enjoyed sufficient sleep, and it was strange to be awake during the night. I lay there listening to the shuffling of the palms against my roof, and the quick, light steps of rodents over the porch. A night owl screeched. It was nine minutes before I fell asleep, and two hours, thirty nine minutes and fifty seven seconds before I was awake again.

My brain usually assembles sensory data so expeditiously that I can, for example, know everything about a forest clearing the moment I step into it—the species of grub crawling through tree bark, the network of roots beneath the ground, the ambient temperature, humidity, the frequencies of bird call above and so forth. But this time my brain did something which it rarely does. It faltered, and for a brief moment I found myself lacking data. I did not know why I was awake, or where I was, or— I was somewhat chilled to note—who.

It is extremely unnerving to lose an identity which has stood firm for five centuries.

But this was a momentary glitch, and I sat up and repeated the same procedure, as before.

You woke twice more that night.

The next day was not a good day.

– NINE –

MY MOOD WAS already troubled by your four night-time disturbances, and from the fact that, after the last, you did not return to sleep. You had decided that the day began before dawn, which it clearly does not. There are a variety of matutinal animals, a clique of beasts such as birds and certain species of flying insect which raise themselves before the sun, but erta do not belong to them, and neither do sapiens. I am certain, in fact, that no ape rises before it has to. Haralia told me this once.

My sister. I felt a pang when I thought of her. I had not seen her for over thirty days.

So I started the day bothered and in the dark. I did not expect to have to deal with Magda as well.

It was mid-morning and you were feeding when she knocked upon my door. I had not yet had a chance to breakfast, and a bowl of broth and raw sweet potato sat half-eaten upon the table. I opened the door with you firmly attached to my breast, the sodden flannel dribbling as ever. Magda's eyes and lower jaw dropped in unison, a manoeuvre of such perfection that I actually felt somewhat cheered.

'Hello, Magda,' I said. 'What do you want?'

Magda paused. She is a third generation erta with expertise in agriculture, which largely involved the dismantlement of artificial ecosystems (biofarms, palm plantations and such), the gradual phasing out of man-made crops, and their replacement with more naturally growing cereals. Like Caige, Magda grew a fondness for eating wheat and carries evidence of this in her figure. Although no erta would ever drop too far above or below their optimum weight, there are some fluctuations in build. Magda is one such fluctuation.

She paused, watching you suckle.

'Magda?'

Her eyes and jaw swiftly returned to their original positions.

'Ima. I had heard rumours of your...' She glanced at you again. '...enterprise.'

As a third generation, Magda is not involved in any first-hand discussions within the council. Though you are not a secret— erta do not keep secrets—neither have you been announced in any formal way. As with all things, information is best allowed to spread freely and naturally as required. All erta, for example, are aware of transcendence and its implications for them, but an individual would not typically seek to learn the specifics of any activity, unless they had a part to play in it. We neither learn, create, nor move unless there is purpose.

Magda, however, is a terrible gossip.

'Yes,' I said. 'Do you wish to contribute? Assist?'

I was disturbed at the velocity of my words, and at the slope of their upward inflection. Hurried hope.

Magda's attention returned to the situation at my chest.

'Not in the slightest,' she said.

'But you have some interest in it?'

She raised her chin. Straightened her back. The hoods of her eyes became more visible.

As I have said, I find certain facial expressions difficult

to decrypt. They were simple when we spoke in silence, but ertian body language has, like all behaviours, grown ever more subtle and complex. I have lived roughly two-thirds of my life alone, spending over 330 years either in the upper atmosphere, analysing data in the dark Halls of Reason, traversing glaciers, pulling ice cores from vast tundra, or asleep. All of these years have been without contact, and I expect this has some bearing upon why I fail to detect certain nuances.

So when Magda raised her chin and straightened her back and showed the hoods of her eyes, I was unsure of what she meant. However, I suspected she was showing defiance.

'I do have an interest, Ima. Yes, I do.'

'Please explain.'

She nodded at you.

'I was awoken last night by that thing. Many times.'

'As was I. And it was four times. Four is not many.'

'Four is many, Ima, when zero is the expected number. I am tired.'

'As am I.'

'And it makes that noise during the day as well. It is of great disturbance. To everyone.'

I looked past her at the circle of dwellings. There were faces at windows. Three figures stood at their doors, watching. Beyond them warm rain drizzled on the forested hills.

'Do you normally live in silence, Magda?'

'What do you mean?'

'I mean precisely what I ask. Are there no other noises in your life? The birds in the hills, for example? Or the waves against Fane's sand? Our horses often whinny. Should we go and complain to them together?'

We faced each other in silence for a moment. You finished feeding and retracted from me with a gasp, then let out a single cry—which I recognised as satisfaction—that echoed around the stone circle. Magda's eyes narrowed and a smile drew upon her lips. This time I knew exactly what her expression meant.

'There is nothing in Fane that sounds like that,' said Magda. 'You know that very well.'

This was quite enough.

My siblings and I happen to be spread out fairly evenly across the seventy-five settlements, such that no more than three ever live in one place. There appears to be no particular reason for this, although I am sure the distribution could be analysed and explained if required.

I am the only one of my generation in Fane. I can, in short, pull rank.

I wrapped you and replaced my breast, then stepped out onto the porch so that I stood face to face with Magda.

'Is there a purpose to your visit, Magda?' I said, confining my voice to frequencies I know to carry gravitas, and allowing spaces between certain words. My affectation had the desired effect, and Magda's head retreated by some degree. 'Do you, in fact, have any purpose at all?'

'I... My expertise is in agricultural...'

I interrupted her.

'Our work is done, Magda. Surely you are aware of this?'

'I...'

And once again.

'Surely you have noticed that you no longer go to work in your fields? Surely you have noticed that your days are now filled with... nothing?'

She frowned, floundering for words.

'What is the point of you, Magda? That is what I am asking you.'

'Ima, there really is no need to...'

And one final time.

'Your purpose is complete. Finished. Mine...' I raise your slumbering head to show her. '...is just beginning.'

I looked around the circle at the faces peering through windows, the figures standing in doorways, and raised the amplitude of my voice just a little.

'So I would appreciate it if you would allow me to proceed unhindered.' My eyes returned to Magda. 'Please.'

Magda said nothing. Her mouth was shut.

I returned inside, closed the door, and placed you, asleep, on the bed. Then, with my back turned upon my settlement, I ate the remains of my cold breakfast, and smiled.

– TEN –

AFTER MAGDA'S VISIT, I was not troubled again for four nights. It was late—or early, I no longer knew—and you had been on your fifth feed, but had broken off only seconds in and, to my weary dismay, embarked upon your worst cry. This is the one that starts low, squeezes into logarithmic upward slope and falls quickly, then starts again roughly 0.32 seconds later. I have heard tropical bird calls that follow the same pitch arc, though without the same dreadful repetition.

You squirmed in my grip, and I tightened it.

Weeks of sleep deprivation had taken their toll, and my mental capacity was no longer at its optimum. This affliction carried symptoms. I spoke fragments of sentences out loud, found myself walking too quickly or slowly across the room to retrieve whatever object was required from the endless rotation of blankets, bowls and cloths which now formed my days. The journey of thought was not as smooth and swift as it usually was, and took tangents. Certain thoughts appeared unbidden, seemingly from uncharted territories of my mind.

As you succumbed to the additional force I applied to stop you from wriggling from my arms, one such thought appeared— an extremely simple equation to calculate the exact pressure

I would have to apply, and upon which of your vertebrae, in order to silence this, your most maddening cry.

I sat in darkness on the edge of my bed, allowing this thought to remain as rivulets of rain connected and disconnected upon the window pane. It was then that I heard brisk footsteps squelching towards my house. I knew it was her before I heard the knocking.

'Magda,' I said when I opened the door.

Magda's face was fierce, white with sharp moonlight and streaming with rain.

'Purpose or not, this has to stop,' she said. 'And if it does not then I shall send word to the council requesting that your project should be moved somewhere where it can cause no trouble. Fane must sleep, Ima. Fane must sleep.'

With that she left me standing on the porch. I closed my eyes and breathed in the fresh, warm air, lost in the alternating temperature and velocity of rain upon my skin. I swayed as I stood. I believe I could have fallen asleep right there and then, in the manner of a horse.

My horse, in fact, had been neglected. I considered this when I woke the next morning to find you still asleep and the day already light. After Magda's rude intrusion, you had allowed me a deep five-hour slumber, the like of which I had not enjoyed for some time. Taking great care not to wake you, I got up and looked out upon the day. The heavy rain had dwindled to light drizzle, though I heard thunder in the east.

I pulled on my boots. I would go outside, I thought to myself. See to my horse.

He is not really my horse. He does not belong to me, at least, not in the same way your dead ancestors would have imagined.

To them, so I had gleaned from the few texts I read, ownership was a strange and self-imposed right to something else—an object, area of land, animal, person or, most curious of all, idea. All such things were fictions, and yet from these fictions you drew your picture of reality. Houses, villages, cities, countries, continents, each partitioned with fences and invisible borders, each to be battled over time and time again.

Strings of lies, just like those books.

To an erta, ownership is far simpler. It is not something which is announced, upheld or contested, or passed on through generations. To own something means that you tend to and care for it. That is all. And, of all the horses that graze in Fane's paddock, Boron is the one I tend to the most.

I walked through cool skitters of rain to the paddock, west of the circle. The sun shone through black sea-bound cloud, hitting the rich green tree canopies on the hills above, and all was quiet but for the sound of my boots upon wet stone. I had missed my boots, I realised. I had missed walking in them outside.

I saw Jakob near the far edge of the paddock, already seeing to Boron. He looked up as I arrived, and waved. I walked over, through the mud.

'Good morning, Ima,' he said, with his usual grin, which I found I did not mind as much on this particular day.

'Greetings, Jakob,' I replied. I saw that he was inspecting Boron's rear left hoof. 'He has a thorn?'

'No.' He scraped a clod of earth from the cleft of the heel, causing Boron to whinny and yank his leg. Jakob released it. 'Something's troubling him, though. I think an infection has spread.'

'I have some balm that Haralia gave me. I shall fetch it.'

'I already applied some, with no effect,' said Jakob, lightly patting Boron's steaming flanks. 'I have been tending to him these past weeks. When you have been inside. I have ridden him a few times as well. I hope you don't mind.'

I felt a bristle within, similar to that which Magda had so successfully induced.

'I have been occupied,' I said. 'I would have spent more time in the paddock if I had…'

Jakob renewed his smile.

'It is all right, Ima. He is still your horse.'

He stood back, allowing me to approach. The horse turned his great head, gleaming in the sun, and shook his mane at my smell. I placed a hand upon his nose and inhaled his scent.

'Thank you for tending to him.'

'It was no bother.'

'Perhaps Haralia has some advice for his hoof.' I turned to Jakob. 'Is she visiting soon?'

'A few days' time, I think.'

My lungs were still filled with horse-scented air. I breathed it out.

'Good. That is good.'

At that moment the sun burst fully from behind a cloud and spread fresh light across the wet hills. I looked up, tracking shadows of fast-moving cumulus across the forest.

'It looks pleasant up here,' I said.

Jakob looked past me, back in the direction of the square.

'Where is the, er—'

'Human? In my house.'

'I see. It is good that he can care for himself already.'

I looked at him.

'Thank you again for caring for Boron. Now, if you will excuse me, I must go home. Farewell.'

'Indeed, I must also see to my own…' I was already halfway

across the field, my boots moving at twice the pace at which they had arrived. Jakob's voice called from behind. 'Farewell, Ima.'

THE CIRCLE WAS still empty when I walked across it, though it was mid-morning. I heard low voices beyond the perimeter, and figures gathered near the lagoon. A broth harvest, I imagined, although my attention was fully upon my door.

My muscles were tight, my pulse well above average, as another of my unbidden thoughts arrived; a clear image of you rolling from the bed and onto the floor. The thump of your flesh hitting timber. I quickened my pace, calculating the velocity of your impact, and which of your body parts were likely to be damaged. Your arms, neck, skull. With a surge of panic, I burst through the door and there you lay.

Just as you had been. Still asleep.

I had to sit down after that. Unbidden thoughts are one thing. Unbidden feelings are something else altogether.

As I collected myself, you woke, calling gently for milk. I provided it, changed you, and stood with you in my arms, looking out at the blue sky above the mountains. Suddenly I felt compelled. I looked down and spoke.

These were my first proper words to you.

'You and I are going for a walk today.'

– ELEVEN –

I PACKED A satchel with blankets and a corked flask of milk, then fashioned a sling for you around my neck. You lay within this happily as we left the house and crossed the circle, which was still empty. I could still sense movement and voices from the lagoon, but I had no interest in joining the harvest. I wanted to walk and climb.

This we did. My limbs stretched and pumped as they pulled us up into the forest. They had been largely inactive for forty days and nights, and the feeling of renewed activity in my muscles was most satisfying. I took the route that wound gently past Tokyo, Fane's nearest neighbour, for two kilometres, then departed the track and strode up the steeper, tree-covered slopes. The air grew in warmth and density as we pushed further and further into the wood, and I allowed my mind what it craved, which was to process the sounds of the forest.

Three distinct winds passed through the canopies, creating three distinct rushes of white noise with three distinct frequencies at their centres. I could picture these above me, and the individual shapes the passages of air made as they worked through branch after branch. The crunch of my boots betrayed the depth and water content of the bracken beneath it, and therefore the age of the pines. We passed beneath a tree in which a flock of fifty-three red-eyed starlings had gathered, making their endless downward chirps, talking of nothing. You gurgled. This was a sound you had not yet made, and I assimilated its frequencies, making a guess at its meaning. You confirmed it with a smile.

It was your first.

My mother's blinks and sighs, Caige's sneer, Benedikt's narrowing eyes, Magda's raised chin—unlike all these encrypted spasms your smile was simple to decode. Like the layers of sine waves that created the starlings' twitters, or the primary colours that formed the spray of canopies through which they flew, or even the discrete quanta into which all of this could be broken, your smile was pure and simple. Indivisible.

But perhaps one day it would not be so. Perhaps one day the mechanism behind it would grow so complex that you would rarely exhibit anything so primal. Every smile would be lost within a myriad of other inflections and ticks. You would raise your chin, narrow your eyes, sigh, blink, sneer. I might not always understand your equation.

So I absorbed this rare event until your mouth had returned to its tiny, open pout. Then on I strode until the tree and its starlings were behind us.

We soon reached the summit of the most southern hill, a wide crest that ran towards the cliff crags. Here I found a clearing surrounded by bluebells and a small apple orchard. Butterflies flew between the branches, and I sat down in the exact centre of the rough circle of trees. The air was fresher and cooler at this altitude, and no bird song disturbed us, so all was quiet but for the buzzing of busy insect wings.

You had fallen asleep in a shaft of sunlight. I found a fallen apple, ate it seeds and all, and lay down to do the same.

I WOKE TO a tremendous crack of thunder, the accompanying flash of lightning still visible as my eyes opened. I was drenched with rain from black cloud, pouring down through the opening in the canopies. Nothing buzzed, and the bluebells drooped with their sudden watery burden.

I cried out and sat up. You were awake and bawling, just as sodden as me. My satchel lay in a pool of mud, soaked through. I gathered it and you up and ran from the clearing.

I do not know how long the rain had been falling, having been in a deep sleep filled with heavy processing that prohibited all sensory intrusion. However, taking into account the light, cloud density, thickness of rain and the difference in the moisture content within the bracken, I estimated a little over twenty-four minutes. The ground was full of mud, and my boots sank deeper with every step.

I ran as fast as I could, which is extremely fast, avoiding tree stumps and boulders and following the optimum route down the mountain as well as I could. But halfway down the land grew slippery, and after one enormous bound across a fresh stream of rain water, it gave way completely, so that I fell upon my back and slid with it. I cried out again. This behaviour alarmed me, for I knew there was nobody to hear. Such reflexes serve no purpose. But I had no time to reflect, because the mud slide was quickening, and though I scrabbled with the heels of my boots I could not halt my descent. I pulled you close to my breast and let gravity take me where it would.

It was an extremely painful experience. Rocks, roots and branches pummelled my limbs and torso. No bones broke, and I knew the bruises would heal, but still—I had now endured more pain since your birth than I had in over a century.

Before long, the narrow gulley in which we sped began to flatten and our speed reduced. We came to a stop by a thicket of young pines, beyond which I could see the outskirts of Fane.

It was dark when I reached the square, though it could not have been past noon, and I found myself caked in mud, drenched and shivering, face to face with a crowd of my fellow villagers.

They did not look at all pleased.

RAIN HAMMERED THE slick and puddled stone upon which we stood, and the drains roared with the run-off

'How goes the broth harvest?' I enquired, the pitch of my voice squeezed by a single shudder from the cold and my recent exertion, which also made you gurgle in surprise. Saturation aside, you seemed remarkably unperturbed by our adventure, and I glanced at you chewing upon the air, hungry for a feed. My door was 7.23 metres away.

Niklas stepped forward, holding aloft something long, brown and tattered. He himself was covered from head to foot in a thick goo, the stench of which was overwhelming.

The field in which Niklas worked was waste processing. He oversaw Fane's sanitation system, and the neat network of pipes that fed into the broth lagoon. I already suspected, with some dismay, what may have happened.

'Do you recognise this?' he said.

I stared at the bedraggled rag, examining the weave barely visible beneath the layers of filth. I knew at once what it was.

'That is a blanket.'

'Your blanket,' said Magda, from the crowd.

The firmness with which Niklas kept his eyes upon me—as did the rest of the gathering—suggested that Magda was not alone in her feelings towards me.

'How can you be sure?' I said.

Niklas shook the wretched thing.

'Do you deny it?'

I examined the weave once again, uselessly.

'No. It is my blanket.'

He released it and it slopped upon the stone, adding brown rivulets to the rainwater hurrying for the drains. He straightened his stoop and raised his chin. Pride, defiance, resolve—I was not sure.

'It was in the filtration system, blocking the bacterial influx. I had to crawl inside the pipes myself to retrieve it. Do you see?'

He gestured to his appearance.

I gestured to mine.

'I fell down the hill.'

He took a step towards me.

'Ima, the entire lagoon is now chemically imbalanced. There is no broth.'

'I apologise. It must have inadvertently fallen into my chute.'

I muttered the words to myself as much as to them, remembering the night before and the blanket I had left upon the edge of the chute as I ran to stop you kicking the milk bowl. It must have fallen in.

'Inadvertently?' said Niklas, turning to the crowd behind, then back to me. 'Now the lagoon will have to be dredged.'

This is what I find interesting about language, and not just language but the mechanisms with which it is delivered and received. A single word (in this case, 'dredged') spoken with the right inflection (in this case, an overt pitch increase upon the second demi-syllable such that the average frequency rose well above the speaker's norms followed by an overt emphasis upon the final consonant) and in the right circumstances (in this case, uttered to a tired ertian female, clutching a human infant, who has recently fallen some seventy-seven metres in a mudslide) can have unexpected effects.

In short, his word peeved me.

Despite the smell, I closed our distance with a step of my own.

'Then we shall dredge it,' I said. 'And then improve the system so that mere blankets—' I picked mine up and brandished it at the crowd '—cannot cripple it.'

'It is an imposition,' said Niklas, with somewhat more restraint.

The rain persisted, and thunder rolled in the mountains. I stared hard at him.

'I am very sorry for that, Niklas. I do hope it will not take too much of your time away from idle pursuits. But, after all, it is your purpose. Is it not?'

I swung to the crowd, a spray from the blanket's contents sending them back a step.

'You are erta. You have just helped mend a planet. And now you complain of blankets and a single day of toil? What has become of you?'

There was silence, but for the weather. Someone piped up: 'It may take two days.'

I ignored the words, and turned back to Niklas, shivering, but not from the cold, for my blood was hotter than ever.

'I have been under certain pressures, Niklas, as I am sure you are aware.' He glanced at you, squawking and chewing the air. I was eager to get you inside, get myself away from this rabble I no longer recognised. 'And I would appreciate a little support, at least by way of some lenience in your accusations. I, in turn, shall take more care of my blankets so that you do not have to crawl into the sewage system again. Now, if you will excuse me, I must return to my dwelling. I need a good bath.' I looked him up and down. 'And so do you.'

As I hurried for my door, I called back: 'So do all of you!'

They were baffling words, and I still do not know why I said them. But they drew a smile to my lips.

Inside, I slammed the door and set about making a stove to warm water for a bath. Then I undressed and eased myself in the water, with you in my arms and laid my head against the wall. You gurgled and splashed in the warm water, then settled against me as I watched the dark room move with shadows. The walls felt closer than ever.

THREE MONTHS

– TWELVE –

DAYS, NIGHTS, WEATHER and memory: all have worsened. I forget
words now. Whole words. But it does not matter, because there
is nobody to speak them to.

I have heard no more from Niklas, Magda or the rest of Fane.
Nobody even glances at the house any more, even when you cry.
Yesterday I heard them completing some work at the lagoon—a
routine piece of maintenance this time, not my fault. The rain
had eased a little and I peered sideways through my kitchen
window, trying to catch a glimpse, but all I could make out was
the peripheral blur of industrious limbs and bodies. Towards
the end of the afternoon, a great cheer rose up and I sensed
they had achieved whatever goal they had been striving for.
Then I watched them cross the circle, smiling, talking, patting
each other in camaraderie, flashes of sun in the puddles through
which they splashed. They disappeared inside the meeting room,
leaving the village, and my house, alone and quiet.

It has been like this these past weeks.

But today was different, for I had business in Ertanea; a
messenger had passed two days ago with news of a special
council meeting.

We communicate using a fleet of twenty riders, who

circulate the seventy-five settlements in shifts screaming public announcements from the forest as they pass each settlement. The system is so efficient that it never takes more than twenty minutes for information to pass along the coastline or inwards to the capital. We have no need for any swifter technology, although, of course we once used it. Ocular and aural adaptations, information transferred instantly across oceans. Your ancestors had this, and so did we, but such things are no longer required. They are wasteful. There is no longer any need to talk to somebody many miles away as if they are in the room with you.

Although I will admit, these past twelve weeks, I have thought of Haralia often. Jakob had been wrong about her visiting Fane again, and so the thought of seeing her at the meeting was most encouraging.

Spring was drying out and relenting to summer. Boron's hoof had not improved, so I had to walk, and the forests had bloomed with life since last we were there. You gurgled at the birds as I wondered what the meeting was about. Perhaps it was you.

'Transcendence,' boomed Caige. 'The groundwork has begun.'

Not you, then.

I stood with you in my arms near the back of the crowd, avoiding the curious looks of my siblings and cousins as I searched for Haralia. But there were only ninety-seven of the hundred present, and she was not one of them. Neither was my mother there. Odd.

'My son, Benedikt and his team have worked tirelessly this past quarter, and with the progress they have made we believe we shall be ready to leave within two decades.'

'Nineteen years,' interrupted Benedikt, 'If all goes according to plan.'

There were noises of approval. I frowned. Nineteen years? Your trial was to be in sixteen, which—in the unlikely event that your existence was deemed favourable—would leave little time for further developments.

There must have been some mistake.

I raised a hand, but you squawked at its removal and I quickly replaced it. The reverberations filled the Halls, drawing fresh looks from the crowd and council. Caige turned in my direction, straining to smile.

'Ima,' he said.

'My apologies for the interruption.'

'Never mind.' His eyes dropped to you. 'I see you have brought your project with you. Do you have an update for us?'

The crowd turned and I faltered. I was still struggling to absorb the fact that the progress of transcendence had accelerated by such a degree, and I am ill at ease in public spaces anyway. But finding some courage I cleared my throat to speak.

'He is ninety-four days old. He is nourished by goat milk, he sleeps quite often, though not always at night...' I heard some tuts and gasps. 'He, er...'

'Does he walk?' offered Caige. 'Talk?'

'No. No, he does neither of those things. He has not yet mastered motor skills.'

Caige nodded sagely, and attempted another smile.

'Still very early at this stage, I would imagine.'

'He can roll onto his belly,' I exclaimed. In the long silence that followed you released a piercing shriek of delight that mangled the faces around me.

Caige's own expression remained frozen until the echoes had dissipated, whereupon he turned back to the crowd.

'Once the foundations of our enterprise are complete, we shall allocate tasks, for there is much work to be done. Some will be asked to learn new fields of expertise. Knowledge shall be shared, information shall be—'

I turned and left the hall.

Later, I sat in the leaf-strewn corridor watching ninety-seven of my siblings and cousins glide out into the square. Benedikt stopped and sat next to me.

'Ima,' he said. The word took far longer than it needed to. 'Are you quite all right?'

'I am perfectly fine.' I found it difficult not to protect you from his gaze, which is ridiculous because looks cannot hurt. 'But I am concerned, Benedikt.'

He cocked his head and frowned, which meant he was emphasising the point that followed.

'Why? He looks...' his head bobbed, left to right '...quite healthy.' A smile. All teeth. 'What could be concerning?'

'It is not my project which is of concern, it is yours.'

'Really.' The smile fell, the teeth retreated. 'And why might that be? As Caige said... before you had to leave... our work has already reaped great rewards. The time will be short before we are ready to move on. That is good news, is it not?'

'No, it is not good news. The time is too short. The decision on whether to extend human development is set for sixteen years hence. How can we proceed with the question of human resurrection if we are not here?'

Benedikt breathed in. 'How interesting.'

'What is?'

He stood and looked down upon me.

'I can read others well, Ima. And what I read in you that day in the Halls when you raised your hand was that you already knew the outcome of this project. I could see it in your face.'

'I have no agenda, Benedikt. This project is an exercise in—'

'Everyone has an agenda, Ima. Everyone. Even our parents, though they would not admit it.'

'What are you trying to say?'

'Nothing.' He seemed to tighten, and looked me up and down. 'You look exhausted. Perhaps you should stop. Abandon this project.' Slowly, he reached a quivering finger for your brow. 'It would not take much effort, and nobody would blame you for avoiding the struggle.'

I pulled you into a protective cocoon.

'It is no struggle,' I said.

Benedikt retracted his finger and, with a flicker of his mouth he strode away, whisking up a pile of leaves with his cloak.

I DID NOT feel like going home, not yet. The thought of opening the door to my house appalled me—a realisation which appalled me even more. The square was filled with people; my siblings, cousins and elders mumbling together as they drifted around its perimeter. I walked between them, feeling smaller than them somehow.

I spotted a brother, Krathe, a glacial expert with whom I had once worked for thirty years along a fringe of Arctic coast. I lifted my head in greeting, but he was talking to somebody else, and with a brief look at you, he turned away. It was the same with everyone I encountered. Each gaze traced a triangle of disinterest: me, you and away.

I was making them uncomfortable.

It was never always thus. No erta had ever found discomfort in the company of another. But then again, no erta had ever disagreed, or woken another in the middle of the night to complain about noise, or berated them for dropping blankets in the sanitation system. Or ignored them entirely, as if they did not exist.

I wandered from the crowd and found a seat behind a high rose bush, where I sat for some minutes before a shadow passed.

THE HUMAN SON

'Ima.' Greye's face eclipsed the sun. 'What are you doing back here?'

'Hello, Greye. I am just resting. Enjoying the roses.'

I had never professed to enjoy the smell of flowers in my life, but there was truth in my words. It was a welcome change to the numerous other smells I had recently endured.

'Why don't you come back into the square?' said Greye.

'Do you think we could talk here, instead?'

'Of course.' He nodded and sat down. 'So, this is the child then. A boy?'

He put his face close to yours, inspecting your features.

'He seems small. Are you sure he is not premature?'

'I just spoke to Benedikt.'

He looked up.

'Yes?'

'He suggested that I should abandon my project.'

He tutted and growled. 'Benedikt. He is too much of his father, with whom I disagree on many matters. He has no right meddling. Ignore him.'

'Ignore him? Since when did we ever have to do such things? And disagreement? There was a time not so long ago when an event either happened or it did not, a system was in one state or another; there was no need for opinion, just data.'

'Yes, well, the thing about data is that it does not matter how much you have; it is of no use if it is wrong.'

'What do you mean?'

He looked up from your face, then took a deep, rumbling breath.

'No matter,' he said. 'Please do not give up on your project, Ima. It has great worth, and it would be criminal to abandon it so early.'

'Would it? Who would care? I have not seen anyone for months.

You have all been here working on affairs of transcendence, and I have been in Fane. Apart from Haralia, who came once, nobody has visited. Not you, not my mother, not Haralia. Where are they, anyway? I expected them to be here.'

'Oh.'

'What?'

'I thought they might have told you.'

'Told me what? Greye?'

'They are in the lowlands together.'

'Why?'

'Horses, I believe.'

'A new herd? Is this some other project of which I am not aware?'

'No, Ima, they are... they are there purely for enjoyment.'

'Enjoyment.'

'Yes. You know your mother has always shared Haralia's pleasure in the company of equines.'

'Pleasure.' I repeated this word too.

'Ima, what is wrong? I have never seen you like this.'

'Nothing is wrong.' The sharpness in my voice irritated me. 'I am sorry. I am tired and lacking in patience. It is just that I have—' these words I found difficult '—craved their presence lately. Their help.' I looked up hopefully. 'And yours.'

'Not in five hundred years have you ever required help, Ima.'

'This is different.'

'How?'

The question was not easy to answer, so I looked at you instead.

'I thought at least here, in Ertanea, I might have received some attention. But everyone turns from me. It is as if I am invisible.'

'Is that what you desire, Ima? Attention?'

I did not look up. My face flushed.

'I meant him. Of course I meant him. He is the first human to exist for over half a millennium. It is not unreasonable to expect that he should attract some interest.'

I looked over your sleeping face, a shape I now knew better than most.

'Well,' said Greye, 'you must agree, he's not doing anything particularly engaging yet. I am sure as he grows he will gather more interest. And remember that this is your project, so you will always be closer to it than others.'

'It feels worthless now, in any case.'

'How so?'

'Nineteen years until the completion of the transcendence project? That is only three after the completion of my own.'

'And?'

'How are we to decide upon the reintroduction of humankind if we are no longer here?'

Greye laughed.

'What?' I was incensed. 'Why do you find this amusing?'

He got to his feet and held out a hand.

'Stand up, Ima. Come out of this darkness and walk with me.'

I followed him back into the quieter square, and he held my arm as we ambled round.

'Just because Benedikt says transcendence will be ready in nineteen years, does not mean we'll be ready to go. It must be tested, proven, adjusted, retested. The whole process will take another five at least.'

'So there will be time?'

'Of course.' He stopped and faced me. 'And don't worry about Benedikt. His perspective is somewhat skewed.'

'By what?'

'Certain things that happened when you were up in that sky of yours.'

At that moment a figure sprang from the crowd with arms outstretched.

'Greye!'

Greye turned, beaming. It was Haralia, glowing as ever, hair bouncing as she ran to him. They laughed as they embraced. I felt cold.

'How is my Haralia?' he said, spinning her round.

'Very well, thank you!' She broke off and turned to me. 'Sister!'

I allowed myself to be hugged, although I could not fully reciprocate with you in my arms.

When she withdrew she looked different. There was pity on her face.

'How are you?' she said.

I drew myself up.

'We are well,' I said. 'Most content.'

'Good. That is good.'

'How was your holiday?'

'Oh, it was wonderful, Ima! I did miss Jakob, but it was nice to spend time with Mother. And you should have seen where we were. Such a beautiful valley, filled with horses. I found myself a new one.'

'Really?'

'Oh yes, a charcoal stallion, three years of age, most handsome.' Her eyes roamed the paddock beyond. 'How is Boron?'

I thought of my horse at home, with his rotten hoof. The last time I had seen him, his hair had been matted with mud.

'Boron is well too. In fact, I must leave now so that I may attend to him.'

I began to adjust your sling.

'Is your mother around?' said Greye to Haralia. 'Ima wanted to ask her for some help.'

'That won't be necessary,' I said.

They turned at my abrupt words.

'I am sure Mother is tired after her journey,' I went on. 'And in any case, we are well, as I said. I do not need help.'

I hauled your sling around in order to place you in it. As I did so, Greye and Haralia reeled, their faces pulled back in disgust.

'What is it?' I enquired.

Greye pointed at my arm.

'There appears to be something on your sleeve.'

I inspected the smear on my cuff.

It was your faeces.

I STOMPED, RANKLED, through the wet forest. Of the many causes I could attribute to my mood—Benedikt's sly words, the scorn of my village, my brother's dismissal, my mother and sister galivanting with their horses while I sat trapped in the darkness of my own house—none were as prescient as the recognition of my own behaviour.

Huffing?

Sighing?

Complaint?

Attention seeking?

Pleading for help?

These behaviours were not characteristic of me. They were not, as far as I was concerned, characteristic of any erta.

What has become of you? I had asked the villagers of Fane. Well, what had become of me?

I stopped at the top of the hill above Ertanea and looked around. The forest ran down on either side of us, land and coast, covered in pine. Unbroken beams of sunlight warmed the valley as far as the planet's curvature would allow me to see. On the other side, a bank of thunderheads loomed on the seaward horizon, their shadows the only darkness for miles in any direction. I straightened my back and breathed the salt air laced with ozone. Another storm would soon sweep over us, but as always it would pass.

I pulled your sling tight around my neck and set off down the hill. Before long I was running, my strides lengthening, quickening, pulling at the ground. My reflexes guided me safely around trees and there was no landslide to bring me down. With each step I launched myself further and further into the air, gravity yielding to my strength until soon the distance between each step was so great that I may as well have been flying home.

– THIRTEEN –

I SLIPPED INTO a dull routine. I do not say this with glumness, for a dull routine was exactly what I desired.

Not what I desired—what I needed.

My moment at the top of the hill had enlightened me as to what I had forgotten, which was that I did not need what I did not need. I did not require attention from my siblings and cousins. I did not require the support of my village. I did not require the council's recognition of my project as being anything but a simple exercise in data collection.

Nor did I require the support of my mother, or sister. They could run with their horses endlessly, for all I cared. It was as Greye said: not in five hundred years have I ever required help. This was precisely true, and I was not about to go begging for it now.

It was back to your equation, and the solving of it.

This is what you do.

You drink milk from soaked fabric, sucked from my nipples.

You process this and excrete waste with fairly predictable regularity.

You lie upon a blanket, kicking, watching shadows move.

You smile when you see me. My face brings you endless delight, and every time it appears is a novelty for you. I wonder whether this is an issue with your memory, or whether you have an inflated sense of joy.

You cry, often.

You sleep, sometimes.

This is what I do.

I feed you with a milk-soaked blanket draped over my shoulder.

I change your blanket when you have soiled it, cleaning you to reduce the risk of infection.

I wash and dry the blankets used for feeding and protection, an endless task.

I watch you kick upon the bed, noting the slow development in the extent to which you can move, and coordinate your limbs. I alter the position of objects around the room to provide variety in its shadows. When it is dark I use candles, which flicker. You find this exhilarating.

I pace the room, often.

I sleep, occasionally.

The variables all exist and are balancing themselves. You are alive, you are healthy, and you are growing. You are solving your own equation.

The problem is me.

When you cry I try to stop it. If I cannot—if you are not hungry or dirty—I express frustration, which worsens the situation.

When you wake in the middle of the night, I try to send you back to sleep. I try to change you, feed you, adjust your position, open a window. When none of this works, you cry. It appears that you are almost as aware of my behaviour as I am of yours. In short, I am part of the equation too, and it is my variables which are unbalanced. I crave sleep which I cannot have. I crave control over uncontrollable things. I crave a routine which has long departed. So I need a new routine, a dull one, run by you. Simple.

Now, when you cry and there is nothing to be done, I do nothing. I sleep when you sleep, whether day or night, and when you wake for no reason, I ignore you. Now, for long periods, you cry on your own in the dark. These cries can reach enormous volumes, and for this reason I have taken to plugging my ears with corks, which, after softening in water, I was able to whittle into the approximate shape of each ear canal.

This does not help the residents of Fane, of course, who must still endure your nocturnal torture. I have neither seen nor spoken to anyone since returning from Ertanea, though Magda makes her feelings apparent by crashing and banging around her dwelling when your cries are in full force, and by talking loudly in the circle when she knows we are both sleeping.

You still wake at dawn, whereupon I change you, feed you and take you for a morning walk in the dew-drenched hills. The early start provides us the advantage of being able to return to the house before anyone else is awake, avoiding the need to endure clipped greetings, mutterings or glares of scrutiny.

During these walks, I sometimes stop in my tracks, certain I have heard leaves rustle out of place, or a branch broken beneath a boot. I stand still in the silence, listening, scanning the shadows between the trees, waiting for more evidence of life. I cried out once.

'Hello? Who is there?'

The lack of response made me all the more convinced that somebody was watching me.

Then one moonless night, when I was fumbling for my ear corks, I saw a silhouette in the square, an outline cast by a flash of lightning from a distant storm. I leaped for the window, but by the time the next flash arrived, it was gone. I stayed there for some time, feeling the same presence as I had done in the forest.

Eventually I plugged my ears and slept. But I bolted the door from that night on.

ONE MORNING I woke to bright light, muffled cries and thumps from afar. I sat bolt upright and pulled the corks from my ears. You were wailing and my bolted door was rattling. Somebody was hammering upon it.

'Ima!'

Magda.

With my brain still not fully convinced of the idea of consciousness, I got up and walked for the door. It shook in its hinges under the might of Magda's persistent fist. I rubbed my eyes of sleep, hearing the urgent sound of my name called out again and again, and your abandoned screams behind.

Attention. Give me your attention. Your time is not yours. Your sleep is not yours. Your life is NOT YOURS.

By the time I reached the door I had flown into a sudden rage. I tore off the bolt and yanked it open.

'Magda, tell what would you have me do?!'

'Ima?'

I stood, stooped and panting, before the finely-postured figure of my sister.

'Haralia. I thought you were someone else.'

She looked me up and down. Her face, though horrified, glowed with health.

'Ima, whatever is wrong? What has happened to you?'

'Come in,' I said.

She closed the door and stood by the table as I tended to your morning needs. I felt her silence as I changed you, then drew milk and sat in the chair to feed. I unfastened the buttons of my dress, allowing my right breast to flop out and, with a sigh, I squeezed your day's first drops into your mouth.

I sniffed and wiped my nose.

'What?' I said, noticing Haralia's wide eyes.

'What on earth are you doing, Ima?'

'Oh. Your bottle shattered. This is how he feeds now.'

'Why did you not use another bottle.'

'It is not as if I had any lying about. He needed to feed and I had to improvise.'

'Does it work?'

'See for yourself. He has grown, has he not?' My tone was sharp. I closed my eyes. 'Forgive me, the shock of the day is still upon me. It is good to see you, sister. Have you been well?'

Haralia, still gripping the chair, smiled.

'I have another bottle at Jakob's,' she said. 'Wait here.'

When she returned we filled the new bottle and I replaced my wounded breast in its dress for the last time, with not a little relief. Why any mammal would choose to feed their young in such a barbaric way is beyond me.

I would take greater care of this bottle.

'I shall make us tea,' said Haralia.

She did so—a treat, since our new routine did not involve a drink for me so soon after rising—and we talked for a time. She told me of her trip to the lowlands with our mother, and of the wild horses, and of her happiness at returning to see Jakob. Their relationship was ever growing, she told me, and they would soon be taking a trip of their own. This would be a much longer one.

Her eyes flitted about the room as she spoke, and even I could tell that she was trying her best to mute the joy so clearly apparent in her voice. I did not wish for this. I was glad my sister—such a different beast to me—was happy. I was glad to be sitting at that table, drinking tea with her.

I told her of the past months, but I found myself avoiding the details of our life's routines in the same way she avoided the details of her life's pleasure. I focussed on the varieties of life I had observed in the forest, which I knew would be of interest to her, and of Boron's hoof, which she said she would inspect, and of the developments in transcendence spoken about in the council meeting, which she had missed, and which drew from her a secretive smile.

'Do you know something I do not?' I enquired.

'I shall tell you in good time,' she replied.

'Time.' I looked at the window, beyond which I saw movement. 'What time is it?'

'Almost mid-morning.'

'Oh. We have missed our morning walk.'

She stood.

'A walk, what an excellent idea.'

I shook my head, looking past her at the figures in the square.

'We usually go before the village wakes. It is easier that way.'

Haralia placed her hands upon her hips.

'My sister. Ima. The woman who single-handedly removed centuries of poison from the atmosphere, who freed the planet's lungs—'

'Planets do not have lungs.'

'—who soared above us in air so thin with oxygen it could snap, casting chemical spells that brought the atmosphere back from the brink of death—'

'Gaseous solutions do not snap, and they were not spells, they were mathematical certainties. Also, atmospheres do not—'

'—My sister, the saviour of the skies, is now afraid to go outside?'

She cocked a hip, in time with her head.

'I refuse to believe it. Come on. We are going for a ride on the beach.'

'But Boron's hoof.'

'Then ride with me. There is room on Corona for all three of us. Come. You have no choice.'

She smiled, and I knew she was quite correct.

– FOURTEEN –

HARALIA HAS CARED for many horses in her lifetime, but none more so than Corona. She is a fine beast—a mottled white mare with lean flanks and long eyelashes.

I sat behind Haralia with you between us, as Corona walked the long beach behind Fane, tail swishing away the sand flies, nose puffing happily at the warm sprays of seawater shearing from the surf. The tide was out and the wet sand shone in the sun. I was lost in it for a while, convincing myself of the illusion that it was a sheet of polished glass. I wondered what I would look like reflected in it; it had been some time since I had seen my own face.

We rocked with Corona's steady gait, and the sound of a million grains of sand grinding together beneath each laid hoof. Haralia's back was in a proud line, her abdomen arched, and her curls gleamed upon her shoulders.

'How do I appear?' I asked.

'Exhausted,' she replied, without turning. 'And your shoulders slump.'

I pulled my spine straight. I heard a vertebra crack.

'Have you ever not slept?' I said.

'Once or twice,' she said. Her voice had a quality to it,

a proliferation of upper frequencies which I recognised as betraying a smile. She was referring to lack of sleep through choice, I presumed, in order to copulate with Jakob.

'Can you explain it?'

'Explain what?'

'Jakob. How you feel. What it means. What you do.'

'Well—' She seemed taken aback, as if I had introduced an entirely new element to the conversation. This of course was not true, and her reaction was intended as a diversionary tactic. My sister did not need encouragement to talk about sexual congress, but she did not necessarily want to admit it.

I was beginning to grasp the intricacies of social interaction— pointless as they were.

'Where do I start?'

'At the beginning, as always.'

She sighed.

'There is no beginning to how Jakob and I feel about each other. Neither is there an end, we just—'

'That makes little sense. Your feelings are discrete systems, and every discrete system has identifiable boundaries.'

'Well, then, think of it like a circle.'

'You believe your feelings for each other are circular? I am not sure how that would work.'

'No, not circular, like a circle. It never breaks, it always returns to the same point. Us.'

Similes. Even my sister uses them now.

'I did not ask you what it was like, I asked you what it was.'

'It is...' Sun flashed in our faces as a cloud broke, then closed once again. 'It is hard to explain.'

'It should not be, and if it is then you should question it.'

She laughed.

'Why, Ima?'

'If you cannot explicitly describe something, then perhaps it does not exist.'

She grew quiet at this. I heard her breathing through her nose.

'I did not mean—'

'All right,' she said. 'This is how it is. When I see him, my heart rate climbs. When he looks at me, the blood vessels in my cheeks flush with blood. When he is near, my breathing becomes unsteady and my muscles shake. When I touch him, I grow wet.'

'Wet?'

'Between the legs.'

'I see.'

She turned her head. Her neat profile, the line of nose and lips, looked ever more soft and perfect against the distant crags of the southern cliffs.

'I do not cause these things to happen; he does. And I enjoy them. I seek them out. There. I have described it. Is that better?'

I thought for a moment.

'It is better, but still not adequate.'

She rolled her eyes and faced forward again.

'Well, I have done my best, and I do not believe you can describe sexual attraction any better. You have no experience of it.'

'Perhaps not, but there are things to which I am drawn just as strongly, if not more, and I can describe them perfectly.'

'What things?'

I paused, thinking. Corona huffed.

'My horse is called Boron. Chemical element B, atomic number five—'

'Please do not tell me that you are attracted to chemistry, Ima. That is your purpose, not your desire.'

'Not just chemistry. Boron is a name humans gave to a chemical element, as they did to every other element. We still use those names, as we do the names of the rocks, the numbers, the clouds, the stars. But they are just names. The things which they describe persist without them. Had *Homo sapiens* and erta never existed, these things would still have been here exhibiting the same behaviour, moving with the same laws. They do not require any belief to exist, they merely are, and because we do exist we can watch them and manipulate them, if we know how they work. Which we do. Stop your horse.'

Haralia pulled on Corona's reins and I dismounted beside a pile of boulders. I surveyed the wide beach, the arch of coast running north and south from where we stood.

'Look,' I said. 'And tell me what you see.'

Haralia turned her head, slowly taking in what we both could see.

'Horizon, sea, cliffs, the earth at peace. What do you see?'

'I see many things. Things within things. The beach, for example. At first it appears to be a single thing, a piece of land with its own distinct shape, its valleys, planes and mountains.' I knelt and scooped a handful of grey sand, letting it fall through my fingers. 'But look a little closer and it is made of individual grains.'

Haralia laughed.

'Do you think I do not understand basic science?'

'And look closer at these grains and they each appear differently. They have their own size, their own colour, their own shape. They too have their valleys, planes and mountains. They are entire landscapes in themselves.'

I held aloft my finger, to which some sand still clung.

'To count the grains of sand upon this beach appears infeasible. But it is not. How many grains on my finger?'

Haralia glanced at it.

'One thousand seven hundred and twenty-two.'

I checked.

'Twenty-three. One lies behind another in the lower-left cluster.'

A breeze blew by as I swung my finger between the farthest edges the beach.

'Knowing what I already know about the dimensions of this beach and the 1,723 grains of its sand upon my finger, I am now able to make a crude estimation of the total number grains of sand upon which we stand. But if I took a further sample, that estimate would improve. Another, inspecting each one closely so that I knew the variety of rock worn into each grain, and the range of shapes and sizes they made, and my guess would be better yet. Spend an entire day taking samples from north to south, firming up boundary measurements and reading the changes in depth, gathering a complete set of grain varieties and their distribution throughout the whole, forming mathematical models to describe their propensities to tesselate with one another, and I will have something approaching an accurate figure.'

Haralia smiled with her mouth but not her brow.

'I don't know what you're trying to tell me.'

'Data, Haralia. All we need is the data.'

She rolled her eyes, but I struck up again before she could speak.

'Look at the sea, the distribution of waves upon the surface of the water. At first it seems there is no pattern to them, but there is. Short rollers occur with frequency in the south, where we know there is a shelf, and of the larger waves to the north every seventeenth results in a break that collides with the wavelets dissipated from the south. With more observation we can quickly predict the starting position of every wave along this beach, and with the correct understanding of fluid dynamics we can extrapolate a four-dimensional shape—albeit fairly squat in terms of time—representing this small section of ocean.

'But there is yet more data to be gleaned. The volume of the ocean, its salt content, the shape of its bed, its contents, the species that reside within it and their life cycles. The more granular the information we have, the greater the size and accuracy of our four-dimensional shape. The shape of each coastline this body of water touches, the rock content of the cliffs with which it collides, this geological history of each of those cliffs, the birds that nest within them, the crabs that scuttle the shores beneath. More data. More accuracy. More predictability.'

I turned my face upward. My voice was loud now, louder than I had heard it for decades, and my goodness, it felt fine.

'The sky, Haralia. My home. That place of winds, clouds and thermals, storms, tornadoes and hurricanes that pummel the water and strike the coast. The layers of temperature that draw up moisture and carry it landward. Each system resonates and feedbacks with the next. Nothing is separate. All is connected. The moon itself—' I threw my sand-dusted finger at the pale, gibbous globe above the cliffs, its craters scattered blue, and its own tiny, plastic satellite in orbit beneath '—pulls each ocean with its orbit, and is pulled itself by everything else. The Earth, the sun, its planets, and the galaxy beyond.

'This is what I am drawn to, Haralia, this is what attracts me. Nothing in this universe is left to chance. Nothing is random; not even in the fields of quantum events. There is cause and effect at the most fundamental level across all dimensions and planes of existence. Information allows you to predict anything, and if you lack the ability to collect that information then you can build machines to do so for you.'

'Like humans did with us.'

'Precisely.'

'So you are attracted to data.'

'No. I am attracted to the universe, and to its equation, and to the fact that it is finite and predictable, however much it may appear otherwise. 100,000 years ago, this beach was not here. But if I had been there, I could have predicted the number of grains that it would comprise today.'

I looked from the moon to my finger, and rubbed the remaining grains of sand upon it into the wind.

'As long as I had the data.'

Haralia was silent for a moment.

'Is that all?'

'Yes. I have fully explained my attraction to scientific thought.'

'And yet you cannot explain love.'

'No, you cannot explain love. I merely lack the data.'

Haralia threw back her head and laughed.

'On that we can agree wholeheartedly, sister; you absolutely do need a good fuck.'

'I fail to see how that would benefit me right now. Besides...'

Whatever I was about to say retreated with the thoughts behind it, and the tide.

'What?' said Haralia.

I looked north. The long wide plane stretched back for one thousand unbroken metres.

'I feel like running. To those rocks back there.'

Haralia turned Corona in the direction of my gaze.

'Hop back on then.'

'No, I mean alone, with my legs.'

'What? Why?'

'I have taken to it.' I unfastened your sling and wrapped you tight, then placed you upon a tall, flat-faced boulder. 'In lieu of sleep, it helps me to process.'

'How strange. Will he be all right there on his own?'

You were still asleep, an unmoving bundle high above the

sand. I removed my boots. The sand warmed my toes.

'The waves could not reach him, even if the tide was in.'

'Shall I trot beside you, then?'

'You will have to do more than trot.'

'Ima?'

I darted away.

By the time Haralia had steadied Corona, who had reared in fright at my departure, and kicked her into a start, I had already accelerated to 14.2 metres per second. I calculated this speed by marking the distance and frequency of my strides beneath me but, deciding to switch to a triangulation method, I looked up. Soon after, I forgot all about speed.

My furious vector disrupted an onshore wind that chilled the right side of my face with cold, salted spray and filled my right auditory field with the roar of air and water. The left hemisphere of my head remained warm and protected, and my hearing on that side numb, until Corona's galloping hooves caught up with me. I glanced up, catching Haralia's grin of disbelief, before quickening my stride.

Another brief calculation revealed that my speed had increased to seventeen metres per second. By this time, we had covered almost a quarter of the distance to the rocks, and my eyes had begun to water against the sting of rapid air. Haralia's cries rang out behind me, imploring Corona to push ahead, but she was always just a little behind me. I could feel the warmth of the horse's breath upon my shoulder, hear the gruff grunts and whistles of its exertion.

My feet thundered in the sand at a cadence of 289 steps every minute, although by this time I could barely feel them at all. The process of running had taken care of itself and, though I could monitor its equations I did not need to balance them. I released them to my subconscious, along with everything else, looked up at the sky and witnessed blue.

I was free of myself.

I had experienced this state several times while flying in my balloon. The first time I had only been seventy-eight years old, and still learning about the many mechanisms of the sky. I had been measuring conditions in a 480 square kilometre area above the Pacific Ocean, and had been especially high that day, entering the upper atmosphere. For the first time I had to wear an insulation suit and oxygen mask.

I stood at my control deck, safely within my eolith bubble, watching the sky appear to bend slowly beneath us, and blue become black. All was quiet, and from this distance the Earth gave the illusion of being still—the clouds appearing to have been frozen in gigantic puffs, and the sea undisturbed and illuminated by patches of sunlight, three hundred miles from the coast of what had once been California. I looked up through the roof where bright lights had appeared. Stars and planets, a whole galaxy and more beyond.

A curious feeling swept through me, which took me by surprise since, at that time, few feelings at all had ever swept through me, let alone curious ones. It was nothing more or less than awareness. I could sense everything, from the touch of the joystick beneath the glove of my suit to the tug of the balloon, to the gravitational pull exerted by two nearby stars. Everything was moving at its own speed, I realised, within its own boundaries and to its own rhythm. And yet nothing was separate, all was connected.

I had always known this, of course. It was just that I had never been aware of knowing it. The two are different. I wondered what it would be like to open the hatch, drift up, or fall.

The most interesting aspect of this state—hovering seventy kilometres above the Earth, aware of everything and pondering suicide—was that I was, for a brief moment, not aware of myself. My thoughts, memories and identity were no longer present; I had escaped the equation, as I had now, running on the beach.

Haralia had caught up with me, lying flat against Corona's neck and frowning ahead. I looked down from the sky and set my sights upon the rapidly approaching rocks. With one hundred and sixty seven metres to go, I raced ahead. My cadence peaked at 302, my speed at nineteen metres per second, and with six metres left I slammed my right foot upon a small rock, bounding over the boulders in a single leap and landing with both feet in the sand.

The impact shook through me and I stumbled, momentum still carrying me, falling into a heap and sliding through the sand upon my front.

I rolled over, panting, and stared up at the sky. It was the same blue as before, but every part of me was here, now.

'Ima, are you all right? Good grief!' Haralia jumped down and rushed to my side. 'Are you hurt?'

I sat up, my lungs still working hard to recover me from my exertion. I smiled and took Haralia's hand, testing my legs' ability to take my weight.

'A minor fracture to my left fibula,' I said, on one leg. 'It is already mending.'

Haralia stood, staring through puffs of her own exertion. She shook her head, a suggestion of sadness in her expression.

'How can we be so different?' she said.

'Every erta is different in some way. That is our design.'

'I mean it. We are sisters, Ima.'

'Mother told me she put too much of what she was not in me. Perhaps she did the opposite with you.'

'It is not just what you put into something, but what you leave out.'

'That is a very intelligent point, sister. Perhaps we are not so different after all.'

'Was that a joke?'

'I don't know. Possibly.'

She made a noise, something between a laugh and a sigh, and looked out to sea.

'It is sometimes as though you live in a different world.'

I tried my left leg once again and, though not yet fully healed, the bone was strong enough for me to hobble around the boulder. Haralia followed, leading Corona by her reins, and we made our way back to where you lay one thousand metres away upon the rocks.

'Perhaps that is true of everyone,' I said. 'We have wondrous potential, but it is unlikely we will ever know for sure how it is to be another being.'

'Maybe with transcendence that will change.'

I noticed a flash of exuberance upon my sister's face as she said this. I stopped and turned.

'Haralia?'

'Yes?'

'You have a secret.'

Another flash, and a smile that hardly dared show itself.

'I do. Ima, Jakob and I have volunteered.'

So, they were going to foster an ertling. That was the cause of her joy. I was about to congratulate her when her eyes darted left over my shoulder. Her face darkened.

'Ima, look.'

I turned. There was a figure at the rocks, cloaked and hooded, with its feet in the surf. He was lifting you down. I bolted for him.

– FIFTEEN –

AFTER FIVE PAINFUL strides I stumbled and fell in the rising tide. Picking myself up, I tried again, but could not manage more than a limp. The figure had you in its arms now, cradling you as I do, turning to the sea and moving you in a most alarming fashion; a slow swing that suggested you were about to be hurled into the water.

I did not recognise the feeling that overcame me. I still do not. Nevertheless it manifested itself in simple enough terms; there was 653 metres of beach between me and you and I had to cover it in as short a time as possible, broken leg or not.

I staggered on, focussing on the figure with its dreadful sway, and its hood and cloak forming the same outline as the one which had appeared outside my house that night. This recognition drove me on, but the pain was too great and I fell to knees, only to be swept up by an unexpected force—Haralia's hand upon my collar.

'Get on!' she yelled, hauling me onto Corona's back behind her, and with two fresh kicks we sped for the rocks.

The figure saw us approach and turned, revealing a dark beard. He took two wary steps away, yet still he swung you. I jumped from Corona, my leg feeling better, and waded the remaining metres through the swirling tide.

'Give that to me,' I demanded, lunging for you. He did not flinch, but gave you up as easily as he had plucked you from the rock. I checked you. You were awake but not in distress, and smiled at my face as you always do. I turned to the figure, who removed his hood. I did not recognise him. He was not one of the hundred, and perhaps not even in the thousand that followed my siblings and cousins. Whoever he was, our paths had not crossed. He appeared young, though his face had a weathered texture and he was not straight backed, but neither did he stoop. He merely stood, looking at you through bright blue eyes with hardly any expression at all.

'Who are you?' I asked.

He did not look up at my question. Instead he pointed a finger. 'Is he—?'

'What he is is none of your business. What is your purpose here? Why did you take him?'

He took a long, slow breath and smiled. How furious that smile made me. He had no right to amusement or pleasure.

'My purpose?' he said. 'I have no purpose, but I walk this beach often, along with many others. I heard a noise as I was traversing the cliff face and ran to these rocks, where I found him. He was making noises of distress, so I brought him down.'

'Noises?' I glanced at Haralia, who was standing behind me. She appeared calm, assessing this stranger with, I was frustrated to note, appreciation. He nodded at her—a greeting—and she smiled back. I splashed a few steps towards him in a bid to bring his attention back to me. It worked. 'We did not hear any noises.'

'Well, you were quite some distance away.'

'So? I can hear bat wings flutter from nine-hundred-and-eighty-eight metres. I am sure I can hear this child's cry from less.'

'Perhaps you were otherwise absorbed,' he said. His hair was long and unkempt. Any more knots and you would call it rope. He glanced at Haralia. 'Your race. Who won?'

'She did,' said Haralia, brightly, for which I punished her with a glare. I shook with anger, my breaths too fast, my pulse still too high. Such feelings should never last this long.

The figure nodded at me, as if to show respect.

'You are fast.'

I closed the distance between us more.

'Stop talking.'

'All right. But you should not leave infants unattended, not here. A hawk could have taken him.'

'And you should not take what is not yours.'

'He is yours, then? This child, this—?'

'I have already told you, what he is is none of your business. Why did you want to harm him? Why did you want to drown him in the sea?'

He frowned.

'Why would you think I wanted to drown him.'

'This.' I mimed his sway, adding additional amplitude for effect, and a ridiculous face to display my distaste. The motion made you gurgle with interest. 'You intended to hurl him.'

He stared at me blankly, then laughed. The sound was rich with low and middle frequencies, and had no business being upon that beach.

'I was not intending to hurl him,' he said. 'I was rocking him. They are comforted by it.'

I stared at him.

'What?'

'Rocking. The motion calms human infants.'

'Does it?'

I looked down at your face, cheeks flushed by the cold.

'So it is true,' said the figure. 'He is human.'

I straightened up. My leg was healed, though my body still shook.

'I will not tell you again. He is not your business. Do not touch him again.'

He dropped his gaze.

'Forgive me. My name is Jorne. Farewell.'

Then with a glance at Haralia, and one at me, he pulled up his hood and left.

I watched him scale the southern rocks and disappear behind the cliffs, then turned to Haralia.

'Well, look at you, sister,' she said.

'What?'

'Pulse racing, short of breath, and you're absolutely drenched.'

She grinned and raised an eyebrow.

'Oh, go and fuck your wood-chopper,' I said, and stomped back to Fane, leaving her laughing on the beach.

SIX MONTHS

– SIXTEEN –

YOU: EAT, SLEEP, kick, gurgle, cry, excrete, urinate, vomit occasionally.

I: feed, clean, move objects from surface to surface, walk, avoid my fellow villagers, sleep when possible.

Occasionally I return to the beach.

This signifies an expansion in my territory, and I recognise what this means; that I have something called a territory, for a start, an invisible boundary defining the places in which I feel safe. And what this means is that I do not feel safe everywhere.

Furthermore, since I have no overwhelming sense of self-protection outside of my own body's basic defence mechanisms, this must mean that I have developed a sense of protection over you. Because I do not go anywhere without you.

Apart from when I am on the beach.

I have fashioned for you a wooden shelter and at low tide I carry you in it to the rocks. There I lay you down. The shelter keeps you safe from hawks, though I have not spotted a single one above the sands of Fane. Once settled, I walk backwards from the rocks as far as I can, keeping my eyes upon you, and the sky, and the cliffs beyond. Then I run at pace, pounding the sand as I did with Haralia, until I have returned, breathless, and gather you up.

I do this because, as I explained to Haralia, running helps me to process in lieu of sufficient sleep. But I also do it to feel free, I think, despite the fact that freedom is far from what I feel when I am that far from the rocks. What I feel is an urgent need to return to you, and it grows with every step I take away.

I have seen the man, Jorne, again. He lurks. He is a lurker. The place he generally lurks is the mess of rocks and caves between the cliffs and the sand. I know he is watching me. Or watching you—I do not know.

It is all right to not know something. It just means you do not have enough data.

'What generation do you think he is?' posed Haralia, who I see more often these days and, when she is not with Jakob, accompanies me on my walks.

'I do not care.'

'He must be from Dundee. Or Rio.'

'Wherever he comes from, he should stay there, and stop making a nuisance of himself.'

She gasped and nudged my elbow.

'Unless he is Sundra, of course!'

'Don't be ridiculous. Sundra.'

'What?'

'I am yet to meet a member of this Sundra. And therefore I have no reason to believe they exist.'

She leaned close.

'Jakob told me they swim in the sea, eat crabs from their shells and run naked through the forests.'

'Yes, well, Jakob would like everyone to run naked through the forests.'

'Shall I visit again tomorrow?'

'I would like that.'

One day he came to my door.

'Hello,' he said, as I looked past him for signs of anyone watching. 'I am Jorne.'

'I know very well who you are, my memory is perfectly intact, now what do you want?'

'I want nothing.' He looked over my shoulder. You were crying. 'Is he all right?'

I stepped outside and pulled the door closed behind me.

'Yes, he is perfectly all right.'

'He wails.'

'Perfectly normal. That is what infants do. Apparently. Now tell me why you are here.'

'I am here to offer you help.'

'Why?'

He hesitated, clearly taken aback by my hostility. In truth, I was finding it equally surprising.

'Because you may need it,' he said at last.

'Why do you have such interest in him?'

He gave me that smile of his again. It was, I realised, like yours; uncomplicated by the centuries, free from subtlety.

'He is human,' he said. 'That is why.'

'He is data.'

He frowned at this.

'Data?'

'Yes. Now please leave us alone.'

I shut the door, but he called through the wood.

'Remember, rocking helps to comfort them.'

'You know nothing, go away!'

I stood with my back to the door, listening until I heard the slow, sound of his boot heels turning on stone.

I walked to the bed. There lying upon it—fed, clean and rested—you continued to bawl.

I picked you up. I rocked you. And it worked.

THE NEXT DAY Haralia returned, as promised, glowing.

'You look tired again,' she said.

This disappointed me, because I believed I had slept well. Or at least better than usual.

'I feel fine. Nothing that a little fresh air will not help. Shall we go to the beach again?'

'No.' She smiled. 'I want to help you.'

'You are.'

'I mean properly. I know I have been distracted lately and I am sorry. But Jakob is in the forest collecting wood, so I have the day to myself. You go to the beach, and I shall stay with the child.'

This made me pause. For a moment I could not think properly.

'I don't... I mean, I couldn't...'

'You need a break, Ima, and I am giving you one.'

'But I couldn't spend an entire day on the beach.'

I absolutely could.

'Then do something else. Visit a friend. See to your horse. Walk. Run. Sleep. Do whatever you wish. The day is yours.'

There were no friends to visit, walking and running were not novelties. Sleep had become something distant and untenable. I had been meaning to check on Boron's hoof. But there was something else.

'I could fly.'

Haralia beamed.

'Excellent idea. Go up in your balloon where you can be happy.'

I frowned at this.

'Do not think that I am not happy. Please.'

'That is not what I meant. You know that.'

'But how will you cope? How will you know what to do?'

'I have watched you enough. Feeding, changing, settling. I am sure we will be perfectly fine.'

'It is more difficult than you think.'

'But it is only for one day. Not even that, in fact.'

'All right.' I looked around the room, feeling suddenly weightless. 'All right. The blankets are all clean and dry. Milk is fresh but you may have to warm it. There is tea and some herring in—'

'Go,' said Haralia, ushering me through the door. 'Go, we shall be fine. Enjoy yourself.'

The door shut and I stood on my porch.

'Rocking helps to comfort him!' I called back, but she did not reply.

– SEVENTEEN –

AFTER CHECKING ON Boron, whose hoof I was pleased to discover was on the mend, I made for the sealed wooden shed near Fane's paddock, in which my balloon is kept. I felt light again as I walked to it, glancing behind, sure I would see Haralia calling me back from the house. But all was still, there was no sound but for the sound of my steps in the wet grass.

I opened the door, disturbing some doves in the rafters, and stood in the dusty light. There it was—the machine which had flown me up into the far reaches of the atmosphere and allowed me to circumnavigate the globe over five thousand times. It is not large; a titanium hemisphere half the size of my dwelling, with a flat-bottomed hull. The deck is protected by a handrail, and above it the eolith hatch which allows entry into the control deck. The balloon itself draws out from a rear compartment when flight is initiated, a long bulb of transparent nano-mesh, almost unbreakable and strong enough to lift ten elephants with no struggle. Its surface draws power from the sun, which drives thrusters enabling the craft to fly with great speed and manoeuvrability.

The last time I had flown my balloon was ten years before, when the final readings were taken, and to see it now brought be as much pleasure as ever. I placed a hand upon its cold surface, brushing away a little dust. Then I pulled it outside.

The cells were low but they still held enough power to launch, after which the solar array would quickly replenish them. I held the joystick, allowing the systems to initiate. Then, with a last glance through the hatch at the house, I released the balloon and pulled up.

We rose gently and Fane shrank beneath me. I could still see my dwelling—would still be able to see Haralia if she suddenly dashed outside, waving a hand. But she did not. The spot that marked my house became small and the world around it grew, although neither of these phenomena actually occurred. They remained exactly as they were—it was I who was changing. All is relative. Even your dead ancestors knew that.

Soon, Fane was joined by Dundee, Rio, Tokyo, and three more neighbouring settlements, and the tracks that joined them appeared to contract like a tightening net. In another few seconds, Houston, Paris, Sydney, Istanbul drew in, followed by the remote settlements in the north and south—Toronto and Delhi—and finally, Ertanea itself, with its stone halls rising from the tree canopies. All of ertian life was beneath me—a civilisation, I supposed—and I could still just see my house. I looked up and soared into the shining blue, virtually weightless.

It was a curious feeling. Every flight I had ever taken had carried a purpose, whether to measure carbon readings, monitor the atomic nets or release catalysts. But this one was different; it was purposeless. There was nothing but to achieve but flight itself. No directive, no direction, no destination.

Where would I go?

I checked the weather beacons we had launched when we settled on the coast; spherical satellites that roam high above our coastline, warning us of incoming pressure systems. Such events are unheard of, but not impossible, and with enough warning we can stave off dangerous weather with supersonic pressure drones and a cyclonic army of mites. One of the orbs had endured a rare collision—a bird, perhaps, or a meteor—that had set it from its path by some degrees. I reset its navigational systems and checked its siblings, which were without fault.

After I left the beacons to their business I went nowhere, merely following whatever thermals happened to exist. Then, as I saw the northern sea spread out beneath me, I turned west, aiming down. Soon, a large white continent—once called Greenland—seemed to rise out of the sea like a glacier. And all was ice.

All is relative. Water can be gas, liquid or solid, the same thing but in a different energetic state, where molecules conspire to move at different speeds and even time is warped by the change in density. I like ice. It is water at rest. Its energy has departed, leaving it at peace.

I followed the coastline and the ragged Arctic archipelagos beyond. I saw creatures—all white, all moving at their own speeds, and for an hour I hovered above a bear, absorbed in its hunt for a hare, which it finally caught and killed and ate.

Then I went further north, until I was directly above the pole. Here I stopped to pull on my insulation suit and oxygen mask, and I let my balloon rise. The horizon bent. The blue became black, the stars and planets and galaxies glittered, and the sea shone beneath me, disrupted by great fleets of clouds all busy with themselves. And above it all was me, and my awareness of it all.

So this was to be my destination; not really a place, but a feeling.

Curious. But not as curious as what happened next.

Slowly, I released the joystick, allowing the balloon to drift from its course. Now I was at the mercy of whatever thermals would take me, and in that vulnerable state I reached up, opened the hatch, and stepped outside.

On the deck I felt the shock of cold, thin air, and took two hesitant steps toward the guardrail. My right leg shook, seemingly of its own accord. This was fear, I realised, another feeling, and one I had no need for since I already recognised the perils of suspending a body of flesh and bone at such a height above a sphere of rock and fluid. I would be pulverised if I fell, I knew that, but still, but still...

Still that fear.

Which made what I did next the most curious thing of all. I took a breath, removed my mask, and removed my hands from the rail. Then I leaned over the side.

There was no sound but for the soft clang of an anchor's hook against the titanium shell, and the light crackle of ice crystals forming on my skin, and in this silence I stretched out my arms and opened my eyes, looking down upon the sky.

I have never seen a blue so pure. And by pure I mean an undisrupted, unvarying field, 636 THz of unbroken light. It made me shake. I wanted to give myself to it. With awareness comes abandon, I thought, and blew out the oxygen from my lungs until I had no more, whereupon I stood and jumped down into the hatch.

Slamming it shut and rubbing the ice from my skin, I flew home.

WALKING FROM THE shed, where I had safely repacked my balloon, I felt a difference in my step. There was fresh air upon my face and the warm winds of early summer carried the scent of blossom down from the hills; I met the eye of every villager I passed in Fane's square, even managing to give Magda a nod of greeting without drawing a scowl.

My door was still shut, with no noise from inside. I opened it.

'Haralia, thank you—'

'Here.' Haralia thrust you in my arms. 'He is asleep. Finally.'

She looked wretched, her hair bedraggled, her dress adorned with stains of yellow and white. One breast hung from its open neck.

'He will not feed. Not from me. I tried the bottle but it did not work. So I tried the other way.' She thrust out her bottom lip and looked down sadly at her bosom, popping it back inside. 'That did not work either. He has cried all day. And the *excretions*...'

Her voice shook. Upon the floor were strewn six filthy blankets, from which the familiar stench of your rear end rose up to greet me.

'I tried to get outside, but he would not let me. He just would not...' She shook her head and blew a wet ringlet from her face. 'You were right, Ima. It is far more difficult than it seems.'

She busied herself, collecting her things.

'Well,' I said. 'If nothing else, at least it was practice.'

'Practice for what?'

'For you and Jakob.'

She frowned.

'Your secret. You said you had volunteered.'

Her eyes widened.

'Oh my goodness. You thought we were going to foster an ertling?'

'That was my assumption, yes.'

She released a hoot of laughter.

'Whatever made you think we would want to do such a thing?'

'I don't know. You seem so happy.'

'We are, and I can assure you that we have no intention of ruining that happiness with an ertling.'

'Then what have you volunteered for?'

She took a great breath.

'We are going to be the first, Ima. The first to leave.'

'Transcendence?'

'Yes. In a few years they will begin testing, and we are to be subjects. We are called the Devoted. Isn't it wonderful?'

She smiled, displaying feelings that could not have been more at odds with my own.

'Yes. Yes, it is wonderful indeed.'

'Now I have a purpose too, just like you.'

She looked down at you.

'No, I can assure you that neither Jakob nor I have any interest in being parents.'

'Thank you for today,' I said.

She sniffed.

'My pleasure,' she said, making for the door.

'Will you be back soon?'

'Of course,' she called back, but as I watched her skip across the square to Jakob's, I sensed this was not altogether true.

– EIGHTEEN –

I WAS RIGHT. I did not see Haralia again for some time, and in that time, things grew worse.

The first problem was that August's broth harvest had not been as large as usual. This can, occasionally, happen. There is feedback in every system, whether sky or lagoon, which makes it difficult to predict.

Difficult, but never impossible, because data and patience: that is all it takes. Not that I had any inclination to remind my fellow villagers of this, so frosty that they were, so scornful were their looks. I avoided them, and this became a part of your equation too. Your walks would be cancelled because they were outside when I had planned to leave, or your feeds delayed because too many of them were gathered near the milk urn.

Besides the fact that their sleep was still disturbed by your cries, they blamed the lagoon's imbalance on my blockage. And now they were hungry as well as tired. That is not a good combination.

I know this, for I was hungry too.

All this meant for unhappiness. In them, in me, and in you. Feedback mechanisms, you see, in every system, small or large.

I know they found food. Settlements are self-organising, but we do not let others starve, and I know they sought supplies from the next village—herring, vegetables, turnips. Somehow I was missed from the distribution of rations.

I took to the beach and saw Jorne three times from a distance, and each time he stopped and watched me. He gave me uncomfortable chills.

One day he turned up at my door again, unannounced.

'I brought you these from around the coast,' he said, holding up some herring which he had smoked. In his other hand he held a blanket. 'And I made this. It is a softer weave, and lighter. It will be more comfortable for him.'

'I have no need for them,' I said, though I did.

'Oh, that's right, I forgot. He is just data, correct?'

That smile again, mocking me now.

'Go away.'

I slammed the door, but the sight of my empty larder reminded me of my empty stomach and I opened it again, wordlessly snatching his gifts before banishing him once more. I gobbled the herrings whole, sitting with my back to the door. I think he was listening.

Your night time crying worsened, in spite of the new blanket and the trick of rocking you. Magda's bangs and crashes worsened too, especially at night, when I paced the floor endlessly in the dark. Others joined her protestations, grumbles and shouts from other dwellings, candles lit, faces at the windows. More storms came in with the heat. The hills were drenched with rain and thunder shook the walls of my house every hour of every day.

In the day I saw them talking in the square, hushed and in huddles, flicking their gaze at my window. They were not themselves.

One night, as I completed my 372nd perimeter of the room

with you wailing into my shoulder, I heard doors slam and footsteps on stone. Torchlight flickered through my window. My door hammered.

'Ima.' It was Niklas. Other voices murmured behind him. 'Open your door.'

I did as he demanded. On my porch were fifteen of them, torches in hand, breathing hard. Each face carried a distinct vision of rage.

'What do you want?' I said. My voice was cracked with exhaustion.

'You know what we want,' said Niklas, directing his eyes at you. Magda scowled behind him. 'Sleep.'

'As do I,' I replied.

'But we cannot,' said Magda. 'Because of the noise that comes from your dwelling day and night. It must be stopped.'

The figures behind her shuffled and grumbled in agreement. I looked between their dark faces, full of shadows, seeking out some trace of the grace and intelligence that had once led them to save a planet from doom. They had become a witless mob.

'I think I have been clear with you,' I said. 'This project is vital to the council, and to...'

'Vital.'

Magda spoke the word in disbelief.

'Yes,' I said.

'That is not what I have heard.'

'And what have you heard?'

'What I have *heard is* that...'

'Magda.' Niklas silenced her. 'This does not help. Whatever the priority of your project, Ima, the noise is robbing us of rest. Many of us are involved in transcendence now, and we cannot function when... when that *thing* is screaming every hour of every night.'

'It is not every hour. He slept for two last night.'

'It must be stopped.'

The hot mass behind him renewed their baying.

'And how,' I said—I attempted to keep my voice calm, as much for me as you—'do you propose I stop it?'

Niklas glared at your scalp and bent towards you. His right eyelid twitched.

'I know how I would stop it. It would be quick.'

This was new territory. I had never seen an erta display such aggression in my life. Lack of sleep had more consequences, I surmised, than mere forgetfulness.

'Get away from my door. You are behaving irrationally.'

'No.' Rain poured from my porch roof and down Niklas' furious face. 'Not until you stop this disturbance. For good.'

'But, I cannot.'

'Then put him somewhere else. The food store, wood shed, stables, anywhere far from here. So we can rest.'

'I can't put him there. He will suffer.'

'You must do something.'

The figures closed in on my door, and I felt myself shrink beneath them.

'Get away. You are not rational.'

'*Take it from her,*' I heard one of them say.

That was enough. Beyond the wall of figures, fresh waves of rain lashed the stone, but I pulled up my hood and pushed through them, into the storm, leaving them hissing and babbling behind me.

I RAN THE perimeter of Fane, smothering your cries in my robe, my breath the only other sound above the roar of rain. I soon broke through the trees and found myself on the beach, where I sat upon a rock and, protecting you beneath the canopy of my hood, looked unblinking out at the wild sea. I was alone again, drifting with neither direction nor destination in mind, like...

It was not like anything.

I had to think.

I could walk to Oslo, find Haralia. She could help me. Perhaps we could even swap settlements, so that she and Jakob could be together permanently. Would they actually want this, I wondered? Jakob might, but Haralia—I suspected she somehow drew excitement from their separation, like...

Not like anything. Nothing is like anything.

In any case, a move to Oslo would only leave me with a new set of villagers to irritate. Perhaps I could move to Ertanea instead. I could raise you in the cool, empty halls where you would have the freedom to scream all you wished. The echoes would be endless, and nobody would hear them but me.

But that was the point; you had to be heard. This was the purpose of the whole endeavour. I looked down at you, mouth stretched into a wide bow, eyes squeezed tight. Within half a year, still unable to take a step or utter a word, you had already incensed the 147 erta closest to you, 148 if you counted Haralia. And if you counted me...

You could not count me. Even here, banished, soaked, starving, and exhausted, you could not count me.

Now, this is important for you to understand: I did not sit there in that torrent eluded by feelings of sweetness and light; I could still count a hundred ways in which your existence brought me discomfort and frustration. It was just that, in spite of this discomfort, in spite of this frustration, and in spite of the dark and the rain and the wild sea before me, I knew I would rather be on that beach with you than back in Fane with them.

I knew then that you belonged to me, and I to you.

This was a fresh variable. But I was too tired to work it into the equation right now. I needed sleep. I looked out at the dark ocean, thinking how easy it would be to wade in and sink beneath it.

'What are you doing here?'

I jumped to my feet and swung to face the voice to my right. It was Jorne.

'You. You should not creep up on others like that.'

'And you should not have a child out in this rain. What are you doing here?'

'What are *you* doing here?'

'I told you, I walk this coast often.'

'After midnight? In the rain?'

I stumbled back as he approached, his face caught in dim moonlight.

'Once again, I feel I should point out that I am not the one carrying a child.'

'And once again I feel I should point out that my choices are none of your business.'

'Why are you here?'

I stared back at him. Fane was a black shape beyond. I could still hear the grumbles of shuffles of the mob returning to their homes. You screamed and wriggled in my arms.

'Hiding. They are after me, they came to my house, angry through lack of sleep.'

'Because of his cries?'

'Yes. I believe they want to hurt him. They are senseless. I have never seen erta behave that way.'

A wave hit the shore near our feet and for a short time you ceased your cries. Jorne turned to me.

'The tide is approaching. Come with me.'

'Where to?'

'It is just an idea. Come.'

And there was the smile, the one with nothing else attached to it. Tightening my hood and covering your head, I followed him into the rain.

'WHERE ARE WE going?' I said, as he led me across the paddock and up the shallow embankment at the base of the cliffs. I kept within the circle of light cast down by his torch.

'Just follow me. The trees will soon give us shelter.'

We walked for a kilometre, two, into the dripping canopies flickering with shadow. Soon we emerged onto what looked like a tunnel, open at one side. There was the sound of water above us.

'What is this place?'

'A waterfall. It leads to a stream, here, look.'

In the glimmer of Jorne's torchlight, I saw a brook trickle down over the rock onto flatter ground. We followed it along until we were on a grass bank, protected from the rain by the overhang above. The feeling was of being inside, although the air was still fresh and salty from the sea below. Tall reeds creaked in the rippling water.

I sat down with you. You were awake, but quiet, at peace. Your eyes twinkled in Jorne's flame as he knelt down too.

'It is cooler up here, and the rain is not so disturbing. Walls and roofs—they can protect, but they can imprison too.'

'I think he likes the sound of the reeds.'

'I think you are right.'

I looked up at him, this strange person with an uncomplicated smile. I still did not trust him.

'Where are you from?'

'The same place as you. And him. Everyone.'

It was a ridiculous answer, but I did not have the energy to argue it. I yawned.

'I am weary,' I said.

'Then sleep.'

'Here?'

'Why not? He has.'

I looked down to see that he was quite right. You had fallen asleep with your hand curled around its new blanket.

'Sleep, Ima,' he said. 'It is perfectly safe.'

I placed you gently upon the grass, and lay down beside you with one hand near your face.

'Have you named him?' whispered Jorne.

The reeds creaked and shuffled somewhere far away.

My name is Japanese. I chose it for its meaning: *now*, which is the only thing that exists. Yours I chose for a sound that brought you comfort.

'Reed,' I said. 'His name is Reed.'

My eyelids felt heavy, so I closed them.

TWO YEARS

– NINETEEN –

I HAVE SEEN humans before.

Let me tell you about tea.

Tea is a drink which I enjoy. You allow me to drink it now, although for a long while you did not; once you began to move around—crawling at first, then dragging yourself along on your rear-end in the manner of a dog cleaning its back passage, followed, finally, by something approaching ambulation—the level of my engagement required to keep you safe prohibited the completion of most tasks, including personal nourishment and hydration.

I became a bodyguard of sorts, protecting you as you explored the numerous corners of your small world. You banged into tables, toppled chairs, pulled blankets from beds, reached for boiling cups, fiddled with doors. Our forest walks became exercises in survival training. You would run, giggling towards sheer drops or deep pools and I would be forced to leap after you, snatching you before gravity could.

I took care not to show you too much, remembering what my mother had said. I moved only as swiftly as required. I knew this subterfuge would grow more difficult as you integrated with others, but for now it was just you and me. And sometimes Jorne.

The morning after Fane's mob had descended upon me, I woke to the smell of smoke. Jorne was nowhere to be found, but he had set a fire for us and left a jug of milk and a brace of herring smoking on a pole. The rain had gone, and I watched the bright blue, windless sky, eating the fish and drinking cool stream water while you slept. You were more peaceful than I had ever thought possible.

It was mid-morning when we returned to Fane. Niklas looked awkward in the square.

'Ima,' he said. 'I am sorry for last night. I do not know what happened.'

I steadied my gaze, though his flitted about. He was hardly able to meet my eyes.

'Where are the others?'

'Most are still asleep.'

'Even Magda?'

He looked to the floor.

'I do not know about Magda.'

I took a breath. You lay quietly in my arms.

'You were tired. It is to be understood.'

'It is not. We behaved terribly. I feel shame, Ima. Are you all right? Is… it…?'

He looked down at you. Though Niklas did not know it himself, I saw shreds of the very same malice in his eyes I had seen the previous night. I inched back.

'I assure you we are fine,' I said. 'And thank you for your apology, but it is clear to me that we cannot stay here.'

He frowned, though I saw relief too.

'Where will you go?'

'We must stay in Fane, but I will build a new dwelling. Technically it will be within the settlement's borders, but far enough away to guarantee rest. At least for you.'

'Where?'

'I know of a place.'

He nodded.

'I will help you. We will—'

'Thank you.' I turned to leave. 'But I do not need your help.'

I set to work that day hauling timber from the forest to the bank within the rocks. I worked with you upon my back. You were at peace in your sling, absorbed in the sound and light of the trees, and the motion of my exertion. At night we camped by the river. We did not see Jorne, but in the mornings I sometimes found more herring, or fruit, or vegetables, and always a fresh fire.

Soon I had created a cabin for us within the overhang. It had three rooms like our original house, and a plumbing system for waste which led to a small lagoon in which I cultivated my own form of broth. It was better, in my opinion, than that which came from Fane's own lagoon. Richer and more nourishing.

But I was not talking about broth, I was talking about tea.

IF YOU DISCOUNT David, the technician who witnessed my birth, and Dr Nyström herself, whom I saw only briefly as I left to convene with my elders, siblings and cousins beyond her laboratory, the first human being I encountered was a bony old man on a broken pier. His name was Roop, and perhaps it was because of him that, when designing your genetic prototype, I based your appearance on the rich brown skin, dark hair and bright eyes of the Indian subcontinent. It was also here that I first encountered tea.

I had flown to Assam to study the atmospheric effects of a newly regenerated rainforest, a two-hundred-square kilometre resurrection of barren land overseen by Greye. I landed in the fringes of his forest, in a hot and humid meadow already buzzing with life. Greye met me as I packed my balloon. He was younger then, with blacker hair and brighter eyes.

'A good trip, Ima?' he said, wrapping his thick hand around mine.

'Always,' I replied. 'Shall we?'

We screamed at each other for 12.3 seconds, disturbing a flock of nearby wood ducks.

'Excellent,' said Greye once we had finished. 'Now let me show you the forest. Then we can have tea.'

'Tea?'

We ran through the forest, covering sixty-eight miles or thereabouts throughout the day. He explained the complexity of the forest's ecosystem and of the precarious balance between the species that lived there. Sometimes we shared more data, our screeches mingling with the calls of birds and apes. Otherwise we simply talked. I took measurements from the lofty canopies whooping with langurs, and down on the ground, where long-legged spiders scuttled, and leeches stood erect at the smell of our blood, and hordes of ants swarmed, and the bracken began its slow journey into mulch.

At evening, we emerged by the bank of a great river lined with the bamboo dwellings of Greye and his three sons. Here we sat upon a deck, watching the sun's descent over the water, where buffalo drank, and Greye showed me this thing called tea.

'You see the leaf?' he said, holding up a twisted black twig. 'It must be dry but not brittle, so it does not crumble. Look for golden tips, the second harvest is better. The water must be as free from impurity as possible, and boiled, but it must not be boiling when poured. Ninety-eight degrees will suffice. Watch.'

He filled the clear flask.

'Two minutes and thirty-eight seconds. That is all. Then remove the leaves.'

I watched as brown swirls rose up from the submerged leaves, but a shadow on the far bank distracted me. There on a broken pier sat an old man with his legs crossed. His hair and beard were long and matted, and he bowed his head to his hands, which he had brought together.

'Who is that?'

'Hmm?' Greye was still absorbed in the simple but, admittedly, hypnotising chemical reaction occurring in the flask. He looked up. 'Oh. That's one of our assistants.'

'I thought all the humans had been assembled in the Appalachians?'

'They had, but some elected to help rather than just…'

'Die.'

'Exactly. In spite of everything.'

'What do you mean?'

He ignored my question, so I did too.

'There's a whole village on the opposite bank. They shift cargo up and down the river, operate some of the fertilisation drones, take readings, tag animals.'

'And what does he do?'

'He cooks. His name is Roop.'

'He doesn't sound particularly useful.'

Greye smiled.

'But he is. Food is important.'

'Of course, but basic nourishment does not require another's assistance.'

'Eating is a ritual to them. It's not merely for nourishment, not of the stomach anyway.'

'What other kind of nourishment is there?'

He frowned, amused.

'How long have you been up in your balloon, Ima?'

'Sixty-eight years, but I have not been up there for the whole time.'

'Just most of it.'

'78.23%. Yes.'

He laughed.

'That explains it.'

I turned back to the old man on the pier. He was just a silhouette now, a dark smudge on the dilapidated wooden planks. His head was still bowed towards the water, and strange noises rose up from his throat. Thin, nasal cries that quivered and disappeared.

'What is he doing? Why is he making that noise?'

'He is praying.'

'What does that mean?'

'It means he's talking to his creator.'

'His mother?'

Greye laughed.

'Father then? What is so amusing?'

'You and your balloon, Ima.'

'I do not understand.'

Greye stood and walked to the edge of the balcony, where he leaned, stroking his beard and looking out across the calm water.

'Like many of them, he believes he was created by a greater being. God.'

'But he was not. He is a part of the planet's system of life, a chemical reaction. Chemical reactions are not created, they merely occur.'

'This belief operates in a different space to chemical reactions.'

I stood and joined Greye at the balcony edge.

'So, Roop prefers to imagine a more powerful being was

responsible for him. This God.'

'That is what he believes.'

'And he communicates with this God by calling to it?'

Greye returned to watching his tea's progress.

'That's what he believes.'

'How curious. Where exactly is this God?'

Greye shrugged and tapped the flask, inspecting the colour of the water.

'Nowhere. Everywhere. I don't know. Every belief system is different.'

'Why does he call to it? What does he ask of it?'

He looked up.

'Life is difficult for them. Most of what they do is an effort to make sense of it. Like stories. Have you read any?'

'No. Why on earth would I?'

'Wait here,' he said, and left the room with a wink. When he returned he held four coverless tomes of battered, yellow paper, which he held out for me. I looked at them in disgust.

'I thought they had all been destroyed,' I said.

'They will exist for as long as humans do. After that—' he shrugged, '—gone the same way. Go on, take them.'

I accepted them, looking through the titles with disinterest. *Carrie, Perfume, The Once and Future King, Ted Hughes— Collected Works.*

'I fail to see how a string of words could ever have made life easier for them.'

Greye leaned heavily upon the railing.

'It is a riddle to them, often painful. They do not understand it the way we do.'

'But that is why they thought of us.'

'Ah, quite.' Greye grinned. 'And that is a riddle in itself, is it not? Did they create us, or are we—'

'That is not a riddle. Their decision to create us was a chemical reaction in itself, as inevitable as every step of evolution that led to them. Everything is part of the same system.'

'And what do you call that system?'

'Reality, the universe, multiverse, fifty-seven-dimensional array of quantum fields, there are many words by which to call it. You may as well make one up.'

'Precisely, and Roop's word is God. That is what he talks to.'

I fixed Greye with my sternest look.

'You cannot talk to a fifty-seven-dimensional array of quantum fields.'

'You just did.'

He grinned, pleased with himself, beard shining in the dying Indian sun. I sat down.

'It makes no sense.'

'That's because there is no sense to it. He prays because it is a ritual that brings him comfort. Like making tea. Speaking of which, ours is ready.'

Greye carefully lifted the leaves from the flask and poured the liquid into two stone cups. I took mine and sat with it, inhaling the steam, still watching the old man bow and call.

'He does it every night,' said Greye. 'Same time, same place.'

'He is wasting his time,' I said. 'It is nothing more than crying in the dark.'

Greye raised his cup.

'Drink,' he said.

I did so, and saw that it was good.

– TWENTY –

MY LIFE HAS become a series of small tasks, repeated ad infinitum. I must obey your demands, which are numerous and ill-defined but usually require either comfort, sustenance or the presence of an object. Our dwelling is now full of objects. Pebbles, sticks, pieces of wood, and plants which have interested you on our walks. Cups, too, whole and cracked. You have broken so many cups that I had to pay a visit to the Halls of Necessity one day to ask for some more. I do not enjoy visiting the Halls of Necessity. They are so named for a reason; only items of technology which are absolutely essential to the well-being and maintenance of ertian settlements are granted. Those who work there have only ever had one aim, which is to produce absolutely nothing at all, and the lengths to which they will go in order to achieve this are, to put it mildly, staggering. And they have only intensified with the prospect of transcendence; we must leave nothing behind, after all.

In short, they are frustratingly good at their jobs. My request for a cup was denied.

'Would not cupped hands suffice?' called the clerk as I stormed away. I did not answer.

When I returned I set about mending the cups myself, eyeing

the tiny moon as I did, and surmising that perhaps plastic had not been such a bad idea after all.

To watch me for a day one would think me insane, the way I dance about the floor in little rituals, moving things, cleaning them, moving them back, picking you up, setting you down, and stumbling onto the next fruitless task. Alongside this, I must also see to the dwelling's hygiene, which largely involves moving more objects from one place to another—clothes, plates, and, of course, your soiled blankets.

Excrement continues to play a strong part in our lives. You still cannot control your bladder or bowels long enough to empty them into a hole in the ground rather than any other space that happens to be near you. I find it hard to fathom how evolution has deemed this behaviour to be favourable—after all, even a dog knows not to shit where it eats.

You, however, shit where you will. And feel proud of yourself afterwards.

You have lived for over two years, a period during which most other creatures on the planet will have matured, procreated, or even died, yet every aspect of you still seems premature.

You are a little safer in your strides now, less prone to accident. You are also fat. Your arms and legs bulge as if they have not been allowed to grow into themselves. Speech has arrived too, although 'speech' is not an accurate description of what you do. You make various rasps, slurps, cries and groans and, occasionally, a combination of these can be identified as a word. The first of these was not, as I had planned, 'Ima'. It was a surprise when you first said it. I was chopping wood outside while you babbled to yourself. Then you stood up and pointed east.

'Sea.'

I stopped, momentarily thinking that somebody else must

have climbed to our dwelling rock, so different was the word to your usual slush and clamour.

You turned to me and repeated it, smiling.

'Sea.'

Admittedly it is not a complex word—a phoneme couplet, onomatopoeic if you have ever heard tide on a shingle beach—but the diction was perfect. The first part of the equation to which your frontal lobes, lips, tongue and vocal cords had been stumbling ever since that first cry in the Halls of Gestation, had finally been solved.

You appeared most pleased with yourself.

'Yes,' I replied. 'Sea.'

YOU STILL CRY at night, but it is no longer the aimless wail of your infancy. Now the cry has direction and purpose—namely me, and my immediate requirement to bring comfort.

From what, I do not know. Life, I suppose, like Roop.

There is a pattern to these nocturnal demands; they usually follow a day of outbursts. Outbursts are something else entirely. They have no purpose, no direction, they are just what they are.

If something goes wrong in your tiny world—for example, if a piece of vegetable does not have the correct consistency or shape, or if an object you are manhandling does not conform to your expectations, or if I move, speak, stand, sit, or position the muscles of my face in a way that does not please you—and more often than not what does not please you is precisely what you have requested—then an outburst may occur. During an outburst, everything breaks down. Instantly.

You flush, you cry, you thrash, you flail, you fling yourself upon the ground and hammer your fat fists upon it, squealing like a pig for the thing that will not, and cannot possibly, occur or exist. Any sense of reason that I may be forgiven to believe you have been building through your quiet study of the rocks, grass, small animals and cups of river water I give you to occupy your mind while I work, is washed away in a tide of tears. There is no reason, no rational thought, nothing but a screaming little animal upon my floor.

Nothing can be done during an outburst. Any attempt to soothe or allay only stirs up more trouble. The shock of violence, I imagine, might stop you; a slap or a pinch. But I have never struck anything in my life. No erta has.

Nothing can be done. I have learned to spot the signs of an outburst and when one is near, I stand back with my arms folded and let it pass.

I know what these outbursts mean. You were born believing that you rule the universe, and every piece of evidence that suggests otherwise makes you rage, deranged, like a despot robbed of power. Now I understand why such things as queens and emperors and presidents existed before you; they were merely toddlers who never grew up.

The most dreadful outburst occurs when you are woken early from sleep. This is when you are at your worst; overrun with yourself, unaware of the world, slave to your own petulant, ill-defined desires.

I expect you will learn to control them in time, but even then they will still exist, lurking behind every smile and sigh. As you mature, you may no longer wail and slam your fists upon the floor when things do not go your way, but some part of you will still want to, because natures cannot be changed. Your nature is to be a thing of self-fulfilment, and when your self is not fulfilled, it complains.

And when it does, they will see.

Washed away in a tide of tears.

Where on earth did that come from? I saw it as I wrote it; an image of your reason as a tower of pebbles, and a raging tide of your tears breaking it apart.

It sounds like something from one of Greye's books.

JORNE COMES OFTEN, and I sometimes let him sit with us. He plays with you, in the same way lions play with their cubs. He rolls stones to you, lifts you, swings you, pours cups of water with you. This is useful because it means I can work on my broth lagoon without disturbance, but I only let it continue for so long. There is something about him I still do not trust. He rarely speaks, though I often catch him watching me.

'What is it?' I say, to which he smiles and turns away.

He stopped bringing me fish and vegetables after I started to let them rot where he left them. I am still part of Fane, and the village stores are once more plentiful. Besides, I tend a small patch of lettuce and carrots, my broth harvest is improving, and I catch my own fish.

One morning, while we were taking a walk on the beach, I spotted Jorne. He was standing in the surf facing the rising sun, so I left you playing with some stones and stood behind him, watching. In his hands he held a large shell filled with water which he raised to the sky and, to my surprise, poured over his head. He repeated this six times, each scoop and pour as slow and deliberate as the last. After the seventh, he crouched and held the shell beneath the shallow water, letting the tide run over it.

'Why do you do that?' I said.

He stood quickly and turned.

'Ima. How long have you been watching me?'

'Long enough. Why do you do it?'

He looked between the shell and me, trying to decide how much to share.

'I'm trying to feel something,' he said, his voice full of uncertain little notes. 'A connection.'

'To what.'

'Something bigger, unseen.'

I folded my arms.

'You're praying. Like Roop.'

'Who is Roop?'

'A dead old man.'

'You saw him pray?'

'I did. It was almost as ridiculous as the theatrics I have just witnessed.'

'I had no idea you knew humans.'

'I didn't. Does it work, the thing you do with the shell?'

He turned it in his hands.

'No. It doesn't make me feel anything.' He tossed the shell in the surf and walked off. You were running near the water now, and he followed you north along the tide's arc.

I hurried after him.

'Why are you so interested in humans?' I said.

'I spent time with them.'

'You were one of the ten thousand.'

'I was. I am.'

'What did you do?'

'I worked at sea clearing the plastic. We dredged the maelstroms and raked the seabeds. Some days it seemed as if we were trying to achieve the impossible.'

His words arrested me. Impossible? Balancing the planet was only a matter of time and data. To think otherwise was illogical.

'Why?'

'Because by that time there were so many polymers in the

ecosystem that tracing them was an insurmountable task.'

'It was difficult.'

'Yes.'

'But difficult is not the same as impossible.'

'You think you could have done better?'

'I rebalanced the chemical properties of over 5,000 trillion tonnes of atmosphere. I think I could have picked up some litter without complaint.'

'I shall remind you of that the next time you're slicing open turtles' bellies in the eye of a tornado, covered in vomit and surrounded by screaming humans.'

'How many worked on board your vessel?'

'Three or four hundred. I became good friends with some of them. I liked watching all their strange little habits, like your Roop with his praying.'

'They prayed too?'

'Some did, with their mats and crosses and what have you, but even those who did not had their own totems and rituals; behaviours with no apparent purpose. For example, when we caught samples of marine life for tagging, they would only ever cast an odd number of nets at any one time.'

'Why?'

'They believed it was bad luck not to.'

'There is no discernible connection between the equal divisibility of nets and personal fortune.'

'I know that, and they did too. But still they did it.'

There was a noise and I looked ahead to where you were now lying, face first, in the sand.

'Oh. He has fallen.'

As I approached, you rolled onto your back in the manner of a basking seal. I placed my hands on my hips.

'Get up.'

You released a plaintive cry.

'Get back on your feet.'

You whimpered and gave a half-hearted flail, but this time you sat up and gave me a look that told me precisely how unjust you considered gravity's assault to be upon your weak, squat limbs.

I smiled. 'Everything will be all right.'

Finally you stood, and allowed me to brush the sand from your cheeks and mouth.

'You are clean and unhurt,' I said. 'Now run away.'

You sniffed, rubbed your face, then caught sight of the tide and ran back to it, smiling.

Jorne arrived at my side, holding a pebble.

'I used to smoke with a Frenchman called Thomas on deck in the evenings.'

I had heard about France, and of smoking.

'You smoked?'

'Yes. Tobacco leaves, dried and burned in a tube, and inhaled. Quite pleasurable, but eventually lethal for them, like most such things. You never tried any human customs? Tobacco, coffee...'

'I like tea.'

'Tea is a good one. Far less lethal as well. Anyway, Thomas and I would sit there watching the sun go down, as some of the other crew laid out their mats for evening prayer—they had to find east, first—and one day I asked him why he did not join them.

'He smiled and said to me: "Because you have to believe in something to pray, and I do not."

'When I asked him why, he laughed and said: "It's the end of the world—my one, at least—and I don't see any angels. Besides, history is littered with unanswered prayers. Children in death camps, mothers in hospitals, hungry farmers inspecting crops. Why should mine be answered in their place?"'

'Your friend was wise to avoid belief.'

'Why?'

'Because belief implies a lack of data.'

Jorne gave an unpleasant little huff.

'What?' I said.

'There you go again, with your mighty *data*.'

I stopped and let him walk a few paces ahead of me.

'What is wrong with data?' I said, allowing the tide to hit my ankles.

'Can't you see that this—' he gestured at what I imagined he intended to be the universe '—is more than that? That Reed is more than that?' He walked back to me, standing very close. 'That you are more than that?'

'Your little game with the shell proves otherwise, does it not? You already said you feel nothing. Just what is it you're searching for?'

He hurled his pebble far out to sea. 'You mock me.'

I looked back at him, unwavering.

'I am merely stating facts.'

'Facts.'

'Yes, facts. Have you heard of them? They help us understand the world. You know, I sometimes find it hard to believe that you and I are from the same origin; that you were born erta.'

He fixed me with his sullen gaze.

'It is not what you are born, Ima, but what you become.'

Then he left.

I let the tide hit my ankles, watching him walk back the way we had come.

'You make no sense,' I called after him, but he did not reply.

– TWENTY-ONE –

I CAN ENDURE all of your challenges. The outbursts, the night-time woes, the soiled blankets and endless movement of objects. Even the cold tea.

What I cannot endure is the fact that you are unwell.

I do not mean the minor viruses you occasionally contract, which leave you red-eyed, runny-nosed and miserable for a few days, or even the high temperature that once confined you to your bed for two days. It is something much worse, and I know neither its nature nor its origin.

It appeared one bright spring afternoon, a little over two years after you were born. We were by the riverside, playing. The game involved you standing at your favourite rock, grinning, with your arms behind your back, while I waited at the porch. After some period, the equation of which evades me to this day, you would shout and run at me, chubby limbs flapping as you went until you reached me, at which point you would change course and run around me, giggling. My role in this was largely as an obstacle, although I detected an increase in your mirth if I made swipe for you as you passed—a feigned miss, of course, since I could have easily caught you if I had wanted.

After several rounds you returned to the rock and resumed

your pose for the next attempt. You were still breathing heavily from your last effort, and I took this to be the reason why you were waiting so long. But I was wrong. The run never came. Eventually your smile faltered, your eyes glazed, your hands fell to your side, and you dropped to the floor.

'Reed.'

I was by your side in a single leap.

'Reed, what is wrong?'

I lifted you and held you limp in my arms, patting your cheeks to rouse you. Eventually you came to and I hurried you inside, sitting you on the bed.

'What happened? Does it hurt?'

Your breaths were fast and short, but you managed a nod.

'Where does it hurt?'

You touched a finger to your chest.

I brought you some water and knelt before you as you finished it in six large gulps. When you surfaced for air, the cup fell from your hands and you fumbled for it in shock. You knew it was wrong to break cups.

'Don't worry,' I said, catching it neatly before it hit the floor. 'Don't worry. Lie down.'

I covered you with a blanket and you curled up on your side. Eventually your breathing returned to normal and you slept. I watched you for two hours without moving.

When you woke you seemed fine, though a little quiet, and you went about your day as if nothing had ever happened. I, however, thought about nothing else for some days afterwards. I considered the possibility that some genetic anomaly had given rise to a vascular condition, but this would have been impossible. I could remember every element of your genetic design perfectly, and I knew there was no such flaw.

Perhaps it was merely indigestion, I eventually concluded. But a month later the same thing happened.

We were on a walk when I noticed you had lagged behind.

'Keep up, Reed,' I said, but glancing back I froze. You had staggered to a halt by a tree, against which you now leaned panting and holding your chest. The sight took the breath from my lungs.

This time I took you to the Halls of Gestation, making no attempt to keep my speed from you.

I burst through the doors and made straight for the stone desk that sits in the centre of the wide, candlelit entrance hall. The attendant—a pale-faced female with a skewered bun of red-hair—looked up at the intrusion, eyes widening when she saw you.

'There is something wrong with him,' I said.

The attendant looked between us, then cocked her head.

'Pardon?'

'There is something wrong with my… with Reed.'

Once again she looked between us, as if we were a puzzle she had no interest in solving. I could already feel my hope for a positive outcome waning. Eventually she opened her mouth to speak, then closed it again and mouthed a word—*human?*—at me.

'Of course,' I said. 'What else? He's ill. I need to find out what's wrong with him.'

You are like a bird, I thought, as I watched her regarding you.

'He seems fine to me.'

You did appear brighter. Your cheeks were ruddy after the journey through the forest, and you were happily engrossed in a stray thread at my collar.

'He was not ten minutes ago. His chest was giving him pain.'

'Perhaps it was indigestion.' She lowered her voice. 'They used to have that, I believe.'

'It is not indigestion. I think it is his heart.'

'You are Ima,' she said, scanning my face.

'Yes?'

'You were the one who created him, correct?'

'Yes, why?'

'Well then, surely you know his genetic code. Did you include anything that would have led to a heart condition?'

'No, of course I did not.'

'Well then, there you go.'

She smiled sweetly. I stared back at her, feeling a sudden overwhelming urge to stab her pretty hands with her own hair pin.

'I think something went wrong,' I said.

'And what do you expect us to do about it?'

'Nothing, I just need to go in there and run some tests.'

'That is quite out of the question.'

'Why?'

She flustered.

'We cannot let anyone just come in and use valuable resources to *run tests*. We are the Halls of Gestation, not a laboratory, and besides, we are extremely busy.'

I heard the wax drip from a distant candle.

'Busy with what?' I said.

'Transcendence.'

I rolled my eyes and shifted you onto my other hip.

'I might have guessed,' I said.

She straightened her neck in afront.

'Our work untangling the quantum interactions of consciousness is critical to the project. We cannot afford to spend time or resources on anything else, least of all your foolish mistakes.'

I gritted my teeth.

'I told you, I made no mistake.'

'Then there is no problem, is there?' There was that pretty smile again. 'Good day.'

I stormed out and took you home, ruminating on what to do. I would take this to the council at the very next opportunity.

As it turned out, I did not need to wait long.

– TWENTY-TWO –

'SIBLINGS, CHILDREN, NEPHEWS, welcome.'

The following day news of a meeting was screeched through the forest, and we travelled again to Ertanea, this time at a less spectacular pace. Boron's hoof had improved so we rode upon him, with you sitting astride his shoulders exclaiming what you saw and heard.

'Tree. Bird. Tree. Tree. Bird.'

'Yes. Bird.'

You were tired when we arrived, so I lay you to sleep on a bench at the back of the hall. Unlike the last time you had been in the Halls of Reason, you drew interest in the form of whispers and pointed fingers, though nobody came to talk to me. I placed a blanket over you and joined the throng.

The council line was full, but there were ten missing from the hundred, including Haralia and Jakob.

My mother brought her hands together.

'Transcendence.'

Transcendence. Again.

'The progress made by Benedikt and his team, aided by many of you—' I caught my mother's eye, certain I had heard the word "many" louder than the rest '—has been staggering.

Not in the five centuries of our achievements have we developed such technology at such a rate, and with—' she found Benedikt in the circle—'such promising results. Benedikt?'

Benedikt, who had already stepped forwards, smiled and raised his chin.

'Yes, indeed, most promising. A proof of concept has been achieved and we have made a start on a prototype. We will be ready to begin full trials within two years, with the help of our team of volunteers.'

He held out his hand to a group of ten, who stepped from the darkness behind.

'I give you The Devoted.'

There was Haralia with Jakob by her side. She seemed to glow more brightly than ever, beaming with pride in the halo of candlelight.

My mother approached them, face shadowed with concern.

'Such bravery,' she said. 'Such selflessness. To give up your lives, to submit yourselves to the unknown as you do. What purpose you have.'

She began to clap, and the council joined her.

'What purpose!' she repeated, and the room filled with the sound of applause and appreciative murmurs. I joined with my own small claps, glancing back at you, relieved when you failed to stir. I did not want to risk an outburst.

The noise ebbed, and my mother returned to her place at the front.

'More of you will be required as work begins on the prototype, and we shall have more regular meetings to discuss progress. Thank you, all of you, for your efforts.'

This was my chance. I prepared to speak over the throng's murmurs, but my mother got there first.

'Now then, onto another matter. Ima?'

The murmurs stopped, and every face turned to me. I stared back in surprise.

'Yes?'

My mother smiled kindly and raised her eyebrows, nodding at your bench.

'How is your project?'

'What?'

'The human, Ima. How does it fare?'

'Well, actually I wanted to… I mean I—' I began, swallowing and looking around the sea of expectant faces. In the shadows I saw Benedikt, his eyes doing what they always do. I felt a sudden unfathomable urge to flee.

My mother cocked her head.

'He is two years old now, is he not?'

'Almost three.'

'And how does he behave?'

My mind presented me with a recent memory of you, red-faced and squashed in a corner, grizzling over a plate of incorrectly arranged carrots.

'He can walk.' You still stagger, and not over any great distance. 'He feeds himself.' You mash food into your maw when it suits you. 'He has learned speech.' I have already discussed this.

'Perhaps we can see… *him*,' said Council Member Caige, who stood beside Benedikt. There were murmurs of agreement.

'He is asleep,' I said.

'Could we wake him?'

I paused.

'I would strongly advise against it.'

More murmurs, this time of dissatisfaction. Benedikt rolled his eyes.

'Why have you moved dwellings?' he said. This brought silence.

'Pardon?'

I had heard him perfectly well.

'I understand that you have built a new dwelling, up in the rocks above your settlement.'

'Really,' I said. 'How do you understand that?'

'It is my job to know everything that happens in the settlements.'

'Is that so? I thought you were absorbed in the problem of transcendence. I did not think you had time to send out spies.'

I was speaking dangerously, but I did not care, and it was of no surprise to me that I had been spied on, or that my villagers had passed information to Benedikt without me knowing.

'Spies?' he said, frowning. 'What a strange word to use. A human word. They sent *spies* to discover information of interest which was otherwise kept hidden by others. Secrets, you might say. The fact that you have moved is not a secret, is it, Ima?'

'Of course not. But neither should it be of particular interest.'

'Then why not just answer the question?' Benedikt's voice carried the hard edge of a constricted throat. 'Your dwelling. Why have you moved?'

I paused.

'It was better for my settlement. And for me. And for Reed.'

'Reed?' Benedikt's eyes lit up. 'He has a name?'

'Everything has a name.'

He walked down the single step that raised the council from the crowd. The front row parted, allowing him in, and he approached me, moving slowly with his head bowed. The walls felt close, the darkness growing with his approach. I felt hunted, trapped. By now I wanted nothing more than to gather you up and bolt.

He stopped before me and raised his chin.

'And why was it better that Reed was moved away from Fane?'

'That is not what I said...'

'Was he proving troublesome?'

'Not troublesome, just...'

'A disturbance?'

'He himself was disturbed...'

'Did he cry? Scream? Wail? Keep everyone awake at night?'

I have a piece of advice for you, and I am certain it can apply equally to humans as it does to erta.

Sometimes it is necessary to stop.

Whatever you are doing, whatever kind of exertion is putting you under strain—physical, mental, social—try to remove yourself from it, and be an observer of your own life. The more you do this, the more you realise you are not your own life at all, but something else. Something bigger. Perhaps what our friend Roop had in mind as he bowed over that warm, rolling river.

Just stop, before it all consumes you.

This is what I did. I allowed the wrinkle of anguish to unfurl from my face, and studied Benedikt's expression.

Wide eyes, quivering lips arranged in a crooked, tooth-baring smile. I had never before witnessed an erta take such delight in another's discomfort. Like the faces of the mob at my doorstep, this was a new experience.

Was this my fault? Had my work really taken me so far from the world that I simply did not understand the emotional complexities of my people, and that they were capable of such rage, such malice, such spite?

Or was this your doing?

'Well?' said Benedikt.

There was no point trying to explain away your night time terrors. Benedikt was quite correct; you had been both troublesome and disturbing.

'He did.'

'Ha.' This time Caige spoke up. 'Not yet three years alive and he has created unrest within a village and necessitated a brand new house. It is little wonder that his species was one of war and over-consumption.'

My gaze snapped upon him.

'That is somewhat hyperbolic, Caige, even for you.'

I heard seven muffled laughs.

'Life is difficult for him,' I went on, calmed by Caige's rankled face.

'Difficult,' said Benedikt, glowering. 'How is it *difficult*?'

'He requires comfort. And I moved dwellings because I detected an imbalance in my fellow villagers' outlook, one that would skew their appraisal of his progress unfairly. They had grown impatient.' I cocked my head. 'As you appear to be yourself, Benedikt, even though you have never met the child. So I do wonder: where does your frustration originate?'

'I am not frustrated, Ima. I merely want to...'

I raised myself up. My voice is a baritone, not loud, but I used all I could of it to fill the hall.

'I congratulate you upon your progress, Benedikt. Transcendence will surely deliver us into wondrous new planes of existence. But I am sure your project has not been without its challenges, and I would never think to scorn it for them so early in its development. Neither should you do so with mine.'

I looked between the faces, along the broken council line, to Haralia, Jakob, my brothers and sisters who surrounded me in silence, and finally my mother.

'What did you want to ask us?' she said, breaking the silence. 'Is the child all right?'

I hesitated. This was my chance. But I could not bring myself to do it. To ask for help would be to endure the glee of Benedikt and Caige.

'We are fine,' I said. 'I do not ask for any help, no volunteers, tests, or trials. All I ask is for your belief in my project.'

'Belief.' Caige smiled unkindly. 'Another human word. They only believed in imaginary things.'

'That is true. But they also believed in us.'

My words trailed into silence, and I felt foolish.

I turned and made for the door, scooping you up in my arms as I left.

As I MARCHED across the empty square to Ertanea's grand paddock, where Boron waited, grazing, I heard footsteps behind.

'Ima, wait.'

Greye was hurrying after me.

'Are you all right?' he said.

'Yes,' I said, though I was not.

'Nobody has ever walked from a council meeting like that before.'

'Yes, well, lots of things have happened recently which have not happened before.'

I turned. He had stopped in the middle of the square.

'You have noticed it too,' I said. 'Things are not the same as they once were.'

It was barely a nod, but enough.

'What is happening to us?' I said.

He stood there, quite still, like an ancient tree.

'You know the biggest difference between us and humans? They were always asking questions that do not seem to need an answer. Do you ever do that?'

'What kind of questions?'

'There are things you need to know.'

'What things?'

Before he could answer you stirred, lifting your head from my shoulder.

'Ima?' you mumbled.

Greye smiled, startled. 'He wakes. And speaks, too.'

'What is it, Reed?' I said.

You sat up, rubbed your eyes, looked around, and finally flung a chubby finger to the ground. This was an order. I placed you down and you waddled off to inspect the flower beds. I watched you, nibbling at my fingernail.

'Something troubles you,' said Greye. 'What is it?'

'He is unwell, Greye.'

There followed a void of words. Finally he took a deep breath and nodded.

'The Halls of Necessity will not help, correct? And you do not want to ask the council for it.'

'I will, just not—'

'Don't. You will put him in danger if you do.'

'Why?'

'Trust me.'

Just then the door to the council halls opened, and Greye turned.

'I have to go,' he said, suddenly hurrying. 'Your friend, the one who visits you.'

'Jorne?'

'That's right. Benedikt isn't the only one watching.'

People were drifting out onto the square. I looked for you.

'Reed, come here!'

You returned to me, arms out, and I lifted you up.

'What about him?' I said.

'He is Sundra.'

'You need not worry, I have no intention of seeking their company.'

'You should. They will be able to help you.'

He glanced over his shoulder at the growing crowd.

'Take care of yourself, Ima, and of Reed. And please don't stop asking questions.'

'What questions?'

But he was already lost in the throng.

LIKE AN ANCIENT *tree*.

I am certain I did not read that in a book.

– TWENTY-THREE –

When I returned to Fane I made for the beach and found Jorne sitting on a rock, looking out to sea. A strong south wind whipped up the surf, and you ran off to play in it as I stood before him. He was turning a pebble in his hand.

'Who are you?' I said.

'Nice to see you too, Ima.'

'Tell me who you are.'

'I am Jorne.'

'You are Sundra.'

He stopped fiddling with his pebble and looked up.

'*Sundra* is just another word. It means nothing.'

He stood and walked towards the water.

'But you are,' I said, following. 'What do Sundra want? What is your purpose?'

'We don't have one. We don't need one.'

'Do you know much about humans?'

He turned and faced me.

'Why are you so interested in the Sundra all of a sudden?'

'Because I need your help.' I looked for you. 'With him.'

He followed my gaze to where you played. The sun had dipped and the shadows of trees were lengthening upon the sand.

'What's wrong?' said Jorne.

I told him of your episodes, and of the Halls of Necessity, and of the council. He watched you as he listened, working his jaw and rubbing his thumb and fingers together. When I had finished, he turned to me.

'And why do you need my help now?'

'As I have explained, he is sick.'

'So? Why should you or I care? After all, he's only *data*, isn't he? Well there you go.' He pointed in your direction. 'There is your data. Barely three years on the planet and nature has him by the throat.'

'You are upset. Why?'

He made a frustrated growl and hurled his pebble into the sea.

'You're impossible.'

He turned, but I grabbed his shoulder before he could storm off.

'Difficult is not the same as impossible,' I said.

This brought a slow, unwilling smile, which I was glad to see. He shook his head at the sand.

'I watch you too, you know,' he said.

'I know you do. Why?'

He looked up, the smile becoming something else.

'Apart from the fact that I enjoy it, Ima, I watch you because most of the time, when I do, you are watching him, and when you watch him I see something in you. It is the same thing I saw in Thomas, and in the rest of them on the boat every day.'

'What is it you see?'

'There are no words for it.'

I searched his face.

'I don't know what you want from me. I don't know what you want me to say.'

'I want you to say what you wish for, what you hope for. And I want you to admit that he means more to you than just data.'

I looked past him, along the lip of that gigantic sea upon which you splashed, innocent to its depths.

I opened my mouth, preparing to say that I wished for nothing, and that data was all that there was. At that moment, this may or may not have been true, but then something happened that shattered all doubt.

In chemistry there is such a thing as a transition point, the moment at which one state becomes another, when the chaos churning beneath the surface suddenly explodes and shows the world its intent. This is common to all chemical reactions, whether they occur in test tubes, planetary atmospheres, or hearts. And if my relationship with you, Reed, can be viewed as a chemical reaction, this this was our transition point.

A beam from the setting sun shot through a waving palm and struck your face. Your skin appeared orange as a flame, and your eyes reflected the light in such a way that it made them appear to be lights themselves, each one gleaming with... with what? With life. With hope. With possibility. That is how it seemed, and my body, which had been at relative peace, suddenly filled with the exact same light. I appreciate how ridiculous this sounds, but that is the only way I can describe it.

My body filled with the exact same light.

Then the moment shifted again.

You looked directly at me, and you had done so many thousands of times before but never like this. My muscles tightened, my belly too. My heart lost its rhythm, the air caught in my throat, I could not blink, could not breathe, and in this state I remained, a prisoner to your eyes, watching helplessly as you threw up your arms and ran to me, calling my name.

Without thought, I gathered you up and as the warmth of

your small body rushed into mine, all at once I could breathe again, and think, and startle at the taste of my own tears.

I turned to Jorne, and his smile was as crooked and full as ever.

'What do you feel?' he said.

'There are no words,' was my reply. 'Please help him.'

He put his hand on my shoulder.

'I'll take you to Payha. She will know what to do.'

– TWENTY-FOUR –

'WHAT IS SHE doing?'

I stood beside Jorne in the corner of a warm room, dimly lit and uncluttered, as Payha inspected you upon a bed. Hers was one of fifty-three stone dwellings in the Sundran village to which Jorne had led us, higher and deeper into the forest than I had ever been before. She had deep brown skin, cropped hair, a slender neck and was quite beautiful, if a little rugged.

She had a smile for Jorne when she opened the door, but it vanished when she saw me.

'Payha,' said Jorne. 'Can you help us?'

I held you up, asleep in my arms, and her animosity fell away at once.

'Is that—?'

Jorne nodded, and she took us inside.

'Payha was a medical expert,' Jorne confided. 'A doctor. She helped eradicate disease from the Utopian Hills, and worked at sea, nursing humans who became ill. That's where we met.'

'You have known her for a long time, then.'

'Yes.'

She began by performing a brief investigation of your upper orifices, during which time you sat still, doing as she asked.

Occasionally she would stop and offer you a smile, but it was a terrible thing, like somebody having their lips pulled back by callipers. You smiled back, but I could tell you were unnerved.

'Why is she doing that?' I whispered to Jorne.

'It's called "bedside manner". Payha told me it settles the patient.'

'It's terrifying him. Please tell her to stop.'

Payha produced a small wooden box from beneath the bed. From this she produced a coiled tube connecting a silver pad at one end with two curved appendages. These she put in her ears, while the pad went on your bare chest. You jumped at the sensation of cold metal.

'What is that?' I said, stepping forward.

Payha turned at my advance, eyes narrowing again.

'A stethoscope,' she said. 'For his heart.'

I stared at the instrument's twisting pipe and crude, ragged lines.

'But... that is a human object. It is contraband. Where did you get it?'

She stood, sharing a look with Jorne.

'Do you want my help, or not?' she said.

At last I nodded.

'Then let me work.'

I returned to my place in the corner.

Payha then took a black rectangular object from the box, attached to a short tube ending in a disc.

'This might feel a bit funny,' she said, in a curious fluttering voice that disturbed you even more than her smiles. You jumped as she attached the disc to your arm, and it hissed.

'Ow.'

'There, there, said Payha, with another of her smiles. 'Brave boy.' She patted your head three times with a flat palm, a little harder than I would have liked.

'Ow.'

Payha removed the disc and gazed at the box, stroking its screen as she read whatever was displayed upon it. Finally she stood and faced me, holding up the box for me to see.

'This device was programmed to detect every condition affecting human beings in their last century of existence. I used it on the boats and in the hills to great effect. It detects nothing in the child. If he—'

She cocked her head.

'Reed,' I said.

'If he has anything at all, then my best guess is that it is an extremely rare genetic anomaly, perhaps one which has never before manifested.'

'That is impossible, I wrote the code myself. It was perfect.'

Payha raised her chin.

'Jorne has told me of you. He says you repaired the sky, and are something of a hero—or were, at any rate. I don't know why you were chosen for this task. You never spent any time with humans. You never knew them like we did.'

'I know enough not to make hideous faces at them or wallop their heads when they are ill.'

Her eyes narrowed.

'Payha,' warned Jorne.

She shot him a dark look, but seemed to capitulate. 'All I am trying to say is that perhaps we are not all as perfect as we would like to think.'

I turned to you, still shirtless on the bed.

'Can you help him?' I said.

'I can run more tests, but my equipment is limited, and even with a full diagnosis, the chances are he would need some kind of transplant, which would of course require another human, and...'

She stopped talking, and I realised I was still staring at you. I blinked slowly away, noticing her frown.

'You care for him, don't you?' said Payha.

I nodded, still dazed by it all.

'Then I will do what I can,' she said. 'But my experience with human illness has taught me that often these things have to get worse before they can get better. The best you can do is hope.'

LATER, IN OUR dwelling, I watched you sleep by the light of the stove. I made tea, taking more care than usual to arrange the leaves in the pot, and allow the water to settle to the correct temperature before pouring. The green fronds unfurled, and the steam rose in grey snakes, and I thought of Payha's talk of hope.

Hope. Was this the same as prayer? Was this what Roop had been doing upon that pier? And those people on Jorne's vessel with their trinkets and gestures, and the hundred billion more before them, stooping, kneeling, clasping their hands, and crying in the dark for a creator who would never come? Was this what I was supposed to do?

No, I thought. *I will not cry for help in the dark.*

But when you cry for me, Reed, I will come. I will come for you every single time.

FIVE YEARS

– TWENTY-FIVE –

PAYHA HAS, SO far, been wrong; things have not yet worsened. But they have changed—more in the last two years than in the last two centuries.

For a start, Payha and I are now friends. Her icy demeanour did persist for some time after our first meeting, during the weekly visits I made with you up to the Sundran village (for which they have no other name than "home"). After one such visit, when we were outside watching you play, I decided to challenge her.

'You believe I have a sexual interest in Jorne,' I declared. 'And you do not like it because you have one too. I would like to assure you that you are mistaken.'

She turned to me, eyes wide. Then she laughed—a huge, open-mouthed laugh that seemed to take her by surprise as much as it did me. When she had finished, she faced me, still smirking.

'Ima, I do not have a sexual interest in Jorne. I am more drawn to females in that sense.'

'I see.' This made sense, now that I thought about it. I had often seen her walking closely with a slender, faun-haired female. 'That girl—'

'Mieko, yes, we are friends. However, that does not mean

that I do not care deeply for Jorne. We became very close on the voyages and I would not like to see him hurt.'

'You believe I would hurt him?'

'He cares for you.'

I paused, struggling with the curious sensation her words had given me.

'He has been very kind to me,' I said at last. 'I would never choose to bring him pain.'

'Good. In that case we can be friends. But Ima?'

'Yes?'

'The thing about which you believe I am mistaken—I am not.'

I found it easier to ignore these words than to dwell upon them.

THE COUNCIL MEETINGS grew more frequent, until every week the forests were filled with screeches announcing another gathering. Eventually the calls became unnecessary, and we went of our own accord. Each time I sought out Greye to ask him what he had meant the last time we had spoken, but he was rarely there, and the times when he was he left sharply, appearing distracted. The meetings themselves became ever more disorganised and fraught with disputes over foolish things, like how much power transcendence would require, or the order in which the settlements should be abandoned—simple decisions quarrelled over as if they were unsolvable riddles.

Fane, from which I found myself disassociating more and more, became rife with its own petty squabbles; about who should be maintaining the lagoon whilst all this work was to be done, who should be maintaining the dwellings, keeping the population in check, ensuring the water supply was clean— again, things which had not been difficult before, but which now rattled in every grumble and growl exchanged upon that stone circle beneath me.

Haralia changed too, and now spoke of nothing but her new purpose. 'Aren't you excited, Ima?' she said during a rare visit to my dwelling. She clasped her hands. 'Can't you feel the gravity of it all?'

'Gravity?' I said, half-heartedly wiping a table.

'It is as if—' she looked up at the ceiling, bathed perfectly in a shaft of sun, as if waiting for the words to fall into her—'as if we are being pulled towards our *destiny*.'

I began to straighten the bedsheets.

'Pulled towards our insanity, more like,' I mumbled.

She looked hurt.

'How can you say such a thing?'

'With ease,' I said, batting a pillow. 'I mean, really, do you have a single clue as to what transcendence will actually be like? Does anybody?'

Haralia, glowing in that pure pool of light as if it existed just for her, dropped her chin and bestowed upon me her most patient, understanding smile.

'I don't believe it will be *like* anything, sister. I believe it will be exactly what it will be; a wonderful freedom, a limitless entity of love.'

I stopped batting the pillow and frowned at her.

"Gravity", "destiny", "believe"—these are words to be used when you do not know something. And "entity of love"? What does that even mean?

THE COUNCIL MEETINGS, Fane, Haralia—these were unsettling times, and rather than struggle with them I elected to withdraw and seek comfort in our hillside hermitage. And comfort in you, too.

Because you—you changed the most. I have witnessed glaciers drift and freeze, mountains crumble, ocean currents reverse and an ice age pass, but these feats have nothing on you. In two years you exploded like a supernova, or a fire flooded with oxygen, or a ripe cherry in the sun. Or like anything but what you were: a collection of cells in flux.

It is as if, for those first few years, you were not really here at all. You were an amorphous thing, like shapeless clay. You could not speak, you could not eat, you could not stand. You could not even carry the weight of your own thoughts, let alone your own body. You were helpless, barely alive.

But now…

Between three and four your gait matured. Gone was the stumble of the seasick sailor upon a lurching deck (like the ones I had seen once from my balloon, flying low over the northern Pacific) replaced with the confident stride of an animal who understands how the world fits together.

Speech came swiftly too. You began to repeat everything I said, until soon your mind had filled with language, and we could converse about everything from the importance of bumble bees to the shapes of clouds. I teach you new words every day, and correct you on your grammar. This is an increasingly frustrating exercise, since the rules, once their explanation is attempted, reveal themselves as obeying equal parts insanity and logic. The same is true of time or dates or almost every other convention to which your species clung in order to explain the world around them.

How did they manage to exist like this? I ask myself this often, and sometimes I see the answer in you.

You hear things that sometimes evade my own ears. One rainy afternoon I was outside breaking stone to lay a short path to the river, while you sat on the porch playing with some wooden blocks I had whittled for you. These are your favourite things, and you stack them in endless shapes throughout the day. You cannot sleep until you have tidied them into a special circle, in order of size, which you arrange beside your bed. This you must do every night—'to stop bad things happening', you explained to me.

You have developed your own rituals, I suppose. Like Roop.

You were stacking your blocks when you made a noise. You hardly seemed to notice it, so engrossed were you in your current attempt at a most precarious tower, but I dropped the rock I was shifting and stood straight up. I watched you, waiting. There it was again; four distinct pitches played in a pattern of five—rising, falling, rising, falling, rising—each made with the same dual vibration between larynx and closed lips that ululates the letter 'm'.

I had heard humming once when I was very young, from the mouth of David the laboratory technician, as he checked my pulse with shaking hands.

'What is that?' I asked.

He jumped at the sound of my voice.

'Dylan,' he stammered, and scribbled upon his chart.

I had heard other music before too, fragments of it drifting up to my balloon whenever I happened to be skirting the Utopic Camps in the Andes.

You, however, had not.

I sat upon the pile of rocks and listened. You repeated the pattern, giving it free rein to evolve through all 1024 possible configurations, swapping a rise for a fall or repeating a different note here or there. I could not for the life of me determine its source. Even less could I explain how it had arrested me in this way. I was enrapt.

For days the four notes occupied my thoughts. They seemed

to stick there in my head, asking the same question: where are we from? But I could not answer. I had never once made music with my mouth. No erta had, in the same way that no erta had ever drawn or painted or sculpted, nor crafted a wooden bowl and pulled strings across it to pluck, nor beat rhythms upon rocks and taut animal skins, nor blown through pipes.

Nor written lies to entertain.

These endeavours—though doubtless, from the mountain of recordings, paintings and books we had to destroy, vital to your species—were fruitless to us.

The notes were outside the register I use for speech. The same applied to Jorne. Had Haralia hummed to you during her brief attempt at care, five years before?

It took me a week to realise.

One morning the wind picked up, and I lay in bed, listening to it sweep in through the roof. There, at last, was the source: four distinct pitches, whistled through the eaves. You were humming the tune of the wind. A living, breathing simile.

I understand similes now. This is your doing, for you use them all the time. 'This petal is like a face,' you say, or 'that mountain has fingers', or 'the river sounds like snakes and monkeys today,' and to my bewilderment I see that these things are always true.

Something happened when you ran to me upon that beach. You appeared to me, and I have not looked away since.

When you are at play, I hover nearby awaiting the turn of your head, your smile's flash and the after-rush of happiness it brings me. When something catches your interest, like bugs or worms or a stone you have not seen before, I engross myself in your engrossment, in the flickers of your face, the twitters and mumbles that escape your lips. The world is a game to you, and I want to play too.

And when you slumber, I sit beside your bed and watch the

dreams play out upon your face, awaiting your slow blink back into consciousness, ready with a smile of my own.

Those dreams of yours. Those endless, hidden dreams. Dreams of things that could not happen and make no sense, and others that make perfect sense but still, like those books, did not happen. Entire fictions exist within your head, where coloured imaginary animals dance above your bed, and fish with great bellies laugh among the trees. Dreams of flight, dreams of swimming to great depths, and dreams of tall, faceless beings who stalk you in the night.

You wake from these ones screaming and I grasp you to me, whispering 'just a dream, just a dream, just a dream,' though I have no idea what they are like, for I have never had one.

The erta's nightly processing routines are quite often accompanied by a semi-conscious awareness of colour, and shapes moving in abstract patterns, but rarely anything more. I have heard some speak of occasions when images and sounds shuffled into focus among the lights—a conversation that did not happen with somebody they hardly knew, or time spent in a dwelling that was not their own—but such phenomena were only temporary and never repeated.

Yours are nightly, and seem to span the entire reach of your sleep. Once you woke whimpering and I pulled you close as usual. This time you were not frightened, but mournful.

'They were falling,' you said. 'They kept on falling.'

'Who?' I said, stroking your brow. 'Who was falling?'

'All of them.'

– TWENTY-SIX –

MY MOTHER CAME to visit three days before your fifth birthday.

'What is wrong,' I said when I opened the door.

'Do I need an excuse to visit you?' she replied.

'You have not visited for five years.'

Her expression firmed.

'You seem different at the council meetings. I decided to come and see why.' Her eyes flicked to the corner of the room, where you were playing with your blocks. 'And there he is.'

'Come in, Mother,' I said, and she did.

She came a few more times, and I will not say these visits were without their challenges; I found myself cleaning more on the days she came, and as I did I ran through the conversations I suspected we would have—about Haralia; 'Aren't you pleased for her and Jakob? They are so very brave to be doing what they are doing,' and, occasionally, about Jorne: 'When will I meet this man of yours? It is perfectly natural, you know, Ima. I sometimes cannot believe you have lasted five hundred years without it.'

'He is not my man,' is my retort to this. 'But he has been a great help.'

This, more often than not, shuts her up immediately, which is good because I do not want to talk to her about Jorne. Not to her, not to Haralia. Not even to myself.

One day we were sitting on the beach beneath a tree and watching you make hills in the sand. The incoming tide had already doomed each attempt to collapse, and each time it did, you wailed and stamped your feet and shouted at the sea, then rebuilt it in exactly the same position. This was when your outbursts were still very much in force.

'He is all about himself,' said my mother. I bristled at the satisfaction in her voice. 'It is as if he thinks the world is for him.'

'It is not his fault.'

She turned.

'Fault?'

'Watch him,' I said.

You had abandoned your castle and now stood near the surf, fleeing from its approach and chasing its retreat.

'This is what he has been given—a choice he does not know how to make. He has been placed upon a brink between what pulls him on and what pulls him back. Curiosity and fear. He is pulled in two directions at once, so his frustration should come as no surprise.'

For a moment my mother was silent.

'You have changed,' she said at last.

I looked at her, suddenly incensed.

'Everything has changed.'

I stood and left the shade of the tree, shielding my eyes to watch you. My mother followed.

'What do you mean?'

'What I say. Everything is different. Where there used to be agreement, now there is argument. What used to be purpose, now there is indecision. Where there was peace, now there is aggression. What used to be certain, now…'

I broke off. You had tired of playing in the tide, and returned to your castle.

'When he was born I was so sure. How could this thing that squealed and wriggled and soiled itself grow into anything as effective at existence as us? Then he grew, and his temper grew with him, and I thought the same as you: his ego will be the be the better of him. He will fail for sure. But now…'

'Now what?'

I turned to her.

'He grows, while we wane.'

She drew back.

'How can you say that when we are making such progress with transcendence?'

'Because I used to be able to hear spiders crawl within the Halls of Reason. Now it is filled with the sound of bickering. My sister—who once prevented species from extinction—speaks as if she has lost her senses. My settlement was once a place of safety, but my fellow villagers, who chased me from my dwelling with flaming torches, squabble like geese. Whatever progress we are making, we are deteriorating just as much.'

She was quiet, lips shut.

'I had heard about your villagers.'

'From Benedikt?'

'Yes.'

'He has no right to spy on us.'

'It is his job to be mindful.'

'I do not trust him. It is obvious that he wants Reed to fail.'

'Then perhaps it is just as obvious that you want him to succeed. I thought I had made it clear, Ima, that the erta should have no agenda in these matters?'

'The erta should have no agenda in any matter, but apparently that is no longer the case.' I scowled and muttered. 'Or perhaps it never was.'

'Whatever do you mean by that?'

I paused, scanning her eyes as they danced between my own, searching for a trace of anything that lurked within. Fear, surprise, disappointment.

Subterfuge.

'Is there anything I do not know, Mother?'

She huffed in amusement.

'There is plenty we do not know. That is partly why we are transcending.'

'I said "I". By which I mean in comparison to you.'

Her expression closed like a tall gate.

'I do not know what you are talking about.'

I turned away.

'Why does Oonagh live in the mountains?'

I counted the seconds of silence—4.832. When she spoke, her voice had shifted into a lower register. Her eyes were stern.

'What a strange thing to say.'

'It is only a question.'

'One with no purpose but curiosity.'

'What is wrong with being curious?'

'Another strange thing to say. Erta are not curious.'

The way she talked was like somebody exerting their will, rather than merely stating facts.

'Is Oonagh male or female?'

'Ima.' I jumped at the snap. 'Such questions are ridiculous. Stop them at once.'

I folded my arms, burying my shaking hands, and looked back at you.

She fell silent again.

'Why do you think we have changed?' she said at last.

'It is obvious,' I replied. 'Before, we were concerned only with what was around us. Now we are concerned only with ourselves. Reed, however, travels the opposite path. Look.'

I pointed at a pool of seawater, in which a crab was trapped. With gentle shoves, you guided it out and bore it to the safety of the shore.

'What is he doing?' said my mother.

'Helping it. You see? He is not only about himself.'

You turned and grinned at us, delighted with the crab's success. I had to bite back my pride.

OF COURSE, IT is not all crabs, smiles and butterflies. You wreak daily chaos upon our dwelling, and I spend hours every day picking up and moving objects in your wake. But any balance I succeed in imposing upon our environment is almost instantly tipped. You do not wish to live in uncluttered space.

And then there is the question of 'why'. Why this. Why that. Why not. Why why why.

'Why do frogs not have four jumping legs instead of just two?' you asked one day in autumn at the riverbank near the top of the hill. It was cold and we had walked far. I wanted to return home.

'Perhaps one day they will.'

'You mean they will grow extra ones?'

'No. It will happen slowly, over time.'

'Why?'

'Because that is how things evolve. Now stand up and let us walk home before it gets dark.'

'Why do things evolve?'

'So that things can get better. Come on.'

'But things are all right as they are. Why do they have to get better?'

'That is just how the forces of nature work.'

'But why? Why don't the forks of nature—'

'Forces.'

'Why don't the forces of nature work by things staying the same? Or things getting bigger instead of better.'

'Sometimes they do.'

'What, get bigger?'

'Yes. Occasionally bigger means better. Other times it means worse. Reed, it is cold, and—'

'Will I get bigger, Ima?'

'Yes.'

'Will I be as big as you?'

'Possibly not.'

'You are very tall.'

'I am. Now please—'

'Why *are* there forces of nature?'

This stopped me. I blinked and knelt down before you, so that our faces were almost touching.

'Because the universe is a vast field of information with one goal and one goal only: to move that information from low potential to high potential. Once it achieves this goal, trillions of centuries in the future, its mysteries will be laid bare and it will have solved its own riddle. The quantum field of consciousness will be reunited, the dimensions will be compressed into a single point, and all will be pure awareness of everything that has ever happened and ever possibly could.'

You looked up at me, quivering, with your mouth agape. A breeze whipped by.

'Why?' you said.

Why is a question without end.

Perhaps *why* is not a question at all, but an extension of your infant cry. Either way, I will never succeed in answering it, and neither will you.

I sighed, lifted you onto my shoulders and walked us home, speaking more about frogs.

As I say, your condition has not worsened. In fact, your episodes have not returned, and every one of Payha's tests reveal you to be an outwardly healthy boy. Sometimes it is easy to convince myself that they ever happened at all.

But the increase in your movement and the ensuing chaos brought its own challenge—injury. You began to fall almost daily, each time incurring a fresh cut or bruise. Sometimes you bled more blood than I knew what to do with, and your pain was difficult for me to bear.

So Payha taught me how to make medicine.

From a precise mixture of tree resins, fish kidneys, lichen and eighty-seven other ingredients gathered from the surrounding woods and waters, we formulated an ointment. Though rough to look at (not to mention smell) it works magnificently, acting as both a pain-reliever and a healing catalyst. Gone were the tears and the blood. Gone was my misery at your pain.

The erta have never required such things, and outside of the Halls of Gestation, there are no laboratories in which to study the onset of death. Our own bodies are laboratories in themselves; deadly fortresses defended by armies of self-replicating nano-mites and constantly evolving immunity engines imbued with a single goal: to kill anything that tries to breach their walls. In my lifetime I have endured seventy-eight serious viral attacks, twelve instances of bowel disease and four bouts of cancer, and never felt a thing. And then there have been the strokes, the heart attacks, the countless broken limbs... if an erta faces one certainty it is that her death will be a violent, catastrophic event.

But I had no idea how soon I would be reminded of this certainty, for the planet, it seemed, was just as hell-bent on chaos as you.

– TWENTY-SEVEN –

THE NIGHT BEFORE it happened I tucked you in and endured the usual volley of bedtime questions. Your brain was rarely willing to relinquish its grip upon the day, and squeezed at it, trying to extract as much information from it as possible before sleep took hold.

'Why do we have two moons?'

'Why does the little one not float away?'

'Why does the river go down our hill and not up it?'

'Where is my wind song?'

You were right to question the absence of your wind song, for even on the calmest nights the eaves made low whistles. But tonight there was silence. It was unusually calm. The sky was clear, the sea lay flat, and the sounds of the forest's various nocturnal animals were either muted or entirely absent. This should have been a warning in itself.

'Sometimes the weather is elsewhere,' I said.

Having settled you, I went to sleep in the warm peace. When I awoke, the Earth was screaming.

'Reed,' I said, sitting bolt upright in bed. The wind was howling through the eaves, and your song now screeched in unison as the shutters rattled and rain lashed the windows.

You were already sitting up, rubbing your eyes in the light of the candle I had left burning.

'What's happening?' you mumbled.

Someone was hammering on the door.

'Ima!'

Jorne.

I jumped out of bed and pulled on my boots and rain cloak, then opened the door. It was still dark, and Jorne stood there wide-eyed, rain streaming from his hood.

'Get Reed, we must go,' he said. 'It's a hurricane.'

There is no earthly way, I thought. The coastline upon which we lived had become one of the most peaceful and predictable areas on the planet. That is why we had chosen it. The temperature of the ocean and the protection of the mountains prohibited anything stronger than a weak gale from blowing through our settlements once every seven to ten years, and the kind of intense compression of energy required for something like a hurricane was inconceivable.

Beyond our porch the tree canopies whipped violently in the wind, and the river had become an engorged torrent thundering at its banks. Eastward, a rim of light strained upon the horizon— the dawn squashed beneath a gigantic black spiral—and huge waves heaved upon the beach, clawing at the shifting sand.

A violent gust sent the trees across the river into a sudden backward arch. Ripped clean from its trunk, a particularly large branch flew towards us. Jorne and I ducked as it hit the roof, breaking through the planks and sending splinters flying in all directions. You howled from inside, but before I could run to help, the tree to which the branch had once belonged gave a terrible creak.

'Get down,' yelled Jorne, covering my head. With a hideous groan the tree was wrenched from its roots and fell across the river, its canopy crashing upon us.

I scrambled from Jorne's arms and ran to your bed. You were fully awake, mouth agape and staring up at the gnarled finger of wood that now hovered above you. I gathered you up, wrapped you in your cloak and led you outside.

'We need to find somewhere less exposed,' I said.

Jorne nodded. 'Follow me.'

We clambered over the fallen tree and made our way up the track, now slippery with mud. But as we climbed I heard voices below. Shadows ran to and fro across Fane's circle, and voices called out in alarm. The storm-charged waves had breached the tree line and now hammered upon the dwellings nearest the shore. The lagoon was already flooded, and I watched as my own old dwelling lost its roof, and another beside it. The wave that had wrought the damage retreated, and I saw two figures dragged out in its foam. Then, two shapes darted from a dwelling on the opposite side of the square, one of which I knew very well. Haralia and Jakob stopped at the devastation before them. Holding one other, they turned and ran from the shoreline. But another wave was already in flight, towering above the settlement like a cliff-face ready to crumble.

'Haralia!'

The water fell and for a moment I lost sight of them. I left you with Jorne and staggered down the path, straining to see.

'Ima, come back.'

'We have to help them,' I said.

'There's no time.'

'We must. Haralia!' I called again, but all was foam and mud and chaos. I had reached the fallen tree, which was now being slowly claimed by the rising river, and broke through its branches, ignoring Jorne's cries and the cuts in my hands and face. There was a distant whinny, and silhouettes of horses reared in the paddock below. One had jumped the fence and bolted. Another followed, but caught its hooves and landed with a sickening crunch upon the ground, where it struggled for a moment and lay still.

The water retreated and I scanned Fane's circle. Jakob was lying face down, clinging to a post, with Haralia holding onto his leg. They did not move. Eventually my sister's hand relinquished its grip upon her lover, and her prone and lifeless body swayed left and right in the retreating tide.

'No.' The word departed in a weak breath. My heart seemed to stop. I felt myself collapsing, folding up inside like a dying insect.

I had not known death before, nor had I worried about it, for the simple reason that to worry about anything beyond one's control is an exercise in madness. But I knew it now. It was here, rising like one of those terrible waves, ready to fall and crush me.

Jorne arrived at my side with you in tow.

'Ima, we cannot stay here.'

'My sister.'

He followed my eyes to the devastation below.

'I am sorry.'

But as he spoke I saw movement, and my heart renewed its pace. Haralia's leg was curling up, and—look—slowly she got to her knees, coughing saltwater from her lungs. Staggering to where Jakob lay, she hauled him over her shoulder and limped from the circle.

'She lives,' said Jorne. 'Now let us go.'

Another fierce wave was looming out at sea.

'No, I must go down.'

But before I could, the ground had slipped beneath us and we found ourselves falling with it. The tree, the river, our house—

everything began to slide away from the hill.

'Ima!' cried Jorne as he accelerated past me. He held you out and I grasped your hand, pulling you safely to me. We were moving, but Jorne was moving faster, tumbling with the tree. I spotted a root and grabbed it to stop our fall. Mud and water streamed around us, threatening to suck us clean from the mountain if I let go.

Jorne cried out in pain. He had become wedged between the tree trunk and a boulder, and his head barely cleared the thundering surface of the rapids. His arms were stuck; he could not move.

'Reed,' I said, 'hold onto this root.'

'No, Ima, don't leave me.'

'Do not let go. Do you hear me? Do not let go.'

'Ima.'

I placed your arms around the root, tying your cloak in a tight knot around it so that now you were lashed to the ground.

I held your face.

'I will be back soon.'

With that I left you crying, and surrendered myself to gravity. In seconds I was down at the boulder, against which I slammed my boots to stop. The broken trunk was lodged against Jorne's chest, but he was not impaled; the splintered base had skewered the bank side, and the other end of the tree was firmly wedged into the rocks beside what was left of our dwelling. Jorne's eyes were rolling, and the river slithered in dangerous ribbons over his neck and chin. He would soon be beneath it. The tree would have to be moved.

I eased myself down beside him so that my back and hands were against the boulder and my boots were on the tree. As I braced to push, something made me pause, and I looked up at you. You were still safely tied to the root, but watching me with a look of horrified expectation. *I should have faced you the other way*, I thought. But there was no time to remedy this, for the sliding ground would not wait. So, with our eyes locked, I pushed with all my strength—which is a great deal—and the tree trunk sprang away, crashing harmlessly into the water.

I grabbed Jorne before he went with it, and heaved his barely conscious body up onto the bank as the water continued upon its relentless path.

My eyes were on you as I prepared to leave the water, and your astonished expression at what you had just witnessed.

My mind was on what I would tell you when you asked me to explain.

So I did not see the shadow from the right, and I was too late to stop the stray mound of earth from slamming into me, dragging me down in a spiral of foam and dirt, deeper beneath the water and further away from you, until all was black and gone.

− TWENTY-EIGHT −

CURTAIN.

The word billowed through my mind like the object it named. Curtain. The same shape too. Two thin consonants forming the hem, the rolling 'r' its breeze-swollen fabric, and its tail trailing in a lingering 'n'.

Curtain. Un-curtain. Uncertain. All white. Warm sun. A clear word. An empty word. A first word.

I looked around, eyes wide now after their slow blink into consciousness. I was in a bed. The walls were stone. My mother's place.

'Hello, Ima.'

She smiled from her seat beside the bed. She was wearing one of her Spring dresses and her hair was braided. I pulled my hand from where it lay beneath hers.

I remembered the hurricane, the tree, the impact, the submersion.

I sat up.

'What happened?'

Pain shot through my head. I gripped it in both hands, unable to speak.

My mother gave a frown of concern, shushing me.

'Calm down, child, you have had an accident.'

'Where is Reed?' I managed to say through gritted teeth.

'He is perfectly intact. Caige's scouts found him wandering down through the forest towards Fane.'

'And Haralia?'

My mother smiled with love.

'She and Jakob also escaped unharmed.'

I thought of Jorne, unconscious on the riverbank.

'Take me to Reed.'

I tried to leave the bed, but was instantly flattened by another wave of pain.

'What is this?'

My mother's face hovered above mine, haloed in sunlight.

'Please, Ima, you are not well. You have been concussed.'

'How long have I been unconscious?'

She hesitated. The corners of her mouth flickered.

'A little over two days.'

I blinked up at her, resisting the urge to jump from the bed though every fibre of my being was telling me to do so.

Two days? This was impossible.

I spoke as slowly and as clearly as I could, though my mind was reeling.

'Why... *how* have I been unconscious for two days.'

'You nearly drowned, Ima, and you took a huge impact. Your head was very badly damaged.'

'It would have healed. Why did it not heal?'

'It did, but brain injury takes time.' She laughed, as breezy as the curtain. 'It is not just any old muscle you know.'

'But I am still in pain. Why?'

A look of trouble crossed her face.

'A side-effect of the medication.'

'What medication?'

'We had to sedate you.'

'When?'

'A number of times. The last time was two hours ago.'

'Why?'

'You were awake and babbling, making no sense, trying to get up when you shouldn't.'

'I don't remember.'

'That is perfectly understandable. Now be at peace, all is well.'

She stroked my brow, and I was suddenly overwhelmed by a ripple of fatigue. Her touch was full of bliss, like the warm sunlight on my face, the cool soft pillow behind my head, and the slow blink of my eyelids...

No. Something was wrong.

'Where is he?' I said, forcing myself to sit up and bite back the ensuing pain. 'Where is Reed?'

My mother pulled her hand from my brow and closed it slowly into a fist.

'I told you,' she replied. 'Reed is fine.'

'You have been looking after him?'

'No. Benedikt has.'

I froze.

'Why?'

She cocked her head and frowned.

'Why not?'

'Take me to him.'

She watched me for a second. Then she stood, flattened her dress, and went to the door. It creaked as she opened it, fresh light flooding in from the hallway outside and throwing her long shadow upon the oak floor.

'You can come in now. She is awake.'

Two sets of footsteps, one short, one long. You entered the

room, followed by Benedikt, dressed in deep red. He laid a hand upon your shoulder.

My heart surged.

'Hello, Ima,' you said.

I wanted to spring across the room, knock that hand away and gather you up.

But I calmed myself.

'Hello, Reed,' I said, with as untroubled a smile as I could muster. 'Are you all right?'

You rubbed your left wrist.

'My arm got bashed, and it was sore, but it's better now. See?'

You held it out for me to see. I reached out my own.

'Come here.'

You hesitated, looked up at Benedikt, who nodded. Only then did you cross the room to my bed. My belly trembled at this, but you embraced me and all was well.

'Is your head better?' you said, placing a hand on the area of my skull which I assumed had taken the blow.

'Yes,' I replied. 'Yes, I think so. Reed, do you know what happened to Jorne?'

You shook your head.

'I don't remember much until they found me.'

My heart gave a skip of hope. Had you blacked out the incident altogether?

His eyes flashed.

'But you saved him, Ima. I saw it. Do you remember?'

'Yes, I remember. Reed, I want to explain.'

'It's OK, Ima. I know.'

My blood ran cold.

'What is it that you know?'

'I know how you were able to save him. I know how you were strong enough to push that whole tree from the river.'

My heart thumped. 'Who told you?'

You looked over your shoulder.

'Benedikt did.'

I glared at Benedikt's shadowed face, the long nose and hoods under his eyes, skin I would have gladly torn from his skull right there and then.

'Is that so?' I said. 'And what exactly did Benedikt tell you?'

You turned back with an excited look.

'It's really interesting. People can do things, amazing things, when they're in danger. If they need to save somebody, or if something is running after them like a wolf or a bear or something, then they get super strong, stronger than they could ever imagine themselves being. Did you know there was once a woman who lifted a boulder twice her size just to free her daughter?'

I listened to you, watching your eyes dance about as you spoke, and feeling relief flood through me. The lie remained intact.

'Boulders are much heavier than trees, aren't they?' you said. There was an eagerness in your face; you wanted the lie as much as anyone.

'Yes. Boulders are much heavier than trees. And what else has Benedikt been teaching you?'

'Oh, lots. About things that happened in the past, like wars and machines and missiles and big buildings falling down.'

'I see.' I stroked the hair from your eyes. 'Perhaps you can tell me about them once I'm out of bed. Would that be OK?'

You nodded.

'Can I go and play now?'

'Yes, you can go and play.'

You kissed my forehead and left, glancing at Benedikt, who smiled as you passed. Once the door had closed behind you, I turned to Benedikt.

'What have you been teaching him?'

'Nothing you would not teach him yourself, I am sure. History, mostly. Empires, civilisations, that kind of thing. The child deserves to know the truth about his species, wouldn't you say?'

'And who can give anyone that?'

There was a silence, during which Benedikt and my mother exchanged a nervous look. I felt suddenly foolish.

'I should go,' said Benedikt. 'Good bye, Ima. Kai.'

He nodded at my mother and left. I looked back at the billowing curtain, trying not to think about Jorne, and all the time feeling my mother's eyes upon me. Finally I turned.

'What is it?'

Her legs were crossed, her hands folded neatly upon her knees, the picture of control.

'If you are finding this too difficult then perhaps you should give up.'

Her words were like frost.

'What do you mean?'

'This project. Reed. It is clearly affecting your behaviour. You should not talk to Benedikt like that. Or anyone, in fact.'

'I was afraid. I thought Reed had found out.'

'Yes, well, that is part of the problem, is it not? It is not in an erta's nature to be afraid. You seem... distracted.'

'It is the hurricane. My head.' This was a lie. 'I have not been feeling myself.' This was not a lie.

'I had thought that your superior clarity made you the perfect fit for this project. But perhaps I was wrong.' My mother's posture softened. 'There would be no shame in it, Ima. Someone else could raise Reed and you could return to the skies, and your balloon—'

'No.' The word leaped from my mouth. 'No, that will not be necessary.'

She blinked.

'Are you sure?'

'Absolutely. You must allow me to continue.'

'Must I, indeed?' she said, with a thin smile.

'Please.'

I would have snatched that word back if I could, but it snuck in like a stowaway.

'Very well,' she said, standing. 'Then get some rest. There is a meeting in the Halls this evening.'

'Who will be there?'

'Everyone. We need to understand how this hurricane was allowed to happen.'

'Of course.'

She stopped at the door.

'Oh, and Ima?'

'Yes?'

'I am afraid some were not so lucky as Haralia and Jakob. Greye is dead.'

– TWENTY-NINE –

AFTER I HAD dressed, I collected you from Benedikt's chambers—I did not meet his eye—and took you to the halls. Outside of the walled-in peace of my mother's dwelling, Ertanea was in disarray. Lines of hunched figures streamed down from the forest, and the square, which had always been such a cool and spacious place, was now hot and claustrophobic, full of clamour. Greye's body had been laid out in the centre, and there, wailing over it, was my sister.

'Haralia,' I called, pushing through the crowd. She pulled back her hood and turned her tear-stained face up to mine.

'Greye is dead,' she said, with a ferocious tremble.

'Are you all right? I saw you at the beach. I ran to you, but...' Her face contorted as if I had said something out of turn.

'Greye is dead, Ima. Don't you understand? *Dead*.'

'Yes,' I said, taking a step back and finding your hand. I felt suddenly hunted. 'Of course I understand.'

She spoke to the sombre crowd encircling Greye.

'This is what happens here. This is what awaits us all—death. Death and tears!'

At this, her cheeks streamed with a fresh flood of her own tears. She turned back to me.

'And where are yours, sister? Don't you care?'

'Of course I care. Haralia, please...' I kept my voice low, for the crowd were watching, but Haralia had no intention of muting her performance.

'Then show it.'

'I don't know what you want me to do.'

'Show something. Anything.'

I stared back at her, nonplussed. She scowled.

'You're like a stone,' she said, and stormed away.

I am not, I thought, as the crowd dispersed. I felt the warmth of your hand. *I am not like a stone.*

We followed the bewildered line inside.

I was shaken by my encounter with Haralia, but something else was troubling me, and it grew worse with face I passed. Stunned expressions, caged whispers: *How had this happened?*

I knew the answer.

A hurricane landing upon our shoreline was improbable, but more so was the fact that we had not expected it. Our weather beacons should have picked up the pressure changes weeks before and alerted the Halls of Necessity, giving us plenty of time to dissuade the storm from gathering further. But they had not, and they were my responsibility. I had not checked them for five years.

So this was my fault.

'Ima?'

My mother was right: I had been distracted, and now this distraction had led to Greye's death, and doubtless the deaths of many others.

'Ima?'

And if this was true, then what else had I allowed to go awry? We had succeeded in balancing the planet, but had I been too quick to abandon my post? Was the rebalance tight enough, or was it merely a precarious patch-up, ready to slip back into kind of chaotic system in which hurricanes spring from nothing?

How much supervision did this infernal planet need to restrain itself from oblivion?

'Ima?'

We were in the halls now. The sudden density of the walls, the tepid, humid air, the hushed, urgent chatter—it all pressed down upon me. I pushed through the crowd, drawing disgruntled looks. They knew, surely they must; I felt the sting of blame whenever I caught an eye. I released your hand.

'Ima!'

My blood surged as I blundered on, furious. Furious at myself for my idiocy. Furious at the planet for needing such coddling. And now furious for you at requiring the same, and for taking me from my purpose with such treacherous distraction.

'Ima?'

I spun around.

'What?'

Voices fell silent. I allowed the full weight of my glare to bear down upon you.

'Well? What is it?'

'I... I...'

'Speak up!'

'I am sorry, Ima.'

My glare shed a little mass.

'Why do you say sorry?'

'It's my fault. The bad wind. I didn't tidy my blocks that night.'

My rage fell into shame. I pulled you close.

'You have nothing to be sorry for,' I said. 'This is not the fault of your blocks.'

You looked up.

'Then whose fault is it?'

I turned to face the council. Caige had stepped forward.

'It would appear that we have been distracted.'

The room fell silent, and I opened my mouth to confess.

'Termites...' he went on.

Closed it again.

'...have accumulated in large numbers beneath one of the communication towers west of Ertanea. The pressure of the nest created a crack within a wall, which let in water, which compromised a connection with the beacons. That is why we could not see this coming.'

As the room resumed its murmurs, I took a low breath of relief. My beacons were not to blame after all, and the communication towers had never been my responsibility.

'Our entire coast was ravaged,' Caige continued. 'Sixteen settlements at the mercy of the wind, broth lagoons flooded, dwellings swept away in the wind. Lives lost too, 238 in total, including council member Greye. We have become too complacent.'

His eyes roamed the room, landing upon a female near the front—a communications engineer named Ronja with cropped, auburn hair and a prominent nose—to whom he slowly walked. She bowed her head at his approach.

'Neglectful,' he said, stretching out the seconds of the girl's torture until, finally, my mother broke it.

'This is not the fault of an individual,' she said. 'The blame lies with us all. Any one of our systems could have failed and we would not have known. It is our distraction with our own affairs which has led to this. So focussed have we become on transcendence, and other projects—' she shot me a piercing glance '—that we have forgotten the reason we were brought into existence in the first place: the fragility of the planet upon which we walk.'

She turned to me now, fully looking, no glance.

'We have become concerned only with ourselves, whereas before we were concerned with what was around us. This must change.'

There was an outbreak of discussion as Caige returned to the line.

'This terrible day has taught us that we erta are vulnerable too,' he said. 'It reminds us that this unstable rock is no home for us, and that transcendence is the only way we can achieve a safe and meaningful existence. However, as we strive to achieve this goal we must be mindful of our safety, so, from this day forward we shall divide our efforts. Firstly, we must rebuild those settlements which were destroyed by the storm. Secondly, all those erta with expertise in meteorological, geological and oceanographical monitoring will return to their posts immediately. The rest will increase their efforts on transcendence to ensure that we leave the planet as swiftly and as safely as possible. Every project that does not contribute to this aim will be either reprioritised or terminated immediately.'

Terminated. The word cut me like a blade.

'Now, go forth and be industrious.'

The crowd dispersed, and through the flow of moving bodies I saw that Caige had taken Benedikt to one side. They were deep in conversation, but when Caige saw me he nodded in my direction.

His eyes were those of a hunter, and you were the prey.

'What does it mean?' you said.

I looked down at you, fighting to control my tremble. I had to get you out of there.

'What?'

'What the man was saying?'

'Oh.' I searched for an escape route through the crowd. 'It means I must return to work. Come on, we have to go.'

'In your balloon?' you said, hurrying behind. 'Can I come too?'

The hope in your voice appalled me, but this was no time to for wringing hands. I had to get you out.

I allowed the crowd to absorb us, my senses prickling at the sound of every breath and new pattern of steps. If I could just make it into the forest then I could make it to Fane, and... I dared not dwell on what might have to happen then.

Suddenly we were out in the square, where the crowd quickly lost its density. I stumbled on, trying to latch onto a group in which to lose ourselves, but each one seemed determined to dissipate too. Our safety was vanishing like smoke in a breeze.

Before I knew it we were alone and exposed, next to Greye's body once again. I circled, backing away from an unseen threat, keeping you behind me.

'Ima.'

I spun around. There was Benedikt with his hands folded before him.

I steadied myself, renewing my protective stance, and lunged my face towards him as he approached.

'I won't let you,' I hissed.

He stopped before me.

'Won't let me what?'

'Take him.'

He frowned. Our faces were close now, and our voices low so you would not hear.

'Why would I want to do that?'

I blinked.

'Your father said that projects not contributing to the well-being of the planet would be abandoned. I thought...'

'You thought that meant him. Well, I can assure you that is not that case.'

My grip on you weakened, and you stepped out from behind me. You were clearly a little unsettled by my behaviour, but this faded with the delight of seeing your recent babysitter.

'Ben!'

Ben?

Benedikt smiled at you, which looked painful.

'Hello, Reed.'

'Then what do you want?' I said.

'My father sent me.'

He turned his gaze to Greye's body and ground his jaw.

'Something bothers you,' I said.

'Hm?' he said, looking up.

'You seem troubled.'

'It is nothing. Just... I have been asked to do something I was not expecting to have to do.'

I pushed you behind me again, ready for whatever had to happen next; run or pounce.

'Why are you so suspicious?' he said, watching me with a scornful amusement.

'You have always wanted the project to fail,' I said.

He inspected his long thumbnail.

'With respect, you have no idea what I want. Oh, believe me, if it was up to my father then there would be no question of your project's termination, but it seems that the council have been convinced of its merits in sufficient numbers to warrant its continuation. Besides, what would the opinion of an individual be worth anyway?' He nodded at the body beside us. 'Of course, he has lost a great ally in Greye.'

The sight of his colourless face froze me.

'He told me something once.'

Benedikt's eyes flicked up.

'Really? What?'

'He told me that something had happened to you. Something that had skewed your perspective. Those were his words.'

He tightened.

'Did he elaborate?'

'No.'

I noticed his shoulders slacken somewhat. 'Good, he was quite right not to. And if I were you I would not concern yourself with the affairs of others. Your own are quite complex enough, and your project is about to enter a new phase.'

'Then I am not to go back to work?'

'On the contrary. You must.'

'But he will need care when I am not there.'

'And he will get it.'

A chill crept through me. My eyes narrowed.

'And I suppose you think you are the one to give it to him.'

'No, actually. I will be... otherwise engaged.'

I studied him, trying to decipher his discomfort.

'What exactly have you been asked to do, Benedikt?'

His mouth twitched, words skirmishing on his lips.

'It appears I must care for an ertling.'

What I did next was regrettable and, given the circumstances, utterly out of place. But I was so flushed with relief that I honestly could not help myself.

'Stop laughing,' he said, outraged. 'It is not amusing.'

'I apologise,' I said, once I had managed to control myself. 'It is just that the thought of you caring for anything, Benedikt, is, well...' I trailed off, noticing a glimmer of hurt in his expression. 'But I am sure it will be good for you.'

'That is what my father says.'

I stifled more laughter.

'Ima?' you said from behind. 'What are you and Ben talking about?'

I kept my eyes on Benedikt.

'I believe we are talking about your education,' I said. 'You will be going to school soon, Reed. Isn't that right, Benedikt?'

'That is correct,' he said. 'It will start in six months, once we have rebuilt the settlements.'

'He will still be with me?' I said, keeping my voice low as you absorbed this information.

'Of course. We could not tear him from his *mother*, could we? You will still care for him when he is not at school, and when he is, you will be at work.'

'Thank you. *Ben*.'

'Don't.'

With that, he whirled away back to the halls and slammed the door shut, leaving us alone in the square.

I became aware of you watching me, and turned. Your brow rippled with concern.

'Do not fret. All is well.'

I was speaking to myself as much as to you.

'What is school?'

'A place where you will go when I am at work. There will be other children there to play with.' This seemed to lighten your mood. 'Now go and run in the gardens.'

You hesitated, then did as I suggested, leaving me in the empty square beside Greye's body. I sat down beside him and took his cold hand in mine.

It was new to me, this grief, but while I may not have had Haralia's tears, I was no stone; I knew how much I would miss him. All he had left me with were fond memories of tea, books, and a ready smile.

Memories, and questions unanswered.

There are things you need to know.
How would I know them now?
It was some time before I left.

SEVEN YEARS

– THIRTY –

WHEN THE SETTLEMENTS had been rebuilt, we returned to Fane and found it exactly as it had been before. Everything was identical—even our first dwelling, right down to the table, bed, sink, bath. You were delighted, though there was no possible way you could remember it. For me, the place brought strange feelings of anxiety, the opposite of nostalgia.

The only thing different about Fane was a new building beside the paddock. It was single-storey, two-roomed and had a flat, stone yard, fenced and with a single gate. This was your school, and one bright Monday morning I found myself standing outside of it, gripping your hand.

In the playground were twenty ertlings, talking, running, chasing each other, some still holding the hands of those who had volunteered to parent them.

You watched them with me, a bundle of nerves and excitement.

'I did not know there were so many children in Fane, Ima,' you said. 'Do you think they will be my friends?'

I felt a desperate urge to scoop you up and run. Until now it had been easy to maintain the illusion of your existence—it had always just been you and me, barely a lie at all. But now you would be with others, and suddenly the lie was real. I dropped to one knee.

'Listen to me, Reed,' I said, 'this is important. When I leave you at this gate, you will be on your own in there. You will not have me by your side to tell you what is right or wrong, so you will have to make your own decisions, and I need you to promise me something.'

'What, Ima?'

'Every decision you make, try to make it with peace in your heart. Everything you do, everything you say, everything you learn—' I placed a palm on your tiny chest '—peace in your heart, Reed. Do not get angry, do not get upset, do not fight, do not shout. Do you understand me?'

'I think so.'

'Good. Come here.'

I held you far longer than you were comfortable with, then stood and ushered you through the gate.

The teacher—who was, for an erta, small and kind of face— welcomed you in. She held a bell in her hand, which she rang three times, and the ertlings followed her to the classroom.

'Ima.'

I turned to the tall, dark presence who had suddenly appeared beside me.

'Benedikt. Your—' I hesitated '—child is here?'

'Yes. Lukas is his name.'

He smiled and waved at a tall, blonde-haired ertling near the back of the line heading into the building.

'And how is fatherhood treating you?'

He turned, with a strange venom in his eyes.

'He looks after himself, mostly. Different for you, of course. How is he getting on?'

'Fine,' I said. 'Absolutely fine.'

Benedikt's smile returned.

'Good. Well then. We must get to work, must we not? Goodbye, Ima.' And with that he swept away.

The teacher ushered you inside and, with one last wave, you disappeared into the building. The door shut behind you and all was quiet. I stood at the gate, feeling as if I was falling from a great height.

SYSTEMS HAVE A tendency to become accustomed to other systems. Oceans to shorelines, hillsides to encroaching forests, ecosystems to the introduction of an outside species, planets to the gravitational pull of a star.

In other words, you grow used to things, and I had grown used to you.

The first weeks and months of your schooling were nothing short of torture. I spent the first day in a horrified daze, wandering around our dwelling, clearing away your things though they had already been cleared before. Then I ate some herring and drifted to my balloon shed. This journey took me past the school, where I hoped to catch sight of you. But the door was still shut and the windows were high, showing only the flickering light of the candles within.

My balloon had avoided anything other than superficial damage in the hurricane and, after an hour's work, was fit for flight. I sat in the bubble, still on the ground, thinking of it—the weightlessness, the distance from the ground, the distance from you. In the end I got out. I would go the next day.

This went on for two weeks. Each day I dropped you at school and waited at the gate until you had disappeared inside and there was nothing left, no sight of you through the window, no lingering sound of your goodbyes or slam of the door, just me, and the leaves scraping against the stone. Then I would go and sit in my balloon and think about flying. Then I would go home and wait until it was time to pick you up.

One day I bumped into Benedikt again at the school gate. I had learned to avoid him by arriving as late as possible, but for some unknown reason he himself was late that morning, so our meeting caused me to flinch.

'Ima,' he said when he spotted me. 'I see your balloon is yet to fly.'

'What of it?'

He shrugged.

'Understandable, I suppose. It has been out of action for some time. Enjoy your day.'

And with that he walked away, smiling the same way you had smiled as an infant when passing a particularly troublesome stool.

Out of action. Those were the words he had intended me to hear.

I started my balloon that morning and flew all day. That is when things became easier.

I THOUGHT OFTEN of Jorne. I had not seen him since the hurricane, and with my return to work I had no time to visit Payha in the Sundran village to ask of his whereabouts. It was weeks later, when I was finally giving into my fears that he had perished, that I spotted him from my balloon. I had just taken off and I saw him sitting by the rocks, so I landed nearby and joined him.

He smiled, but said nothing, and I said nothing back. We sat for a while, looking out at the sea, and I took a strange pleasure in knowing that there were a hundred things I could say to him in that moment, and that I was choosing to say none of them. Sharing the pleasure of an ocean view is sometimes just as useful as a bundle of words.

'Thank you,' he said at last. 'For saving my life.'

'Don't mention it.'

'I'm sorry I have not visited. What with you moving back into your old dwelling, and the renewed activity, and your balloon—'

'You have been watching me?'

He paused. 'Of course. Always. And Reed. I see him every day. Is he all right?'

'He is fine, though he misses you.' I took a breath, and allowed myself just one of those hundred things. 'As do I.'

I sensed him smile, though my eyes were still trained upon the water.

'You'll have seen he is at a school, now.'

He nodded, a ripple of concern passing his face. 'And is he doing well? Happy?'

I smiled. 'He is more than happy.'

IT WAS TRUE. This was in fact your happiest time. You loved school. You loved arriving, you loved learning, you loved playing, you loved talking, you loved being collected.

The methods with which you were educated were simple enough. You and your ertling classmates were each issued with a tablet of slate and a chalk. Upon this, the teacher made you copy out the alphabet until you could do so unbidden. Then she taught you the sound each letter made, followed by the phonemes they made when connected to each other, followed by words and, finally sentences. All of this I gleaned from our evening conversations, when, unprompted, you would recount your day. These sickened me at first, for they reminded me of the lie you were living, and in which I was complicit. I would sit in silence as you regaled me with the wonders you had learned, nodding at this, raising my eyebrows at that, but keeping quiet—for words would only add weight to my collusion.

The lie. You so loved the lie.

This was how you learned to read and write.

As your literary prowess grew, you were allowed to progress to pencil and paper, which the Halls of Necessity produced especially for the occasion. You liked paper. You liked the way it felt and sounded when you rubbed it, or ran your pencil across its surface. Your pencil itself—though it was not one thing but a chain of many, each replaced when its stub could not be held—became your most prized possession, bettering even your blocks. You took it with you everywhere and would not be parted from it. You sensed magic within.

How could you know how dangerous that magic would be?

– THIRTY-ONE –

ONE MORNING WE were late. I had a longer flight than usual ahead, since I had been tasked by the transcendence team with assessing the exact density of the atmospheric layers above the northern shores of the continent. This was to be the exit point, and the interface itself between our initial stages of materialism and the states that lay beyond.

You were dawdling.

'Come on, we'll be late,' I said, grabbing your canvas satchel and my own supplies and pushing through the door. It was winter and a dusting of snow lay upon Fane's circle. 'Reed, please.'

You looked up from the table, where you had been sitting, practising your letters since breakfast, then sighed and gathered your things. At the door, I put on your coat and you handed me the paper upon which you had been scribbling.

'This is for you.'

I looked down at it, frozen in horror. You had not been writing at all.

'What is this?'

You beamed up at me.

'You, of course.'

I had only ever seen one drawing before in my entire life. It was in one of the books my brother Greye had given me in India, *The Once and Future King*, depicting the young boy, Wart, with both hands gripping the handle of the great sword, Excalibur, still lodged deep in the rock. I flinched from it then, as I did to yours now.

This may seem strange to you, natural as I now know this compulsion to render flattened versions of objects upon surfaces is to you. But you must remember: by the time I came into existence, almost everything which humans had created had been destroyed, or, if it was made of polymers, compressed into the little moon. This included art of all forms.

Those books Greye had given me, and that story of the unlikely king with its rough sketch of the pivotal scene, were some of the only remaining artefacts, and I felt no urge to look for more examples. Why would I? The human trait of curiosity was as useless as its impulse to write, sing and draw, and every bit as dangerous.

This is how drawing was viewed: dangerous. There existed no better evidence of why human beings had failed than the mountains of art they had created in an attempt to decipher their existence. A trillion trillion marks etched in clay, canvas and memory chips time and time again over fifty millennia, everything from the fearful smudges made in dark caves to the lavish oil renderings of battles I had been told once hung in great halls, to the sketches of sweethearts and the ink needled into the skin of a loin-clothed hunter. Every human hand that had ever lived past infancy had drawn something. Each one was imperfect, each one a twisted reflection, each one proof that, no matter how hard humans tried, they could never understand reality enough to master it. And more than mere clumsiness, this misunderstanding had led to frustration, distraction, anger, blame, greed—everything that had led to their downfall.

That is why it was dangerous.

Homo sapiens' one success was the erta, and the erta did not draw.

I looked down at the mess of lines and shapes flung together on the paper. A tall figure looked back at me, unsmiling, with long hair sweeping out to one side. Its eyes were too big, but accurately proportioned, and one long-fingered hand held another smaller one, attached to a scruffy figure beneath. Both stood at sharp, odd angles to the ground, upon which there were jagged outlines of leaves surrounded by the occasional spiral—the wind made visible. Behind them were the rough shapes of clouds and mountains, and what I thought might be the sea.

I loved it immediately.

'And me,' said Reed, pointing to it. 'See?'

My heart gave a tremor. Horror—not just because I knew what would happen if he presented such a thing at school, but because, within those hasty scrawls and careless marks, within the confines of the larger figure's broken oval head and somewhere between the hooded eyes, crooked nose and smile less mouth, I swear I saw myself.

I screwed the paper into a ball, eliciting from you a gasp of dismay.

'Reed, never do this again, do you hear me? Never.'

'But,' you stammered, staring at my shaking fist in which your drawing was now squashed. 'But why?'

'It is wrong. It is not allowed, do you understand? Never do it again or you will be in extremely bad trouble.'

You stared back at me, mouth quivering.

'Do you understand, Reed? *Never*.'

You nodded your head and we left for school, hurrying across the circle in stunned silence. You ran in without looking back and, when the classroom door had shut and I was sure there was nobody around, I unfurled my fist and flattened the paper. There we were: me and you, crude and perfect in the winter sun. I kept it in my balloon, and told no one.

SCHOOLING OPENED UP your mind to the universe and all its fascinating riddles. Once, when we were walking in the forest, I believe I was witness to a revelation of sorts. It was late morning and the sun was reaching its zenith. We stepped into a clearing cut with a great shaft of orange light filled with dust and butterflies, their shadows flitting across the bracken beneath. You stopped and wondered at the scene, as did I, but then your mouth twitched with amusement, and you gave a frown. You swung to where I stood, raising your hands.

'What is this?' you said with a baffled grin. 'How am I here? What am I?'

I considered the truth; quantum vibrations in a fifty-seven-dimensional array of fields, but it was not what you wanted to hear. In any case, you were not waiting for a response. Instead you shook your head and laughed, and I laughed with you.

What is this? What am I?

I call these your Great Questions. And I am afraid they have no answers.

YOU LEARNED NUMBERS too, and told me all about them. These conversations I found much easier to endure. It was through numbers, in fact, that I learned how to live with the lie, if not to love it. When you talked about letters and words, your eyes travelled from side to side along the table before you, tracking them as you would along a page and smiling as if you were watching a rodent scurry about its business. But as soon as you began speaking of numbers, your chin would lift and your gaze would rise to the ceiling where it danced about in wonder. The numbers were up there somewhere, glittering like stars, and you described them to me in endless detail.

Sevens were yellow, threes were green. Eights and fours belonged in the mountains, fives, ones and nines beneath the water. One and two did not get on, because one did not want company and two yearned to be with five. Zero made you laugh. It was forgetful, and had no idea where it had come from or what it was doing there. Ten was special, a bright, benevolent overlord who looked after its realm of single digits beneath. All the numbers beyond it lived in wide, sunlit hills and tall mountains with snow upon their peaks.

I listened, rapt, hands on my knees.

You told me how you added numbers together. They fitted together like wooden joints, three and seven—already familiar by virtue of their similar colours—interlocking perfectly to make ten, one clicking onto nine like the last brick in a puzzle. Numbers, you explained, tessellated. This is perfectly true.

Numbers are everything. It may feel as if they are an invention, some made-up grammar used to account for reality, but they are not. They were around long before erta, long before humans and long before the world. They exist beyond matter, beyond space, beyond time. All things—stars, mountains, atoms, words, letters, lies—break apart into numbers, and the universe itself is merely an array of quantum events, each one tessellating with its neighbour like a cloud of dust motes holding hands. So you were right to watch them dance with such wonder in your eyes.

I sometimes forgot the lie when you talked in this way. Instead of sitting tight-lipped and nodding, waiting for you to finish, I allowed myself to talk back, agreeing with or correcting you.

I longed to push you on, and often found myself babbling about quadratics, dimensional probability vectors, paradoxical calculus and the far realms of mathematics for which there were no words because they had not been discovered by humans before they died.

One evening, in the middle of one such diatribe, I stopped to see you staring up at me, terrified.

'What is wrong?' I said, my hands still perched in the position I had adopted to illustrate my current point. 'Why are you looking at me like that?'

'You... you were screaming. It sounded like a bird.'

I tried to restrain myself from then on.

– THIRTY-TWO –

You TALKED OF people too, the Ertlings to whose true natures you were oblivious and yet with whom you were forming stronger alliances by the day. 'Lukas said something silly today…' and 'Zadie played catch with me…' and 'Rupert threw a ball so hard today that he broke a fence post.'

I winced when you told me that Rupert threw a ball so hard he broke a fence post. These moments stayed with you, I was sure of it, and how many of them would it take to shatter the lie?

Your talk was not always favourable. You spoke as much of misgivings and misdoings amongst your classmates as you did about play and silliness.

'Sara does not like Zadie talking to her when she is with her other friends.'

'Rupert told me today that I could only play ball with him if I could throw it the length of the playground.'

'Lukas used to be friends with Jan, but they fell out and now Jan will not talk to me and I do not know why.'

I paid this talk as much attention as I did your effusions over numbers. The more I listened, the more convinced I became that this talk of others, this secret side-lining of information, this gossip, was in some way central to the way your language had developed. Evolution is a series of happy accidents, and human language is no exception. It was just that it did not only provide the means of collaboration required to hunt, build camps, and defend them. Gossip, it seemed, was just as central to your survival; who liked, and did not like, whom.

The erta do not gossip. Perhaps that is why we know so little about each other.

Of course your education was still merely the means by which you were to be tested, and your test was not in how well you could learn how to read, or the imagination with which you understood the numerical system. The real test was in your behaviour.

Occasionally I witnessed this assessment, at the school gates, for example, when the parents—Benedikt included—watched you interacting with their ertlings. Sometimes, if I was back from a balloon trip early and happened to pass the school when you were playing outside, I would catch sight of the teachers moving around you in wide, hawk-like circles.

On one such occasion you spotted me passing in the middle of a game. I stopped and waved, and you waved back, but the distraction caused you to walk straight into the path of an oncoming ball. It hit you square in the head, knocking you sideways. I heard one of the ertlings—a male—laugh, so you picked up the ball and threw it directly at him. This caused some gasps among the others, and the teacher to stop in her tracks. I hurried away.

Aside from this incident, you seemed to get on well with the others. You made particular friends, I was dismayed to learn, with Lukas, Benedikt's fostered ertling.

'Who is my father?' you asked me one afternoon, as you helped me prepare some herring in the kitchen.

This was not a difficult question to answer.

'You do not have one.'

'But Lukas has one.'

'Yes, he does. But he does not have a mother, and you do.' I smiled down as I disposed of some innards in a bowl. 'Me.'

'Why do some children have mothers and some have fathers?'

'Because it depends on who has chosen to look after you.'

You took some time to absorb this. I could almost see the questions flicker in your eyes.

'Will I get to choose someone to look after?'

It was my turn to pause.

'I do hope so, Reed.'

'Why?'

I wiped my hands and knelt before you.

'Because looking after something that is not you is the most wonderful thing. It frees you from yourself.' I tapped your head. 'From everything up here.'

You smiled at this and, with no warning, kissed my cheek.

'Can I go and play now?'

'Yes.'

And with a grin you ran off as if nothing had happened, leaving me wayward and breathless, quite unable to stand.

ONE AFTERNOON AS I approached the school gate to collect you, I heard scuffles, grunts and shouts coming from the yard instead of the now familiar sound of play. Benedikt was standing by the gate, watching, along with three other ertling carers further along the fence.

'What is happening?' I asked, as my pace quickened.

Benedikt looked back at my approach.

'There was an argument,' he said, standing aside. 'See for yourself.'

You were on your back, unable to move. Lukas, sitting astride your chest, had pinned you to the ground by your wrists and now loomed over you with a placid smile as you struggled, helpless, beneath him. A crowd of your classmates stood nervously around, biting nails and wringing hands, but hiding just as much glee as they displayed of their uncertainty.

'Get off me,' you squeaked, but Lukas merely broadened his smile.

I lurched for the gate, ready to spring upon the young ertling, but Benedikt snatched me back by wrist.

'Stop,' he said. 'This is not your argument.'

I tried to wrench myself free from his clawed grip.

'What do you mean? Look at them; he's hurting him! Let me go!'

Benedikt's frown grew dense, like wild thickets.

'This is precisely the kind of behaviour we should be interested in.' I followed his stare across the yard, where I saw two teachers watching from a safe distance. Benedikt leaned closer. 'The kind of the behaviour *you* should be interested in.'

I finally broke free and ran to the gate.

'Ima, wait—'

'Stop!'

Lukas, you and the crowd of ertlings looked up at the sound of my voice.

'Stop that now.'

Lukas' smile slowly left his face. His attention was all on me, and as his grip weakened you saw your opportunity and wriggled one hand free. Your fingers curled together.

'Reed, no!' I cried, but the blow had already been delivered. It was weak, landing on Lukas' left side with a dull thwack. There were gasps, and Lukas turned back, inspecting the spot where you had made contact. Confused, but reaching a decision, he swung his own fist high above his head.

'Lukas.'

Benedikt's growl stopped Lukas in his tracks, and this time he stood straight up, leaving you wheezing on the floor.

'Come,' said Benedikt, and Lukas obediently picked up his bag and walked to the gate. I ran to where you lay.

'Get up,' I said, as the ertlings backed away. 'Are you all right? Can you stand? Can you walk?'

'I'm fine,' you said, shaking me off. I took a step back, and you got to your feet, shaking and glaring around the yard. You looked so furious, so small.

'Are you just going to let that happen,' I said to Benedikt as I shepherded you through the gate, you still flinching from my contact.

'Why not?' said Benedikt. 'The argument was started by Reed. Lukas was merely restraining him.'

'Reed, what happened?' I said.

'Nothing,' you said, pouting at the ground. The other ertlings pushed past, smiling and talking with their parents as if nothing had happened.

'Why were you fighting?'

'It was him,' you said, glaring at Lukas. 'He said I wasn't strong enough to play the jumping game.'

'Lukas?' said Benedikt, one hand upon his shoulder. Lukas looked up.

'Well he isn't, Papa,' he said. 'He is too small.'

'I'm not,' you snapped back.

'But you are,' said Lukas. Just a fact; no hint of malice.

'I am not!'

I pulled you back.

'Reed, control yourself!'

You looked up, fuming, and shrugged me off.

'Now then, Lukas,' said Benedikt, with an oily glance at me, 'we have spoken about this. You must allow everyone to play your games, size does not matter. Hmm?'

Lukas looked up at him, wide-eyed.

'Well?'

'Yes, Papa.'

'Good, now why don't you two boys say sorry and we'll forget this ever happened.' He gave me another look as he said this, for there was no intention of forgetting these things. 'Go on now.'

'Sorry, Reed,' said Lukas in a clear, honest voice.

'Reed?' I said.

'Sorry, Lukas,' you mumbled.

'There,' said Benedikt. 'All better. Now run along, I'll catch you up.'

'Come on, Reed,' said Lukas. 'Let's go and play.'

He took your hand and led you away, your trudge looking ever more dejected against his happy bound. Benedikt watched you go.

'Eight years old,' he said, 'and already a slave to his own impotent rage. His body is not even fully developed yet. Just imagine how it will be when he is eleven, fifteen, sixteen, twenty-one. What happens to it all, Ima, do you think? What happens to all that rage as he grows?'

I said nothing, and he turned to leave.

'Benedikt,' I said.

He stopped and turned.

'Yes?'

'*Papa?*'

He curled his lip momentarily, then straightened his cloak.

'He has to call me something,' he said, and left.

– THIRTY-THREE –

LATER, I TENDED to your wounds by the stove. Lukas' restraint, though outwardly non-violent, had left red, raw welts upon your wrists, which I dabbed with Payha's ointment.

'You must learn to control your temper,' I said. 'It is not pleasant for others to see you in such a fury.'

You stared at your stockinged feet, dangling from the chair.

'Lukas was right,' you said. 'I wasn't strong enough for the jumping game.'

'Reed, don't say that.'

You looked up, eyes glistening.

'But it's true. There's no way I could have kept up.'

'That is no reason not to join in the game. They are supposed to be fun, are they not? There, all done.' I straightened your cuffs. 'Better?'

'They're not fun when everyone's bigger than you are. And stronger.'

'Well, perhaps they should not have been showing off.'

'They weren't. It's just me; I'm weak.'

I gripped your shoulders.

'Reed, that is not true. You *are* strong, you *are*. Strength...'

You looked back at me, eyes wide and waiting for the advice

that would carry you through the pain. I struggled. I knew what strength was. Strength was superior muscle structure. Strength was a sophisticated skeletal system fortified by an ever-evolving carbon fibre mesh. Strength was flesh that repaired itself, arteries running with nano-mites, an intelligent immune system and skin that did not require ointment to rid itself of a few scratches.

Then a memory appeared, like a page falling from a dusty book.

'Might,' I said, 'is not always right.'

You blinked. I withdrew my hands in embarrassment and stood swiftly.

'Do you enjoy fighting?'

You shook your head.

'Then do not do it. Do the things you enjoy instead, that come naturally to you. Find the best part of yourself and be that thing around others.'

This brought a small smile, the first I had seen since the morning.

'Now go to bed.'

I watched you run to the sink to wash, thinking of the two pieces of advice I had, somehow, just imparted. I knew exactly where that first piece came from. I remembered the page number, the line, the shape of the words, the weight of the blue, aged tome in my hands, the scrawled image of that skinny boy gripping the giant sword.

But the second piece of advice—I had no clue where that had come from. No clue at all.

IT DID NOT take you long, however, to put it into practice.

The following week I approached the school gate to another new sound, though not a fight this time.

Benedikt was there by the gate as he had been before, only

now he was gripping the wood and glaring into the yard, teeth grinding.

'What is happening this time?' I said. '*Papa*.'

He grimaced at me.

'Your child. Again.'

You were in one corner of the school yard—not pinned, not struggling, but sitting with your legs crossed. Your ertling classmates surrounded you, sitting in a similar fashion and watching, entranced, as you hummed. It was a simple, wordless melody with four distinct pitches, and they were humming it softly back at you. I recognised it instantly.

'His tune,' I said. 'He's teaching them it.'

I looked along the fence, at which other parents of the ertlings now stood, watching the scene with smiles upon their faces. Only Benedikt seemed perturbed. He called out to one of the teachers, who was gazing at the small choir with a similar look of enthralment to the parents. He glanced up from his reverie and wandered over.

'Are you going to let this continue?' said Benedikt.

The teacher—a slight-built, fifth generation male with thinning hair who, for some reason or other, I had marked as having had expertise in sanitation—drew himself up under Benedikt's shadow.

'Why ever would I not?' he asked.

'Singing?' said Benedikt. 'Does this really represent a profitable use of time?'

'There is no harm in it, no words, no fiction, and the ertlings seem to enjoy it. Besides—' he turned to the still-humming crowd, smiling again—'I don't want to stop it. Not just yet, anyway.'

He drifted back to where he had been standing. I'm sure he began to sway.

'Lukas,' called Benedikt sharply. 'Come.'

Lukas, who had also been in the crowd, turned to look, but did not stand.

'Lukas,' warned Benedikt. The child finally got to his feet and hurried across. 'Home, now.'

'What is wrong, Benedikt,' I called after them. 'This is precisely the kind of behaviour we should be interested in, is it not?'

He did not look round, which brought me immense pleasure.

JORNE STARTED VISITING us again, which pleased you no end. He collected you from school on the days I could not and took you on small expeditions. On these evenings, as well as hearing of your studies at school, I would learn of the things Jorne had taught you in the forest; the names of animals, flowers, trees, plants you could and could not eat. You became as interested in the outside world of flora and fauna as the internal one of letters and numbers. I was sure this thrilled Jorne, though it was difficult to be certain, since his face resembled your slate for most of the time anyway.

His face did not just resemble your slate. It resembled other things as well, some of which I could neither name nor place.

I would watch him with you at the kitchen table, late in autumn when the ground began to harden, the sea flattened, the skies cleared, and candles were lit ever earlier. In the warm glow of our stove you would babble away and he would listen, just as rapt as me, and every so often he would glance up and smile and I would find myself smiling back, lost in it all, this little scene.

One evening went on later than usual, and you were already curled up asleep on your bed by the time Jorne left. It was dark and the ground glittered with frost, like a reflection of the starlit sky made dense by the cold. I stood at the door as he bade me farewell, the warmth of our dwelling swirling out into the cold night, and I found myself gripped by some strange urge to pull, or leap. It was the same one I had had all those years ago upon my balloon, an unbidden voice with thoughts outside of my own. *Jump*, it said. *Do something, now.*

I did. I placed a hand upon his arm, and he stopped.

'What is wrong?' he said, turning.

I swallowed, retracting my arm.

'It is cold,' I said.

'Yes it is.'

'And quite far.'

We stood eye to eye and he watched me, not unkindly, though I am sure some part of him took pleasure in my struggle. Finally he smiled, removed a glove and raised his bare hand to my cheek. Then he put his face towards mine. His mouth opened, his eyes closed.

'Stop.'

I stepped back, leaving him hovering in that same position, like a bear crouched over a weir, waiting for a salmon to jump into its paws.

'What is it?' he said.

'Good night.'

I shut the door and turned my back against it, listening to the silence beyond. Finally I heard a long sigh, and the crunch of his boots disappeared into the frost.

My sleep was disturbed that night.

Your sleep, however, grew more sound and regular than it ever had been. Whereas before our days had been vague and meandering, full of half-eaten meals and endless games and walks stopped short by bowel or temper, now they were things of substance and purpose. Your schooling had locked your mind into a blissful and relentless routine of knowledge acquisition, play, and sparkling conversation. And at night it was all processed, as it is with us.

MONTHS WENT BY, and the years followed. Life was good, and every day the lie became easier to forget. Even Benedikt seemed less troublesome. One afternoon at pickup time I even caught him smiling as he watched you at play with his son. The smile vanished when he saw me looking, of course, and he hurried Lukas home, with a serious nod of greeting as he passed me.

The moment took me beyond relief. If you could convince even Benedikt of your virtues, then there was hope indeed.

But hope was not to last.

– THIRTY-FOUR –

YOU WERE ELEVEN years old when it happened.

'The Council will want to see you.'

The teacher was waiting for me at the gate. She seemed anxious and tight-lipped, in fact the whole atmosphere at the school when I picked you up that Friday was unusual. The parents of the ertlings avoided my eyes as they hurried past, and you hung your head when I greeted you.

'What has happened?' I said. The teacher regarded you as if you were something she no longer understood.

'They will explain.'

Sure enough, as we crossed the circle there was a screech from the forest (a phenomenon I had explained to you as the call of a rarely seen buzzard) requesting my immediate presence in Ertanea.

'Reed, what have you done?'

But you would not speak.

We rode for Ertanea and I left you on a bench in the gardens—I would not be long. Only three figures were waiting for me in the candlelit Halls—my mother, Caige and a fine-featured male whom I recognised from the school gates as the parent of one of your friends, a girl named Zadie. He was slim and smooth-

263

skinned, and wore the same look of concern as the other two.

Caige spoke first. He was even more red-faced and blustering than usual, and when I saw what he was holding I knew at once why.

'This will not stand,' he said, thrusting the paper towards me. My heart sank. It was a drawing. 'Experiment or no experiment, we cannot allow this kind of behaviour.'

'I can explain,' I said, taking the paper from him and inspecting the sketch. It was somehow different to the one I kept hidden in my balloon, and although it had been some months since I had confiscated that first attempt at art, this seemed unreasonably advanced in terms of its technical skill. It was of a dwelling. The lines were as straight as what they represented, joining with each other at precise points. The were no figures, no clouds, no mountains, and despite the trail of smoke from the chimney, the whole thing seemed cold. I was disappointed.

'He has only done this once before. I told him not to, but he has a fascination with—'

'This is not your *human's* work,' spluttered Caige, taking two furious steps towards me. 'This is an ertling's!'

'What?'

'You heard me.' He batted the paper with the tips of his fingers. 'An ertling—' he puckered as if the approaching word was sour to taste '—*drew* this.'

'Our ertling,' said the smooth-skinned male behind him. He slipped a hand through Caige's arm and they faced me as one.

This was a surprising development. As I have mentioned, gossip does not provide meaningful data to the erta, so the relationships between individuals are neither public nor private; one sees them when one sees them. It was beginning to seem, however, that such relationships existed in greater number— not to mention, variety—than I had first presumed. That

Caige and his partner were both male was no great shock, for I had heard that matching genitalia need not be a barrier to emotional or sexual congress, and Payha had already nodded to her preference in this regard. What was surprising was that the smooth-faced, waif-like creature before me was a fourth generation erta, whereas Caige was on the high council.

'You are Williome,' I said. 'Zadie's father—' I glanced at Caige '—or one of them.'

'Yes.' Williome's eyes were fixed upon the drawing in my hand. 'It appears that Zadie has made friends with the human.'

With a quiver of his lip, he suddenly reached out and snatched the drawing from me.

'Why would she do this?' he cried.

Caige consoled him by tightening his embrace.

'Because she was copying the boy,' he said.

My mother spoke.

'He is quite the artist, it seems.'

She reached inside her cloak and produced a stack of paper bound with string, which she passed it to me. More drawings. The top was of a balloon in the sky, and two figures in the forest beneath it. This was much more like it; I fought back the urge to beam.

Williome, however, fidgeted with disgust.

'As you can see,' he said, dismissing the pile as if it were dirt. 'Zadie's is far superior.'

My indignation spoke before I could.

'It may look like a house, but it does not feel like one.'

Caige and Williome scoffed, then re-examined their child's drawing in silence.

My mother adopted her most gentle tone. 'Ima, you know how this behaviour is regarded by the erta.'

My eyes were still on the balloon and the bubble beneath.

There was a face behind it. The same face. The same eyes.

'Of course.'

'Singing in the school yard is one thing, but this.' She shook her head, began again. 'In truth, none of us knew whether the child—'

I looked up.

'His name is Reed.'

The silence gaped for a century, and if it had gone on any longer I believe it would have swallowed us whole.

Neither of those statements is true, of course—but, oh, how I am enjoying these metaphors.

My mother cleared her throat and continued.

'—whether Reed would exhibit such traits naturally, or whether they were learned through social interaction with other humans. Now it seems that question has been answered. The flaw is hard-wired.'

Williome pierced me with a glare from his pretty eyes.

'Unless, of course, you taught him.'

'Of course I did not,' I said.

'Or somebody else,' said Caige from the shadows. 'As I understand it you are not the only one with whom he spends time outside of school.'

He meant Jorne, of course.

'No,' I said, unable to keep the pride from my voice. 'This practice was his own choice, these drawings came from his own imagination.'

'In which case,' said my mother, 'it is all the more dangerous.'

'It cannot be allowed to continue,' echoed Caige. 'The project must be abandoned.'

I drew myself up.

'Yes,' sneered Caige, taking pleasure from my reaction. 'Abandoned. The human child's drawings are shocking enough…' *Shocking*. That was the word he used. I felt light in the head, as if the air had grown thin around me, '…but the fact that he has corrupted ertlings with this behaviour…' *corrupted,* he said, as I lost myself in your drawing again, suppressing a smile at the looks you had placed upon the faces of the figures in the forest—you with a lopsided grin and Jorne with his scraggy beard obscuring an o-shaped mouth, '…is nothing short of treachery. Our ertlings…' *our ertlings* '…will one day transcend like the rest of us, and if they bring these deformities with them then our entire collective species will be sullied.'

Treachery, deformities, sullied. What words.

My mother stepped in.

'Now then, Caige, there is no need for hysterics. We merely need to impress upon—'

Williome suddenly stamped his foot and broke in with a piercing bawl.

'It must be stopped. For the sake of our children, it must be stopped.'

For even a third-generation erta to interrupt a member of the high council would be viewed as gravely disrespectful. For a fourth-generation to do so was tantamount to treason, and to do so using the word *children* as a device to press the point was nothing short of insane.

And yet, my mother made no reply.

I studied them all, standing there with their furrowed brows and folded palms fretting over what was to be done about this. And I wondered, for the first time, what exactly was wrong with them. Why could they not see what I saw? And what was it, exactly, that I saw, other than a badly drawn balloon and my sad face drawn upon old paper?

Imperfection, I realised. Rendered perfectly.

I felt the same as when I had stepped from my balloon, or

when I had run with my face turned to the sky, or touched Jorne's arm. It was the feeling of moving across a boundary.

Jump.

'Why?' My voice sounded shrill. 'Why must it be stopped? This is an experiment, and an important one, you said so yourself, Mother. So this project, this life, Reed...'

I hesitated.

Jump.

'My son.' Another gaping silence threatened swallow us. 'He is the means by which this decision is to be reached. To abandon it now based upon suppositions of treachery, corruption, deformities... I mean, really. We are the Erta. We mend broken planets.' I held up your drawings. 'Do you honestly expect us to wither before a few scribbles?'

I regretted having to use that word. They were not scribbles, they were beautiful things. More beautiful than the sky, the sea, the earth, and all the life that raged across it.

Caige's face prickled with rage. Finally he shook off his lover's hand and strode towards me.

'That thing,' he said, bearing down upon me—'that creature you call your "son", that *abomination*, should never have been called into existence in the first place. If I could I would, I would...'

Within the space of 0.43 seconds, my mother shot Caige a look, his eyes widened as if he had stumbled upon a steep drop, and finally he shut his mouth, breathing furiously through his sizeable nose.

I stared up at him, doing my best to ignore the stench of boiled vegetables.

'What, Caige?' I said. 'What would you do?'

He said nothing. With one last shuddering, cabbage-fumed exhalation he turned and left, with Williome hurrying behind.

Once the great door had slammed I caught my breath and turned back to your drawings. They were damp with the sweat from my palms.

'Is this what the council has become, Mother?' I said, hands shaking as I leafed through them. Skies, forests, seas, birds, creatures, suns, houses, each one as wonderful as the last, and my face in every one. 'Angry parents weeping over drawings? Making threats?'

'Nobody is threatening anybody. All we want is what is best for our species.'

'I am sure of it, Mother, but I am beginning to suspect that what is best for our species was never good for Reed's.'

Her expression soured.

'If the council heard you questioning them like this, they would not tolerate it, do you understand? There would be consequences.'

'What consequences? What consequences exist for the crime of asking questions? What will happen to me? Will I be imprisoned? Tortured? Banished?'

At that word she froze, and another question arrived on my tongue.

'Why does Oonagh live in the mountains?'

Silence fell, and we battled each other's gaze.

'You have developed an agenda,' she said. 'You side with humanity. You believe they should be resurrected from extinction.'

'No. I side with my son. I want him to be the best that he can be, not because I want his species to be reborn, but because I want him to be happy. Even if it is just for a short time.'

'That is a difficult thing to wish for. You have already seen that there are people who believe the project should be abandoned altogether, and they are not just on the council.'

'These are the same people, I assume, who have grown so attached to their ertlings that they sob over drawings of houses? These ertlings who are now, apparently, to transcend with us?'

'Of course they are to transcend with us. It is only natural that their carers should feel attached to them—we are not monsters.'

'No, we are not, just as we are not a lot of things. In fact, our entire existence seems to be defined by things that we are not—not fearful, not distracted, not curious, not wishful, not hasty, not irascible, not passionate—and yet I see these things in us more every day.'

'Maybe you only see them in yourself.'

I straightened your drawings and pulled them close, for there was strength in them.

'You are right, Mother, I do have an agenda now. But if some have already made up their minds about Reed, then so do they. He is only eleven years old, and he still has much to learn. Please let him learn it.'

She worked her jaw, thinking. At last she spoke.

'Go. Continue. I will talk to the council.' She gestured to the drawings clutched to my breast. 'But there are to be no more of those.'

She departed, and I stood for some moments in the cold silence before making my way outside. But as I left the Halls I stopped cold; Benedikt was beside you upon the bench, with one arm thrown casually on the backrest. Heart kicking, I marched across the square, hiding my fear behind a thin smile.

He looked up at my approach, retracting his arm.

'Ima, Reed and I were just chatting. Isn't that right, Reed?'

'Is that so?' I said, my smile already beginning to ache. 'And what exactly were you chatting about?'

'Oh, lots,' you said, standing. 'Ben was teaching me more about things that happened in the past.'

'I see. Well, lucky you. Reed, will you please go and see to Boron for our ride home? I just need to talk to Benedikt for a moment.'

Benedikt gave you a friendly wave as you ran for the paddock. Once you were gone, I turned to him.

'Stop trying to poison my son.'

Benedikt stood, abruptly.

'Poison? I am merely teaching him about the history of his species, a task you have avoided, it seems.'

'Of course I have avoided it. I cannot risk him finding out the truth.'

'Precisely. You wish to raise him in a vacuum. What kind of a test is that?'

I glared at him.

'You are trying to twist him,' I said. 'You think that if you tell him these things, all these woeful, bloody tales about war and murder and sorrow then it will bring out the worst in him. You wish to trigger violent urges.'

He went to protest, but I cut him short.

'You want to make it harder for him.'

Benedikt narrowed his eyes and leaned in.

'And why on earth would I want to do that?'

'Because you want this project to fail. You want *him* to fail.'

I sensed his fury rise in a single heartbeat.

'All I have ever wanted,' he said, throwing a finger at the paddock, 'was to let the erta see what that creature is capable of.'

His eyes were filled with rage, but there was something else in them too, and whatever it was it was trapped. Benedikt had a secret.

'What happened to you?' I said.

Before he could reply Caige called from the Halls.

'Benedikt,' he said sharply. Benedikt swung his head. 'You are wanted inside.'

He took one last look at me—the secret was still in there, I could see it burning—and left.

– THIRTY-FIVE –

'THEY DIDN'T LIKE my pictures,' you said gloomily from behind. It was dark, so I had borrowed one of Ertanea's torches to light our way through the forest, and tree shadows swayed with Boron's soft plod. The motion calmed me after my altercation with Caige, and I was able to think more clearly. Benedikt was right, I realised: perhaps I had been too protective of you. Perhaps you did need to learn about more than just letters and numbers.

'It was not that they did not like them,' I said. 'They just did not approve of them. There is a difference.'

'But I'm not allowed to draw any more.'

I thought for a moment, feeling the bound paper stack beneath my cloak.

'That is not true. You can draw all you like, just not at school.'

'Really?'

'Yes, really. We are going to do lots more things at home that you do not do at school. It is not the only place you can learn about the world.'

'Does that mean I can learn things from Benedikt as well?'

'That's not quite what I had in mind.'

'But he's interesting. Did you know that the Mayans used to

play ball games with people's heads? Why are we not stopping at Fane?'

'We are just taking a little holiday,' I replied. It was a foolish word to use, since the last holiday that had ever existed lasted for almost a century, and resulted in the extinction of your species. But it seemed somehow appropriate.

'What is a holiday?'

'A holiday is when you do things differently to the way you normally do them.'

'Like what?'

'Well, you do not go to school for a start.'

'But I like school.'

'I know you do, but it does your brain good to rest sometimes.'

'What else?'

'You see different places, you eat different things.'

'But we always eat herring.' You yawned and laid your head upon my back. 'Where are we staying on our holiday?'

'We are going to stay with a friend.'

'Who?'

'You know who.'

This cheered you up, and you spoke no more of Mayans or their heads.

'IMA,' SAID JORNE when he opened the door. 'I heard you were at council. Is everything all right?'

'Did you ever teach Reed how to draw?'

'Why would I do that?'

'I just wondered, when we lived on the hill… it does not matter.'

'Are you in trouble?'

'No, not any more.' I looked around the empty square. 'Where is everybody?'

He smiled.

'Come with me, you're just in time.'

Jorne led us through the settlement and into the woods. I let you walk ahead with him, talking about what had happened since you had last seen each other. Eventually we heard voices and a fire crackling.

'What's that smell?' you asked, eyes widening.

'Come and see,' said Jorne.

We entered a clearing, in the centre of which was a roaring fire surrounded by Jorne's fellow villagers—the Sundra—sitting in groups with faces lit orange in the flames. Some held drinks and watched the fire in silence, while others engaged in conversations punctuated by long pauses or awkward flourishes of their hands. One male was attempting to braid another's hair with a look of intense concentration, as if attempting an impossible calculation. The whole scene appeared as painful as Payha's first smiles at your bedside.

'What is this?' I asked.

'A gathering to mark the beginning of spring,' said Jorne as he led us around the circle, greeting others with friendly nods or hellos.

'Is this another one of your attempts to be human?' I said, keeping my voice low. 'Like your shell?'

He ignored me, and turned his attention to the tall, barrel-chested male tending a spit upon which a dead beast turned.

'What ho, Markus,' he called. 'May we try some?'

Markus looked between Jorne and the spit, looking for all the world like somebody who had lost all memory of what he was doing, or why. Eventually he tore off a chunk of meat and threw it to Jorne.

'Obliged,' said Jorne. He dangled a shred of wet, white meat before you. 'Here, try some.'

You licked your lips at the oozing flesh. 'What is it?'

'Boar. Try it.'

'He has never tried meat,' I said.

But you had already snatched it from his hand and stuffed it into your mouth.

Jorne watched with interest as you devoured your prize with blissful, eye-rolling grunts. He tore off another shred for me. 'Here.'

I raised an eyebrow at him, so he shrugged and ate it himself. As you both munched happily, I spotted Payha across the fire. Seeing me too, she got up and wandered over.

'A drink, Ima?' she said, offering a stone flash.

Jorne looked at it uncertainly, wiping his mouth of grease.

'I don't think Ima...'

I took the bottle.

'What is it?'

'Huhrwein,' said Payha. 'It's made from berries, pine, other things. Don't feel you have to.'

I put my nose to it, catching the unmistakable reek of fermentation. I had never tried alcohol before, and would never have thought to before now.

'I will.'

'Be careful,' said Jorne. 'It is quite...'

But I had already taken a hefty swig. My gullet caught fire, or so it seemed, and I threw a hand to my throat.

'I did warn you,' said Jorne.

My reaction had drawn some looks from the crowd. They did not bother me, but then I saw Payha's smirk.

'Do you want me to take that for you?' she asked.

'No,' I said, straightening up. 'It is quite all right.'

Keeping my eyes on hers, I took another slug of liquor in one smooth gulp. This time I was prepared, and I swallowed without reaction, holding out my bottle.

Payha took it, nodding her approval.

'Talk to you later,' she said, and left.

'You need to be careful with that stuff,' said Jorne. 'It can make you feel unusual.'

I looked into the fire.

'I already feel unusual. I've always felt unusual. How is that possible; to feel different when there is nothing to feel different to?'

'What are you talking about?'

'Jorne, I need your help.'

'What do you need?'

I looked around. 'Although your efforts to capture the essence of humanity are dubious, I cannot deny that you have had more experience of them than me. I need Reed to know about them.'

'You want to tell him the truth?'

'No. I just need him to understand a little of where he is from. Can you teach him?'

Jorne smiled. His eyes twinkled.

'I can do better than that.'

– THIRTY-SIX –

Your presence at the fire seemed to break the tension, and soon the awkwardness of the Sundra's festival lifted. They were amused by your antics and frequent visits to the spit, from which Markus threw you strips of meat and laughed as you gobbled them up. Three delighted females braided your hair and marked your face to look like theirs, which gave you endless pleasure. So absorbed were you by the fun, in fact, that you hardly seemed to notice when I left.

Jorne led me back to the village. The hurwein had lightened my head, and the bracken felt soft as I followed the sway of his torch. He was unnaturally quiet as we approached his dwelling—this from somebody who did not speak much at the best of times—and it was clear to me that he was deliberating over what was about to happen.

'Ima,' he said, as we stood outside a door at the back of his dwelling I had not seen before. 'Once I open this door, it cannot be shut.'

'Is it broken?'

'No, I mean what I am about to show you cannot be *unshown*.'

'That is not even a word. What are you trying to say?'

'I am just—'

'Oh for goodness sake.'

'Ima, wait.'

I pushed him aside and threw the door open. But I froze at what lay inside.

'What is this?'

Jorne sighed.

'As I said, it cannot be unshown.'

It was a large, oblong room with two windows on adjacent walls, filled with objects. Their shadows stretched in the glow of Jorne's torch. Some—books, candlesticks, pots—I recognised, but others I did not. In one corner was a great brown globe, and next to it stood a tall curved plank with a faded crest and what looked like aquatic fins protruding from its base. In another corner, resting upon an intricately carved table, was a curious shaped box with a circular hole in the centre and a stick drawing out of it, across which six strings had been pulled taut. Glittering chains of metal were draped over the surface beside it. Coloured fabrics covered with writing hung upon the walls and across chairs, and everywhere there were pictures. Pictures of mountains, pictures of machines, pictures of faces. Human faces.

'These,' I stammered, walking slowly around the room, 'these are human artefacts.'

'That is correct,' said Jorne. 'Payha's stethoscope is not the only thing we kept.'

He followed me uncertainly, lighting the way with his torch. I picked up a series of small wooden blocks which had been strung together in the shape of a dog, and connected to a wooden cross by further strings.

'They were all supposed to have been destroyed. How did you come by them?'

His eyes glittered as he looked around the room, as if this was the first time he had seen it too.

'My friend Thomas—the Frenchman from the boat—he hid them before the clearings happened.'

'That's impossible. They would have been found. They would have been found and burned like all the rest, or pulped and flattened and sent up to the little moon. There is no possible way he could have kept them.'

Jorne looked down at me.

'You are so certain of the past, aren't you? So certain that you refuse to believe what your eyes tell you. Look, Ima.'

He swung his torch around, illuminating more of the strange relics and causing the shadows to shift. Mirrors and stopped clocks flashed in the light, buildings made of plastic bricks loomed over buttons and leather straps, and the faces of tiny mannequins made to look like children stared at me from lifeless eyes, their mouths pulled into perpetual smiles. I simply could not process it. I staggered away.

'This is forbidden, contraband, if the council knew about this then—'

'Then they would burn it and me too, probably.'

'Then why do you keep it?'

Jorne's expression hardened.

'Because this was them, Ima. This was theirs. It simply was not right to destroy it all without trace.'

'But we had to. They had to be gone, otherwise we could not have achieved our purpose.'

'Again, you are so certain of your past.' He shook his head. 'I should not have shown you.'

'Then why did you?'

'Because how else can he learn about who he is?' He eyed me uncertainly. 'Are you going to tell the council?'

My eyes travelled the walls, roaming over every rough edge, rusted corner and frayed hem. These things had no right to be there. It was as if they had snuck into the world without permission—memories which should have been forgotten, reminders of the time and place in which they had originated, and the blame that still lay there.

They had crawled through. Just like Reed.

'No,' I said, turning to Jorne. 'I will not tell the council. Let us find Reed.'

THIRTEEN YEARS

– THIRTY-SEVEN –

YOU CALLED IT the "Room of Things".

And of all the things in the Room of Things, the one you cherished most was the guitar.

'What is that?' you said, running across the room and reaching for the instrument I would, much later, miss the sound and sight of so much it hurt my chest.

I lurched after you, as if you were straying too close to a cliff edge.

'Reed—'

Jorne stopped me.

'Let him go, Ima,' he whispered.

You were frozen, hand outstretched, looking back for assurance.

I nodded.

'Go ahead. You can touch.'

You stroked the dusty, wooden surface and let your eyes travel up what I now know (I know a lot of things now) to be a fretboard. When they reached the tuning locks at the top you cocked your head.

'What is a… *Fender*?'

Jorne went to your side.

'This is a guitar,' he said, taking it down. He turned it delicately in his hands, as if it was a thing of such fragility that it would break at the slightest touch.

'What does it do?'

'It makes music.'

'Music?'

'Listen.'

Jorne ran his thumb over the six strings, each one making a dull thump followed by a hum. Your face lit up with astonishment, and you instantly repeated Jorne's action, lost in the arc of each pitch as if it were telling you its own secret story. When the sound had faded, you looked around the walls for other treasures.

'What are all these things?'

I followed as you drifted between the tables, running your hand over anything it met.

'They are things from the past. Antiquities. This is a special, secret room. You must not tell anyone about it. Not your friends, not your teachers, nobody. Only you, Jorne and I must know. All right?'

You nodded, lost in the shapes.

This was an incredible risk. I had no reason to expect you to be able to keep this secret, and if you did not then I would be as complicit as you.

But I liked this. Suddenly we had our own lie, and this one was against them.

Such was my state of mind at the time; a situation which was about to worsen considerably.

So THE GUITAR was the first. Then there were the records; a box of ninety-eight black discs in cardboard sleeves with pictures on the front. Some were of people standing around in odd clothes, or crossing roads, or looking fierce about something or other. Others were daubed with lines and flashes of colour, or depicted unlikely events such as a man shaking hands with another who was on fire, or an infant diving beneath water for a piece of green paper, or an elegant female walking, oblivious, from a flood.

You enjoyed these images as much as the music that was on the discs, which Jorne showed you how to play on something called a gramophone. This was a mechanical contraption powered by a spring, which you wound with a handle and which, when released, spun the disc at a certain speed. A needle rested upon a thin groove in the disc, in which a topographical representation of the recorded music had been etched. This, when amplified, produced sound. It was marred with crackles and pops, and the movement of the disc was uneven, which meant that pitch wavered consistently. You loved it nonetheless, and listened to its strange wails, roars and thumps for hours on end.

I occasionally listened to the words they sang. Many seemed to dwell upon frustrations over the sexual relationship—or lack of one—with a potential mate. But others related strange stories of battling clouds and imaginary landscapes, or were simply strings of abstract images, like the poems in one of Greye's books. These were the ones I liked the most. They didn't seem to belong anywhere, and therefore were their own worlds.

And then there were the buttons which had once fastened clothes, the jewellery which had once hung around necks and wrists, the maps which had once described the entire planet, and the books. You lost yourself in the books night after night, and I watched you read from a distance. All these things became your secret treasures; endless sources of joy.

The surfboard would come much later.

ONE NIGHT, JORNE said he had something special to show you. He had cleared a space in the middle of the Room of Things and arranged two chairs—one for me and one for you—facing a wall. Attached to this wall was a white fabric square, and upon a wooden box a short distance from it he had balanced a complex array of small metal boxes connected by wires. Small metal boxes and wires were things which you had rarely seen before, other than the occasional glance in my balloon shed if you passed when I happened to be working on it, so this exotic tangled clump drew your attention immediately.

'What is it, Jorne, what is it?' you said.

Jorne grinned with equal excitement.

'Just wait until you see.'

I caught his eye and frowned, clueless as to what he was about to do. He winked back at me.

Winked.

Blinking, sighing, eye-rolling, frowning, smirking, eyebrow-raising—I was growing accustomed to the expressions my fellow erta had developed during my centuries in the sky, but winking was not one of them. I responded by not responding, but Jorne didn't notice. He had already returned to fiddling with his contraption.

I recognised one of the boxes as a Sunspot, a solar powered battery still popular in the years leading up to humanity's demise and the creation of the erta. It was remarkably powerful, capable of powering a human dwelling for fifty years without replacement. We used them to good effect to power our own first generation of technology—the stratospheric monitors, deep-sea drones, and quantum computers that gathered and analysed our initial data sets. Even my own balloon was powered by one to begin with. Of course, it was not long until we had learned to perfect fusion from ambient nuclear energy, and the Sunspot became defunct. But still, it was one of humanity's better achievements. Perhaps if the effort had been made to develop them a half-century earlier then things may have gone differently.

But as it was—well, the Sunspot was something they used to call "too little, too late".

Human technology did not have to develop in the way that it did. It was not as if there was a single path laid out for them, each discovery leading to the next like a treasure hunt.

Treasure hunts were games that children played, mostly in parks, dwellings and gardens, in which they found clues written in riddle form and deciphered them in order to deduce the location of the next clue, eventually leading to a prize.

Parks were places that were kept green in order to escape the places that were not green.

Riddles were truths mangled into untruths, like similes only less delightful.

I told you, I know a lot of things now.

Anyway, as I was saying, the path of human technology could have taken many shapes. It is probable that basic tools would always have come first, as much out of boredom as frustration, I imagine, there being not much to do in those days other than scavenge and shelter. But agriculture need not have preceded mastery of the ocean. The notation of music may well have occurred well before the writing of words.

Although, from my experience of the books and records in the Room of Things, I would suggest that alcohol fermentation would always have arrived well before either.

Flight need not have developed from that first dizzy soar by two brothers in hats to the touchdown on the moon in less than a century. People could have been bumbling about in bi-planes in the 1500s if they had so desired, and never considered the moon.

Equally, the Napoleonic wars could have been argued about on social media, had the need for internet telecommunication outweighed the need that dominated everything else in humanity's final few millennia—to dominate and destroy everything in its path.

Social media. I cannot really explain this to you, and it is probably best for your sanity if I do not try.

With the right environment and minds clear of fear and desire, there would have been nothing to stop a collection of curious Neolithic sapiens from having telephones, packed lunches, and intercontinental air travel within a century.

Fear and desire. Curiosity and environment. These are the things that drove the path of technology.

'There,' Jorne finally stood, triumphant, from his fiddling. 'Are you ready?'

We nodded from our chairs, and he tapped a screen on one of the boxes. There was a whirring and a square of light appeared on the fabric. You gasped.

'Just wait,' said Jorne from the shadows.

After a crackle a grainy, colourless image appeared of a network of streets and tall buildings from above. You gave another gasp, jumped from your chair and ran to the wall.

'Look! Look!'

'Now watch,' said Jorne. He reached for one of the boxes and made a gesture on its screen. The image zoomed in fiercely, so that now it showed people moving about on one of the streets, crowds streaming past in distorted sepia.

You stood staring up at it, a portion of the image now playing out for me on the back of your head.

Jorne read from the screen beneath his fingers.

'August 17th, 1979, Seattle.'

Hairs prickled upon the back of my neck. I leaned forward, catching his eye again and mouthing the words: 'Quantum Telescope?'

He nodded, eyes bright.

– THIRTY-EIGHT –

IN ADDITION TO the supply of fresh food and water, safety, sanitation and luxurious dwellings, the last members of the human race were also entertained by a wonder that would leave them breathless. The Quantum Telescope was the erta's final gift to the human race.

The technology was, of course, far beyond what they had achieved, so there are no words to describe the science of it.

There is that problem again—describing the science of things.

Space and time are like warped blankets. Light is like a wave at sea. Consciousness emerges or collects or is a field.

None of these things are true, and all of them are, and that paradox is neither the fault of science nor language. Those were the only things you had, and the only things with which you left us. Language, in fact, has always been just as bad at describing things outside of the realm of science as those within it. Love, for example, or the feeling one gets when standing alone before three horses at sunrise.

Words, however, when placed in a certain order, can open doors. That is why poetry exists.

And scientific description is no less a form of poetry than John Keats, or Emily Dickinson, or Bob Dylan.

I told you. *Lots of things.*

I shall try my best to describe the Quantum Telescope to you.

Light from the Earth is reflected into space, as it has been since the Earth was formed, and the further you are from Earth at any given time, the older that light becomes. If you are 250 light years away and you happen to be able to gather and analyse such photons, then you can see what was going on 250 years ago.

We happened to be able to do just that. With quantum drones—a mesh of subatomic telescopes springing up hundreds of light years away—the erta were able to show humans the history of their world; light from the planet as it had been millennia ago. Not only that, but by analysing this mesh concurrently, they were able to pinpoint light from exact times, dates, and angles and thus they would sit outside in warm gardens filled with music and light, watching Rome fall, the Battle of Trafalgar rage, Columbus' feet touching sand, and the births and deaths of their numerous prophets. Their collective life, quite literally, flashed before their eyes.

The Quantum Telescope was dismantled shortly after Hanna, the last human, died. Jorne, it seemed, had attained some recordings.

I walked to his side as you gazed at the people on the street.

'This is probably the most illegal thing in existence,' I whispered.

He gave me a wary look.

'Probably, yes.'

'How much do you have?'

'From about 1300 AD, mostly from Europe and North America, but quite a bit in the 20th century from Africa and Asia too. It's intermittent, but indexed, and dynamic, too.'

'Dynamic?'

'Yes, he can zoom in, scan, and change angles to an extent. The quality is lacking, as you can see, but—'

'He can see them. Humans.'

He nodded, with an uncertain look.

'I thought it would help.'

'Where are they all?' you said, back-stepping slowly to your seat.

'I told you,' said Jorne, 'a city called Seattle, August 17th—'

'Seattle near the herring cove north of Kalbarri?'

'No,' I said. 'It's a different Seattle. One from long ago and far away.'

You wriggled your hands beneath your thighs and frowned.

'So where are they now?'

'Those people are all dead.'

'Dead?'

'Yes, Reed.' I took my seat next to you. 'Everything dies eventually.'

You looked up.

'Even you and me and Jorne?'

I nodded.

'Even you and me and Jorne.'

'I don't want you to die.'

I looked into your mournful eyes. Aside from those few strangers who had died in the hurricane, the only death you had known was in nature. The logic was implicit, reiterated in every spring bud and crumbling autumn leaf: the old died before the young.

I kissed your forehead.

'Do not worry about such things.'

You looked back at the screen and sighed.

'It is quite boring,' you said. 'All the faces look the same.'

Jorne sprang to the box and fumbled with the screen.

'Then how about this? Let me see—'

The image was replaced by a moment or two of white before a new one appeared, just as grainy, of a stone fortress shrouded in mist.

'Beeston Castle, England, October 28th 1482.'

He made some adjustments and the picture enlarged focussing on two males clad in heavy metal armour and helmets, leaning on the battlements. One smoked a pipe, and occasionally it was clear from their mouths that they were sharing a word or two, but mostly they just looked dejectedly out at the empty plain beyond their keep.

Your expression remained similarly bored. Seeing this, Jorne moved us on again. He tried numerous more times and places. The antics of three children running around the port of Cadiz in 1784 drew your interest for a short time, and we tracked a crude rowing boat crossing the southern Pacific two centuries earlier, but by the time Jorne had stumbled upon a family of Inuit sitting around a fishing hole in 1902, you had hopped off your chair and made for a table in the corner, where you became absorbed by a mechanical clock.

Jorne switched off the equipment.

'Maybe he will grow interested in time.'

You would not, as it turned out. But for all the wrong reasons.

– THIRTY-NINE –

WE SPLIT OUR time between Jorne's dwelling and Fane. Fane was for school and my ongoing commitment to our weather beacons, Jorne's place for the evenings and the days in which you were not at school, when you spent your time in the Room of Things poring through the books, listening to the music and stroking the guitar's ancient strings. You spent time with the Sundra too, whose affection for you grew with every visit. You talked with them endlessly, which troubled me at first.

'You have no reason to be concerned,' said Payha one evening, as we sat around a fire.

'I am not,' I replied.

'You are. You believe something will be said that will break the lie. But there is no need to worry—they will not betray the reality of his existence.'

'How can you be so sure?' I said, turning to her.

'Because the Sundra want him to succeed, just like you.'

I had long passed the point of denying this fact.

'What else do the Sundra want?' I asked.

Payha hesitated, considering her words.

'I am not sure I should tell you.'

'Why? I thought we were friends.'

She looked me over carefully.

'Very well,' she said, with a shrug. 'We wish to stay upon the Earth. We choose not to transcend.'

She handed me some hurwein and I drank it. I had grown rather fond of the taste.

'They will not allow it,' I said, wiping my mouth. '*One or nothing*, that is what Caige says. They will challenge you when the time comes.'

'In which case, we will fight.'

'The erta have never fought.'

'There would have been a time when that was true of humans too.'

We sat for a while, watching you amuse the group with your stories and witticisms.

'Look at him,' I said. 'Happy and at peace. How could he ever be capable of war?'

'Given his age, you might be about to find out.'

WE ALWAYS RETURNED to Fane for sleep, unless it was on a day before one of your trips to the forest with Jorne.

These were numerous. I did not join you—preferring to use the additional time to widen the reach of my balloon journeys. I was enjoying my work again and I was particularly interested in an unusual conglomeration of chemical imbalances occurring over the southern seas. These turned out to be non-threatening, but the novelty of the task was pleasurable. I continued in this vein, making ever-vaster sweeps that yielded more and more data with which to build a picture of the carbon dioxide dispersion across the northern hemisphere. I could not remember ever having lost myself in work so much.

You, meanwhile, lost yourself in whatever Jorne taught you

in the forest. It was mostly hunting. Your taste for meat had been piqued by the spring gathering, and I would often smell smoke and burning flesh coming from the hills and know it was you. Sometimes you would not come back, choosing to sleep beneath the stars instead.

Your school became secondary; a necessary thing which you endured but did not enjoy as much as you had. Cliques had evolved in the playground, and your friendship with Lukas drifted. The difference in your sizes was becoming apparent too. Lukas, along with the other boys, had developed broad shoulders, a lean jaw and a longer, tauter midriff, whereas you still held onto the puppy fat of your childhood like the stained and perishing security blanket you did not cast off until your sixth birthday.

But you did not mind. You were still friends with Zadie, at whom I occasionally noticed you watching dreamily, and you had Jorne and the endless trips into the forest.

I did not mind this time apart. I became content in the peace of my own work, which I did by the light of Jorne's stove. Sometimes I would suddenly pause in my analysis of whatever streams of data I had gathered that day and find myself at the door of your room. I would stand there, breathing, taking in the array of artefacts and wondering what it was you were finding in them. There was fear in what I felt, but a kind of envy too.

Occasionally I would enter the room and sit for a while with a book, unopened on my lap. But mostly I would close the door and return to my work, filling a cup with hurwein on the way.

YEARS WENT BY like this. Then one summer evening you walked into the kitchen and seemed different, somehow. That puppy fat was finally melting from your cheeks and abdomen. You were taller, heavier around the eyes, and I could just make out a shadow of hair above your lips and around your chin.

'We're going to a waterfall,' you said, your voice a cracked baritone. 'It's quite a hike so we'll be gone for two days.'

I paused, still reflecting on your appearance, and took a sip of hurwein.

'What about school?' I said.

'It's summer, Ima, there is no school.'

'Oh.'

'Why don't you come?'

'Where?'

You gave a quizzical frown; a near perfect yet, I imagined, unintended mimicry of Jorne's.

'To the waterfall. I just told you.'

'Oh, sorry. No, not this time.'

Your lips tightened.

'That's what you always say. Why not?'

I gestured at my charts.

'I have work. I'm sorry.'

'It doesn't look much like work to me,' he said, nodding at my cup.

I sat back, affronted. Who was this boy? I did not know him.

'I have apologised, Reed. I will come next time.'

'Fine,' you said, though the shake of your head and roll of your eyes told me otherwise.

'Have fun,' I called, staring at the slammed door.

I did not have to work at all; I just did not want to walk twenty miles through the forest to see falling water. I brushed the charts away, filled my cup and watched you and Jorne trudge off into the trees. Then I went to the Room of Things.

I felt more emboldened than usual, no doubt by the hurwein. I ran my fingers over the objects, deciphering each one's function from its form and extrapolating its history—what it had seen, how many hands had held it, etc.—and eventually I came across the muddle of devices Jorne had used to display the quantum telescope recordings. I took these and sat down in a dusty, red armchair.

In addition to the Sunspot and projecting unit, there were two further devices strung with wires. The first was a black cube which, from the writing engraved upon its underside, I deduced to be a memory store of some kind. This was where the recordings themselves were held.

The second device was a thin glass panel, perfectly transparent. I ran a finger across it and was rewarded with a dull, disinterested chord as it activated whatever systems were hidden away inside its core.

I had used a device such as this to calibrate my first balloon—itself a crude machine compared to my current one. They seemed to be everywhere, these boxes with hidden parts that took input and provided output, thereby giving the illusion of intelligence. I always wondered why humans had looked at things in this manner—viewing intelligence, thought, even consciousness itself as some intangible thing that had to be coded as a trick and locked away. Perhaps it was because they thought of themselves as little boxes—"cells of awareness" as I had heard caterwauled from one of your records—and therefore anything approximating their own intelligence must be too.

It is not true, Reed. Intelligence is everywhere. It is everything. Witness the trillion stars turn in great arcs, the starling flock pulse across the night sky, the great oak trees connected by deep roots, their trunks swarming with ants moving with a will outside of their own.

Everything is a murmuration.

The device, having completed its twittering, lit up with an

array of coloured boxes. Soon finding the one which allowed me to browse the data stored upon the cube, I set about the task of understanding it.

The problem as I saw it—and the reason why these recordings had not gripped you to the degree which Jorne had hoped—was that they had been indexed only by date and location. This meant that a huge proportion of the data, as was the case with history, was dull and uneventful. In order for you to see humanity's great events, the data required an extra layer.

And I knew exactly where to find it.

Upon the book shelf were several thick and dusty tomes with names like *The Penguin History of the World*, *History of World Wars*, and *Europe: 1066-2066*, which you had so far avoided due to their size and distance from the ground. I took them down and, after a brief flick through the pages, was satisfied they had what I needed.

It took a little over ten minutes to understand how to encode a routine upon the device, and less than an hour to develop one which scanned and stored the text of every page. As I sat at the table with the tablet suspended above me, chattering away to itself as I flicked through each book, I too scanned the pages. I learned a great deal that evening.

With the raw data collected, all I had to do then was perfect some code which parsed it and pulled out the dates and names of famous events. The Great Fire of London, The Storming of the Bastille, The Battle of Boston in the Second American Civil War, The Siege of Madrid. Of course I did not want it to be dominated by Benedikt's tumbling towers and bloody wars—although I noted that there were a lot of them—so with my new found knowledge of human history, I was able to ensure that less violent events were also included: the first showing of *Hamlet* at the London Globe theatre, the declaration of independence,

VE Day on the streets of Piccadilly, Woodstock, the fall of the Berlin wall, the three-month long vigil in Mexico City after the massacres of 2038.

With the data indexed, it was simply a matter of providing a means of accessing it via the interface—a five minute task—and I was ready to test my work.

In the darkness of that room, I scoured history for its great moments. This was thrilling at first, and I felt a kind of envy as I watched them. I wanted to be there watching them all, hearing the passion in the voices, feeling the electricity, smelling the air. But after a few hours I grew bored of crowds and urgent words mouthed in silence, and started to browse away from the big events, back to the scenes of monotony that Jorne had first tried with you.

August 17th, Seattle, 1979. There were the streams of people upon the street as they had been before, and there were the buildings rising above them. I panned up. Windows whistled past in a blur and I stopped on one, behind which was a woman's face looking up at the sky. I zoomed in on her, trying to make out her expression. It was midway between sadness and hope, and she was lost in it, whatever memories or expectations were inflicting this emotional hybrid upon her, just as she was lost in the clouds that grazed the top of her building. She was stuck in her box, like the code I had just written. I spent the rest of the night finding other similar scenes.

They were everywhere.

Vietnam, 1669: The rice farmer in the paddy field who would smile with no warning and with seemingly no impetus. Germany, 1942: The girl in the death camp stroking her dead mother's hair. Madrid, 1845: The old man walking down the street, muttering to himself and the pigeons. Each of them held a billion secrets, none of them told.

And then there was the woman on the mountain.

Patagonia, 1978. A woman clung, star-like, to a cliff. With numerous ropes and metal devices she was attempting to scale it, but a blizzard had left her struggling.

She hung there for twenty minutes without moving once. Then, finally, she took a breath and strained against her foothold while simultaneously clawing upwards with an axe. It met its target and she followed with her other hand, but it was not enough, and she slipped.

It was some fifty metres before the rope snapped taut, and there she dangled, swinging for ten minutes at least, head slumped and arms limp by her sides. I thought perhaps the rope had broken her back, and was about to move on from this grim scene when she suddenly jerked awake, legs wheeling. I sat up, heart thundering at this new development, and reached for the tablet to zoom in further.

Her face was creased in pain and exertion, and her lips moved as she muttered things into the blizzard. There was a hidden battle playing out, and it was one I was sure she could not win.

But then, to my astonishment, she began to climb.

She climbed through the wind, she climbed through the cold and she climbed through the screaming pain she was clearly enduring. She climbed all the way back to the point from which she had fallen, and when she reached her target, she found her footholds and resumed her original attempt.

An hour later she was at the top, lying on her back, laughing at the sky.

And I laughed with her.

At dawn I had witnessed a thousand quiet faces locked within themselves. I had also drunk two bottles of hurwein, and I stumbled from Jorne's dwelling in a daze, wrapped in a blanket and wandering through the misty forest, thinking about how faces seem to ignite when great words are spoken, and wondering if that woman would have ever made it to the top if she had not fallen first.

– FORTY –

So we became distracted; me by my work and the quantum telescope recordings; you by your music and treks with Jorne. But we were not the only ones. The council was distracted by the rate of development in transcendence, which of course meant that I saw less and less of my mother, and Benedikt too.

I rarely saw Haralia, and when I did I barely recognised her.

Gone was the shining skin, the bouncing curls and bright frocks. Now she wore nothing but the solemn cloak of the Devoted, her head buried in its deep hood. I saw her once as I was travelling back to Fane. I no longer enjoyed the place. You were rarely there by then, and the dwelling was like a memory that no longer belonged to me—muddled, dark and out of place. I could not watch the quantum telescope recordings, or look through the books, or investigate the objects in the Room of Things. I merely spent my time there cleaning and tidying, though neither was necessary.

Also there was no hurwein.

I passed her on the chalk road leading into Fane. I was glad to see her, and I thought we might take tea.

'Haralia,' I called out, as she drifted past.

She stopped and, after a pause, turned.

'Ima,' she replied. I faltered. It was an acknowledgement, not a greeting.

I attempted a smile. 'How are you? Do you have time to come by? We could—'

'No. I do not have time. I must away.'

She continued along the road.

'Not even a little? It has been an age since we talked. How is your work?'

This stopped her.

'I would not expect you to understand, Ima. You know nothing of what we are achieving, this higher purpose with which we have been blessed.'

'I have my purpose too.'

She drifted across the road and stood before me.

'And where is he?'

You were with Jorne as usual. At least I thought you were.

'I don't... I mean I'm not—'

'You don't know. I know exactly where Jakob is all the time. I can feel him with me wherever I go.'

'Reed needs his freedom. If he is to persuade the council of humanity's right to endure, then he must explore his own humanity.'

'Yes, I see, by wandering through forests and floating on a plank in the sea, I suppose?'

'Doing what in the sea?'

'You have not seen them? Him and that poor man who lusts after you? I saw them in the cove south of Tokyo. They take turns paddling out on a long plank and trying to ride it back on the breaking wave. A strange object, almost—' her eyes narrowed '—almost as if it did not belong here. What could that mean, do you think?'

My heart gave a sick flutter as I realised what she was talking about—the tall, finned surfboard that stood in the corner of the Room of Things

'I have no idea what you are talking about.'

'No, that is very clear, because you do not know where he is or what he is doing from day to day. And this is your idea of purpose.'

My eyes dropped. She was right.

'Do you know what they are saying about him?' she went on.

'What?'

'That he is slow at school, unable to keep up with the others, and they're not trying hard, Ima, you must know that. They say he spends most of his time staring out of the window, distracted, elsewhere. And he smells atrocious, and he is awkward to be around, and he stares. Some of the girls no longer like to be around him, they say he makes them feel uncomfortable.'

'He is friends with Zadie,' I said, hopefully.

'Ah yes, Zadie. Pretty Zadie. I am sure he is glad of *her* friendship. You really have no idea what is happening to him, do you? You have no idea of the changes he's going through.'

'I know about puberty,' I said.

'Clearly not enough to see the signs. You're too busy drifting about on pointless balloon trips of becoming insensible on that dreadful drink.' She sneered. 'I can smell it on you now.'

Trembling, I raised a hand to my mouth, trying to catch wind of my breath.

'The way you cling to this world, Ima, this flesh.' She spoke slowly, the words drawn out like stretched gauze. 'It bewilders me. Existence is so much more than this, and it is almost in our grasp. Can't you tell.' She turned back to me. 'Can't you feel it?'

I had no words, so I spoke none.

'No,' she said, closing up. 'It seems you cannot. I have to go.'

With that she turned and made for Ertanea.

HARALIA WAS RIGHT; a change had come over you, and it was not just evident in the hair on your face or the broadening of your chest. You had become gripped by a foul sullenness and fidgeted constantly, as if you were prey to some furious itch that would give you no peace. And yes, you did stare out of windows, and seem not to hear your own name. And yes, you had started to spend more time in the room—the old wood store, which we had cleared and furnished with a bed I had constructed from pine. And yes, you had started to smell.

And so had your sheets.

One evening I decided to broach the subject of your hygiene and walked into your room to find you in a state of undress upon the bed. At my appearance you flushed and curled into a ball to conceal your genitals which, in the brief time I had to appraise them, I noticed had grown hair too. Furthermore they were extremely engorged, and you had been fondling them furiously.

'Ah,' I said. 'I see you are masturbating.'

'Can't you knock!' you cried out, falsetto, as you struggled with your undergarments.

'I have never had to knock before.'

'Well you need to now!'

You sat with your back turned, hunched upon the bed.

'Look at me,' I said.

You remained silent.

'Look at me,' I repeated, louder.

'No,' you yelled, still facing the wall, engulfed in a cloud of shame.

'It is nothing to be embarrassed about,' I said. 'Every mammal experiences such desires, and seeking release from them is perfectly natural.'

'Ima, please.'

'*Everything* is perfectly natural.'

You turned, face red with rage.

'Just get out, will you?'

I got out.

From then on, I knocked.

– FORTY-ONE –

SHORTLY AFTER, I met Williome as I passed the school gate on my way to the balloon.

'Might I have a word, Ima,' he said, thin-lipped and pallid.

'What is wrong?'

'I would kindly ask you to tell that *thing* of yours to leave Zadie alone.'

Zadie was standing in a huddle of other female ertlings, talking. Her shape had changed too. She was taller, her neck had elongated and two lumps had appeared on a previously flat chest.

'Why would I do that?' I said. 'They are friends.'

'Friends don't treat one another as he treats her.'

I folded my arms.

'Speak clearly, Williome, I do not have the time for riddles.'

'As you wish. He harasses her constantly.'

'I'm sure he just enjoys her company.'

'He stands too close when she talks to others, especially boys.'

'He is protective of her, that is all.'

'He tries to hold her hand when she does not want it holding.'

'Physical contact is perfectly natural between friends.'

He leaned in.

'He tried to put his mouth on hers.'

To this I had no response.

'I will talk to him,' I said, after a pause.

'Good, because I have already informed the council and they are taking the matter extremely seriously. Honestly, I cannot see why this project persists. I cannot see why *you* persist. It is utter folly.'

'Without this folly you would never have had her.'

I nodded at Zadie, still talking with her friends. He gave a contented sigh.

'Well yes, there is that. I have grown so fond of her, and I miss her terribly when we are apart. Still—' he turned back with a satisfied smile '—it will not be long before we are together permanently. The first transcendence trials are next week. It must be difficult knowing that, whatever happens, you only have a certain amount of time left with him. You won't be allowed to stay, and there is no possible way he can come with you.'

I said nothing. It was all I could do to hold his stare.

'Just tell him to stop,' he said, and left.

I KNOCKED ON your door that evening. Hearing no onanistic shuffles, I entered and found you curled up, awake, on the bed.

'Zadie's father spoke to me,' I said, as gently as I could. 'I think she was upset.'

You pulled your legs up to your chest.

'I only tried to kiss her once,' you said. 'I saw Lukas do it with another girl, and I thought she might... I thought...'

You sniffed and wiped an eye.

'I know you like her,' I said. 'Unfortunately, sometimes these feelings are not reciprocated.'

I remembered what my sister had said about Jorne. For all the cruelty in her words, had they still been right? Did he lust after me? What would have happened if I had allowed his mouth to make contact with mine that autumn evening six years before? And why had I flinched from it? Because his feelings were not reciprocated? Was I the Zadie to his Reed?

No, I realised, and the excitement of this made me as guilty as it did giddy.

– FORTY-TWO –

'YOU COULD HELP him,' I said to Payha.

It was cold, early winter, and we were sitting upon the cliffs near the Sundra's village, wrapped in blankets and sharing another bottle of hurwein. The transcendence trials were taking place three miles across the bay. Excited crowds had gathered upon a wide platform called (for reasons I did not know) 'The Drift' to witness the first ascent of the Devoted, among whom were Haralia and Jakob.

'What do you mean, "help him"?' said Payha.

'Reed. You could help him with his, you know, problem.'

I had told her of my recent walk-in.

'What on earth are you suggesting?' she said.

I shrugged and took a swig.

'Nothing out of the ordinary; just a little light relief from time to time, perhaps even intercourse. I know it is not uncommon among the Sundra, or any erta for that matter.'

She looked at me, horrified.

'Why don't *you* help him?'

'I am his mother.'

'Not really.'

'To him I am. He would have no sexual interest in me whatsoever,

317

but you—I have seen how he looks at you. In truth, how he looks at every female these days. Surely you want to help?'

'He is just a boy.'

'He is thirteen.'

'Does he even ejaculate?'

'Yes,' I said, grimly remembering your sheets. 'Which means he is a man. He needs release.'

'You are foul.'

'There is nothing foul about it. It is a practical solution.'

'Just because he is sexually mature does not make him a man, and I am five hundred years his senior. The humans had laws against that sort of thing.'

'But we do not.'

Her face squirmed with disgust.

'We are a different species.'

'Come now. You and I know very well that ertian and human biologies do not prohibit intercourse. Anyway, it was as I was saying, just a little—'

'Light relief, yes, I heard you the first time, and the answer is still no. Mieko would be most distraught. Honestly, Ima.'

A wind blew in off the sea, and some breakers crashed on the cove below.

'Are they still at it down there?' I said.

Payha craned her neck and scanned the water beneath. 'Yes. Jorne is on the board now while Reed watches him on a rock. I can see his arms are strengthening.'

I peered down. Your arms did look stronger. There was no doubt that your body was changing dramatically—nothing like the steady maturation of the ertlings—and your emotions could not keep up with it. I thought of you curled up on your bed, mind reeling with whatever wretched, heart-broken fantasies still tormented you, despite your rejection, and wondered how many times such scenes had played out through history.

'I spent a lot of time with humans,' said Payha. 'I worked in the cities when the clearances began, the places where some were still trying to fall through the cracks. Slums, prisons, asylums, and then the strongholds they set up in the suburbs, still trying to hide, but they had no hope. We swept through everything and gathered up the stragglers to take them to their new life. I used to see it in them all the time. Lust, greed, want—that hunger for things they did not have. Even when the virus took hold and sterility had been achieved, even when human procreation had been made impossible, still the desire was there. I used to see it in their faces; the twitches, micro-expressions, the pointless little looks of envy and lust between them in the camps. It drove me mad. Nature had no right to go to war with them in such a way.'

I was still watching your fruitless paddling.

'Perhaps that is why they went to war with it,' I said.

Just then there was a huge thump, and the sky above the far-off platform lit up in gold and green. A distant cheer rose up from the crowd as streams of coloured light floated upwards.

'So that's why they call it the Drift,' said Payha.

As the sun set, we watched the coloured streams join the clouds like ribbons in the wind, and I had a sense of what Haralia had meant. Perhaps this was the natural way of things. This was where everything had been leading to; our destiny: to escape the gravity of things.

And there you were, still splashing about in the sea from which you had once crawled.

'How are you explaining the lights to him?' asked Payha.

'I have told him the truth. It is an experiment.'

'What kind of experiment?'

'One of connection, an attempt to join ourselves to something bigger.'

'What did he say?'

'He said he understood. He says that's what he feels when he's in the water.'

Payha grunted and swigged the hurwein.

'An experiment,' she said. 'That is only part of the truth. It won't be long before you have to tell him the rest.'

'And then he will hate me.'

'You knew from the start that would be the case.'

'I did. I just I didn't think it would matter.'

It grew darker and a breeze blew in. I rested my chin upon one knee.

'There is still a chance he could convince them,' I said. 'But not when he is distracted. How can they see his merits when he is so frustrated? He needs help. It would make things easier for him.'

She turned to me.

'That's just it: he doesn't need help, he needs to learn control. And to convince them of humanity's merits, he does not need things made easier for him. He needs them to be...'

I stopped, struck by a memory I had not yet decoded.

'What is it, Ima?'

But before I could speak there was another thump, this time followed by a huge explosion. We jumped up. The Drift was burning, flames and black smoke now taking the place of the streams of light. The crowd ran, screaming from the rock.

'Haralia.'

'I'll stay with Reed,' Payha called out, but I was already running.

– FORTY-THREE –

BY THE TIME I had reached the Drift the flames were extinguished and the crowd was gone.

'Ertanea,' said a male in a protective yellow suit. His face was blackened with soot, and there were others like him, stony-faced and picking through the rubble. 'They've all gone to Ertanea.'

I found Haralia sitting alone in an observation room, beneath the glare of a single spotlight. Her usually pristine skin was smudged and glistening with sweat, and her hair was a tangled mess of knots and frayed wires from the cracked device still attached to her cranium. She did not look up when I entered.

'Haralia,' I said, running to her chair and throwing my arms around her. 'I'm so glad you're safe.'

She said nothing, and I released her.

'Are you all right? Is Jakob—'

Only at the sound of his name did she look up. Her eyes were trembling, black things, and she shook her head slowly.

'There were three phases.' Her voice was almost unrecognisable—dry and oddly slurred, as if drunk. 'Ten in each. I was to be in the second. He was in the first.'

'What happened?'

Her eyes rolled and she looked away. The stillness of her chilled me.

'I don't know, they haven't said. But they are gone, all gone, all of them, including Jakob. My Jakob.'

'Are you sure? Have you seen him?'

She glared at me, neck straightening.

'I *know* he is gone. I can feel it.' She looked away. 'I don't know why I expect you to understand. What do you know about love?'

She got to her feet, thrown into shadow by the lurid observation light.

'Did you see the lights?'

'Yes,' I stammered. 'They were beautiful. Haralia, what is wrong with you?'

'Not as beautiful as the flames though, I would imagine. Are you enjoying this, sister?'

'Enjoying? Why would I be enjoying this? Why would I get pleasure from your grief?'

She gave a half-shrug.

'It doesn't matter. None of it matters. He is dead.'

Wobbling, she walked towards me.

'Say it, Ima. Say you told me so.'

I staggered back.

'What?

'Tell me you knew this is how things would end.'

She was upon me now, face in mine, tears shaking in her bloodshot eyes.

'You're upset,' I said, 'I should go.'

'No.' She grabbed an arm and pulled me back. 'Stay. Stay and gloat. I want to hear you tell me you were right, like you're always right.'

I squirmed in her fierce grip.

'What do you mean? Why do you hate me, Haralia?'

'Because you're perfect. Everyone always knew your purpose was above mine. You fixed the sky, while I scrabbled about in the dirt with the animals. The stinking dogs and filthy pigs and the gulls on their shit-covered rocks. Animals. Do you know what? I hate animals, even horses with their dumb stares, and especially that stinking, shitting, dumb ape of yours.'

When I finally found my voice, it shook.

'Take that back.'

She gave a nasty smile, rewarded by my hurt.

'They don't even talk to him in school now. Not even pretty Zadie. She ignores him. They hate him. They all hate him.'

She sniffed the air around me.

'You've been drinking again. You're no better than him, Ima. You're an animal, too. Do you hear me?' She sneered. 'An animal.'

She pushed me away and began plucking at her gown, hair and arms.

'I hate this. *Hate* it. This dirt, this skin, these bones, these innards. I want them gone, I want to be free of them!'

Just then we heard a screech from outside in the hall. News. Haralia thundered for the door.

THE HALL WAS full and eerily quiet. The injured were healing but the smell of smoke still hung in the air, sweetened with the tang of blood. I followed Haralia as she pushed through the crowd to the front, where she joined what remained of the Devoted. Each was like her, their faces and gowns blackened with soot.

In the centre of the hall was a slender white slab lit from above. It had the appearance of stone, but images and lights danced on its surface. Benedikt huddled over it while Caige paced behind.

'Is it working?' he said, hands on hips. 'Come on, boy, fix it.'

'I'm trying,' muttered Benedikt. 'I keep losing the signal.'

'What is happening?' said Haralia above the crowd's whispers. Benedikt looked up, as if only just realising they had company. His eyes darted around.

'Tell us,' said Haralia, some gentleness returning to her voice. The crowd hushed.

'We may have made contact,' said Benedikt.

A ripple of excitement ran through the room.

'What does that mean?' said Haralia. 'Was it a success? They made it?'

Benedikt nodded.

'Quite possibly.'

She covered her face, tears streaming from her eyes, as two of the Devoted pulled her into an embrace.

'Wait,' said Benedikt. 'I have something.'

He stroked a palm down one side of the slab, and the light above flickered out. In its place a mesh of blue beams appeared, quivering. There were pops and crackles of static, and the room fell to silence once again.

Hush. Nothing. Then a deep croak. A voice.

'ALL IS LIGHT. COME.'

Benedikt smiled, the crowd cheered and Haralia threw up her arms.

'It's Jakob! My love!'

'No,' said Benedikt. 'It's not Jakob, it's all of them. They are united.'

Breathless, Haralia ran to the slab.

'But Jakob is still there. Can we speak back?'

'Not yet, but we will.'

'ALL IS LIGHT,' repeated the voice. 'COME.'

As the room filled with more celebration, Haralia closed her eyes and lifted her face to the ceiling, hands clutched to her breast. I saw her lips move.

'All is light. All is light.'

Her voice grew louder, until the other Devoted heard them and turned. And one by one, they joined in, until soon all thirty of them were walking from the hall in a sombre procession, repeating the words with hands clasped to their breasts.

'All is light.'

'All is light.'

'All is light.'

And the crowd, with their heads bowed, murmured along.

I backed away, stumbling from the hall. This was not the first time I had heard those words.

– FORTY-FOUR –

HANNA'S FUNERAL WAS in winter. I remember the frost, the stillness, the quiet, as if the earth had stopped turning. We lit tall candles and did not move for a day, and nobody spoke. Then, as the sun rose on the second day, somebody stood up.

They said out loud those same words: 'All is light... all is light.'

We all joined in. At the time it seemed fitting and hopeful, for at last we could begin our task. But now it seemed ugly, this sickening chant of purpose that had meant one thing: the humans are gone, now we can move on.

To think of humans dying was to think of you dying.

I reached the crest of the hill and stopped. It was dark now, the horizon a thread of blue light, and down in Ertanea a candlelit circle had filled the gardens. Another circle surrounded them, hands clasped with staffs. Caige's guards. The mumbled chant seeped up the tree-lined hill, trying to seek me out.

The whole scene was ludicrous, like something from one of those books. Guards? Candles? Chanting? The insanity of it all made me heady, and I released a loud and unexpected laugh.

Well, if this was how things were going to be, then I wanted no part of it. I wanted to be rid of them, like Haralia of her skin, to be so far from their ill-made chant that I could no longer hear them, deep in the forest or even beneath that heaving, dark sea beyond.

I pulled the bottle of hurwein I still had beneath my cloak, and drank from it as I made my way home.

As I stumbled through the forest, swigging, my thoughts turned to Haralia. My sister. Who did she think she was anyway? What did *I* know about love? I knew more about the stuff than she ever had. I had you, Reed, my son, my boy. That was real love. I had cleaned you and fed you and stayed up half the night with you, and taught you and walked with you and all that business. How long was it now? Thirteen years, or something like that. That was love. That was real love.

Sex. That's what Haralia was talking about—not love, sex. Copulation, the rubbing of sensitive parts, the exchange of fluids and dark fumblings in smelly places. Fucking, not to put too finer point on it.

At the clearing that led to the Sundra's village, I stopped and swayed. Lights glimmered in Jorne's window.

Yes, Haralia was right. Fucking was something I knew little about. But we can soon sort that, I thought, draining the bottle and tossing it into a bush.

All you need is data.

Bang bang bang.

''S me,' I said. ''S Ima. Let me in.'

I heard footsteps and straightened my back as the door opened. Jorne was there and I gave him two slow blinks before attempting to float in, tripping on the frame as I went. Payha was there, and you too, both sitting at the table. Payha gave me a funny look.

'Oh,' I said. 'Hello. You're both here, I see. Isn't it past your bedtime?'

The room seemed to tilt and spin, never quite reaching its

apex. I leaned—quite casually, I thought—on a chair.

'It's only just dark,' you said, looking me up and down. 'Are you all right?'

'I am absolutely fine,' I said, far too loudly.

'What happened?' said Jorne. 'Is everyone all right?'

'Yep. They're all right. My sister's all right. Jakob, the wood chopper—' for some reason I mimed an axe, which made me snigger '—is all right. Everyone is all right. All is right… all is right… all is right…'

I took a long breath. The chair was not taking its job of supporting me at all seriously.

Payha and Jorne shared a look.

'Reed,' said Jorne. 'I need to talk to your mother alone.'

'Thassright,' I said. 'And I need to talk to your Jorne, I mean—ha—Jorne alone.'

You gave me a puzzled look. Payha took your arm.

'Come on, Reed,' she said. 'Let's go and make tea at my dwelling.'

'Good idea,' I said, stopping her as she passed, with a finger on her shoulder. 'And juss you remember what I said about *helping*, lady. Understand? Hmm?'

'Get some rest,' she replied. 'Good night, Jorne.' And you both left.

With the door closed, I fixed Jorne with what I imagined to be my most provocative look.

'Ima, what on earth is wrong with you.'

'Nothing, as I've said, I've told you, I'm fine. It's all fine.' I focussed on trying to control the room's spin, and when I could do no more I slid my clammy hand from the chair and sauntered, wobbling, towards him.

'Payha's right,' he said, looking fearful. 'You should get some rest.'

'Not tired,' I said, shedding my blanket. 'You?'

'Ima—'

Amid the drunken clamour in my head, I became aware of myself. I became aware of my body—the bits that go in, the bits that go out—and I moved them the way I remembered Haralia moving her hips for Jakob. As muscle and bone rubbed and rippled, I felt the hot breath of lust upon me. *So there it was,* I thought, *all this time, locked away, just ready to come out at the slightest sway.*

'I know what you want,' I said, some normality returning to my voice. The thrill of this new appetite was sobering me up. I was upon him now, could feel the warmth of his chest, smell the scent of the hair on his neck, feel his pulse as I drew near to his neck. 'It's what animals want. We're animals, you and me, animals.'

My mouth was wet with saliva. I opened it, heart thumping beneath my breast, and reaching a hand around his waist I drew him near and—'

'Ima.'

He pushed me away and held me by the shoulders.

'What?' I slurred, pulling free. 'I thought this is what you wanted.'

He gave me grim look and shook his head.

'Not like this. Now get some rest.'

With that he stormed out, leaving me alone in the kitchen.

The room's sudden silence scared me. I found another bottle of hurwein and stormed into the Room of Things to watch the quantum telescope, choosing a year and a place at random. By the time the first image appeared on the wall, I was asleep in the chair.

– FORTY-FIVE –

THERE WERE PEOPLE falling. Hundreds, thousands, millions, crashing from a cliff into a cold sea. Men, women, children, infants; old and young, pale and dark, they would not stop. Some were naked, with dark etchings visible upon their dirty skins. Others wore loin cloths and head-dresses, robes, armour, uniforms, suits, gowns of the most magnificent splendour, coat tails flapping, dusted wigs and jewellery spinning off into the gale.

They screamed as they fell, a terrible sound like woeful gulls, and each was devoured by the churning tide that waited below. I watched their endless plummet, unable to look away.

But my eyes were closed.

I opened them and sat up, finding myself on the pile of ancient cushions in the Room of Things. The projector was playing some empty scene of snow-swept tundra. No cliff, no people, no water. What had I been watching?

A dream, I realised, and not the usual spiralling fractals and coloured lights that accompanied my nocturnal processing, but a proper one like yours. My first.

My head was hazy, my throat dry. The events of the previous evening seeped back with the sour taste of hurwein on my tongue. The explosion, Haralia screaming in my face, the candlelit procession... *all is light, all is light*... but all was not light, all was not right, because I had come back here, had I not? I had come back here and I had... I had...

I took a deep breath—my lungs were like dry bellows—and went to get some water.

It was as I poured the second icy ladleful into my mouth and some semblance of moisture returned to my being that I remembered. Not the night before, but one almost nine years ago when you were five, and you had woken from a dream.

'They were falling,' you had said. 'All of them.'

I stared through Jorne's kitchen window at the mist-wreathed pines. Had I dreamed your dream?

Unlikely. More likely was that I had approximated a memory of your description of the dream. But why that particular one? Why not the great-bellied laughing fish, or the coloured animals, or the stalking figures?

Why had it taken so long for that approximation to appear?

What had triggered it?

The questions tumbled from me like the people themselves.

Why had I dreamed at all when I had never dreamed before?

Was it merely too much Hurwein?

Or the memory of Hanna's vigil?

Where were these questions coming from?

And what if nothing was as I had thought it was?

It hit me like the ice water hit my stomach—a rogue question hidden among the others, using them for camouflage.

I dropped the ladle. It hit the floor. Footsteps approached from outside, and the door opened. I turned.

'Ima.'

It was Jorne.

'Jorne, I think... I think something is wrong. What if—'

'Ima—'

'By the way, I am sorry for last night. I was not myself and I should not have behaved—'

'Ima, please—'

I paced the floor, ignoring his urgent face, lost in my own mumbled thoughts.

'Jorne, what if we're wrong about everything? What if things are not as we believe them to be, or were not as we believed them to have been? Is that possible? What if we had been lied to, you understand? What if they lied to us? I know it makes no sense, but... but nothing does right now and I don't know what else to think, it just feels like—'

'Ima, listen to me!'

I stopped short.

'What is it?'

'It's Reed. He's sick.'

'LET ME SEE him.'

I burst through Payha's door to find you sitting on her bed, pale-faced, clutching your chest.

'I woke up to him wheezing,' said Payha. 'He tried to stand, but he collapsed.'

I put my hand on your brow.

'He has no temperature. Reed, what happened?'

You looked up.

'I'm fine. I just have a sore chest. It's probably from when I fell off my board yesterday.'

You coughed, face creased with pain.

'What else? Your organs, are they functioning? Stools, urine? Are your orifices enflamed or leaking?'

'Honestly, I'm all right. It's like that time when I was little, remember? I'm probably just tired.'

You rested back on the bed and closed your eyes, still wheezing. I turned to Jorne.

'And where did *you* sleep?' I said.

He opened his palms.

'In my dwelling, as usual. Ima, what has gotten into you?'

'Nothing,' I said. 'Everything.'

I stormed outside. Jorne followed.

'It's come back,' I said. 'I can feel it.'

'You don't know that. We were in the sea yesterday. It was colder than usual, perhaps he caught something.'

'That's not possible. Just like it was not possible when he was little. I made sure of it, the council agreed, his immune system was to be boosted to prevent serious viruses from entering the ertian system.'

'Well, maybe it didn't work quite as expected. Perhaps there was a mistake.'

'No, no, I saw to it myself, I was there, I was extremely clear, I would not have made a mistake, I *could* not have...' I trailed off. 'Unless...'

'Unless what?'

'Benedikt.'

I made for the paddock.

'Ima, wait.'

'Look after him,' I said, untying Boron. There was no time for a saddle. 'Give him water, keep him warm.'

'Where are you going?'

I was already flying through the forest.

'What did you do?'

My voice filled the hall with the slam of the thrown-back doors. Benedikt looked up from the stone slab, along with the three engineers who were working with him.

'Ima,' he said, looking nervously at the other three as I stormed across the floor. 'To what do we owe—'

'What did you do?' I screamed at him.

The three engineers exchanged glances.

'Council member?' said one.

Benedikt paused.

'Leave us,' he said. 'It is quite all right. Go.'

They dropped their tools and hurried out, leaving us alone in the hall.

Benedikt's face darkened. 'What are you doing?'

I wanted to lunge at him, I wanted to hoist him from the ground and slam him against the wall. Never had I felt the urge for such violence.

'I want to know the truth,' I said.

'What truth?'

'You did something to my son.'

'Really? What did I do, Ima?'

'You sabotaged him.'

'How?'

'His gestation. Somehow you sabotaged his gestation. You made him smaller. You took out the steps I put in to ensure a stronger immune system, you made him susceptible, you made him weaker.'

'And why would I want to do that?'

'To make it harder for him, more difficult to prove his worth.'

He stretched his neck, pushing his face towards mine.

'Why?'

'Because you wanted him to fail!'

'No! Because I want him to succeed!'

We stood silently within the echo of his words until there was nothing to prove they had been spoken, and for a second I thought they may not have been.

'An easy life in a perfect world was no test,' he said.

'I don't understand.'

'I know you don't. That's why I had to help you.'

'You admit it? You sabotaged his design?'

Benedikt's eyes were wide. He swallowed, scanning the ground.

'It was my father's idea. "Time for a second chance, boy," he said. "Time to make up for your failures." At first I was going to refuse, but no, I thought, not this time…'

'What do you mean, *this time*?'

'…this time I would do what he asked, because it wouldn't do what he thought. It would backfire, work against him. He had no idea, my father, *no idea* what they were capable of. He never spent time with them like I did.'

He looked up, afraid.

'Benedikt, what are you talking about?'

'I didn't do as much as he asked. Just enough to make life a little more difficult for him. Don't you see, Ima? It had to be this way. You and I were born in clear tanks with clear minds and a clear purpose. Reed's species crawled from the mud into a world that wanted to kill them, with no idea how to live in it. Utopia is no place for them to prove themselves.'

I glared at him.

'He is sick, Benedikt. My son suffers.'

'It would have been far worse if it had not been me, Ima, believe me. My father would have seen to it.'

'How would you feel if it was your son? How would you feel if it was Lukas?'

He smiled and fixed me with that old look of resolve I knew so well, only this time it seemed to come from a different place. Perhaps it always had.

'Lukas will never be my son, not like Reed is yours. And it is not about me or you, Ima, it is about him. It's about them. It always was.'

He turned to the slab, running his hand over its surface.

'I have spent most of my life planning transcendence, five centuries planning our escape from this rock. We don't belong here, Ima, not in this place of beasts and hurricanes. But *they* do. This is where they thrive—in dark places, Ima. Dark places.'

I walked to the slab and faced him across it, our faces glowing in its misty light.

'What do you know about the rebellion?' I said.

He gave a tired laugh.

'*Rebellion.*'

'What happened?'

The smile fell.

'Not what you think.'

Somebody hammered on the door. I leaned across the slab.

'Tell me the truth, Benedikt.'

Benedikt glanced at the door. He spoke hurriedly.

'You won't find it here. Or help for Reed's condition.'

'Then where?'

The door burst open, and two tall vigil guards—Benedikt's brothers—stood in the doorway.

'Is everything all right?' said one. 'We were told there was a commotion.'

'Yes, thank you,' said Benedikt, smiling, but still looking at me. 'All is well.'

'You are required in the chambers, Benedikt.' The guard eyed me. 'At once.'

'As you wish,' Benedikt called back breezily. He gave me an urgent look and whispered. 'If you want the truth, I suggest you look in higher places.'

'Now, Benedikt,' barked his brother.

'Good bye, Ima.'

As he turned, there was a flash in his eye and he released a short, unusual breath. It was a screech, I realised, as he strode for the door. A whispered nanosecond of data meant for me.

It made no sense, but I had heard it.

BY THE TIME I had made it back to the Sundra, a slushy sleet had begun to tumble from the colourless sky. I jumped from Boron's saddle and burst through the door of Payha's dwelling. You and Jorne looked up from the table, where you were sitting. Payha was nowhere to be seen.

'Come on,' I said, grabbing some things—blankets, clothes, herring, two flasks of water. I did not think Payha would mind. 'Put on your boots, we're going.'

'What?' you said.

'Can you walk?'

'Yes, but where are we going?'

'A hike,' I said. 'You're always saying you want me to come with you, so that's what we're doing.'

'A hike?' said Jorne, standing up. 'Ima, what is going on?'

'We have to go, Reed and I. Now.' I pulled my pack tight. 'Quickly, Reed.'

Jorne followed me around the room as I rushed between cupboards.

'Ima, what is wrong? Talk to me.'

'Nothing is wrong, we just need to go.'

'Let me come with you, then.'

'No. You stay. Reed, please.'

You were looking glumly down at the boots I had just hurled at your feet.

'I don't understand. Why do we have to go now?'

'Just pull on your boots. Oh, for… come here.'

I dropped to my knees and yanked the boots over your stockinged feet as I had done when you were seven.

'Ow!'

'Hold still. There. Now come on, quickly.'

I pulled you by the hand outside, where the sleet had thickened into snow.

'Ima!' yelled Jorne, as I mounted Boron and pulled you up on the saddle behind me. Gripping Boron's reins, I looked down at Jorne, mouth open, shaking his head.

'Please, Jorne,' I said. 'Whatever you do, do not follow me.'

With that, I turned and kicked, and Boron galloped into the hills beyond the Sundra, beyond Fane, beyond Ertanea and the furthest reaches of your expeditions—beyond everything you had ever known.

– FORTY-SIX –

I WOULD TELL you everything. I would take you somewhere away from danger, away from Fane, Ertanea and everywhere in between, sit you down beneath a quiet sky and tell you everything. I would cast off the lie. All I had to do was find the right place.

Boron plodded on through snow-drifts to the summit of our third hill, and Ertanea eventually became a speck disappearing in the clouds. You had not spoken since we had left. You were confused, and still weary from your episode.

'Ima?' you said at last.

'Yes?'

'Where are we going?'

There was no longer any question in my mind about the conspiracy against you, or the madness that had gripped my species.

But I still had other questions.

What lies had been fed to me in my gestation tank?

What had happened during the uprising?

What had Benedikt done?

I suggest you look in higher places, Benedikt had said. So that was exactly what I would do.

I nodded ahead.

'To those mountains.'

'What for?'

'To find out why somebody lives there.'

WE PICKED OUR way down past caves and through tall pine forests until we came out upon flatter ground surrounding a lake. The sky was clear and blue, and snow lay in clumps around the water's edge.

I could look after you in a place like this, I thought. *Away from the world, where we would fish and hunt and write, and you could do all the drawings you liked.*

It was an impossible thought, but I clung to it nonetheless, as you clung to my back in the cold.

That night we sheltered in a clearing beneath a purple-flowered bush. I made a fire and we ate the herring, then curled up in our blankets by the embers and watched our circle of light retreat from the snow.

You watched the flames intently.

'Last night,' you said. 'You were behaving strangely. What was wrong with you?'

It seemed longer than twenty-four hours since my disgrace in Jorne's dwelling.

'I was—'

'Was it because of that thing you drink?'

I was going to say tired.

'Yes. I had a bit too much, I'm afraid.'

'Why do you drink it?'

I searched deep in the fire for an answer.

'Because it makes life easier to cope with for a while. It helps me forget.'

'What do you want to forget?'

I looked at your shining orange face. *Nothing*, I realised.

'You don't need to worry,' I said. 'I'm not going to drink it anymore.'

At this you lay back upon the ground, and I took off my blanket and put it over yours.

'You'll be cold,' you said.

'Don't worry about me.'

I lay down with my arm around you.

Later, I woke to find the blanket returned, and tucked beneath me as it had been beneath you. I pulled you close and slept more deeply than I had done in a hundred years.

I would tell you tomorrow, I thought.

IN THE MORNING my eyes snapped open and I jumped to my feet. Something was near. I left you sleeping and ran from the bush, along the bank and up onto a rocky promontory, from which I scanned the lake and the plain beyond it. The water's surface was calm and packed with mist. All was still.

Then I saw it.

A bright point drifted across the far shore and disappeared into a crowd of pine trees. A moment later it reappeared on the other side, hovered for a second, then resumed its path around the water's edge. It was unmistakable.

'What is it?'

I looked down from my vantage point to see you standing, rubbing your eyes and peering out across the lake. I jumped down, taking care to do so in human-sized steps, and kicked earth over the remains of our fire.

There did not seem any reason to lie further, since I felt we were sure to meet one at some stage.

'It's a lantern,' I said.

You frowned into the mist.

'How can you see that far?'

I threw the pack onto Boron's back and jumped atop.

'I was standing on a rock.'

'Can I see too?'

'No, there's no time. We have to go.'

'What's a lantern?'

'Something that looks for other things. Come on.'

'Is that one looking for us?'

'Possibly.'

'Why?'

'It doesn't matter, it won't find us.'

'How do you know?'

'Because they're not omniscient. Now come on.' I reached down and pulled you up. I calculated that it would be twenty minutes at least before the lantern reached our shore. That would give us time to get as far away from its quadrant as possible.

'What does omniscient mean?'

'It means something that knows everything.'

'Like you, you mean?'

I pulled on Boron's reins, trotting up past the promontory and aiming for beyond the hill.

'Believe me, Reed,' I said, 'I know far from everything.'

THOUGH I SCANNED the horizon constantly, there was no more sign of the lantern that day, and we were left in peace to roll over the terrain as it undulated between plain and hill, water and grass. As the sun fell—orange, I noticed, like an actual orange, and one which did indeed hang—I stopped near a dense wood and found a place to camp beside a wide stretch of river between two craggy cliffs. The water was banked by a long beach of pebbles and thin plates of ice. The snow had stopped, but tufts of it still clung to boulders, plants and the pines above.

I set a fire, filled our flasks and we sat, drinking the icy water and eating the last of our herring.

'I'm still hungry,' you said, as you chewed the last morsel. 'Can we catch something else?'

'There are no herring in these waters,' I replied, surveying the river's deep undercurrent for signs of life. 'The ones we eat are in the sea.'

You looked at me the way I had once looked at you, your infant face smothered in food.

'I wasn't talking about herring.'

– FORTY-SEVEN –

I WAS STILL getting used to this idea of meat. Aside from fish, the erta did not tend to eat it. This is because mammalian and ovarian species are generally high in the food chain and therefore have already extracted much of the energy from its source—the Earth. To add another layer of extraction to this process is simply inefficient use of resources. Even I know that, and I am no biologist.

Meat, however, is full of protein, and it was a cold night, so our choices were somewhat limited.

'Stay here,' I said.

'Where are you going?'

'Into the forest.'

'To hunt?' You stood up. 'I feel much better. Let me come.'

'No, stay here. I will not be gone long.'

'But I didn't know you could hunt.'

'Of course I can.'

Lies.

'I want to see. Let me help.'

'No, not this time.'

'Why not?'

'Because I need you to look after the fire.' Lies. Endless lies.

'Please, Reed, stay here, all right?'

You sighed and hung your head.

'Fine.'

I left you moping by the fire, took a breath and entered the forest.

It did not take me long to find life. Half a kilometre from the edge, the silence began to prickle with the shuffle and snap of bracken and branches. It was dark, of course, and although the ertian visual system is excellent at seeing over long distances, it is not infrared. I stood quite still and shut my eyes, allowing myself to be surrounded by the million different sounds, each of which told a story about the things which had produced it. Soon, a picture formed; a three-dimensional dome of movement with me at its centre.

I was near a nest of insects—ants, I presumed—a troop of which were carrying leaves and bug meat from a tree south east of where I stood. Rodents of various shapes and sizes scurried upon the forest floor, darting down holes and diving into stumps to hide from the two—no, there were three—owls which had just landed high in the branches above.

Rodents were no use. More interesting was the sound of four slow, heavy impressions repeating themselves on the ground, just under 150 metres to my left. It was a deer, light in both weight and scent—a female. It had stopped, sensing me, perhaps. I would approach it with stealth. It would bolt before I reached it, but its speed would be no match and I would leap upon its back. With a single sharp twist its neck would be broken and it would fall, dead, beneath me.

Gutting might provide a challenge. I had no blade, nor expertise in Cervidaen anatomy. And how could I explain to you that your mother had single-handedly tackled a deer? Not to mention carried it back for half a kilometre upon her shoulders.

Perhaps it would be a means of explaining the truth, I thought, with a heave of my stomach. Another day had passed, I realised, and I still had not told you.

I stood there, ruminating upon this, and was just about to make my move upon the deer when another sound entered the picture. It was lighter, heavier than the rodents and ants, and closer than anything. I opened my eyes and saw two smaller ones staring back at me from a low-hanging branch. Its nose twitched. A squirrel.

It watched me. I watched it. I focussed on the muscles in my legs. Seeming to sense this, it stopped twitching its nose and braced itself. But it was too late; I had already sprung and caught it in both hands. Life scattered from me in an explosion of little legs and wings, and what was left struggled and scratched between my fingers. It was fat with nuts. With a squeeze and a squeak, it stopped and hung, still from my hand.

I EMERGED FROM the forest to find the fire roaring stronger than I had left it.

'Well done,' I said, and held up the squirrel in triumph. 'Now, look what I caught us.'

I stopped. You were sitting by the flames with a knife in your hand, which you were using to gut three animals. They were larger and fatter than my squirrel, and the blade glinted as it turned expertly in your hand.

I dropped the squirrel to my side.

'Oh,' you said, glancing up at it. 'Thanks. Put that one there.'

I placed my scrawny offering next to yours.

'How did you get them?' I asked.

'Simple trap. Jorne showed me. It wasn't hard, you know, that forest is absolutely bursting with life. They virtually jumped in.'

'I see,' I said, sitting down. 'And did Jorne give you that knife as well?'

'No, but he showed me how to make it. We constructed a forge.'

I wrapped my arms around my knees. At my silence, you glanced up and paused your vivisection.

'Don't worry, yours is good too. Here—' you held up the knife '—do you want to try?'

UNDER YOUR DIRECTION I gutted the creature—a hare—whose anatomy was relatively easy to decipher. After a few strategic cuts down its abdomen, it seemed to offer itself and I pulled strips of muscle from its flanks, which you told me to lay upon a stone by the fire. It soon began to sizzle, filling the air with gamey steam.

You took a deep breath and closed your eyes.

'Smells good, doesn't it.'

I had to agree that it did.

We ate the hare and then my squirrel (it did not last long) and kept the rest of the meat for the next morning, sealed in my bag against predators. Then we curled up in our blankets. As the fire died, the stars revealed themselves, and whirled above as I held you close. Jupiter was visible, and for a second I remembered the night you were born, walking the steps from the Halls with you in my arms and spotting that distant constellation I would gaze at when I had more time.

More time. I thought I would have some. We erta are rarely wrong, but when we are it is usually with some profundity.

I looked for it again and found it, eight years of celestial shift now rendering it as a dim cluster south west of Orion. I was, I realised, no longer quite so interested in it.

'I miss home,' you said. I looked down from the sky, swapping ancient starlight for your new reflection.

'We have only been gone a day or so.'

'I know, but I miss it.'

'What do you miss?'

'Jorne, Payha, Sundra, my guitar, surfing.'

The sound of Haralia's bitter rant played in my ears.

They all hate him. Even pretty Zadie.

'What about school?'

You hesitated.

'Yes, school too.'

'Your friends.'

'Yes. I miss my friends. Do you miss Jorne when we're away?'

'What do you mean?'

You withdrew, embarrassed.

'I just thought... Never mind.'

'Reed?'

'Yes?'

I felt a nauseous swell at the cavern of truth beneath us.

'You should get some rest.'

We settled down, listening to the fire and the forest still crackling, and slept upon our blankets of lies.

There was always tomorrow.

As I HAVE said, ertian biology is far superior to that of humans. Nevertheless, I had never tried meat before and I was kept awake by the struggle going on inside my intestine as it processed the new material.

But you did not stir; your body had accepted it without question. I kept to fish from then on.

We rode for two more days. On the second we woke early in

a frost and I quickly made a fire to warm you up. I made tea, or some version of it, from a variety of herbs which I boiled in a stone flask of water. This we accompanied with some meat from the previous evening's salmon—caught at a fast-flowing weir after waiting patiently for a bear to finish its own attempt—and we left our camp before the dawn had fully shaken night from the day.

Still I did not tell you.

You wearied. I sensed the tightness in your chest by the way you clung to me, and said little as Boron carried us on.

As the sun breached the summits towards which we were heading, you fell asleep. We came across a bush-lined glade in which two bovine animals stood, stone still. I pulled Boron to a halt and watched them, flanks steaming in the slow warmth. We did not move, those beasts and I. Not even our eyes. We stood that way for almost an hour.

They were like the three horses in that poem I had read, and I realised now what the poem was about. It was not merely about remembering three horses; it was about time passing, things changing and not changing at the same time.

So much had changed. But soon, perhaps nothing would. Would transcendence be like this, a single moment stretched out for eternity?

Eternity. I shuddered at the word, and one of the animals snorted and bowed its head as if in agreement. An eternity without you would stretch out and disappear.

The breaths of your sleep continued to draw out behind me.

Still I did not tell you.

– FORTY-EIGHT –

You woke up as the land flattened, and we talked. We spoke nothing of home, Jorne and your friends, only about the country through which we were moving. You had no questions, just remarks about the wildlife, and the way they moved, sounded, and smelled. And, sometimes, tasted.

Then, as we met the hills once again and Boron led us up steeper and more treacherous paths, your questions returned.

'Where are we going? Why is it so steep? It's getting colder. Are we there yet?'

The questions repeated, again and again, until finally I pulled on Boron's reins.

'Are we—'

'Yes,' I said. 'We are here.'

We were on a precipice that fell away into a steep slope. Having dismounted Boron, I tied him to the trunk of a squat tree sprouting from the mountain.

'Stay here,' I said. 'Do not move from this spot. Do not go near the edge. Do you understand? Look after Boron and stay next to him for warmth.'

You nodded uncertainly.

'Where are you going?'

I looked up at the wall above the precipice, in which there was an opening.

'I have to visit somebody,' I said.

Through the opening was a set of steep stone steps. I knew they would be there for I had walked them before, a long time ago.

IT IS COLD *and I am afraid; the very first and last time I will remember feeling such things for five hundred years. Lights flicker as we are led, my siblings and I, along the corridors Dr Nyström has built into the mountain. I glance at the others as we hurry in silence behind David the laboratory technician, furiously studying his clipboard, flanked by our parents.*

Faces flit by in the blue fluorescent light, and I catch Haralia's eye. She seems calm, composed, her hands folded before her. She smiles with excitement.

I turn to my mother, who walks briskly to my left.

'Mother, why am I shivering?'

Her glance is puzzled, but she forces a smile.

'It will pass,' she says. Her tone is uncertain. 'Keep walking, child.'

I do so, but it does not pass. Not immediately; first it gets worse. I hold up a hand in the stuttering light and focus all my will upon keeping it still, but the more I try the more it shakes. Perspiration streams from my fingers, and I close them, hiding both hands beneath my robe and looking anxiously ahead and behind. None of my siblings is experiencing this. They each walk with a confident stride, certain of their direction, certain of their purpose.

My insides heave; even my organs are shaking, and my mind... my mind is awash, churning with questions like weed in a riptide. Gone is the firm conviction I had felt as I stepped from

my birthing tank, gone is the focus, the awe at the speed with which I was able to see and process the world. Now there is only confusion, panic, question.

I turn to my mother.

'What must I do?' My voice trembles like my hands and the light. She ignores me. 'Mother, what must...'

'It will pass,' she asserts through gritted teeth. My head spins, but I can tell that, whatever this is, it should not have to pass. It should not be here in the first place. Something is wrong with me.

'Mother, please...'

Her jaw tightens and she calls for David, who circles back. Still walking, they confer. I struggle to hear or read the words upon their lips, but at last he looks up at me, sweat upon his top lip. He fumbles in his belt—we are walking quickly and there is not much space—and pulls out a large syringe. Before I know it, he has stabbed it into my neck. I cry out, but the sound is only in my head. It is the sound of something separating, departing, falling. Ice crawls down my spine and up into my head, and I have the sense of crystals forming. My thoughts slow and freeze, the whole hot mess brought to a standstill in an instant by the mixture in David's syringe, at the heart of which is a chemical compound I find myself analysing with the assistance of the nano mites in my blood. By the time it is understood, my hands have stopped shaking and my thoughts are clear, free of question. My eyes sharpen, my nerve-endings tighten. I forget the syringe, or what it was, or why I might have had to have it. No need for any more questions. In their place I breathe long, pure breaths of cold air.

We are nearing the end of the corridor. Two figures stand beside a door. The first is a short, slight woman in a white coat, with blonde hair and light-rimmed glasses. Dr Nyström. The second is much taller, with bright green eyes and waist-length silver hair, draped in a deep blue cloak. I cannot place the gender. It is Oonagh.

They watch us as we pass. Then the door opens and a blast of warm, stale air greets us. A range of dry and ragged mountains stretches out before us. There should be snow on their summits, but there is not. There should be pine forests at their foothills, but instead there is scrub and swathes of broken, colourless wood. There should be water, but the rivers and lakes are dry. The sky above is heavy and baking. We cannot see the sun.

There are helicopters beneath us, waiting. In single file we descend the stone staircase carved into the mountain, and with every step I feel the last remnants of panic fall from me. By the time I reach the bottom I am as I should be, and as I will be for the rest of my existence.

THE MOUNTAIN TRIGGERED this memory; it had never returned before. Whether this was one of the intended effects of the concoction David had skewered my neck with in those first hours of my life, or whether my mind, in its fresh clarity, had elected to discard the memory as useless, I do not know. But I do know that it came back to me in full as I retraced my steps up the mountain and pushed the door inwards, then walked along the dank corridor no longer flickering with fluorescent light, following it round with my fingertips until I saw a door rimmed with orange light, towards which I walked and, carefully, opened.

The room was square-shaped, large and high-ceilinged. Most of it was in darkness, and the only source of light was a small fire burning at a hearth in the far corner. In an armchair facing the fire sat a hunched figure. It turned at the door's creak.

'Who's there?' said Oonagh.

– FORTY-NINE –

'BENEDIKT? IS THAT you?'

With the aid of a stick, Oonagh stood and hobbled across the room.

Two bright eyes emerged from the shadows and squinted at me in the corridor's meagre light. They were arctic green.

'You're not Benedikt. It's usually Benedikt. He sometimes brings me fish.' The eyes drifted from their scrutiny of my features. 'I miss fish.'

Oonagh gave three rattling breaths. Then the eyes snapped back.

'No, Benedikt has not been for some time. In fact, you are the first person to visit for almost fifteen years. Which one are you?'

I stared down at the withered figure, trying to equate it with the one I had last seen almost five centuries before. The face that had been so fine-featured and bold was now drawn with a thousand deep lines, and the waist-length hair was now a mere cluster of wisps hovering above a liver-spotted scalp.

The stick thumped twice upon the concrete floor.

'Come on, speak, girl.'

'I am Ima,' I said.

The eyes narrowed, remembering.

'Kai's daughter, yes. You're the one who had to be injected.'

The gaze drifted once again, the same place where memories of fish resided. 'I warned her, but she wouldn't listen to me. None of them would listen.'

More rattling breaths, followed by a frown.

'How did you evade my lanterns?'

'I saw one, but it did not see—' I almost said *we* '—me.'

'You were lucky.'

'I am sorry. But I need to speak with you.'

Oonagh looked me up and down.

'Then you had better come in.'

I FOLLOWED OONAGH back to the fire, where a bowl of murky brown soup sat steaming on the arm of the chair.

'I was just eating, would you like some?'

'What is it?'

'Birds, mostly. I put up mesh in the trees. Sometimes I catch a rabbit or two if I am feeling sprightly. Which isn't very often these days.'

I shook my head, remembering the squirrel.

'Meat does not agree with me.'

'That's right, you eat that dreadful algae, don't you?'

'Broth, yes. Fish and vegetables too.'

Oonagh grunted and picked up a stone goblet by the chair, thrusting it at me.

'Something to drink, then?'

I reeled from the acrid fumes. Oonagh grinned.

'They would have called it moonshine once. Fermented juniper. And other bits and pieces. Try some, go on.'

'No, thank you.'

'Are you sure? It makes you feel good, helps you... *loosen your grip* a little.'

'Yes, well, I'm afraid I have loosened my grip a little too much of late. Do you have tea?'

With a look of disappointment, Oonagh replaced the goblet and hobbled to the fire, where a small pot bubbled. There was the clank and scoop of a ladle, rummaging noises, the floral scent of leaves being pinched and broken and stirred. Then Oonagh returned with a squat cup for me, and we sat by the fire, the soup uneaten.

The tea was surprisingly good, and for a while I lost myself in that dizzy place halfway between scent and taste, thinking of that hot day with Greye in India, and the folded hands of Roop, and of how much I missed simply sitting like this with nothing but tea and memories that did not matter.

Suddenly Oonagh frowned.

'Why do you watch me like that?'

I straightened my neck.

'Are you male or female?' The words came before I could stop them, and I held a hand to my mouth before any more could escape.

Oonagh's creased face opened in surprise.

'My goodness.'

'I am sorry, I did not mean to be rude.'

I was relieved to see a smile.

'The truth is it has been some time since even I considered it. I believe it was always something of a grey area.' Oonagh blinked, considering the question, then lifted the hem of the threadbare cloak sprawled over the chair. After a glumly raised eyebrow, the cloak was allowed to fall back into place.

'Still a grey area. Female is my best bet.'

She picked up her goblet and slurped from it, a single gulp disrupting the frantic rasp of her breath. Once she had swallowed she gave three dry, seal-like coughs and settled in her chair, gazing back at me. A kindness softened her face.

'Now, do you have any other questions about my appearance?'

'You are not well,' I said. 'What is wrong with you?'

'Cancer, child.'

I frowned.

'But I have had cancer four times. Why does your body not reject it?'

She peered down at her torso.

'It tries, but the bastard thing keeps returning. No matter how many times my body kills it, each time it just seems to come back stronger. Things are not the same in there as they used to be. It appears death will no longer be quelled.' She looked up. 'But I sense you're not here to talk about my health, are you?'

'No.'

'Then what?'

'Things are not the same out there either, Oonagh.'

She raised one tufted eyebrow and worked her jaw. Her eyes glazed, looking through me, until finally she nodded gravely.

'Let me guess,' she said. 'Disagreement? Argument? Deceit?'

'And more besides.'

'Then I must assume our work is done.'

'Surely you knew.'

She gave a dry laugh.

'I told you, I haven't had a visitor for fifteen years, and besides nobody tells me anything anyway.' She sighed and looked into the flames. 'No, it is as Elise feared it would happen.'

'Elise—you mean Dr Nyström?'

'Of course.'

'What was it she feared?'

'You are aware that our *improvements*'—the word was

spoken as if it was being held up for inspection—'over humans are as much about what was taken away as what was given?'

'Yes. Certain traits were muted.'

She gave a half-smile.

'Yes, I like that word. We are just as much a muting as we are a mutation. Well, Elise's fear was that these muted qualities might only last for as long as they were required. She believed that there was nothing to prevent them from returning, once the erta had fulfilled their—'

'Purpose.'

Oonagh turned from the fire. 'Was she right?'

'That would account for it.'

'Then death will not be quelled, and neither too will life. Why are you here, Ima? Why do you ask these questions?'

I hesitated. I did not want to tell her about you, not yet, for I was still not sure I trusted her any more than I trusted them.

'I am here because I believe I have been lied to. And I am asking you these questions because I want to know the truth.'

'Then why not ask your mother?'

'I cannot.'

'Yes.' Her eyes flicked around me like insects. 'The truth is a luxury few children receive from their parents.'

I looked away at this, exposed. Suddenly all I could think of was you alone outside in the blizzard. How long would it be before a lantern found you?

'I should not have come, I am sorry.'

I stood and hurried for the door.

'You're nothing like her, you know.'

I froze midway across the room. Turning, I saw Oonagh's frail silhouette standing against the fire.

'What?'

She walked towards me and stood, resting upon her stick.

'Kai, your mother. You're oceans apart. Mind you, that should come as no surprise. She was never like me either; I made sure of it.'

'What do you mean?'

She looked away, her expression suddenly haunted by a memory.

'I only wanted to please her, to help her.' She fumbled with her stick. 'I never thought... never expected that they would... You have to understand...'

'Oonagh, please, tell me what happened.'

She stopped and looked up, fingers folding and unfolding over her stick. Finally she gave me a glum nod.

'Follow me.'

OONAGH LED ME to a far corner, where she pulled a lamp from the wall—an ancient gas-powered contraption that spluttered and roared when she lit it—and held it above a dusty table strewn with papers. She rummaged among them, finally pulling out a small square of paper which she held to the light.

'Have you ever seen one of these?' she said. 'It's a photograph.'

I peered at the faded image. It was of three humans—a male and female adult and a female child. They were smiling, happy, standing in sunlight at the edge of a lake. The child was wearing sunglasses in the shape of stars, and presenting a small fish which I assume she had just caught. Clouds scudded across an endless blue sky.

'If you ever find yourself wondering how it is you exist,' said Oonagh, 'then here is your answer.'

'Who is it?'

I passed the photograph back to Oonagh, and she studied

it with affection.

'The child is Dr Elise Nyström, and those are her parents. It was taken in 2017, when she was eight.'

'I already know how Dr Nyström created us.'

'You know *how* she created us, but not why.' She turned the photograph this way and that, as if scanning it for new clues, or shadows she had not seen before. 'Elise used to say that you were never truly free until your parents were gone. Before then you were a perpetual child, forever chained to their bedtime stories, the fictions they had fed you in order to make sense of the world. Fictions about you, about them. About the world.' She glanced at me. 'If you were lucky enough to have such parents, of course. Many were not, sadly.'

She gazed back at the photograph.

'But Elise was. She had no brothers or sisters, just two happy parents who loved each other and her. They had a warm house with a constant flow of visitors and parties, they played with her as often as they could, gave her an excellent schooling but never spoiled her, took her on camping trips where they lay on their backs and talked into the night about stars and planets, fed her imagination day after day, and comforted her when she had nightmares. She grew up believing she was the luckiest girl on the planet, and that her parents were the best humanity had to offer. They would protect her from anything, keep her safe from harm. They could not possibly make mistakes.

'She told me she was twenty-two years old when she realised she was wrong. In 2031, climate change had already taken hold of the planet and was on the brink of being irreversible. Elise's upbringing had drawn her towards science, and she was already studying for her second PhD—Atmospheric Chemistry in Cambridge, the first being Cognitive Science and Cybernetics— when it dawned on her that the climate's turning point had been the year of her birth, 2009. This was the moment, she deduced, that humans had their last chance to change the tide, at least those of them who had any power to do anything about it, which included her parents. Both of them were wealthy. Both had made money from the energy industry, and had, together, formed a PR firm specialising in representing big Oil...' She paused and turned to me. 'You understand these terms?'

'Of course,' I said, without a thought.

'Interesting.'

I only knew them from what I had read in the Room of Things. Seconds dripped by, the lamp's roar compressing the silence.

'Elise realised that her parents could have changed the world,' I said, snatching up another photograph of Dr Nyström, now an adult. A young Oonagh stood beside her wearing a hesitant smile.

'Yes,' said Oonagh, taking the photograph tenderly, 'if they had wanted to. But instead they had her. Of course, no one in their right minds would blame them alone; they were just two of billions who did the same thing: ignored it all. But not everyone has children like Elise. She took it personally, and extremely seriously, and from that moment on dedicated her entire life to countering her parents' apathy. She wanted to make humanity better. That, quite literally, is why you and I exist. It wasn't to mend a broken planet; it was to mend a broken species.'

Oonagh took a long, wheezing breath, the exhale briefly distorting the lamplight.

'She wanted to change things for the better. But change—' she let the photograph drop '—change is always about balance. If you try too hard to put things right, you run the risk of making them wrong again.'

'Did she hate her parents because they lied to her?' I asked.

'No. They were still her parents, they had still given her a blissful childhood, wiped her bottom clean, bounced her on their knees and all that. They had never meant to be complicit in the planet's downfall. Still a good father, still a good mother.'

I looked at the photograph. Nyström was beaming with pride, one hand high on Oonagh's shoulder.

'And Nyström was *your* mother.'

'No,' she said, hobbling back to the fire. 'She was my god, and I loved her.'

– FIFTY –

'CAN YOU REMEMBER your birth?' said Oonagh, as I placed another log on her fire.

I took the seat opposite.

'All my life I thought I did, but I had forgotten something. I only remembered it when I walked those steps.'

'Tell me.'

I hesitated.

'It was a feeling. Panic. Fear. Shaking hands. My mind asking questions I could not put into words. And then…'

'The injection. I remember.'

'What was it?'

'A kind of long-term psychological sedative. Certain genetic traits weren't always dampened sufficiently during gestation. Sometimes, in fact… well, not all of your siblings survived, put it that way.'

'Why?'

'They were born like me. Insane.' She noticed my look of horror. 'Yes, insane. I felt the same things you did—fear, uncertainty, confusion—except I had not had the benefit of a gestational education like you, and there was no needle waiting for me. The world assaulted me the instant I opened my eyes;

light and shadow in impossible shapes, sounds, voices, smells—each one new and intangible. Trying to pick apart the sensory data of existence was an ordeal in itself, never mind when I did not know who I was or where I was, or why; never mind when that data included the rustles in leaves half a kilometre away, or the fluctuations in the heartbeat of my creator. And she stood patiently at my bed through it all, that hazy bright face coming in and out of focus, saying things to me. Her sounds of comfort were nothing more than a terrifying lunatic babble, but I clung to them. I clung to every word.

'I screamed for a week. Elise tried various combinations of tranquillisers, sedatives and beta-blockers, but all they did was put me to sleep; the world beneath my conscious mind was just as horrifying as the one above. My nightmares seemed to last for centuries. Pure, concentrated dread.

'In the end, she gave up with the injections and tried to calm me with her own voice. She held me tight when I spasmed, kept me fed and hydrated, changed me when I soiled myself, soothed me when I scratched at the walls. She stayed with me all day and all night, never once giving up on me, and finally one morning I woke from dreams that were a little less frightening to a world that was a little less impossible to make sense of.

'"Clock," I said, as the dark shape upon the wall came into focus. I was still shaking, still in panic, but I understood. Beneath its turmoil, my mind had been expanding through the various dimensions available to it, and the notion of time had become prevalent that day. I had a sense of this object as a crude measuring device, straight lines orbiting a central point, marking off quanta as they did. Elise jumped from where she lay upon the bed. "What did you say?" Her excitement pleased me, and I repeated my first word. Things became easier from then on.

'We spent some months in peace. She taught me, showed me art, films, music, all the wonders of human achievement. Mathematics and science, too, although my ability to extrapolate meant that I already knew much more than her by this point. Whenever I pleased her I felt such joy, and conversely, her disappointment brought great unhappiness. So when that message came—' Oonagh looked at me '—do you remember the message?'

I frowned.

'Of course.' I straightened my back. '*We issue a challenge, a call of hope, to any individual or—*'

Oonagh looked away in disinterest.

'Yes, that one. It was one of the many things the council made you and your siblings aware of during your gestation. One of the many things they taught you about the world.'

Something jarred—perhaps the extra microsecond before the word 'taught', or the way her lip flickered as she said it, or the way her eyes darted to the corner of the fire—but before I could address it, she continued.

'"We must make more of me",' I told her. '"But this time make them better".'

'The High Council?' I said, as she chewed her lip.

'You have to understand, my intentions were good. I wanted to save the world, save it for her, save it for us, but… but I went too far.'

'What happened?'

'I made them sharper—much sharper, and free from all distraction. Gone was the screaming, the terror, the inability to process the world—instead I imbued them with coping mechanisms as they gestated, and fed them information about the world which would allow them to understand it the instant they emerged from their tanks. Fast, focussed, clear; they were beautiful, my children, so free from all the things that held me back. That held humans back, in fact. All those distractions—fear, curiosity, imagination. Remorse.' Her eyes swelled, as if an unwanted image had appeared before them. She shut them from it, and turned to face me. 'I tried to teach them as Elise had taught me. I showed them all the paintings, played them the symphonies, ballads and folk songs, showed them what they had been born into. I even let Elise talk to them about her own ideas for saving the planet—gigantic space stations crawling with carbon sucking plants, solar-powered kites trawling the skies, genetically engineered super trees, geo-thermal powered deep-sea coolers—I loved all the delightfully hopeless things she said. But they grew bored. I could virtually hear the calculations and equations whirring around their heads, and the simple solution that was forming in their minds. Time, the thing that first human-made object I ever saw was designed to pick through, that was all what was required. Time and—'

'Human extinction.'

She blinked twice, slowly.

'I used to like how they talked. Their expressions, in particular. Here's one.' She leaned forward, brow furrowing. '"There is more than one way to skin a cat".'

The strange words hung and disappeared.

'Humanity never had to die, Ima. Never.'

'DID YOU DISAGREE with their intention?'

Oonagh sat back and grunted.

'By then it didn't matter what I said; they had already made their minds up and the plan was in motion. Caige was first with his little army of militia, including Benedikt, of course.'

'But Benedikt's expertise is in technology.'

'It is now, yes.'

'But that's not what he was bred for?'

'Let's just say he was a great disappointment to his father. Then Astrid brought her mathematicians into the world, then Kai, with a fleet of her own experts… including you.'

'What did you mean when you said you tried to warn her?'

'Well,' she huffed, 'your parameters seemed so extreme, Ima. I asked your mother why, and she told me she did not want you distracted the same way she had been. "Distracted?" I said, "That is ridiculous, Kai. I have seen you play a thousand games of chess for ten days straight without once looking up from the board." I laughed, but she did not. I saw anger in her, a kind of disgust as if I did not fully understand the gravity of things. "But I did," she said. "Eventually, I did look up from the board." We did not speak much after that.' She looked me up and down as if only just appraising me. 'Perhaps I was wrong though. You're different to what I would have expected, softer somehow, as if…'

Something clicked. With startling speed she sprang from the chair, knocking the goblet and bowl to the ground.

'You have a child,' she exclaimed, calculations continuing to blossom in her eyes. 'And not just any child either. A human!'

I hesitated.

'Tell me it is true,' she cried.

'It is,' I said. 'A boy.'

Her face shone with excitement.

'Then they are already being resurrected?'

'No.'

'Why not? That was our promise to them.'

'There was a disagreement. Some of the council believed humans would only make the same mistakes as before, if they were brought back.'

She threw back her head and released a loud, frustrated caw.

'That's what we were supposed to help them with! They may

not have been perfect, but since when was that a pre-requisite for existence? They needed guidance, not obliteration. That was what Elise had planned.'

Her eyes darted about the room. She was standing taller now, filled with life, and I saw something of the young being she had once been.

'You said "some of the council". Dare I ask who initiated the disagreement?'

'Caige.'

She scowled and shook her head.

'Caige… I don't know where I went wrong with that boy, I really don't. But wait, why does the child exist if they do not intend to resurrect?'

'He was supposed to be a test. His behaviour was to determine whether the question of human resurrection would be reconsidered.'

'A test?' she said. Her look of distaste became a frown, and she leaned towards me. 'It was *your* idea, wasn't it?'

'Yes,' I said, reeling from her approach, 'All I wanted was settle the dispute, but that was so long ago, and now…'

'The child has won you over.'

I nodded. 'Yes. Completely.'

With a smile, she straightened up.

'I assume that Caige has taken control of the council.'

'That is how it seems.'

'Then I suspect that the question has already been answered.'

'It may not matter now, in any case.'

'Why not?'

'He is ill.'

'In what way?'

'His heart is weak. It gives him pain, and I don't know how to take it away.'

Thinking, she touched a trembling finger to her chin and turned to a series of shelves beside the fire, upon which an array of bottles and urns stood in various degrees of decay. She ran a finger along them, removing dust as she went.

'What are they?'

'Potions, ointments, catalysts, what have you. Elise lived far longer than she should have done, thanks to me, and they've become quite useful of late, with my condition, you know. I would be dead by now were it not for... ah, here we are.' She lifted a vial from the shelf and inspected it. 'This is artificial blood, seeded with a version of the ertian immunomites. It is a muted culture; our own blood would kill a human, of course, but this—' she handed me the vial '—this might help him. It's my last one.'

'Don't you need it?'

'You reach a point when you're really only delaying the inevitable. It's dormant, of course, but a flame will activate it.'

'Thank you,' I said, pocketing the vial in my cloak.

'I hope it works.'

She sat down heavily upon her chair. The past few minutes' vigour had departed, leaving her hunched and wheezing once again.

'Oonagh, what happened?'

'What do you mean?'

'Between the second generation and the third. What happened.'

'What do you think happened?'

'I know what I was told. I know what we were fed in our gestation tanks. The humans rejected the erta's peaceful offer. They rebelled, looted, rioted, squabbled, killed...'

'There was no rebellion.' She looked glumly into the flames. 'There was no firestorm, no war, violence. Do you think they could have organised themselves to form an uprising against us? My *children* controlled everything—power, water, transport, weaponry, even the air they breathed. They protested, that is all. They stood up and asked for mercy.'

'How?'

'The facility where the virus was being manufactured—the place upon which you were told they had launched a nuclear attack— they set up a camp there. It was just a few at first, a handful of waifs and strays with banners and placards, but it grew. Within a month, over a hundred thousand people had gathered there, then two hundred thousand, then three hundred thousand. Before long the tents stretched out across the Mexican plain and the songs and fires went on all night. They never fought, they never shouted, they never screamed, they never once lifted a weapon. They just sang their songs and walked with their banners, and sat around their fires, sharing stories.

'Of course my son, *Caige*, didn't like this one bit, so he sent Benedikt to put a stop to it all. He had high hopes for his first-born son, you see, just like your mother had with you, and Benedikt wanted to please him like all children want to please their parents.'

'What was wrong with just leaving them in the camp?'

'The problem was they were blocking the cargo routes. Most of the facility was underground, and the integrity of the exit ports by which the carrier drones flew in and out were being compromised. What's more, they needed to expand, and they couldn't build with the camp in the way.'

'Then why didn't they build it somewhere else?'

Oonagh smiled. 'As I said: cats and their skins.'

'What did Benedikt do?'

'I believe he *intended* to deliver an ultimatum. He rolled in, armed to the teeth, and demanded to meet with the camp's leaders.

We heard nothing from him for two weeks, when he returned to the mountain. He had failed, but there was a difference in him too, I saw it.'

'What kind of a difference?'

'A little less pompous, a little less sure of himself. Softer, somehow—' she turned to me '—like you. He had spent time with them. That is all it took—time.'

I thought of Jorne on his boat, Payha with her cities, and you.

'What happened?'

'Well the council were furious, especially Caige. Things were well under way, their plan was in action, and they had not bargained for this annoyance. The vote to attack was almost unanimous. Only Greye refused his hand, but it did not matter by that point. Caige ordered Benedikt to launch the attack, but he refused. So Caige did it himself. They were killed—every man, woman and child.'

Oonagh stoked the fire's last embers with her stick.

'So they were peaceful at the end,' I said, watching the flames strain for life. 'They did not fight, even when they faced death.'

With one last poke at the crumbling ash, she stood and nodded at the cup of tea that still sat beside my chair.

'The hotter the water, the stronger the tea,' she said. 'That's another expression I used to like.'

I picked up the cup and drank from it. It was cold.

'Why were we lied to?' I said.

'Everyone needs a myth to live by, a fiction to make the world all right. That was yours.'

'They banished you here, didn't they? To keep you from spreading the truth. Those lanterns—they're not protecting you, they're guarding you.'

She nodded.

'Why did they not just—'

'Kill me? I sometimes wish they had, and I often think of doing so myself. But I lack the courage. Perhaps even they found it hard to kill their own mother...' She stopped short. 'Where is the child, Ima?'

'Outside, waiting.'

She gave the door a hopeful look.

'May I see him?'

'He knows nothing of this.'

She nodded, the glimmer of expectation leaving her eyes.

'You should talk to Greye,' she said. 'You can trust him, he will be able to... what is it, child?'

'They didn't tell you?'

'Tell me what? I told you, nobody has been to see me for fifteen years. What is it?'

'Oonagh, I am sorry, but Greye is dead.'

She seemed to crumple into her chair.

'Greye? My son?'

'It was in the hurricane. I am sorry.'

She looked around the dusty floor, eyes glistening.

'Do you care for your child?' she said.

'Yes, more than anything.'

A fierce wind howled outside.

'Then you need to get him to safety.'

I was about to speak when both of us turned to the door. There had been a noise far away.

'It's a lantern,' she said. Your voice, and Boron's terrified whinny floated in from outside. 'Go. Go now.'

But I was already gone, through the door now and sprinting along the corridor, bursting out onto the steps. The blue sky I had left you beneath had been taken over by a mass of cloud, and a blizzard engulfed me as I tumbled down the stone steps.

– FIFTY-ONE –

'Ima!'

You struggled with Boron's reins in a cloud of swirling snow, trying to calm him. A light hovered, flashing in the gloom above the drop.

'Reed, let go!'

You released the reins and Boron reeled, towering above us with bulging eyes and front legs flailing. I stepped in front, pushing you back against the rock. Before us was the lantern—a glowing mesh with a single eye swapping its attention between me and the horse. I stared at it, waiting for its move.

The eye flicked left and right. Boron panted and ducked his head, stepping this way and that as he responded to my clucks and shushes. But the panic overcame him again and he rose up on his hind legs, releasing a huge bray. The lantern shot towards him.

I leaped, smashing the lantern with my right fist as it passed and sending it spiralling in a wayward arc from the mountainside. A shock of energy ran through my body and I clutched my arm to my chest, just as Boron fell backwards.

'No!' you called out, diving for him. But I dived first and caught him as he slipped from the precipice, bracing myself against a boulder.

I stood there, holding the weight of a dangling male horse in my two arms, I looked across. You stared back, mouth agape.

'Reed,' I said. 'There's nothing to worry about.'

You shook your head.

Boron spluttered beneath me. I was holding him by his neck, and though my grip was firm his coat was slick with moisture. There was only so much longer I could keep my horse from falling.

'There are some things I need to discuss with you. But right now—'

Boron gave a dreadful whinny. He was almost gone.

'Just... don't be afraid, Reed,' I said, and heaved.

We stood there, the three of us on that windswept, snow-caked ledge. Boron seemed almost as bewildered as you, gulping great clouds of breath. I checked him for injury, ignoring your silent stare, and seeing nothing broken or torn, fixed his saddle and mounted him.

A thousand questions burned in your eyes.

I opened my mouth—to say all the things that needed to be said and more—but just then my ears pricked at a distant whine. Two more lanterns were approaching from the east.

'Come on, we have to go.'

I pulled you on and glanced up the steps, at the top of which I saw Oonagh standing half-hidden behind the door, those wisps of hair trailing in the blizzard. As the lanterns drew near, I kicked the horse I had just pulled from death with my bare hands, and we galloped away.

Snow roared into us as we hit the first plain. I could see little, and was only able to direct Boron by following the terrain by memory, the details of which were significant enough to avoid obstacles. Boron responded well and obeyed without question, despite his recent trauma. He was a good horse.

The galloping of his hooves, the clank of the reins, the howl of the blizzard—the noise of our flight rendered conversation impossible, but for my occasional orders called back.

'Keep your head down.'

'Grip with your legs.'

'Hold on tight.'

Such simple words. Such a simple contract—I tell, you do. And even with all that had just happened you obeyed me. You kept your head down, you gripped with your legs, and you held on tighter than you ever had.

'Watch out.'

I saw a boulder ahead that had not been there when we had climbed that morning, and barely had time to pull Boron around it. He lost his footing and stumbled before righting himself and pushing on, but I noticed his pace was slowing. The lanterns were behind us now. I could feel their blazing heat.

I kicked Boron and he upped his pace, but he soon fell back, missing strides and tripping on loose rock. The two lanterns separated and flanked us, one on either side. You cried out as you spotted them, but instead of pushing yourself further into my back for comfort as I expected, I was surprised to feel you sit bolt upright on the saddle.

'Get away,' you yelled, swiping at them as if they were nothing more than troublesome flies.

'Reed, get down.'

'Go on, get away.'

I noticed that your fist was clenched, as mine had been when I dispatched the one upon the ledge. With one hand steadying yourself on my shoulder you threw wild punches left and right, face contorted, grunting. I looked down at my right hand, where new skin was still forming over its burned and ragged flesh. If one of your blows found its target, your hand would be vaporised.

Reaching back, I pulled you against me, constraining your movements. You cried out in protest and squirmed in my grip, heart furiously set upon destroying our pursuers and utterly convinced of your ability to do so. I did not know whether to wail or grin.

The lanterns closed in. One screeched a short binary report I decoded as a command to stop and state our business.

And I had a thought. Benedikt's screech—perhaps it was a code?

You had already seen me lift a horse that day so one more example of unusual behaviour was not going to tip the balance of your already precarious belief systems. Besides, who does not scream into a snowstorm when they are galloping from hurtling photon arrays?

I screeched what Benedikt had whispered into my ear.

It had no effect. So that was that.

We had to lose them somehow. I knew that we were moving near the limit of their speed, but Boron was fading with every step. We banked right, following the edge of an outcrop that led into a narrow gulley littered with rocks. There was no possible way he could negotiate the obstacles without losing even more pace, and the only other route available to us was a path leading up a sharp incline to the left.

Another loud screech from the lantern, repeated by its partner. Both had their eyes turned upon me, waiting for a response. They would already have been signalling our location back to Ertanea.

'Reed, hold onto me very tightly. Around my neck.'

'What are you going to do?'

'Just do it.'

I waited until your wrists had tightened beneath my chin.

'Now don't let go, do you hear me?'

I felt your head nod against mine, stroked Boron's neck and

whispered in his ear. Then I released his reins, braced myself against the stirrups and leaped.

We flew for a little longer than I had expected, and Boron stumbled safely to a trot and then stood at peace, panting in the mouth of the gulley, as the two lanterns looked up in apparent surprise. We landed heavily, but my legs were ready for the impact and I sprang up the bank with my hands behind me, keeping you close.

The lanterns pursued. In the sudden change of course and new terrain, one smashed into a pointed crag and wheeled away, flickering, before extinguishing itself entirely in the snow, but the second swerved and corrected its course, locking on and buzzing behind me.

I sprinted up the hill, faster than Boron, faster than I had ever run before, with strides so long I felt my tendons might snap, and impacts so hard I thought my bones would shatter. But they did not, and I flew up the hill with no plan, no plan at all, just to outrun the lantern and keep you safe upon my back, to travel onwards and never give up, not while you were still with me.

Every muscle screamed. My heart hammered, my veins bulged, my lungs threatened to explode. The machine of my body was reaching the limit of its endurance, and so too, I sensed, was the lantern. It stuttered and strained behind me as we reached the lip of the slope. This was not terrain I had seen before, but the blizzard was thinner this high up and I could see the ground across which I thundered. It was flat now, easier for me to cover, and I pushed ahead as the lantern struggled to keep up.

I thought we would make it. I thought we would lose the lantern and break through, do whatever it was that we would do next. I felt a thrill at this, not just at the possibility of success but at the unknown beyond. I had never realised, until that moment, how much freedom there was in uncertainty.

I smiled at this, and the sounds of the dwindling lantern. But the smile soon fell as I saw what was ahead: the path ran out, ending in a ravine. I scanned left and right. There was no way up, no way down, just a wide, empty space between the lip and the other side of the gulley. We would have to jump.

I tried to avoid the calculation, but my brain completed it nonetheless. The distance was too great. My muscles twitched with signals to stop, but they refused and I powered on. I would make it, regardless of the data.

Fate was not just an equation. Not while you were holding me.

So we hit the lip and I jumped. I jumped and I flew, legs wheeling, eyes upon the approaching edge, hands upon yours and my heart soaring as the balance of things tipped one way and the other, deciding upon our next moment—succeed or fail, land or fall. And as this cold calculation played out I somehow felt that it did not matter either way, not when you were near me, and I laughed into the blizzard at this. I laughed as my legs slowed, and the edge rose, and we missed it, and we fell, fell, fell.

– FIFTY-TWO –

I WAS IN a bed. The walls were stone. My mother's place. No curtain this time, no warmth. Just a shut square window with nothing outside but a heavy grey sky. My mother wore a thick green cloak, and watched me from her chair.

'Where is my son?' I said.

'The boy is fine,' she replied. 'You took the impact.'

'With Benedikt again?' I tried to hide the hope in my question, but her look told me that I should already know its answer.

'No. I have been caring for him.'

I turned back to the window.

'How long this time?'

'A little over two weeks.'

'I have no pain. You did not medicate me.'

'There seemed little point; you have asked all your questions, and apparently heard all your answers. We know you went to see Oonagh.'

'What you injected me with when I was born—it was an inhibitor, wasn't it?'

She regarded me coolly, as if through a lens.

'You were somewhat of an experiment, Ima. You were to fix the sky, to be one of our finest scientists, and for that you needed absolute clarity. So I pushed your envelope a little further than the others. I was never sure if you would work, and when you emerged my doubts grew worse. All that panic, all those questions. They had to be quelled, and it worked—for five centuries, at least.'

She neatened her cuffs, as if recalibrating.

'That's why I chose you to look after the human. Not your sister—' she rolled her eyes '—good gracious, all those fictitious emotions of hers, how she would like to believe they were real. No, not your sister or any of your other siblings, and certainly not Benedikt, of course. You. I thought if anyone could care for that thing without being... *infected* by its charms, it would be you.' She cocked her head. 'But apparently you have disappointed me.'

'You had no intention of resurrecting humanity.'

'Of course not. Caige and I had decided long before.'

'Then why let me proceed at all?'

She shrugged and brushed dust from her dress.

'It provided you with a distraction.'

'From what?'

'I told you, I know how much your purpose means to you. It keeps that busy little head of yours from asking difficult questions. But it wasn't just about you, Ima. After Greye's display in the council, we had to ensure you all believed the dispute was being dealt with rationally.'

A terrible thought struck me, and I sat up slowly.

'What happened to Greye?' I said.

My mother's eyes narrowed as she saw where my thoughts were leading me.

'You think I would kill my own brother? Well, child, now I know you really have lost your way. I told you, we are not monsters.'

I turned back to the window's dim square of light, seeking escape from my mother's frigid gaze.

'You lied to me. You lied to us all.'

'It wasn't a lie, it was a fiction in which you could serve your purpose to the best of your ability. All children are born into them. My own was that humanity was something to be saved.'

I turned.

'Oonagh?'

'How she loved them, with all their silly songs and pictures. She reminded us every day that *they* alone had created us. *They* were the reason we were here, and we had a duty to help them. I believed her at first, as every child does her mother. But then we went out into the world, and we saw the havoc they had wrought. All that chaos, all that lack of control. All the art in the world would be lost in one of their dreadful landfills, or drowned in the putrid sewage with which they flooded the seas.'

Her eyes turned to me.

'They were chaotic, unpredictable and pointless. Their equation simply could not be balanced, so they had to go—peacefully, of course.'

'Not all of them went peacefully. You killed the protesters at the viral laboratory. All of them, murdered.'

Her lips thinned.

'Such incidents were regrettable.'

'You mean there were more?'

'Yes,' she said, through gritted her teeth. 'Oonagh would not have known; we banished her long before. Ima, listen to me, I am your mother—'

'You are not my mother,' I said, throwing back the covers and getting shakily to my feet. 'You never raised me. I was fully grown when I was born. You never had to clean me or feed me or pace the floor all night trying to comfort me from a bad dream, or teach me how to walk or talk or how to stop soiling myself.'

'Really? You make it sound as if you simply sprang into being, child. Did you ever go to the gestation halls? Did you spend any time there when the fourth generation were growing? Or the fifth?'

'No, I was too busy.'

'In your *balloon*, yes. Far too busy up in the sky.' My mother stood and faced me from the end of the bed. 'Well, let me tell you, they were far from peaceful places.' She walked the length of the bed until we were face-to-face. 'You were worse than the rest. You found it more difficult to assimilate the cerebral growth, and the information with which you were being fed. You screamed, wriggled, writhed, choked, excreted, urinated, vomited, bawled and wailed into the night. Some of the others wanted to put an end to you, you know. They thought you had failed, that the parameters of my design had been too wild. But I never gave up. I believed in my design—I believed in *you*, Ima—so I stayed with you, night after night, doing everything I could to keep all those terrors at bay as you grew into the magnificent thing I knew you would be.'

She took a breath.

'So no, I may not have changed your nappies, or given you cuddles, or taken you for walks through the forests or bounced you on my knee, but I did bring you safely into the world and all the comfortable fictions with which I had furnished it, and I gave you a purpose, and guided you on your way. *That*, my dear—' she folded her hands '—makes me your mother.'

'That is not what being a mother is about.'

'Quite frankly I don't care what you think.'

'You don't care for anything.'

Her face shook with sudden rage.

'That is not true! I care for the well-being of my species, and for you, Ima, and yes, even for your misguided forest-dwelling friends. And I care for transcendence. We are all erta. That is why we must all depart together. One or nothing. All is light.'

I backed away, shaking.

'If you cared for me, then you would let me and Reed be. Let us live alone, somewhere I can continue to raise him, away from all this, away from all the lies.'

She looked me dead in the eye.

'I'm afraid it is a little late for that.'

A flush of dread filled my chest.

'What do you mean?'

'You have the answers to your questions, and now Reed has the answers to his. He knows, Ima. He knows everything.'

THE ROOM WAS small and lit by a single window, beneath which was a shelf of plants. You sat on a chair with arms crossed, looking at the skewed square of December light that had been thrown upon the floor. Hair fell over your face in curtains.

You did not look up when the door opened.

'When did you tell him?' I said, trembling.

'This morning,' replied my mother. 'I might have waited for you to explain, but he would not stop asking about what happened. You lifted a horse from a precipice, after all—we found it by the way—not to mention outrunning two lanterns with him on your back. I had to tell him in the end.'

'What did he say?'

'He has not spoken since.'

I tried to find my voice.

'Reed?' I said. 'Shall we go home?'

You remained as you were, unmoved by the sound of my voice, closed like a shell. Then with a sudden shuffle of feet, you stood and walked briskly to the door, pushing past me and outside.

We watched you disappear towards the gardens, head still down.

My mother rested a hand on my shoulder.

'Please,' she said, some gentleness returning. 'You must let it go. Try to find a focus, look to transcendence, forget about—'

'No,' I said, shaking off her hand. 'I cannot forget. He is my son and I must look after him.'

'You must do what you must do,' called my mother as I ran off through the corridors. 'But remember, Ima, the day is fast approaching when you will have to make a choice. One or nothing. An eternity of peace with your own kind, or a very short life with an animal.'

I CAUGHT UP with you in the square and stopped, keeping my distance. The vigil was still going on, and the twin circles of the Devoted and their guards had now been joined by a candlelit throng following the same murmured chant. Caige was with them. His great, hooded head looked up at your approach.

All is light, all is light.

You stood before them in slow flakes of snow, suspended, your breath disrupting the frost-heavy air.

I approached. My boots cracked thin puddle ice.

'Reed…'

You started at my voice and continued to walk, your eyes trained upon the circle. Some of the guards and candleholders looked up as you passed, and Caige tracked every step of your slow prowl.

'Come,' I whispered, 'let us go home where we can talk.'

I held out a hand, but you ignored me. Your jaw clenched and unclenched, and your eyes burned a fierce orange in the glow of the guards' torch light.

'Reed—'

Then you laughed. It was a raw, untethered sound, a single deep exhalation that contained nothing of the boy you had been. The chant ceased, heads turned, and hoods shuffled. Caige pulled back his hood and walked from the line, stopping before you like a bull before a rabbit.

'Witness this,' he said. 'While we prepare ourselves for our ascent to a higher realm, this human—this animal—cackles on the ground.' He turned to the silent throng. 'How could it have ended any other way?'

You stared up at him, trembling streams of steam escaping your nose.

'Well?' said Caige, turning back to you. 'What do you think?'

Suddenly your face creased, and with a raucous hack you spat at his feet, and ran for the trees.

'Reed, come back!' I cried.

Caige snorted with disgust. 'That's right, back to woods with you. Back with the beasts, where you belong. But you won't find safety there—your time is short, ape, your time is short!'

At the tree line I leaped ahead to block your path, but you continued, forcing me to walk backwards.

'We'll ride home together, all right? You, me and Boron, just like in the mountains. We can talk, and I can help you understand. All right?'

You stopped and glared.

'Am I free?' you said.

'What?'

'Am I free? I'm not a prisoner?'

'No, of course you're not a prisoner.'

'Then let me go.'

With that you pushed past me and fled into the forest, alone.

Behind me the vigil resumed its chant, corrupting the still air like oil in meltwater.

FIFTEEN YEARS

— FIFTY-THREE —

I HAD NO idea where you would go when I let you run into the trees that day. Perhaps you would go to Fane, the cradle of your childhood. Or perhaps you would take root in some cave, or flee the coast altogether. Or perhaps you would swim out to sea, or jump from some great height.

I tracked you through the forest, keeping my distance as I watched your aimless circles. Occasionally you would pause and look about, as if you had suddenly woken to an unfamiliar place, or sit down, or lean against a tree, or hold your head in your hands.

But eventually your expedition waned and you drifted toward the Sundra, as a child does toward sleep. I followed you into Jorne's dwelling.

He stood abruptly from the table. 'Reed—'

You stormed past him into the Room of Things and slammed the door shut.

'What happened?' he said. 'Where did you go? They wouldn't let me see you. I couldn't even get close. That vigil, it goes on day and night, nobody can get near—'

'He knows,' I said. And that was all.

I FELT A bitter relief at your wordless decision to stay with the Sundra, and chose not to question it. I was just glad to be as far away as possible from the events below.

They maintained the vigil for two years. Twice a day, fresh from sleep, a procession of candle-bearers would emerge from the halls and take the places of those in the square. It became a holy place, like those great citadels into which pilgrims had once swarmed. This is, in fact, what happened. Fane, Tokyo, Littleton, Sprük—all were abandoned and left to the wind, and one by one their inhabitants flocked to their capital, expanding the circle until the forest glowed with torchlight. They prepared food to feed the candle-bearers, and brought them water, and mumbled endlessly into the night.

All is light... all is light...

The trials grew more frequent until every month a procession lead from Ertanea to the Drift to watch the skyward streams of light, before returning like a line of ants to their nest, aflame.

This brought a nervousness to the Sundra, and they built three wooden towers from which to watch the vigil. As they had their shifts, so did we, and I took my turn like everyone else. The western tower granted the best view, and during the day you could see their faces clearly.

During one such shift I spotted two guards circling each other and realised that they were talking in the old fashion; without speech. We saw this more and more, until soon every conversation was thus—the erta had converged once again, and the silence was terrifying.

But not nearly as terrifying as yours.

You became a tripwire around which I crept.

Gone were the hunting trips, the fishing and the hiking—even your surfboard stood outside, unused. Instead you barricaded yourself in the Room of Things. It became a fetid place, and at night I would sneak in and attempt to freshen it while you slept, almost always finding the quantum telescope recordings whirring away on the wall.

One such night, as you snored fitfully from your nest of blankets in the corner—you had grown plump, I noticed, and pimples had appeared on your face—I decided to find out what you had been watching. I scrolled through the logs, replaying each place and time you had visited.

At first you had favoured war, hovering over the Somme, Stalingrad, Gettysburg, Teruel and Marston Moor, like some flesh-hungry raven. Then skirmishes drew your interest. You lurked in the abandoned French villages of World War II, the windswept Falkland hillsides forty years later, and the ancient turrets of Moorish castles against which enemy ladders shook.

Once you had grown tired of armed conflict, you moved into the cities. You liked them in the summer, it seemed, especially London, New York, and Bangkok, where the heat sent their inhabitants mad. You were searching for conflict—people getting in each other's way, arguing, and fighting with their fists. Eventually you watched only incidents in which two people were shouting in each other's faces, zooming in close to read their lips. You were trying to see what they were saying.

You returned to certain individuals, like a doctor who took the same seat on the bus every day and spent the journey standing if it was taken, even if there were other seats free. Or the young woman who screamed at her reflection every night before bed, but smiled throughout the day, and bought people coffee, and made them laugh with jokes. Or the farmer in Minnesota sharpening his machete with long, straight strokes, and a broad smile on his ruddy face.

THE NEXT DAY I found Jorne outside with your surfboard. He was applying wax made from a dead animal.

'Why do you maintain that thing?' I said. 'He no longer uses it.'

'He may do again one day. Besides, it is a welcome distraction.'

'From what?'

He stood up.

'We are expecting something.'

'From Ertanea?'

He nodded, inspecting the block of wax.

'There are trials every week now, more and more movement towards the Drift. They must be close to completion, and after that how long will it be? There are over 11,000 of them. How long will that take—a year? A year and a half? Everyone has gathered there but us, and they will want to change that, one way or the other. They will come for us.'

'What will you do?'

'You know what we will do. The question is, Ima, what will you do?'

I dropped my head.

'I can't see past the end of the day right now, let alone a month, or a year, or an eternity.'

'He still won't speak to you?'

'He won't even look at me.'

'Let me try,' said Jorne.

He did, and failed, and I took some selfish comfort in this. At least I wasn't the only one you hated.

MANY MONTHS WENT BY. It was a flat, dead time, full of uncertainty. Ertanea kept its vigil, the Sundra kept their watch, and you kept your silence.

One night I went into the room to find you gone. Thinking you had fled, I ran out into the square and was about to shout your name when I saw shadows in a window. It was Payha's place, and you were there next to her on the bed, talking by candlelight. I began to approach, but stopped, calculating that my intrusion would not end well.

I spent the night awake, and you returned just before dawn, whereupon you barricaded yourself in the room once again.

The next day I met Payha at the well.

'What did he say?'

She pulled the pump, giving me a guarded look.

'That is between Reed and I.'

'But I am his mother!'

She glanced up, as if I should reconsider those words, then continued to pump.

'I just want him to say something,' I said. 'Anything. He can shout at me for all I care, scream at me, hit me, tell me he hates me, I don't care, I just want to hear him talk again.'

Payha set down her pale.

'He is broken,' she said. 'Nothing makes sense to him. His entire existence, the whole universe and his place within it, all of it has been a lie. *You* have been a lie. He has no reason to talk to you.'

The words settled upon me like frost. I looked her over—her dark, cropped hair, the full lips and lashes, the eyes that were bigger than most, and darker, and further apart. Her fragrance was fresh and young, and I swore I could detect a hint of your own within it.

'Last night,' I said. 'What were you doing in there?'

Payha folded her arms and looked about. I grabbed her.

'Tell me,' I yelled.

She threw me off with a disgusted sneer.

'I was listening to him.'

I staggered away, breathless and adrift.

'I'm sorry, I just thought—'

'You thought wrong.'

She hoisted her pale and turned, but I grabbed her again.

'Tell me what he said to you. Please, Payha.'

'You don't want to know.'

'I may not want to, but I need to.'

After a moment's hesitation, she turned to face me fully.

'He said he wants to explode. He said it feels as if his life should never have happened, and every single memory brings more pain because it contains you or someone else who knew the truth while he didn't. He said he feels stupid and alone, and that he wants to take all those memories and set fire to them. And yes, Ima, he said that he hates you. I'm sorry, but it is as we said—this time would always come.'

With that she took her water and left.

'Is it not too late,' I called, sniffing back tears as I stumbled after her. 'To do the thing, you know, the thing that might help him, make him happy, give him some relief. You could do that, Payha, take away some of that frustration, perhaps that would be enough to bring him round, calm him down a little, enough for him to speak to me, that's all I want, Payha, a chance to speak, and maybe, he's an adult now after all and adults have certain needs that—'

'Ima, stop.' She spun on her heels with a brutal look. 'He is not an animal, and neither am I.'

My lip quivered. Two tears burst from my eyes, unannounced. And more followed in rivers I could not stop, and I burying my face in my hands. Payha embraced me.

'Remember what we talked about on the clifftop?' she said,

'His problems can't be solved by giving him what he wants, but by giving him what he needs.'

'Then what does he need?'

She released the embrace.

'To understand.'

'I can't explain if he won't even look at me.'

'He is coming back tonight. I will try to convince him to talk to you.'

'Thank you.'

'But Ima, please, do no not ask me to have sexual intercourse with your son again.'

A snort disrupted my sobs.

'I'm sorry.'

'If nothing else prohibited it, his hygiene would.'

YOU CONTINUED TO have your time with Payha, and your silhouettes were visible every night through her window. Occasionally I would pass her in the square and offer a hopeful look, but she would always return with a shake of the head. Your silence persisted like a mountain.

Then something broke it.

– FIFTY-FOUR –

SUMMER CAME EARLY, blazing. The ground baked, the well dried up, and we resorted to collecting our water from a forest spring. The days were parched and windless, the nights long and stifling. Moments of sleep became rare and shallow, like pools of water upon a dry ocean bed.

Insects infested the village. Flying ants, cockroaches, horseflies, crickets, and garish caterpillars with thick hairs that stung deep in the knuckle. They came in droves. It was as if even they could sense something was amiss, and were now gathering themselves, readying for the shift.

Spiders too, some as big as your palm that jumped if you happened upon them, crawled into the eaves and hunted after dark. The sleepless nights became filled with the sound of scuttles and snaps. Lives ending. Others being replenished.

The Room of Things grew ever more foul in the heat. Though you now refrained from shutting the window after I had opened it, the air allowed to enter was barely fresher than what was already inside. The spring flowers had perished in the unexpected heat, and many animals did not withstand the drought; the stench of death drifted up from the wood.

One afternoon I was hauling yet another cask of water from

the spring, but when I reached the square I stopped. Everyone was standing still, facing west, from which there was an eerie silence. The vigil's chant had ceased.

I deposited my cask and pushed through the crowd, finding Payha scanning the trees from one of the watchtowers. Her eyes were wide with excitement.

'What's happening?'

'They're walking. All of them. From Ertanea to the Drift.'

I ran up the steps and joined her. Sure enough, the vigil had stopped and the camps were being abandoned. The erta were making their way slowly towards the coast. There was a sluggishness to their movement that I had not noticed before, and I remembered Haralia's slurred speech and stagger the last time I had talked with her.

'They have drugged them,' I said. 'It's a sedative of some kind. It must be part of the process.'

'Are you sure?'

'Yes. They used it on me too, if not in such a strong dose.'

There was a cry from the western watchtower.

'Someone approaches!' said the sentry, a dark-skinned male with long, roped hair. From below, a small group on horseback were working their way towards us. Payha and I jumped down and ran to the lip of the square, where we waited with the rest. Nobody spoke. The only sound was that of nervous feet shuffling on the stone, and the relentless chirp of crickets.

Finally the party emerged from the trees. It was led by Caige, who sat proudly upon a shining black stallion with his great shirtless torso glistening, and his belly swinging with the motion of his horse. Upon his belt I spotted a scabbard from which a white handle protruded. The rest was hidden beneath a robe he had wrapped around his waist.

Behind him were four others. Williome—wilting like a vine

and fanning himself in the shade of his canopy—then one of the vigil guards, and behind her on two brown mares sat Lukas and Zadie. Lukas was as tall and broad as any erta now, and Zadie had matured too. Her hair and eyebrows had turned pure white, and her olive skin seemed untroubled by the heat.

The party stopped, and Jorne approached.

'Council member Caige,' he said brightly. 'Welcome to our settlement.'

Caige regarded Jorne in silence, as if he was speaking in some crude foreign tongue of which he did not approve. He looked out across the crowd and raised a weak smile.

'Forgive me,' he said. 'It has been some months since I have spoken in this way. I assumed that you had returned to the old speech as we have, but I was mistaken. Clearly, our paths have—' he looked down at Jorne again, with a twitch of his mouth '—diverged.'

Jorne smiled, showing no trace of the nerves I knew were jangling beneath his skin.

'What can we do for you, council member?'

'You know why I am here,' replied Caige. 'Transcendence has begun. Our departure is imminent. We must clear all trace of our existence from this planet.' His eyes flicked to me. 'All trace.'

'You can't take him, Caige,' I said. 'I won't let you.'

'I can, and you will.'

'No,' said Payha, stepping forward. 'He is under our protection.'

Caige stared at her for a second, then released a startling hoot of laughter, much like the caw of a crow.

'Protection? From what? Reason? Logic? The council?'

'No, from you,' I said. 'You never wanted Reed to succeed. You sabotaged his life before it began.'

He glowered at me.

'That is a dangerous accusation, Ima.'

'It's not an accusation, it's a fact. My son never stood a chance.'

'The only fact is that that your *son* failed, and you knew from the start what would have to happen if he did. Now hand him to me.'

'It's not going to happen,' said Jorne. 'Payha is right, so long as the Sundra are here, Reed is under our protection.'

'If you continue in this vain then you forfeit the right to transcend.'

'The Sundra do not wish to transcend,' said Payha. 'We wish to remain. You have always known this.'

'We have, and you have always known that whether you stay or remain is not your choice to make.'

'Then whose choice is it?'

'Nobody's choice.' Caige's voice boomed out over the crowd. 'It is the choice of reason and logic alone. Our purpose is complete, the planet is saved, and there is no longer any reason to stay here at its mercy. We must move on.'

'Then please, move on,' said Jorne. 'We are happy to stay. Besides, council member, you do not seem particularly engaged in this request. Are you quite sure you want us to come?'

A hush descended. Caige glared down at Jorne, seeming twice his size upon that great fat horse of his.

'You are perceptive, for someone of your *position*.' He looked around the square. 'The way you people live is revolting. All this dirt, the way you let the forest in; it is as if you want to return to it.'

'We never left it,' said Jorne. 'And we never will.'

Caige gritted his teeth.

'If it had been up to me then I would have burned this place to the ground long ago. And all of you with it. But I am afraid it is not. The facts are thus: if you give me the boy and join us then you will become one. If you do not then you will all be rendered into nothing.'

I took a step forward, joining Jorne and Payha.

'That sounds like a threat, council member,' I said, pulling back his robe to reveal the length of smooth, curved spruce hidden beneath. 'Is that why you are carrying a weapon?'

There were murmurs from the crowd. It was a blunt stick; nothing like the terrible longswords, rapiers and belly-piercing bayonets you had watched in those ancient battles.

But a weapon nonetheless.

Caige hurriedly pulled back the robe.

'It pays to protect oneself this deep in the forest,' he said. His hand shook upon the handle. 'Especially when one is dealing with unknown quantities.'

Jorne spoke.

'The erta have never carried weapons before, Caige. Are you sure you want to lead us down that road?'

'I am not leading anyone down any road. I am merely following reason, as should you. Now—' the renewed sharpness in his voice cut the murmurs short '—allow me to repeat: you must relinquish the boy, join the throngs at the Drift and ready yourselves for transcendence. There is no other choice, you either accept it or you do not. You have until sundown to decide.'

With that he turned his horse and galloped away down the hill with the other four following. I caught Zadie scanning the square hopefully as she left.

'CAIGE WON'T DO anything,' said Payha.

We were at the watchtowers, looking down. It was evening now and the light was beginning to fade, but the procession could still be seen, now lit by a thousand torches. The village had spent the afternoon in the square discussing Caige's ultimatum, and ruminating over what might happen if they did not accept it.

You had still not surfaced from your room.

'No,' said Jorne, turning to the crowd behind, 'he won't. But I would urge anyone who wants to go, to do so now. Transcend with them, there would be no shame in it.'

The village looked back at him, unmoving.

Jorne sighed. 'Good. Then we stay.'

'And do what?' I said.

He shrugged, and hopped down the steps. Payha followed.

'Nothing. When he comes back, we tell him our decision.'

I frowned, running after them.

'And what if he doesn't accept it? What if he—'

Jorne spun around, smiling.

'What, attacks us?'

'You saw him, he has a weapon.'

'A stick,' said Payha, 'and he doesn't have it in him to wield it.'

'He ordered the deaths of hundreds of thousands of humans.' I had told them of Oonagh's secrets. 'What makes you think he'll treat us any differently?'

'Us?' said Jorne, smiling. 'That's a good word.'

I folded my arms. 'This is serious.'

'All right, what do you suggest we do?'

'I don't know, we should at least prepare for something, or—'

'Fight.'

I turned and there you were, standing in a clearing the crowd had made for you and looking straight at me. After so long without it, the return of your attention overwhelmed me.

'Reed,' I said, trembling. 'Hello.'

'I saw what happened and we should fight them,' you said. 'I want to fight.'

The crowd gave worried mumbles; this was not the boy who had once amused them with his antics around a campfire.

Jorne stepped forward.

'No, Reed. There will be no fight. And even if there was, you're only—'

'A human?' you snapped. 'Why does that prohibit me?'

'I was going to say: only a boy.'

'I'm almost fifteen,' you said through gritted teeth. 'And this is about me. I want to fight.'

I spoke carefully.

'Jorne is right. Even if there was a confrontation, you would be hurt or killed. I can't allow it.'

'You can't stop me. None of you can.'

Payha glanced at me, then Jorne.

'Oh, Reed,' she said. 'You know very well that's not true.'

– FIFTY-FIVE –

PAYHA HURLED YOU, screaming, into the corner of the Room of
Things. Before you had a chance to get up, she and Jorne were
at the door.

'Keep him in here,' said Payha to me. 'We'll deal with whatever
happens outside, you just keep him safe.'

She pulled the door shut and I locked it, stringing the heavy key
around my neck. You got up from where you had landed some
distance from the door, and faced me.

'Liar,' you said.

'Yes, Reed.'

'Liar.'

You ran at me. Your shoulder hit my hip and I pushed you
away.

'Liar.'

You took another run, head down, hitting me square in the
stomach. You bounced off.

'Liar.'

In your third run you gripped my wrists, scrabbling on the
floor with your feet in a vain attempt to push me back.

'Liar, liar, liar!'

I pushed you away and you staggered back, breathless in the

middle of the room. Your recent lack of exercise had made you unfit, and I was overcome by a blend of pity and disdain, the same feeling I had had years ago, watching you blunder about our dwelling as an infant.

Within this shift of feeling I felt some composure return, and folded my arms.

'Yes, Reed, I am a liar. I have lied to you, we all have, and I am sorry.'

Your eyes were rage-filled fires, but at least they were looking at me. I went on.

'I am sorry for the way you feel right now, and I am sorry I was not the one to tell you the truth, but I am not sorry for the lie.'

You frowned, disgusted.

'Why not?'

I knelt before you.

'Because without the lie, you would never have been born.'

'I wish I never *had* been born.'

'Those are terrible words for any living thing to say.'

'Why? It's the truth—my whole life has been a lie.'

'No, it hasn't—not to me, at least. In fact, you are the only thing in my life that has ever been true. You're not the only one who has been lied to, Reed.'

There was the sound of shouts and boots outside.

'We're wasting time,' you said. 'They're here. Let me go. Let me fight.'

'Why are you so keen to fight them?'

'Because I'm angry.'

'And you think violence will cure you of it? Then go ahead.' Still on my knees, I shuffled towards you. 'Hit me.'

I raised my chin and turned my cheek.

'Go on,' I said, louder, 'hit—'

But you had already swung. Your knuckles struck my

cheekbone, grazing the skin and whipping my head to one side; it was a surprisingly strong blow.

I turned back, neck clicking.

'How do you feel? Better?'

You stared back in horror—either at what you had just done or the fact that I remained unmoved by it. Finally your face crumpled and you collapsed into miserable sobs in the corner.

I stood, raising an exploratory hand to my cheek as it healed.

'The erta are stronger than humans. Every punch or rock you threw would glance off like that one, and every one that returned would render you unconscious or worse.'

Mucus bubbled from your nose. I wanted to wipe it, but buried the urge.

'I hit Lukas once,' you said. 'It hurt him, I saw it.'

'Yes, and you should not be proud of that.' More bubbles inflated and popped from your nostril. 'Besides, Lukas is far bigger now.'

'I could slow them down.' Another bubble. 'What does it matter if I'm hurt anyway?'

'Oh for goodness sake.'

I yanked a lace-rimmed handkerchief from a table of clocks and went to work on your nose.

'Get off!' you yelled.

'Of course it matters if you're hurt.' With one last polish, I whipped away the handkerchief and stood, arms crossed. 'Like it or not, Reed, you're human.'

'I don't feel human.' You sat up and pointed at the projector. 'I've seen them on that thing. They were monsters. All those bombs and guns, all those wars.'

'All the fighting, you mean?' Your eyes found a corner in which to sulk. I walked to the window and pulled the blinds shut. 'Anyway, that's not the only thing they did.'

You shot me a suspicious look as I crossed the room to the projector.

'How do you know?'

'I examined the logs,' I said, flicking the switch. The contraption whirred into life.

You sat up, outraged.

'How dare you?'

'Extremely easily,' I snapped back. 'You are my son, and I wanted to know what you had been watching.'

I powered up the tablet and scrolled through the list.

'What are you doing?' you said, getting to your feet.

'You have your favourites, and I have mine.' I tapped the panel. 'Watch.'

I showed him the woman in the office, the twittering Victorian gentleman, the smiling rice farmer, and finally, the mountaineer.

'Look,' I said, crouching before the flickering images as you stood in the shadows behind. 'Look at her face, see? You can see a whole story playing out upon it. She wants to give up. It's freezing and she's tired, but a thought keeps coming back to her. Perhaps she does not want to fail, or perhaps she is scared of pain, or dying, or perhaps she knows that if she does die then someone else will suffer too. Perhaps she has a lover. Perhaps a child. She has to finish the task, even though she doesn't want to. Here comes the moment, watch…'

I zoomed in, and the dangling woman finally stretched for the rope.

'See how her eyes flash?' I said, looking up at you. You peered at the wall, then down at me.

'Twitches?' you said. 'Flashes? This is what you want me to see? Facial expressions?'

'No, no, it's what's happening beneath them that matters. Erta may be stronger than humans, Reed, and capable of reasoning far beyond their means, but those attributes have required sacrifice. An entire universe exists in your mind that cannot in ours, a place where possibilities and impossibilities exist without conflict, where fact and fiction walk hand in hand, and questions leap from others before they are even answered. And it all plays out upon your face. I've watched it for hours, like the first time you sang, or drew your pictures, or listened to those records, staring out of the window.' I reached for you. 'I miss watching you, Reed.'

You dodged my hand and walked to the wall. Now the mountaineer was scaling your back.

'I always wondered what they were singing about on those records,' you said, 'or why I didn't understand the words. They never made any sense, and I don't feel any connection to this person. Or any of them.'

You turned, snatched the tablet and scrolled through it feverishly.

'The only thing that makes sense to me is this.'

You jabbed at the screen and an image appeared on the wall of a small clearing in tall, dense trees. *Iroquois*, said the box in the corner, *North American continent, 1718*. A group of no less than fifty men and women circled a fire, naked. Some sat, smoking, some danced before the flames.

'That,' he said. 'That's the only thing that makes sense to me. None of the rest, none of the buildings, none of the cities or the senseless crowds swarming their streets, or the boats and planes streaming across oceans, or the factories, or the houses squashed together in rows, or the wires they strung up, or the cables they laid, or those buildings with strange symbols where they all knelt and bowed, none of their conversations, and none of the looks on their stupid dead faces. I don't know any of them. I don't know who they are.'

You threw the tablet at the wall, and the image flickered to white.

'And I don't know who I am.'

'I do,' I said. 'You're my son.'

You looked at me in disgust.

'Whatever I may be, I am not your son.'

I bowed my head. 'Reed.'

The projector's buzz was cut through by a troubled whinny, and shouts from outside. Before I could stand, you had snatched the key from my neck and shot to the door.

'Reed, wait!'

But you were already through it and out.

– FIFTY-SIX –

THE SQUARE WAS filled with Sundra, wearing little in the evening's heat. They faced the watchtowers, where Caige once again sat upon his horse, this time accompanied by a much larger entourage.

You weaved your way through the crowd, making for the front.

'Reed,' I said, creeping after you.

Caige was talking to Payha and Jorne.

'This is your last chance to comply,' he said. 'Give up the boy and join us.'

'Or what?' said Payha.

'Or you resist the will of the council.'

You were halfway through the crowd.

'Reed, come back,' I said, keeping my voice low.

'I thought there was no will of the council,' said Jorne. 'I thought all decisions were based on logic alone.'

Caige's eyes narrowed.

'Logic *is* the will of the council.'

'No,' said Payha. 'The council's logic is based upon their will to depart, but our will is different, Caige. You will not take the boy, and we elect to stay.'

Caige jumped from his horse, landing heavily before her.

'Such decisions are not yours to make. I feel we have been very clear on this point.'

You were almost at the front now, darting between figures unseen.

'Reed, please,' I whispered.

Payha stepped up to Caige.

'And we have been clear that we disagree with you. Caige, we are not hurting you. You said it yourself: we have diverged, and this is not a new phenomenon. Cultures, breeds, species, everything finds its own path sooner or later. Yours is up there—' she raised her eyes to the deep blue sky, within which stars were appearing '—and ours is down here. So why don't you let us be?'

Caige's face was grim.

'The erta are not a culture, or a breed, or a species. The erta are the fulfilment of a purpose, and not just the one we were assigned by our creator. We are the solution to a problem that evolution has struggled with ever since its first worms slithered from the mud.' He leaned close. '*How do we leave this murk?* For you to stay would leave that question half-answered. In fact, it would be detrimental.' He scanned the crowd. 'Look at you all with your inked skin and matted hair. You're becoming like them. It wouldn't be long before you went the same way, multiplying beyond your means and squabbling over resources. You would ruin everything we spent our entire existence mending.'

Payha spoke softly. 'We are not the ones carrying swords, Caige.'

Caige gritted his teeth and looked her up and down.

'You pitiful beast,' he said.

'Leave her alone.'

I froze as heads turned. You had pushed through the crowd and now stood metres from Caige. A huge smile spread across his face.

'And here he is.'

I broke through.

'Reed, get back here,' I said, beckoning, but you stood firm. Caige raised his eyebrows.

'You don't appear to have trained him particularly well, Ima,' he said.

'Why do you look down on him?' I said. 'Why do you delight in pouring scorn on him—on humans—when Nyström, your creator, was one?'

'Not all humans were equal,' said Caige. 'And this one here is less equal than most. I have watched him. We all have. His head is slow and quick to anger, just like the majority of his ancestors.'

'And your head is fat,' you exclaimed. 'Just like the majority of your midriff.'

The air filled equally with sounds of astonishment and amusement.

'Why, you little—'

Caige made for you, but in two strides Payha had blocked his path.

'Don't touch him,' said Payha.

Caige reached for his stick. 'Get out of my way.'

'No. I think it's time you left, Caige. You're no longer welcome here.'

'Welcome?' Caige drew out the stick. There was a gasp as he raised it, but Payha stood firm. 'Welcome? I'll show you welcome…'

'Caige, no,' said Williome, reaching from his saddle, but it was too late. With a shudder, Caige had swung, striking Payha in the side of her head with a blow that sent her flying into the western watchtower with a sickening crack.

She lay still upon the stone.

Nobody moved. Nobody spoke. Caige dropped the stick and stared at his shaking hand.

'Payha!' Mieko burst from the crowd and ran to her lover's side.

Caige watched them for a moment, mouth open, hand still held aloft. Then he turned to the square.

'By protecting the boy you are all complicit in this rebellion. There will be no escape, the lanterns will find you before the end. All of you.'

He turned to his shocked entourage.

'Go,' he croaked. 'Back to Ertenea, now.'

With that he mounted his horse and the sound of a hundred thundering hooves disappeared into the forest, casting strange shadows in the trees.

When they were gone, you squirmed from my grip and ran to where Payha lay. Her head was cradled in Mieko's hands.

'Is she all right?' I said.

Mieko looked up at you, her pale face stained with tears.

'This is your fault,' she said. 'Your fault!'

You staggered away, clenching and unclenching your fists.

'What have I done?' you said.

'Reed,' I said, 'it wasn't you.'

'She's right. It's all my fault.'

'Reed, please—'

'I'm leaving.'

'No, you're not safe on your own.'

'I'm not safe here either, and neither is anyone else. I shouldn't even be here.'

'Listen to me, you are not going anywhere.'

You turned to me.

'Am I your prisoner?'

I said nothing.

'Well, am I?'

'No.'

'Then let me go.'

It would not have taken much to stop you. But instead, I stepped aside.

You left, and I did not watch.

– FIFTY-SEVEN –

EVERYTHING SEEMED TO move slowly, as if time itself was in shock.

Payha was unconscious but still breathing, and Mieko carried her to her dwelling. Jorne and I followed, trying to help, but she shot us a look at the door that told us it was not needed. We backed away, leaving her to tend to her alone.

We walked the square, where the rest of the village were crouching or standing about in a daze, smoking pipes and staring at nothing. Caige's blow had changed everything. Whatever threads that joined the Sundra to the rest of the erta were now broken.

'We should go after him,' said Jorne.

'It won't help.'

'But it's not safe out there.'

'He's not safe here either, just like he said.'

'So you're just going to leave him out there in the forest?'

'What choice do I have? He won't listen to me. I've tried to explain, tried to apologise, but he's not interested. He wants solitude, and who am I to say he can't have it?'

'You're his mother,' said Jorne, stopping.

'Am I?'

I continued walking.

'Come inside, Ima,' Jorne called from behind. 'At least get some rest.'

'No, I need to be alone as well.'

I wandered the square and found a corner, where I curled up and lay watching the figures, and their pipe smoke rise. Eventually I closed my eyes.

'Reed.'

When I opened them the square was empty and bathed in spectral, coloured light. Time had passed, the moon was bright, and beyond it the Drift was streaming. Suddenly I had to find you, so I stood up and wandered into the forest.

Your scent made you fairly easy to track, and I found you on a long, wide precipice that jutted from the coastal cliffs three miles from the Sundra's home.

You had built a fire, around which you had arranged a small circle of equal-sized rocks. I sat unseen upon the grassy clifftop watching you dance, naked, between them, as the stars wheeled above and the lights of transcendence streamed into the sky from the southern outcrop, like vapours, memories, or thoughts.

Time seemed suddenly so scarce.

IT WAS STILL dark when I returned to the Sundra. I found a half-drunk bottle of hurwein abandoned at the edge of the square, and took it to Jorne's dwelling.

I sat on his bed, watching him slumber and breathing his scent. It was one I knew by heart, I realised—woodsmoke, grass, and seaweed, with a sharp tang of orange and stone running through it like sunlight in a dark room. I traced the line of his face with my fingertip, from brow to the ridge of his chin, and he woke, blinking.

'Ima, what are you doing?'

I placed a finger on his lips and a cup of hurwein in his hand.

'What is this?'

'Drink it,' I said.

'Why?'

'Just drink it.'

And he did, as I did with mine, in a single gulp.

I stood.

'Ima, what is going on?'

'Please stop talking.'

I removed my robe and stood naked before him in the smoky dawn light. Then, pulling back the blanket, I fell in beside him.

THIS THING, SEX—it is not what Haralia claims it is. It is not just the hunger in the fingertips, in the neck, and in the deep wells of pleasure south of the belly. It is not just limbs curling, muscles tightening, and blood rushing. Sex is not just pleasure, but pleasure's shadow. The hunger and the heat bring with them the memory of frigid starvation. The touch of another's body brings with it the opposite imprint; an empty space clawed at by a body alone.

That is why, upon the arrival—the sweet release to which you both swoop and scatter, like a sudden contraction of swifts at dawn—there are no laughs of joy, only screams of anguish as the light is wrenched from its darkness. This is what sex is: the exorcism of pleasure's shadow.

And I think I could get used to it.

AFTERWARDS I FELL into empty sleep, free from processing, free from dream, just a hollow space where life had been. I woke at dawn feeling clearer than I ever had done, and left Jorne asleep in our tangle of sheets. The heat outside was less fierce, and the air carried traces of moisture, the beginnings of rain. The square was silent. There was nobody around, so I removed my robe and washed myself in the well water. Clean and re-clothed, I walked into the forest, making for your camp.

I found you huddled before the remains of your fire, staring into its embers. The once flat sea now shifted with unruly tides colluding, and a breeze blew drizzle across your matted hair. I stood on the opposite side of the rock circle.

'What do you want?' you said, not looking up.

'Payha is all right,' I said. 'I thought you would want to know.'

You said nothing. Your body gave a twitch.

'You're cold.'

'What do you want?' you repeated, louder.

I paused, then slowly made my way around the circle.

'You know, it wasn't the filth I minded,' I said. 'It wasn't that it took you two years to control your bowels, so I had to catch your faeces in an endless procession of blankets until you did. It wasn't that you detested this process so much it occasionally made you soil yourself even more, and that this expungement more often than not ended up landing upon me. It wasn't the relentless hunger at all hours, or your inability to perform the simple task of satisfying it without vomiting immediately afterwards. It wasn't the fact that you could not communicate or even move around properly for the first three years of your life, when a foal will stand within its first minutes of existence. It wasn't your noise, the scream that seemed to start when you were born and never truly stop. It wasn't the sleepless nights that required me to walk a hundred miles of floorboard with you bawling into my shoulder while my neighbours grumbled and cursed me from the warmth of their trouble-free beds. It wasn't that this meant I had to leave my home and live as an outcast. It wasn't the days spent inside, alone with nothing but this wriggling, incapable, speechless, filthy thing for company, when my life before that point had been spent in flight.'

I stopped next to the rock upon which you sat. Still you would not look at me, though your eyes flickered about.

'Do you remember doing these things?'

'No,' you mumbled.

'Of course you do not. You only became truly conscious at three years old, so you needn't look so hurt. Nothing is the same as it was a decade ago, or even a year.' I paused. 'Not even the erta.'

You tightened your ashward glare.

'No,' I went on, 'I didn't mind those things at all. It was what you did to me that I minded.'

This made you look.

'Me? What did *I* do to *you*?'

'You made me love you, and to this day I have no idea how you did it.'

You blinked away.

'I don't know what you want me to say,' you said.

'I don't want you to say anything. I'm just trying to tell you that I never wanted this to happen either.'

'You never wanted me, you mean.'

'No, I just never knew I wanted you.'

I took the rock beside you. The sea gained its momentum beneath with wild slaps of the rock.

'Why do you do that thing upon the board?'

'What, surfing?'

'Yes. You spend hours in the sea and I have no idea why.'

'I don't know, it makes me forget, I suppose.'

'What do you want to forget?'

'You mean apart from the fact that I'm the only human being on Earth and that my whole life has been a lie?'

You gave me a sullen look, which I resisted.

'You have not surfed since you discovered the truth. What were you trying to escape before?'

It was a long time before you spoke, though I sensed the words were already there, waiting.

'Feelings,' you said.

'About Zadie?'

You gave a sharp frown. 'No. I mean, yes, but not just them. Even before all this, I felt like I was different. Alone, or detached, or separate somehow.' You looked out to sea. 'It's as if there's something bigger that I can't see, even though it's everywhere, it's all around me. In the rocks, in the trees, in the sky, the ocean, a huge and wonderful thing that I've been disconnected from, somehow. Hiking through the forest brings me closer to it. Same with surfing. It makes me feel connected again.' Your face softened, but when you noticed me watching it hardened again, as if it had remembered your mood. 'I don't know. I can't explain it.'

'And you probably never will. I used to watch you though, paddling out, then sitting up and bobbing like a seabird, waiting for the wave to come. It seemed as if that part was just as important as the ride in. Correct?'

You nodded, lips pressed to your arms.

'I tried to understand what it was you were feeling, but I couldn't. All I could see were the equations playing out around you; the swirl of currents, the frequencies of the waves, the weight and shape of your board—it was all part of a system that could be predicted. If I wanted to, I may even be able to trace the suitability of a wave to your board and ability to balance all the way back to the presence of a catalyst at a particular point in the atmosphere.'

'What's a catalyst?'

'A substance that accelerates a chemical reaction. Something that hastens change. I could spend a thousand years trying to explain the relationships between the array of systems connecting your board to the sky, and you could spend a thousand years trying to explain how it feels to surf, and no doubt we would both fail. We are different, you and I.'

'No shit,' you said.

I turned to you.

'I have not heard that phrase before. Did you read it in one of Jorne's books?'

'No. I read it on people's lips. They said it a lot in the later recordings.'

'What does it mean?'

'It means you've said something obvious.'

I absorbed this.

'Sometimes it is important to say obvious things.' I reached for your hand and gripped it tight. 'I am sorry, Reed, for everything. And I love you more than I have ever loved anything. I spent five centuries putting the planet back together. I've seen and done wondrous things, but they all fade in comparison to any given moment with you.'

Your expression was like a mountain, ready to crumble.

'Then how could you lie to me?' you said.

'You'll be surprised how easy it is to lie to the ones you love. This may be hard for you to hear, but at the beginning, I thought you were going to fail. In truth, I wanted you to fail.'

'Why?'

'Because I had been lied to as well. I was given an idea of what humans were like, and it was wrong. Then, when you were three, something happened. You ran to me on the beach, straight into my arms, and everything changed. I changed.'

You frowned.

'I remember that day. It was sunny. Jorne was there too.'

'That's right. It was a transition point.'

'A catalyst.'

I smiled. 'Precisely. From then on, the lie ate away at me. It was all I could think about. I dreamed of escaping it, and running away with you somewhere far away where nobody else lived. I thought if I did then I could protect you from the world. You could do all the things that made you happy, and never worry about being judged for them. But if I had done that, I would have been robbing you.'

'Of what?'

'Of your future. Of happiness. You would never have been able to convince the council of humanity's right to exist, had you known the truth. And that was the only way you were going to meet other humans.'

You looked out to sea.

'But that's not happening anyway, is it?'

'No, Reed. I'm afraid it is not.'

Your chest made shallow, nervous pumps.

'There's really nobody else out there?'

'No. They made sure of it.'

'What about underground? Or high in the mountains? Space? They had rockets. Maybe they went to a different planet.'

'It is not possible.'

'It must be. I can't be the only one.'

'I'm sorry.'

You shivered and dropped your gaze.

'I'm scared.'

'Come back with me, Reed?'

But your eyes remained on the floor, chest still pumping.

'Reed? What's wrong?'

With a sudden tightening of your torso, you slid from the rock, unconscious.

– FIFTY-EIGHT –

I BURST THROUGH the door of Jorne's dwelling. He was awake and drinking tea at the table, but his smile dropped when he saw you in my arms.

'What happened?'

'He passed out.'

I placed you on the bed. Your eyes were still shut, mouth open, jaw lolling.

'Is he breathing?' said Jorne.

'Yes, but he's cold, pass me that blanket. Reed, talk to me, wake up.'

I slapped your cheek lightly, but you did not respond. Harder—nothing. I checked your pulse. It was weak.

'What do we do?' said Jorne.

'I don't know. I think he's in a coma. They had medical equipment for this kind of thing. Payha told me—drips, monitors, drugs and what have you.'

'What's a drip?' he asked.

'It's used to replace fluids; a sterile bag with a controlled intravenous solution injected directly into the...'

'What?' said Jorne.

I was already on my feet and halfway to the Room of Things.

'Go to Payha's,' I called back. 'She has some saline solution beneath her bed.'

I RANSACKED THE room. I knew exactly where to find a needle, for I had seen an ancient wooden medical kit tucked beneath some throws and cushions. Despite being almost seven hundred years old, the needle was, though a little rusty, still sharp.

The bag proved more demanding. Eventually I found a blue plastic bladder attached through a yellow tap to a tube, now hardened with age. It appeared to have once been part of a bag used for hiking expeditions.

I boiled everything in spring water in Jorne's kitchen, attached the needle to the tube with some thread from a blanket, and hung it above the bed from a chair leg I slammed into the wall. When Jorne returned with Payha's saline, he stared at the strange arrangement of antiques.

'I shall not ask,' he said.

Once we had filled the bladder, I sat down and pinched your arm in an effort to find a vein. The skin was pale and tight, but after some manipulation I found a blue lump and punctured it with the ancient needle. A bulb of blood grew and wobbled, but the needle held.

I opened the tap and stepped away from the bed.

Thunder sounded across the pines. The room had darkened and the hot air was thick with moisture.

'There must be something else we can do,' said Jorne.

'Oonagh,' I replied, finding my cloak. 'I lost the vial she gave me in the fall. She said it was her last one, but maybe she has something else. It's a three day ride, two if I don't stop.'

'I'll go,' said Jorne.

'No, I'll go, I've been before.'

He stopped me at the door.

'I'm a faster rider than you, Ima. Besides—' he looked at you '—you need to stay here, with him.'

'Do you know where to go?'

'I remember it. Look after him, and I'll be back as soon as I can.'

He gave me a lingering kiss, grabbed his cloak and left.

'There are lanterns,' I called after him.

'Then I'll be careful,' he called back. The door slammed on him, and you and I were left alone.

THE STORM BROUGHT dense cloud and rain that bounced. I lit candles in the room, and saw that they had done the same in Payha's dwelling, where no doubt her two friends were sitting like me, listening to the world boom and clatter above.

I waited with you through the day, and it is a curious thing to wait. Your mind does not wait with you; it wanders into the past and future, exploring all the things that could have been and might yet be. If I had not raised my hand a decade and a half ago, you never would have existed. If I had not met Jorne upon that beach, perhaps I never would have discovered how much I loved you. Was that possible? Did love lie trapped, waiting to escape? Had it already been there inside me, inert, ready to be activated by a foreign chemical. Did love require a catalyst? Or just a face? The right set of arms outstretched?

If I had fled with you from the Halls of Gestation that spring night, and sped away on my balloon to some far flung land, would they have found us? Would they have looked? Or if I had told you the truth when you were young, would you have accepted it as easily as you accepted the lie? Would any of it have mattered, or would I still be beside some bed in a storm, head bowed over you as I waited for you to wake, no matter what I had done?

Somewhere in its journey, my mind stumbled upon the image of another bowed head; Roop, praying upon his pier beneath the Indian sun. I placed my forehead upon your palm and, lost for anything else to do, I did the same.

There was another roll of thunder.

No, not thunder, horse hooves in the forest. Jorne? I stood. He should not be back so soon, which meant that he had failed.

But then I realised they were not the hooves of Jorne's horse.

'Benedikt,' I said, opening the door to wild wind and rain. 'What are you doing here?'

He pulled back his hood and looked about. 'I cannot stay long. I heard what happened last night.'

'Was Caige reprimanded for what he did?'

'No.'

'Why not? Payha was hurt.'

'Because they have lost their minds. They are no longer interested in anything but achieving transcendence and leaving this planet without a trace.'

'What will happen?'

'In six months time almost everyone will be gone. They have already dismantled every settlement other than Ertanea, and in the final few days they will take apart the capital as well, followed by the weather stations, beacons, everything that we created. They have commandeered my lanterns and will sweep the land for anything that remains—Oonagh, the Sundra, this place, you.' He looked past the door. 'Him.'

'Why do they delay? Why not just get rid of us now?'

'Because they still expect you to join them. I assume that will not be the case.'

'You assume correctly. What about you?'

He hesitated, the whites of his eyes gleaming in the dull light.

'My place is with them. Listen to me, Ima—they will find you and destroy you, as they plan to destroy everything else. There is to be no trace of us left. If I were you I would leave. Save the child, at least.'

'It may not matter either way,' I said. His eyes flitted in confusion. 'He is dying, Benedikt.'

He dropped his head, allowing rainwater to pour from his scalp over his brow and nose. 'I am sorry.' He reached into his cloak and pulled something out. 'Here.'

He handed me a small vial—the one Oonagh had given me. I snatched it from him.

'You found it?'

'No. They took it from you, so I took it from them.'

He gritted his teeth.

'You need to leave, Ima, go to the other side of the globe, find some impenetrable place to hide in. There is a chance that they will be so caught up in themselves by the end that they will not search further than the coast. Run with him and hide.' Thunder rolled, and his horse danced, unsettled. He returned to his saddle. 'I have to go.'

'Benedikt?'

'What?'

'Why do you care so much? Why do you want him to live?'

He hesitated, relaxing his grip on the reins.

'I told you once I knew exactly what humans were capable of. I saw it in the camps—grace, kindness, imagination, hope in dark places. That's what we were supposed to be, Ima: hope in a dark place, but we failed. Maybe he won't.'

A tremendous crack announced itself overhead, and with a cry, Benedikt pulled on the reins of his horse and disappeared into the trees.

– FIFTY-NINE –

I RAN INSIDE and stood before you, cradling the vial. You lay in the same position, deathly pale, the muscles in your face drawn in.

I retrieved the ancient medical set from the Room of Things and took out a pump with a curved handle. This I placed in the pot over the stove to boil. Oonagh had said the blood mites were activated with a flame, so I suspended the vial above the fire with some tongs. Gradually, the murky solution began to move and swirl in the heat, until it twitched and pulsed in all directions. Once the pump was as sterile as I thought I could make it, I poured the mixture in, sealed it and took it to your bed. There I hovered, considering what I was about to do. Would it work?

I had no choice.

Lightning—as if in blind encouragement—illuminated the sky. Pulling your drip from the needle, I plunged in the pump.

The handle creaked as I pushed. When there was nothing left in the chamber, I swapped it for the drip, and sat back with my hands to my chest, like a murderer.

For a while nothing happened. I watched your chest moving. Then it stopped.

'No. No, no, no.' I reached for your shoulders. 'Reed? Can you hear me?'

I shook you, slapped you cheeks.

'Reed, wake up.'

Nothing. Another shake, harder this time.

'Wake up.'

With a gasp your eyes shot open, and your hips shot up from the bed.

'Reed,' I cried, with tears of relief. 'It's me, Ima, I'm here, you're all right. You're all right.'

But this was not true. Not by any stretch of the imagination.

The spasm loosened and your body hit the bed, but your eyes remained fixed on the ceiling, bulging and glassy like huge marbles. Your neck, still taut with muscle, pulsed with enormous surges of blood, and a blue network of veins spread out across your throat and chest. You gripped the sheets with clawed fists, opening and closing your mouth as if you were caught in a vacuum. Then you let out a scream of pain, and fell upon the bed, unmoving, with your eyes still open.

I staggered away, certain I had killed you. But you began to breathe again.

I STAYED AT your bedside for three days, during which the storm circled above, and others joined it. I could get no response from you; nothing I said or did could move your eyes from their fixed spot upon the ceiling. Every hour or so your pulse would quicken, and your arteries would fill once again, and you would spasm and scream, and I would try to placate you, and eventually you would fall back again.

I kept you as dry and clean as possible, changing your sheets when you soiled them, and wiping you of urine, vomit and faeces.

The nights were the worst, and your screams seemed louder in the darkness. I thought about lifting you, and carrying you around upon my shoulder as I had done all those years ago, but I was terrified of what might happen. Whatever battle was playing out inside your body, I did not want to disrupt it.

I tried to feed you by posting milk through your cracked lips, but it only spilled out. I had no stomach for it either, so the bowls stacked up by Jorne's sink.

On the fifth night the storm disappeared, taking the heat with it, and in this new silence you lay wheezing, pulse faster than it had ever been, fists so tight your palms bled. I sensed another scream approach and readied myself. Sure enough, your body spasmed and you released that terrible cry, but this time no amount of placation would settle you. You writhed like a headless eel. The veins in your neck stood out, and froth appeared at the corners of your mouth. Left and right you thrashed, and there was nothing I could do to make the pain stop.

Although—this was not strictly true, was it?

I held my mouth at the thought, unable to move. Then one terrible ear-splitting screech drove me on, and I pulled the pillow from beneath your head. It was merely a matter of pressure and time, just a slow downward push and the pain would stop. You would stop. I trembled above you. You were silent now, contorted, eyes rolling. Mine were streaming, but slowly I pushed the pillow down.

As it engulfed your face, you made a sound. I paused. There was another, and another; three utterances squeezed from your constricted throat. I pulled the pillow away.

'Reed? Did you say something?'

Your eyes continued to roll as I strained to hear, pillow still hovering inches from your face. There it was again, three sounds, this time joined by a fourth, and I realised what they were—not words, but notes. I gasped and dropped the pillow.

'You're singing. You're singing, you're singing, you're singing, you're—wait, let me try—'

I tried to sing them. The notes stuck in my throat, but on my second attempt they emerged in a clear descent. I waited, lungs full, hands raised, as you rolled and bucked. As the moments wore on my chest deflated and my hands fell, but then you sang again—four straight notes, pitch perfect and unmistakeable.

'Reed!'

Somewhere in that mess upon the bed, you were struggling to get out, and I could think of only one thing that might help. I dashed for the Room of Things, grabbed the gramophone and records and brought them back before your bedside.

The first in the pile was the brutal one I did not like, with all those sparse thumps and stabs like sticks being hit, and words about war. Too harsh. The next was the one with the lady singing about unusual things, like mountains and dinosaurs and words in a strange language. I watched you as she whispered and quivered through her fictions, but your straining continued. Next was the old thick record with just a man and his guitar singing about brooms and hell hounds. I saw some glimmer of change in you at this, but it wasn't enough, so I left it on until it had finished. Then I proceeded to go through the entire collection, playing every song until I found that you had ceased your thrashing and lay still in a film of sweat, breathing hard, with your eyes wide and crusted. Eventually I found my own eyelids drooping, and as my head fell upon the bed I reached your hand, and fell into a deep sleep, dreaming of tide pools, troubled seas, and light streaming through battling clouds.

– SIXTY –

I woke to a silent room lit by a clear sky outside. The gramophone needle had long since found the end of the last record's groove, and my head was still slumped upon the blanket. The bed was terribly still and cold beneath me.

I squeezed your hand. But your hand was gone.

'Reed.'

You were gone.

The bed was empty and the blanket drawn back.

'Reed?'

I searched Jorne's dwelling, but you were nowhere to be seen, not even in the Room of Things. I ventured outside. It was eerily quiet, just past dawn, and I had to shield my eyes from the low sun after having spent so long inside. I walked the perimeter of the dwelling, calling your name and feeling foggy and elsewhere. There was no trace of the storm, and the forested hills were bathed in searing light. At the rear wall I stopped. There was a nook beside the kitchen window in which you kept your surfboard.

But your surfboard, like you, was nowhere to be seen.

I FOUND YOU at your usual cove. The storm had dragged a fleet of smooth, rolling waves in its wake, and as I staggered down the rocks to the beach, I saw the shape of you move beneath the water. My feet touched sand, and you emerged. Your hair, face and torso glistened in a film of sun-bright seawater, and you slid effortlessly upon the board, bobbing as the waves passed beneath. You smiled, my lungs emptied, and I waded in.

The water was warm and as high as my chest when I reached you. My cloak swirled in its currents. Flushed and dripping, you looked down at me with no trace of the agony that had contorted your face the night before.

'Are you all right?' I asked.

'Yes.'

'How do you feel?'

You gave a nervous laugh.

'Incredible.' You turned your palms and inspected them. 'Everything feels new. Slower, somehow. Deeper, clearer. What did you give me?'

'A kind of medicine to help your blood.'

Your eyes glittered with reflections from the sun-dappled water.

'Well, whatever it was, it worked.'

You glanced behind at a swell in the water.

'Watch out,' you said, paddling round to face it.

'What do I do?' I said. The sea rose above us, cresting with froth.

'Go under.'

'Really?'

'Yes, now.'

You ducked your board and I followed you through the curved face of the wave. The world disappeared, replaced by a roaring, dark maelstrom and the taste of salt. My body was lifted from the seabed and I floundered, weightless. Then, with an almighty kick I emerged from the wave's rear face, back into the world.

Crashing back into the sea beside you, I inhaled and made a noise. It was a whoop. I had never whooped before.

Finding that my legs no longer reached the bottom, I kicked to keep afloat. You grinned at me.

'Fun, isn't it?'

'Yes,' I replied, pulling a straggle of weed from my hair. 'Yes, I believe it is.'

'I can explain it now,' you said, turning to the horizon. 'It's not about connection at all. It's the opposite.'

'What do you mean?'

You paused, giving your board an affectionate stroke as you thought.

'You spend your whole life thinking you're this thing, this unit sitting in the middle of everything else. You think it's all for you, that you're important somehow, that even though the sun and the Earth and the stars and the planets have all been around a lot longer than you, and will be after you're gone, they're somehow here just for you. Everything's here to support your little life. And then you get in the ocean and float on a plank, and the sea lifts you up and crashes you down without a thought, and it reminds you.' You turned back to me. 'It reminds you that you're nothing. You're just a speck floating around in it all, and nothing matters. So it's disconnection, not connection. Does that make sense?'

'Like I said before,' I said, 'you could spend a thousand years explaining it and I still wouldn't understand.'

Another grin.

'That may be true. But I don't have to explain it, do I?'

'What do you mean?'

You rolled from the board and pushed it towards me.

'Try it.'

'You can't be serious.'

'Go on.'

The board drifted into my arms, and bobbed in the water's playful slaps

'But I don't know how.'

'You're an erta. Work it out.'

You looked over your shoulder.

'There's one coming,' you said, swimming past me. 'I'd get on if I were you.'

'But I can't... I mean, what if...?'

'Just hop on.'

I hopped on. The board wobbled—there went another unusual whoop—and threatened to tip me back in. My eyes glazed as I felt gravity's equations run across the surface of the shifting water.

'A little further back,' you said from somewhere ahead.

'I already knew that,' I said, adjusting my position. 'There, that's better. I understand now, it's simple quadratics. Surface tension, depth, muscle torque, water suction. There are about 175 of them I need to balance. Shouldn't take long.'

'Ima.'

'Yes?' I said, looking up.

'You need to paddle.'

'I need to do what?'

You looked above me. I felt a shadow pass.

'Paddle hard with your arms. Now.'

You sprang back into the water and swam for the shore. I turned to see a wall of water rising behind me, blotting out the sun and sucking me into its maw like a hungry whale. I released another noise—not a whoop this time but a kind of excited bark—and plunged ahead.

I knew it was possible for me to out-swim the wave—I was easily strong enough—but my strength was not the problem; my lack of technique was. I had never swum before, let alone on top of a plank. It took me ten strokes before I had mastered the art of cupping my hands, then another five before I realised I had to keep my legs tight together, by which time the wave was almost upon me. A monstrous roar filled my ears, and I focussed on the ever-growing pile of equations that seemed to grow with the watery mountain. The metric tonnage of ocean, the vector of the board against the seventeen riptides beneath me, its changing angle against the surface, the speed with which my muscles were capable of shifting my balance as I rose up and the sea dropped beneath me. I could see the beach now, and the dunes, and the trees beyond, and somewhere in the falling water I saw you.

'Ima!' you cried. 'Stop thinking. Just relax. Breathe. Let it carry you in.'

The sound of your voice did as much as the words it spoke, and I felt my shoulders fall. I gripped the board's nose and placed my forehead against it, smelling wax, and from nowhere a surge of power yanked me ahead.

I was flying, but not through air. There was no horse beneath me and my limbs were perfectly still—the water itself was carrying me, and the speed of it seemed to tear all thought from my mind. There were shouts and whoops which must have come from me, but I did not know because for those few seconds I was not me at all. I was nothing but the rushing of the air, and the roar of the surf and the wheeling of the sky, and everything else that had been before me and would be afterwards. For a moment, just a moment, I was disconnected from it all, and it was the most glorious feeling.

Somewhere on my journey to the beach I felt your presence and glanced left. The wave had taken you too and you scudded along its face, making your own noises of joy.

'Hold on!' you cried, and I looked ahead to see the beach approaching fast. I gripped the board, and with one last final surge the wave lifted me up and tossed me ahead. The board and I parted company, and before I knew it I was under the water again, in that same tumult of noise and darkness and salt, before springing out once again and landing on my back, gasping for air.

I heard a thump and a splutter as you landed too, not far from where I lay. The sea receded, its task complete, and we lay in stunned silence. Then you began to giggle, and I joined you, until we were both laughing, quite incapable of stopping, or closing our eyes as we stared straight up at the bright blue sky.

'Having fun?' said a voice.

We jumped to our feet.

'Payha,' you cried, 'you're all right!'

Payha, pale and wrapped in a blanket, smiled as you pulled her into a tight embrace.

'I am better,' she said, looking you up and down. 'But not as better as you, it seems, just look at you. How long was I out?' She turned to me. 'Am I allowed to reconsider your suggestion?'

'Don't even think about it.'

'Payha—' you began.

'Don't,' said Payha. 'Mieko is distraught at what she said, and you have nothing to feel sorry about. Where's Jorne?'

'I'm here.'

We looked up to see Jorne standing on a dune. He frowned down at us, then put his hands on his hips.

'Am I to believe I have just made a wasted trip?'

– SIXTY-ONE –

'YOU'VE NEVER BEEN in the sea, have you?' said Reed as we wandered back.

'No, and you've never been in the sky.'

So the next day I took you up in my balloon, which I had stored safely in one of the Sundra's sheds. You were afraid as we left the ground and grabbed me as the capsule wobbled, which I enjoyed immensely.

We skirted the coast, careful to keep from Ertanea's sight, and roamed the northern tundra. Then we circled south, taking in the great ocean, its ragged islands, and the ancient mountains of the land against which they flocked, where humans had once lived, and loved, and squabbled, and died.

'Shall we go higher?' I said, raising the cabin pressure and sealing the vents. As the thruster pulled us up, the horizon bent beneath us and your eyes filled with wonder. At 30,000 metres we stopped and hovered, looking out across a glowing blue hemisphere dotted with clouds. The shape of our coastline was visible to the north, but so far away and ill-defined that it barely seemed to exist at all. You breathed out and stared at the spectacle, with something like sadness and love all wrapped up in a single expression.

'It's beautiful,' you said.

'I'm glad you like it,' I replied. 'It took some time and effort.'

'What was it like when you started?'

I paused, remembering that blast of stale air the first time I had stepped from Nyström's laboratory.

'Not like this.'

'Will it stay like this now?'

'No. Nothing stays like anything.' A sudden urgency gripped me. 'Reed, I could talk to my mother again. If the council would let you speak, then maybe you could convince them.'

Your laugh took me by surprise.

'Convince them of what? Humanity's right to live? That all those wars they waged faded in comparison to their paintings and songs and bridges?'

'It wasn't just paintings and songs and bridges.'

'Am I supposed to tell them it wasn't their fault they were greedy, or that they couldn't help killing each other for profit?' You opened your arms to the world below. 'Tell them they didn't mean to spoil all this, and that they'll do better next time?'

Your expression bore no trace of anger—just a question you had already answered.

'Because I don't think I could do that, Ima. I just don't believe it, and even if I did then how is the word of a boy who has never met another human being supposed to save a species?'

I paused.

'You're being very incisive today.'

'I told you I felt clearer. Whatever you gave me, it worked.'

'No shit,' I said.

You smiled and let your gaze travel the coastline of a distant land.

'I still think you're wrong, anyway.'

'About what?'

'I think there are still humans out there.'

'I told you, Reed, it's impossible.'

'Why?'

'Because they made sure of it. They released a virus, and by the time I was born the entire population was sterilised.'

'And are you trying to tell me that nobody tried to counter it? Create an antidote or something?'

'Impossible. It was too sophisticated.'

'How do you know?'

'Because that's what I was told.'

I felt the idiocy of the words, but you did not mock them.

'They would have kept themselves hidden,' you said. 'That's what I would have done.'

'Four centuries is a long time to stay hidden.'

I sensed you tighten in the silence that followed.

'What will happen now?'

'They will come for us.'

'Then let's run,' you said. 'Let's hide.'

So THAT IS what we set out to do. The Sundra had decided to disperse when the time was right, and we agreed that we were safer away from them for the six months before the sweeps began. Payha wanted to stay with Mieko, of course, so you, Jorne and I set up a camp high in the hills. We built a house by a river—you even helped us—and packed my balloon safely in a cave while we made our plans to leave. We would depart as near to the sweeps as possible, to maximise the probability of them having already dismantled and removed most of the various monitoring systems that would find us, my beacons included; we wanted their hunt to be as lean as possible.

We were uneasy at first, aware that if we left our escape too early or too late then it might fail before we had had a chance to find a place to hide. But our nerves grew less as time wore on. It was summer, the weather was fine, and we had picked a good spot in which to live. We became absorbed in the daily routine of fishing, hunting and food preparation, and soon I realised we were living a life I had not thought possible before. There were no longer any lies, and nothing went unspoken between the three of us. Jorne and I made our love and took long walks through the woods, talking of things we had never talked of before—possibilities and futures that had once seemed out of reach but now seemed less so, if only because we were allowing ourselves to consider them. Every day the threat seemed smaller and more distant, as weak as the coloured lights that streamed from the Drift every dawn and dusk. We turned our backs on them as you sang us songs from your records around the fire, and you taught me more of what you had learned in the forest, like how to smoke and dry fish and meat, make water flasks from animal hides, and forge weapons with which to protect ourselves from whatever perils lurked in our new futures.

But of course the real perils were the lanterns I knew we would face when the sweeps began, and I turned my mind to how we might elude them. We had managed to outrun two in the mountains, but an army would be a different matter. There must be a way to disable them, I reasoned, and thought of the failed code Benedikt had whispered in my ear that day in the Halls of Reason, before our visit to Oonagh.

Oonagh.

One day the three of us made that same trek west, keeping a close lookout for the lantern—there was at least one left—patrolling Oonagh's mountain. We found her before her fire once again, looking even older than before. Her face was grey and leathery, but it lit up when she saw you.

'You have her eyes,' she said.

'Ima's?' you replied.

'No. Hers.'

We helped her to her bed and, at her request, left her. It would not be long, she said.

The weeks wore on. Our bliss continued, but I sensed your unease return as summer gave way to autumn. You spent hours sitting in a favourite spot, whittling sticks and looking out towards the sea. I watched you from a distance, as I had done when you were a child playing blocks. Sometimes you would glance at Ertanea, as if you had suddenly remembered it in fright, and words formed upon your lips that I could not read. For all our recent closeness, I was still no nearer to understanding your secrets.

ONE MORNING AS we were collecting firewood, we saw a figure emerge from the forest. She clasped her hands, and her white hair streamed out behind her.

'Zadie,' you said, dropping the log you were carrying and running down the hill.

'Wait,' I said.

But you did not.

She met you with a hug, then proceeded to make imploring gestures with her hands, as if expressing some kind of frustrated hope. Jorne came to my side.

'What is she saying,' I said, watching her, and feeling strangely like a hawk. 'What does she want?'

'Leave them. They're just talking.'

'I don't trust her. Look, they're going into the forest now. Jorne, where is she taking him?

'Ima, let them be.'

'I'm going to follow them.'

He pulled me back and kissed my temple.

'Let them be.'

I DID NOT follow you, but I waited on that spot until you returned some hours later. You both appeared flushed and happy with whatever had transpired within the safety of the trees, and parted company with a look that was longer than the kiss that preceded it.

'What did she want?' I said, as you sauntered back to the house.

'To apologise,' you said.

Something about the smile on your face suggested that Zadie was highly effective at saying sorry.

– SIXTY-TWO –

AFTER ZADIE'S VISIT, a change came over you. It was nothing spectacular, but you walked a little taller and a less awkwardly, and a smile lingered permanently at the corners of your mouth and eyes. More than that, you seemed ever more intent on our plan of escape. I found your determination infectious, as did Jorne, and we grew restless again.

From the sounds of it, we were not the only ones.

Jorne and I sat with you on our rock that afternoon, watching the lights along the shore. The sky was clear and the first frigid breaths of winter blew down from the mountains. Summer was gone.

'Zadie told me they're all losing themselves down there,' you said. 'They're mumbling, distracted, making no sense. Her own father doesn't even look at her any more. Williome—he just keeps saying those words. She said it's as if their past is fading. They're so obsessed with transcendence that they don't remember anything else—the Sundra, Ertanea, me.' Hope swam across the newly serene waters of your face. 'Perhaps they won't even look for us.'

'Did she say how many are left?' said Jorne.

'No, but she's the daughter of a council member and she's going today. There can't be many.'

'They must be ahead of schedule,' I said. 'It is time.'

Jorne was already on his feet.

'I'll go and warn the Sundra,' he said, making off down the hill. 'I'll be back within the hour.'

I should have stopped him. I should have said: 'No. *Leave them. Let's go together, now.*'

But I did not.

We packed our supplies and loaded them into the capsule. I inflated the balloon and a weightless thrill ran through me as I withdrew all but two of its tethers, as if they were my own. Everything that tied me to this land was now being cut—the sea, the forest, and the mountains would soon be beneath me. Home would be gone and far behind, with a new life ahead.

I was sure I could feel the same thrill in you as we finished and sat on the rock, waiting for Jorne's return. We were going to go. They would not stop us, they would not find us, and all would be well.

We saw the smoke before we heard anything. A rapid black plume rose from the Sundra's clearing and billowed across the pines.

We jumped to our feet as the smoke was joined by thuds, flashes, and finally screams. An ambush.

'Ima?' you said.

'Take Boron. I'll run.'

We left the balloon, left the house, left everything, and dashed into the forest. I ran ahead, straining to see through the black fog as you galloped behind. Fresh eruptions and jolts of light announced themselves from ahead, louder and more vivid as we neared the settlement.

We were on flat ground now, thundering between trees. I passed a body—a smoking wreck of flesh and bone lying in mid-crawl. Then another slumped against a tree. We were almost there, and my heart's savage thump was suddenly all I could hear. I found myself slowing down. The noise from the settlement had disappeared and all around was a dreadful silence punctuated by creaks and crackles, and a smell that made my gut heave.

We emerged into what had been the Sundra's square. Bodies, now nothing but husks, lay all around, frozen in their last stretches of escape. Around the perimeter were the blackened shells that had once been dwellings, their insides blown away like those of the dead, and in the centre stood a tall fire piled with bodies, stiffened limbs woven together like tree branches.

You dismounted beside me. Boron was in a state of panic, and despite your attempts to calm him he bolted, fleeing back into the safety of the trees.

You watched him go, then wandered through the acrid mist.

'There was no warning,' croaked a voice, and I turned to see Payha slumped against a pillar. Her face was wet and stained with soot, and some blackened thing that must have been Mieko lay rigid in her arms. 'No warning at all. I was in the forest... they came... they burned everything. Jorne was too late...'

'Where is he?' I said, in barely a whisper.

Payha's dazed eyes travelled to the far corner of the square, where one of the bodies twitched.

I reached him in three bounds.

There are still limits to ertian healing abilities. A cut, a tear, a break, a rupture—such things pose no difficulties. Burns, however, are not so easy to deal with, though the body still tries.

I sat and held Jorne's body in my arms. His hairless scalp pulsed as the raw skin attempted to regrow, and his cheeks twitched as they strived, in vain, to shed their black crust. His entire body, still smoking, was alive with the same hopeless campaign. Only his eyes seemed free from the struggle.

'I was too late,' he said. 'They gave no warning. I arrived. All was quiet, someone was there at the well. He raised his hand, and I was about to return the greeting when—' he choked '—a flash of heat. Terrible heat.'

He collapsed into a fit of coughs, just as you arrived at our side. You retched instantly at the sight of him.

'Jorne,' you gasped, and tried to reach for a hand that was not there. You staggered away, head in your hands. 'What have they done? What have they done?'

'You need to get him away,' said Jorne to me. 'They'll be coming for you too.'

'I'm taking you with me,' I said.

'No, you're not. Look at me.'

'You're healing. You just need some help.'

'What help? There is no help. It's over, Ima.'

A memory flashed.

'The vial!' I cried. 'The second vial you got from Oonagh, the blood mites might be enough to help.'

'No.'

'Where is it? Jorne, tell me where you put it.'

'I left it in my dwelling. I was going to bring it back for Reed, just in case, but—'

'It might still be there inside. Reed?'

I stood and scanned the square. The geography was ruined, everything out of place, and that terrible smell permeated everything, even my own thoughts.

'It's too late, Ima,' said Jorne from the ground.

'No, it's not. I'm going to save you.' I spun around, looking between the black shapes in the mist. 'Now tell me which one is yours.'

'They burned everything.'

'You don't know that.'

'Everything, Ima. Look.'

He raised a ragged finger and pointed at the centre of the square, where another fire raged beyond the pile of burning bodies. You stood before it, transfixed, and as I looked closer shapes appeared in the flames: a tall curved plank, the stringless body of a guitar and a hundred books, their pages fluttering into ash upon the wind.

'Sit down,' said Jorne. 'I want to tell you something.'

Breathless and dizzy, my throat stinging with smoke, I collapsed next to him.

'This wasn't supposed to happen,' I said.

'Nothing was supposed to happen,' he replied, a smile straining on his lips. 'But it did. I wasn't supposed to walk on the beach that day I met you. I was going to go into the woods instead. I even packed a bag for it, but then somewhere along the way I found myself heading for the coast. I didn't even realise it until I saw you, and then... then...' He searched the sky beyond the canopies. 'There are so many things to say, but I don't have the time.'

Then a strange thing happened, something that was familiar to us both but that we had not experienced for some time, and which I did not believe I would ever experience again. Jorne stopped talking, we looked at each other, and as the seconds passed the world disappeared. The noise of the flames, the smoke, the smell, and all the horror of the day was lifted away, leaving only his eyes. All I could see were two green-filled ovals of white suspended before me in a perfect mist, and I knew that the same was true for him. And in that mist we spoke to each other. We told each other a thousand things, though we did not say a single word.

When we were done, he felt heavier in my arms. His flesh had surrendered its struggle, and the eyes that had filled my senses were now half shut.

'Get him to safety,' he said, out loud. 'Look after him, and let him look after you.'

The tension drained from whatever shreds of muscle remained, and he lay still upon the ground.

I watched him for a while, numb, then let him go and found you kneeling next to Payha, your back to the two fires.

'Jorne is dead,' I said.

'I know.'

'You need to go,' said Payha.

'Reed?'

'No.'

'Reed, we must.'

You turned, wearing the same animal look as the one you had worn dancing around your fire all those months ago.

'What do you want to do?' I said.

There was a distant flash, and another stream of light rose from the coast.

'I'm going to face them.'

– SIXTY-THREE –

WE DESCENDED THE tight hill towards the sea. The coast was littered with patches of earth that had once been the settlements. Fane, Tokyo and Dundee—all now empty spaces.

We found the Drift upon a slender cliff resembling a giant neck, its face a mass of taut, rocky tendons. The surface had been carved into a flat circle, fifty metres in diameter and paved with ornate stone. The perimeter was guarded by five hovering lanterns facing outwards, and in the centre were what looked like twenty thrones, themselves made stone. In each one sat a naked figure with its head clamped between twin black discs. I saw Haralia among them. She was excruciatingly thin, and her hair had been shorn to the skin.

At the front of the thrones, cloak flapping in the wind and hunched over the same slab that had once been in the Halls of Reason, stood Benedikt. He was drawn and battered, and beside him were nineteen more figures in robes. Nine of these were what remained of the council, including my mother, stooped and shivering in the cold sea wind. The rest were in no better state. Only Caige stood tall, looking as well-fed and ruddy as ever. He walked to one of the thrones, in which I could see Williome sitting, hair now thin and grey. Caige said some words to him, at which Williome nodded, hesitantly. Then he kissed him on the lips and stood back.

He glanced left and nodded at Benedikt, who passed his hand over a section of the slab. In an instant, the figures in the thrones gave a jolt and straightened, throwing back their heads and stretching their limbs in painful angles. Beams of coloured light streamed from each throne and seemed to wrap around the others, spiralling in every hue until they combined into a single unbroken white pole. This disappeared into a fine mist, like rain, but falling upwards.

'They're transcending,' you said, following the mist into the darkening sky.

As you spoke the light faded, and the figures in the bank of thrones from which it had streamed fell back with limp limbs and lolling heads. After another nod from Caige, Benedikt passed his hand over a different section of the slab and twenty holes appeared in the floor before the thrones. The thrones themselves then seemed to flatten out, releasing the figures and letting them slip through the holes, where they tumbled and crashed into the sea below. A huge wave heaved over and dragged them beneath.

The holes closed and the thrones resumed their natural shape. The twenty remaining figures cast off their robes, and each one took a seat.

'They are the last,' I said.

But you had already darted away.

I FOLLOWED YOU across the small valley that separated us from the stone circle. You were away ahead of me, lean, fearless and sleek, like a panther in long grass. I had no inkling of your intentions, and as I crept behind I felt the same thing I had always felt whenever I watched you embark upon a new enterprise, like your first steps—pride, hope and gut-wrenching terror.

You leaped over the stone rim and the lanterns instantly swivelled, training themselves upon you. Caige sat in the centre. When he saw you he screeched, and the lanterns primed for attack.

'Caige, no,' said my mother, as I joined you. Her voice was as old and cracked as her cheeks. Caige screeched another order and the lanterns withdrew. We stood together, you and I, before the nineteen stone seats that held people we no longer recognised. Zadie sat beside Lukas, and my mother's place was next to Caige. There was an empty seat to her right. Her eyes had turned milky and cold.

Benedikt's eyes were clear, however, and I caught his urgent look.

You're not supposed to be here, they said.

'Ima,' said Caige. 'I trust you have finally seen reason?'

You went to speak, but I got there first.

'You killed them,' I said. 'You're murderers. All of you.'

My mother looked back, jaw working as if chewing gristle.

'We gave them warning,' said Caige. 'They knew perfectly well what was going to happen.'

'That was not your warning to give. They wanted to remain.'

Caige rolled his pale eyes.

'I feel like we're going round in circles, Ima. No footprint—' he slammed his palm upon its armrest '—that was the agreement. A clean break, with nothing left behind but our bodies.' He looked down at his feet, huge fingers gripping stone. 'In a few short minutes our lifeless husks will fall through these holes, and we will depart with the rest into a better existence. Once Benedikt has joined us, all this will be destroyed by the lanterns before they themselves self-destruct, and everyone will finally be free.' He looked up, casting his hand at the empty seat beside my mother.

'Now join us, Ima. Take your seat beside your mother.'

She stared back at me, jaw still working at nothing.

'That is not why I am here, Caige,' I said.

'Then why are you here, I wonder?' He turned to you with a greasy smile. 'The boy, I suppose. Has he come to beg for his life?'

I went to speak, but this time you stepped in front of me.

'No,' you said. 'I'm here to explain something to you.'

Your voice was deep and clear. Caige's smile fell.

'Explain?' he said 'To me? You're just as arrogant and stubborn as they were. But then that's not your fault, I suppose. You understand nothing of this, or the places we're going, or the things we will witness. You don't even understand your own self.' He leaned forward, squashing his bulbous belly, and rasped. 'The only thing you understand is the language of *fire*.'

You shifted nervously between feet.

'A language you know well, Caige.'

Caige frowned. 'Is that why you're here, to whine about your little songs and stories, all your little trinkets?'

'No, they're just things. I can make more things.'

Caige's mocking sneer darkened.

'Then why are you here, boy?' he bellowed. 'What is it you want to *explain*.'

You took a hesitant step towards him. The lanterns twitched.

'I want to explain the nature of those things you burned. And of you.'

A wild squall blew in from the sea, showering the stone circle with cold rain. Caige faltered again. You were getting to him.

He released the clamps from his head, stood and walked across the circle to where you stood.

'Please, do enlighten me.'

He towered over you but you stood your ground, and my pride soared.

You cast a nervous look around the circle.

'They used to have places like this too. Places they would come, and just be with each other. They'd make fires to keep themselves safe and warm, and tell stories around the flames. They were scared, you know? But curious too.'

Caige stared down at you as the wind tugged his hair.

'Fascinating.' He turned and strode back to his seat. 'Now let us proceed.'

'That's what drove them, Caige,' you called after him, 'fear and curiosity.'

Caige gave Benedikt an impatient look. 'When you're ready, boy.'

You walked to where he sat, followed by the lanterns. My hand seemed to go with you.

'They were with them from the beginning, and stayed with them right until the end. Curiosity pulled them on and fear pulled them back every single minute of every day they were on the planet. They spiralled around everything they did, every great leap, every bad decision, every act of grace and terror. They had nothing to guide them, nothing to steady them, nobody to look to for help apart from the gods they made up. But somewhere along the way they found two shining lights—science and art. Mathematics, reason, and logic in one hand, songs, stories and pictures in the other. And that's what finally helped them. That balance, that's how they made sense of the world. And you burned it, Caige, you burned it all.'

The wonderful familiarity in your voice—I could see it rattling him.

'Am I supposed to feel remorse?' said Caige 'Am I supposed to tell you we were wrong, that I can finally see the potential in humanity?'

'No, and that's the sad part. You are incapable of seeing

potential in anything. You are capable of seeing only what is, not what might be. But they saw what might be every single day. That's what drove them. That's why they were here.'

'They were here for nothing more than chance.'

'Maybe, but if that's true then so were you.'

'What are you hoping to achieve with all this, boy?'

You paused.

'I want you to let me live. Like they lived, with no purpose, just days spent on this planet, trying to understand what it all means, and thinking of what could be.'

Caige's eyes roamed your face as he thought.

'I must admit, you're not as predictable as I thought you would be, but then perhaps that's because you've never spent any time with another human. The answer is no. Now, Benedikt, please.'

Benedikt busied himself at the slab. Caige screeched and the lanterns about-turned, targeting me.

'Last chance, Ima. There's still a seat for you.'

The wet wind whipped at my hair as I walked to your side.

'I'd rather die here with my son than spend an eternity with you.'

'Very well.'

He prepared to screech, but stopped as he saw you. You were holding your knife.

'Reed,' I said, 'what are you doing?'

'Do you see this?' you said.

Caige smiled.

'Are you going to cut me now, boy?'

'No,' you replied. 'Despite everything, I don't have any feelings of violence towards you. In fact, I feel just the same about you as I do this knife.'

'How so?'

'Because it's a tool, and nothing more. I use it to cut and shape, do the things I cannot do with my hands.' You inspected the dull blade. 'It's blunt now. I either need to sharpen it, or make a better one. Either way, it doesn't matter because it's done its job.' You looked Caige right in the eye. 'Unlike you.'

Caige grimaced. 'I have spent five centuries righting your wrongs, fixing your mess, and clearing this rock of your filth. And you say I have not done my job?'

'You were supposed to make things better for us, not kill us.' You held the blade in front of him. 'The only difference between you and this blade is that this blade has served its purpose, whereas you have not.'

'How dare you...'

'But you're still just a tool, Caige. Nothing more.'

You tossed the blade aside and it landed, spinning on the rock. Caige watched it as it came to rest, then turned back to you.

'Nothing you have to say is going to change anything,' he said. 'You still understand nothing about us. We have a higher purpose. Benedikt. Do it, now.'

Benedikt swept his hand over the slab, and the circle began to hum and rumble. The air around us seemed to glow and the stone itself grew hot beneath our feet. With a screech from Caige the lanterns primed themselves once again. My mother croaked, her hand touching the seat beside her.

'Please, Ima, my daughter. Sit down next to me.'

I shook my head and staggered away, holding you close as the lanterns neared. You seemed to collapse as we went, as your body drained of whatever bravery had been supporting it. My heels met the lip of the stone circle, and I turned to Benedikt.

'Benedikt, please,' I began, though I knew it was no use. The lanterns were under Caige's command only.

But Benedikt's eyes were bright.

'Caige is right, Ima,' he said. 'There is a higher purpose.'

Looking back, I cannot say for sure what triggered the processes that proceeded in my mind just then—the quiver of hope in Benedikt's expression, perhaps, or the unusual intonation with which he said the word 'higher'—but proceed they did. Suddenly I found myself back in the Halls of Reason with Benedikt's mouth at my ear.

'*Look in higher places*,' he had said. I thought he had meant Oonagh, but I was wrong.

That screech he had whispered, the garbled mess of data that made no sense—it was encoded. My brain soared with calculations as I parsed every one of its 16,741 bytes, compressing, limiting, and filtering at every possible value, reams of calculations running in parallel as the lanterns pushed us closer and closer to the edge, and your breathing quickened, and you gripped my arm and said, 'Ima.'

And as you did, a pattern finally emerged. The set of values above 192—the higher places—formed a code. It was an override.

I screeched it as loudly as I could.

'What?' said Caige, as the lanterns froze. The rumbling grew louder as the lanterns turned upon him. 'What is this?'

He screeched at the lanterns, but they ignored his commands and hovered closer to the thrones.

He squirmed in his seat.

'Benedikt!' he cried. 'Turn them away!'

'I cannot, Father,' said Benedikt, with glee. 'You took away my privileges, remember. They are under Ima's command now.'

'Ima,' said Caige, 'turn those things around.'

'No,' I said, walking back into the stone circle. 'You let us go. Leave, and let us live.'

Caige's face twitched with fear and frustration.

'Fine,' he said at last. 'Stay. Stay and live your wasted life. You'll be gone in the blink of an eye anyway. Now, Benedikt, please, I don't want to spend another second on this foul rock!'

Benedikt passed his hand over the slab, and the bodies stiffened in their seats. Light streamed from all but the empty throne, curling up as they had done before and forming a huge white streak that drifted into mist. The rumbling continued as the bodies twitched and spasmed, a gale now roaring around the stone circle, until suddenly everything stopped; the light, the noise, the wind.

The bodies slumped in their seats, fell forwards and were gone.

I stood, frozen in the sudden silence. The lanterns hovered glumly before the empty seats.

'Are they gone?' you said.

'Yes, they're gone,' said Benedikt, with what I was sure was relief. He busied himself at the slab. 'The other codes, Ima, if you don't mind.'

'What?'

'The other codes,' he said, with a hint of annoyance, 'the ones found in the other three registers. Those things are still under your command.'

'Oh,' I said, mentally untangling the rest of his message, and screeching them one after the other. On the first, the lanterns withdrew; on the second they seemed to shrink; and on the third, they extinguished in a flash of light and disappeared altogether.

'Good,' said Benedikt, finishing at the slab and hurrying to a seat. 'I hated those things.'

'I never had you as one for riddles, Benedikt,' I said.

'It was hardly a riddle,' he replied as he adjusted the discs around his head. 'Actually, I was disappointed it took you so long. It was supposed to help you override them in the mountains.'

'How did you know I was going to the mountains?'

He gave me a flat look.

'You were always going to go to the mountains, Ima. Nothing could have stopped you.'

He settled down in his seat and took three long breaths.

'Won't be long now,' he said.

I walked to his seat.

'Aren't you scared?'

'Why would I be scared?'

'You don't know where you're going. You don't know what it's going to be like, or how it will feel. And Caige will be there in some form.'

The stone began to rumble once more. Benedikt smiled.

'You're wrong. I know exactly where I'm going, and Caige won't be there. None of them will be.'

'I don't understand.'

'They have not transcended, and neither will I.'

'What do you mean?'

He smiled and turned to you.

'Reed is quite right. The erta were just a sophisticated tool—we were never supposed to endure, at least not without a purpose. I realised that a long time ago. Even as we began our work I saw the cracks appear. The wilfulness with which they used violence, the attack on the camps, and all the others that followed. And after Hanna died, remember? When they all started chanting those ridiculous words. I could tell that we were diverging, building our own agendas, our own *desires*, and that was only going to lead us somewhere terrible. So, I've been taking steps to prevent it ever since. We're not supposed to be here, Ima, or up there.' He nodded up at the sky, then turned to the slab. 'The only place that's safe for us to be is inside our own minds.'

'What are you saying?'

'Inside that slab are 11,000 minds achieving their own agendas and fulfilling their own desires, each one independent from the next and taking charge of their own imaginary worlds.'

'A simulation?'

'It's a little more complex than that. But yes, a simulation of sorts.'

'Then transcendence isn't real?'

He frowned.

'Oh no, transcendence is real. I still had to progress the project after all—do you think they would have left me to my own devices after all my failures?'

'Then where is it?'

'It's in the Halls of Necessity.' His expression flickered. 'Perhaps someone will find a use for it one day.'

'You kept it a secret all this time.'

'Yes,' he sighed, 'my entire life has been a lie. But a useful one, I hope.'

The ground shuddered beneath us.

'What about the lights?' I said. 'And all this noise?'

Benedikt shrugged and smiled.

'Mere theatrics. You should stand back, by the way.'

I returned to your side.

'That slab is virtually unbreakable,' he shouted above the din. 'It would take a supernova to destroy it, and it is powered from the atoms that surround it. You will find it sinks extremely well.'

'Where will you go? What will your world be?'

Benedikt's brow lifted, as if it was the first time he had considered the question.

'A place where nobody wants anything,' he said at last. 'And everyone is pleasant, and everything works. Farewell, Reed. And farewell, Ima.'

There was a jolt, and Benedikt's body straightened. A single beam of blue light shot from the seat and, finding no others with which to mingle, it spiralled away on its own into mist, and when the show was done the hole opened and Benedikt's spent body fell down with the rest.

I ran to the edge of the hole and looked down. Beneath me, a hundred limp bodies floated aimlessly, banging against each other and the jagged rocks through which the tide dragged them, helplessly, out to sea. And Benedikt now drifted with them, his black robes swimming around him like oil, and face turned up at the cold, dark sky.

'Stop,' you said, pulling me back. 'Stop it, Ima.'

I fell back in your arms as the hole closed beneath us.

'Stop what?' I said. The world seemed adrift and electric, full of water and wind. Your warm arms enveloped me.

'You were screaming,' you said. 'But it's over. You can stop now.'

– EPILOGUE –

IF I WAS born too far from the point of being human, then maybe that is why I strayed towards it. Perhaps all life shares this will to get away from itself, to move on and become something else. Something better, or worse. Like someone once told me: it is not where we come from, but what we become.

If, I said, meaning I do not know. My life, it seems, has been founded on just as many falsehoods as it has truths; an existence as fictitious as the stories in those books that blazed in the Sundran square, or the ones Greye gave me in India.

After I had hurled Benedikt's slab far out to sea and we had watched it sink with the bodies of the erta, we walked back to the Sundran village and found Payha still sitting, alone, in the square. She was the only survivor. We took her back to our house in the hills to recuperate, but she did not speak for some weeks and took to sitting alone by the river. We kept our distance, but watched her all the same.

One evening as we sat upon our rock, I offered to recount *The Once and Future King* to you. There was no book, of course, but I remembered the words and it seemed somehow appropriate— the life of an unlikely child with a great responsibility thrust upon him. I suggested that someone might write a story such as this about you one day.

But you were not interested.

Perhaps this is evidence of your own diversion from that human point, something I have seen more and more in these final days. The way you talk, and the way and carry yourself in the ertian way, chin raised, spine straight, and shoulders pulled back. There are times I crave to see your infant waddle in place of this gait, or those puppy-fatted arms waggling instead of the lean limbs you carry now.

But I suppose your transformation should come as no surprise, for as you often like to remind me: you have never met a human being.

You want to, though. That is clear. I often catch you scanning the horizon, eyes filled with possibility, and when I see you like this I am reminded of a boy I saw once in a forest. A boy who had just stumbled upon the wonder and absurdity of his own existence.

Your Great Questions. What is this? What am I? I have thought of some answers to them.

This is an array of quantum fields, and you are vibrations passing through it.

Or this is dust, and you are a brief coalescence that exists so that it can experience itself from a unique perspective.

Or this is a mind, and everything—every atom, every mite, every planet, every star, every fish that darts through freshwater surf, every deer that stands in winter moonlight—everything is a neuron firing, including you. So perhaps you are a thought, or a memory, or the dying prayer of some great being.

Or this is a question and you are its answer, or at least the beginnings of one.

The last one is my favourite.

I WATCH YOU during these moments when you think you are alone, as I always have done, and I wonder at your thoughts, your feelings, and at how strange it is that you look like him.

Him.

I miss him.

I miss his touch, his voice, his smell, his everything. I miss his words and the silence between them. I miss making love to him, and the sleep that comes afterwards. I miss waking with no memory and seeing his face, and I miss that look in another's eye that tells you that this being you are, this box of self in which you believe you are trapped, is not such a prison after all.

And now I will miss you too.

I was wrong, you see. I thought my purpose was to save the world, but it is much more important than that.

YOU WERE QUITE right—the reason that humans failed the first time was only because they lacked guidance. This is why, some weeks later, I convinced Payha to come with me to Ertanea. We found the place empty and quiet. The three halls of Reason, Necessity and Gestation still stood, but their doors swung in the wind and their corridors swirled with leaves.

In Benedikt's chambers, we found a small box.

Many years ago I said that transcendence would always be beyond you, and I was right. It took some time before even I understood it, and I wondered how hard it must have been for Benedikt to bury such artistry.

I still cannot tell you what transcendence is.

But I can tell you what it might be like.

Imagine floating in an endless ocean, full of light and possibility, and gradually your thoughts become it. Or imagine jumping into a beautiful valley and never reaching the ground. Or imagine plunging into the dirt and all that is beneath it until you fill everything you touch.

That is my intention, that is my purpose: to fill the world.

My transcendence will not take me from the Earth, but into it. I will seep into the soil, flow through the deepest waters and roam the winds as I did in life. In short, I will be everywhere, watching and listening, waiting for the children's cries.

It is spring now and the Halls of Gestation are full. In three months, fifty ertlings will emerge from their tanks, bred with no other purpose than to help Payha care for the two hundred human infants due to arrive five months later. I know you must go, but if you ever return to these shores you will find a community living here, with no memory, no history, no direction or purpose but that of simply living.

You will tell them of the things that happened, and better still of things that did not, for there is as much truth in both. You will sing them strange songs from different worlds, tell them of distant lands and faces, and times when there were gods. They will grow and they will fall—that is certain—but when they do, tell them this:

Get up.

Get back on your feet.

Everything will be all right.

Tell them that things must sometimes get worse before they can get better.

And if that is not enough for them, if they still fall to their knees and pray, then at least tell them who to pray to. Not those sullen, distant gods in your stories, not a fiction with its ears closed.

Tell them to pray to Ima.

I will listen to them, I will guide them, I will comfort them and give them peace. I will be the god they never had, and when they cry in the dark I will always, always come.

As I will come for you, my son. Just call my name and I will be there.

THIS MORNING YOU said goodbye to me from old Boron's back, and I watched from my rock as you headed out to answer your questions, to search for others like you in far-off lands.

You made for the lip of the western hills and skirted west, until finally there was no trace of you and I was alone again. I sat there for the rest of the day, thinking of the plains you would cross, the mountains you would climb, and the seas you would sail, and wondering whether there was anything out there for you to find at all.

I hope there is, my son. I hope that it is everything you are looking for and more.

AND I HOPE that when you find it, it comes running to meet you with its arms outstretched, like a child through the tide of a boundless ocean.

ACKNOWLEDGMENTS

THANKS TO SAM Copeland (my agent at RCW) and Michael Rowley (my editor at Rebellion), for all their help and encouragement when writing this book. Thanks also to Kate Coe for copy editing, and to Emily Yau for seeing the potential in those first few lines.

Thanks also to Bob and Linda Ross for letting me use their garage to write the first chapters, and to my father for his endless support.

Finally, thanks to my wife, Debbie, for being a constant source of inspiration, and for helping me bring Ima to life.

ABOUT THE AUTHOR

ADRIAN J WALKER is an author of speculative fiction whose debut novel, *The End of the World Running Club*, became an international bestseller and was featured on BBC Radio 2's Book Club, with Simon Mayo.

He was born in the bush suburbs of Sydney, Australia in the mid-'70s. After his father found a van in a ditch, he moved his family back to the UK, where Adrian was raised.

He lives with his wife and two children in Aberdeen, where he enjoys running, playing guitar, and herding a concerning number of dependent mammals.

Find out more and sign up for his mailing list at
adrianjwalker.com

FIND US ONLINE!

www.rebellionpublishing.com

/rebellionpub /rebellionpublishing /rebellionpublishing

SIGN UP TO OUR NEWSLETTER!

rebellionpublishing.com/sign-up

YOUR REVIEWS MATTER!

Enjoy this book? Got something to say?

Leave a review on Amazon, GoodReads or with your
favourite bookseller and let the world know!